"De la Rosa deftly weaves together a delicious slow-burn romance with danger, intrigue, and sisterly bonding. Full of riveting details, *Ana María and The Fox* is a breath of fresh air in historical romance!"

—Alexis Daria, international bestselling author
of *A Lot Like Adiós*

"De la Rosa's writing sparkles, and her characters are both admirable and memorable. With plenty of humor, history, and, of course, spicy love scenes, *Ana María and The Fox* is an absolute must-read for fans of historical romance."

—Elizabeth Everett, author of *A Love by Design*

"Liana De la Rosa fulfilled every historical romance craving I had and then some with *Ana María and The Fox*. The Luna sisters are the headstrong, politically savvy, and intelligent Mexican heroines I have always dreamed of reading about!"

—Isabel Cañas, author of *The Hacienda*

"When a historical romance can combine a swoon-worthy love story with a rich historical setting, it goes on my keeper shelf. *Ana María and The Fox* does this and so much more. It was absolutely delightful to watch Ana María's bond with her sisters grow all while the reserved hero is falling head over heels in love with her."

—Harper St. George, author of *The Stranger I Wed*

"Thrillingly different . . . a new direction for historical romance."   —*Kirkus Reviews* (starred review)

Isabel
and
The Rogue

A LUNA SISTERS NOVEL

Liana De la Rosa

BERKLEY ROMANCE
NEW YORK

BERKLEY ROMANCE
Published by Berkley
An imprint of Penguin Random House LLC
penguinrandomhouse.com

Library of Congress Cataloging-in-Publication Data

Names: De la Rosa, Liana, author.
Title: Isabel and the rogue / Liana De la Rosa.
Description: First Edition. | New York: Berkley Romance, 2024. |
Series: Luna Sisters ; 2
Identifiers: LCCN 2023042080 (print) | LCCN 2023042081 (ebook) |
ISBN 9780593440902 (trade paperback) | ISBN 9780593440919 (ebook).
Subjects: LCGFT: Romance fiction. | Novels.
Classification: LCC PS3604.E12266 I83 2024 (print) |
LCC PS3604.E12266 (ebook) | DDC 813/.6—dc23/eng/20231011
LC record available at https://lccn.loc.gov/2023042080
LC ebook record available at https://lccn.loc.gov/2023042081

First Edition: June 2024

Printed in the United States of America
1st Printing

Book design by Tiffany Estreicher

For the bookworms. The wallflowers.
The quiet ones . . . who roar so loudly.

Isabel
and
The Rogue

1

London, late May 1865

For the entirety of her life, Isabel Luna felt invisible. Overlooked. Uninteresting and uninspiring. Every time a pair of eyes skipped over her to focus instead on her charming and beautiful sisters, she experienced a sharp jab to the heart.

But now she considered that invisibility an asset to be exploited.

Isabel pondered this change in perspective as she stood at the perimeter of the ballroom, watching as her younger sister was swept onto the dance floor for a minuet. Gabriela—or Gabby as she was known to family and friends—had a serene smile on her face, looking to all in attendance as if she couldn't be happier to partner with Lord Jeremy Townsend, the second son of a marquess. But Gabby's smile was tight and more than a little brittle. Her younger sister rarely suffered fools, but her good manners often dictated that Gabby do just that.

Not for the first time, Isabel wondered if the attention, the adulation, her sister received was worth being treated as a commodity by all who admired her pretty face. Oh, Isabel knew Gabby would say no—accompanied by a curse word—and she couldn't blame her. Still, perhaps it would be nice to be admired, to have her company sought after . . . but then being the center of attention had always made Isabel uncomfortable. She had experienced that overwhelming feeling only one time since she had arrived in London, when a mean-spirited young woman had attempted to embarrass her at a poetry reading, but thankfully Gabby had rescued her. Isabel hoped, rather earnestly, that the ton would never have cause to look upon her again.

For however would she accomplish her covert task if they did?

Noting Lady Yardley, her guardian, stood chatting with a group of ladies and was not looking in her direction, Isabel placed her glass on the tray of a passing footman and blended into the milling crowd. Several people dipped their heads in greeting to her, but no one interrupted her walk. Once it would have disappointed her that no one wished to converse with her, but now her palms tingled and her heart raced. She didn't possess the time or interest to engage in mundane talk about uninteresting topics simply for the sake of being polite. Not when there was so much more to do . . .

Swallowing her nerves, Isabel stepped into the corridor that led to the ladies' retiring room. She encountered no one on her short walk, which allowed her to linger outside a door at the end of the hall. After ensuring she was alone, Isabel laid her cheek against the cool wood, closing her eyes as if it would somehow aid her hearing. Any sort of scene could be waiting for her in dark spaces—gentlemen conducting covert business, amorous assignations. During one such memorable encounter, Isabel had been searching a desk when the door suddenly burst open, revealing a man and a woman locked in a passionate—

No. Isabel refused to think about that particular memory. Refused to think of *him.* For if she did, her face would flush and her mind would go down avenues better saved for dark nights alone in her chamber.

Hearing only silence in the closed room, Isabel pulled down on the handle, finding it locked. Huffing a breath, Isabel studied the lock. Perhaps Lord Meadows had locked his study door to prevent attendees from using it as a retreat from the festivities. More likely to dissuade frolicking couples from treating his desk like a bed. Or . . . maybe the earl possessed personal records or information he'd prefer the public not be privy to. A fair request, honestly, but then Isabel and Mexico no longer had the luxury of fairness.

Isabel plucked a hairpin from her coiffure and bent it with her teeth into just the right shape. Confirming the hallway was still empty, she inserted the pin into the lock, wiggled it about, and grinned when the tumbler rolled free. *Yes, only a* wall-flower *would be at liberty to perform such a task,* she thought as she pushed the door open and slipped inside. Once again, Isabel was thankful she had insisted on having the skirts of her gowns designed with a simple A-line silhouette instead of the fashionable bell style that made movement cumbersome. Lady Yardley had complained bitterly over the request, but Isabel knew such skirts would make it impossible for her to squeeze into and out of tight spaces, and fashion was never her priority.

Closing the door with barely a snap, she leaned her back against it as she surveyed the dark room. Bookshelves ran along both sides of the space, although she noted some of the shelves were bare. A large oak desk sat on one side of the room, the top devoid of papers or anything personal aside from a lone paperweight in the shape of a round disk. Isabel paced to the shelves and gave them a cursory glance, not finding much of interest. It was clear someone needed to assist the earl in building up the contents of his library, because his current collection—or lack thereof—was an embarrassment.

With her eyes narrowed, she changed course to the desk. Lord Meadows was a long-standing member of Parliament and served as a chairman on the Foreign Affairs Committee. Surely if anyone had information worth stealing, it was the earl.

But after a fifteen-minute search, picking through every drawer, examining every corner, nook, and cranny of the desk, Isabel had found nothing. Nothing of worth, and nothing she could send back to Padre Ignacio to assist their fight against the French.

A lump burned in her throat, and Isabel fought the urge to plop into an armchair and cry out her frustrations. Instead, she patted down her skirts and filled her lungs until her corset bit into her flesh. Releasing the breath in a long sigh, Isabel glanced around the room one last time, ignoring the disappointment that singed the backs of her eyes.

A quick peek into the hall revealed her escape route was clear, so Isabel rearranged her expression to one she hoped reflected eagerness to rejoin the festivities. Not that anyone would notice her absence. Isabel was as invisible as the wallpaper—

A hand shot out and grabbed her wrist the moment she set foot inside the ballroom. Panic clawed up her spine, and out of instinct, Isabel brought her hand up to ram it into the perpetrator's nose, when a familiar scent wove about her. A stupidly alluring scent she'd know anywhere, for the man it belonged to was also stupidly alluring.

"Snooping again, I suppose." Captain Sirius Dawson slid his arm around Isabel's waist while his left hand grasped her right. "After everything, it seems you've yet to learn your lesson."

Isabel bristled . . . because of his accusation or his proximity she didn't know, for Captain Dawson had an annoying talent of leaving her decidedly off-kilter.

She almost despised him for it.

As he effortlessly spun her into the swirl of dancers, part of Isabel realized that the captain had never danced with her before, thus she'd never been this close to him. Her skin tingled with awareness at every spot he touched. Isabel hated that she was apathetic to most men but that every part of her body seemed to stand at attention whenever *this* man—with his golden beauty and perceptive azul eyes—appeared.

Willing her muscles to relax, Isabel allowed him to move them to the strains of a Chopin waltz. Feeling gazes pressing upon her—whether Lady Yardley's or Gabby's, or possibly one of the scores of Captain Dawson's admirers—Isabel raised her chin. She'd danced a waltz with any number of gentlemen in the time she'd been in England, but never with him. For all that he was her brother-in-law's friend, or that Isabel had spent more than a fortnight at Captain Dawson's country estate, he had seemed to go out of his way to ignore her presence. Being shunned by such a man should not bother her half as much as it did, but her chest went tight whenever she saw him.

The amused look on Captain Dawson's face now reminded Isabel that he had said . . . something. She was sure it was a scold, because when he did speak to her, he liked to point out her bad behavior. Isabel replayed his words in her mind.

"I don't know what you mean. I was merely returning from the retiring room when you waylaid me into this waltz." She arched a brow. "If you wanted to dance with me, you could have asked politely, like everyone else."

Isabel managed not to cringe through her bluff. Everyone else? Hardly. While her dance card was never empty, for rumors of her fortune had encouraged many a cash-strapped second son to seek out her hand, her reserved nature was not particularly inviting. She'd learned quickly that if she spoke of a novel she'd read or a new scientific discovery she'd heard about, eyes would glaze over and attentions would wander. More often than not, Isabel held her silence during such dances, answering the gentlemen's questions politely but volunteering nothing else, for truly, what was the point?

But something about the captain always made her speak without thinking. It was a very vexing thing. The captain was very vexing.

His blue eyes bored into her now, his lips a confusing slash between displeasure and amusement. Surely Isabel was reading him wrong and she fought not to squirm. She had always believed her father possessed the most intimidating stare, but she'd been wrong, for nothing made her want to share all her secrets—or confess all her sins—like Captain Dawson's steely gaze. It was a fortuitous thing, then, that Isabel's stubbornness was more than up for the challenge.

"I don't see why you should care about me or what I do when you and I are not friends," she said archly.

"We aren't?" The captain's brows rose. "Whatever gave you that impression?"

Her own brows dipped low over her narrowed eyes. "You did, sir. In all the months since we departed Dancourt Abbey, you've not spoken with me once. Nor my sister or Lady Yardley, that I am aware of."

"Well, that's not true," he murmured. "I chatted with Lady Yardley in the park just the other day."

"How nice for you." Isabel pinned her gaze on a perfect blond curl near the nape of his neck. "Yet the fact remains that we have never been friendly, Captain Dawson, even while my sisters and I were at Dancourt Abbey that summer. You have never taken any interest in me—" Isabel clamped down on her tongue so hard she tasted copper. She had no intention of hinting at her hurt feelings over his disregard. She never wanted any man to think he could maim her pride. *Especially* this man.

His chest rose and fell with a sigh, and Captain Dawson shifted his gaze from her face to a spot over her shoulder. "That's not true. I assured Fox I would keep an eye on you and Miss Gabriela—"

"And I assure you, Capitán, that my sister and I do not need anything from you."

Isabel did not raise her voice, nor did her tone hint at the anger his indifference had sparked within her. But Captain Dawson seemed to know anyway, for the angular planes of his face softened. Just a tad.

She refused to soften in return. The captain may be her brother-in-law's close friend, and he may have sheltered her and her sisters from Mexico's enemies after Ana María and Gideon were wed. But Captain Dawson had shown her time and time again that she was not worth his notice.

Being a wallflower had its benefits, but Isabel was so very tired of being overlooked.

"I'm well aware that you and your sister are capable of taking care of yourselves. You've proven it more than once." His jaw worked on a pause. "But I fear there may be others among the ton who would wish you harm, and I find the idea of that happening quite . . . unpalatable."

Damn it, what was it about this shrinking violet that made him share all his thoughts as if he'd just stepped into a confessional box?

Sirius had not given Miss Isabel Luna much thought when he'd first seen her. He'd heard she was the shy, wallflower Luna sister, often boring her dance partners with talk of books and discussions of obscure topics. From Sirius's experience, most gentlemen could not be bothered to think about much aside from gossip, horseflesh, and women, so of course an awkward debutante would be of little interest.

But it wasn't until he encountered her in the darkened interior of Lord Ratliff's study that Sirius had been reminded it was always the quiet ones that needed to be watched.

It had been almost two years prior. Sirius had been at some gathering or another—the myriad of events he was required to attend often blended together—where he had finally managed to catch Lady Attwell alone, without the hovering presence of her husband. The Home Office had been certain that if Sirius were able to get the countess alone, she would reveal what she knew about Lord Attwell's French financial holdings that had alarmed officials. Charming the countess had proven easy. The second wife of an old earl, whose heir and spare from his first wife were already at university, the young and comely Lady Attwell had been bored and looking for excitement . . . something Sirius had been more than happy to exploit.

And it was with Lady Attwell pressing hungry kisses to his neck, hands fumbling with the placket of his trousers, that Sirius had seen *her*. She had been crouched under the desk, only the barest glimpse of her crinoline underskirt peeking into view. With careful maneuvering, Sirius was able to crane his head to the side until a pair of large doe eyes blinked up at him, light sparkling in their dark depths. This anonymous woman appeared neither abashed nor frightened to have been discovered, and instead stared back at him as if he and Lady Attwell had interrupted her.

Sirius wasn't sure how he'd managed to end the encounter with Lady Attwell. She had not been happy, but in that moment his interest had swung wildly from her to this unknown variable.

After the countess had angrily quit the room, Sirius propped his hip against the desk, crossed his arms over his chest, and patiently waited for his quarry to come out of her hole. It seemed she was in no rush, however, for he waited five minutes before her head appeared over the desktop. She didn't gasp or seem the least bit surprised to find him still there. Instead, she climbed to her feet, brushed out the fall of her skirts, and met his gaze directly.

"Well, what do you have to say for yourself?" she'd said, in a voice oozing with condescension. It took him a moment to even register her accent.

Sirius slowly quirked his mouth. "How amusing. I was going to ask you the same thing."

Her snort was soft. "Of course you were. Are you the sort to think a man is never at fault even when he very obviously is?"

"Of course not. But then it was you who failed to announce your presence when my . . ." He cleared his throat. "*Friend* and I entered the room. Rather, you hid, as if you'd been caught doing something you weren't supposed to do. Amusing, that."

"Not amusing at all." She paced a step closer, her blithe

mask not slipping an inch. "You and your *friend* caught me off guard, and before I could say a word, you had fallen on each other like frothing beasts."

"Frothing beasts?" Sirius snorted. "There's no need to exaggerate."

"Only a person described in such a way would consider it an exaggeration." Her head cocked to the side. "Amusing, that."

Sirius had bit down on his tongue, whether to contain a laugh or issue a rebuttal, he didn't know. But as he stared at this spitfire, with her blazing dark eyes and rich golden skin, he was struck anew by how arresting she was. He blinked, his mind connecting her accent with her sun-kissed looks.

"Am I to assume you are one of the ladies visiting from Mexico?" His gaze skipped over her face. "It's Miss Luna, is it not?"

She nodded primly. "I see my reputation has preceded me." A pleased sort of smirk settled on her lips. "And now I've seen *your* reputation in action, Captain. I appreciate the lesson."

"You know who I am?" Sirius had been surprised, and people so rarely surprised him. How was it possible this wallflower knew who he was, but he'd been clueless of her existence until that moment?

"Of course I do." Miss Luna stepped away, the skirts of her green gown swishing about her legs. At the door she paused, glancing at him over her shoulder with a quirked brow. "I'm always aware of those I should avoid, even when an introduction proves unavoidable."

It had taken Sirius several minutes after that parting response to recover his composure and rejoin the party.

And his subsequent interactions with Miss Isabel Luna had continued in much the same vein. It was clear she considered him a speck on the bottom of her shoe, and Sirius did his best to ignore her presence. Their mutual indifference would have continued if she hadn't been forced to stay at his country estate, Dancourt Abbey, for several weeks. Their forced proximity had shown Sirius what he suspected he'd already known but had carefully avoided: that the quiet Luna sister had fascinating depths to her.

Sirius considered her now as he spun her around the dance floor. She was not pretty in the lauded English rose sense, but something about her sharp cheekbones, the proud tilt to her jaw, and the expressive nature of her dark brows drew his eye again and again.

It was annoying, really, how he'd noticed these details about her.

Which was why he had done his best to put Isabel Luna far from his mind. For Sirius had no time or inclination to befriend a young, unmarried woman, no matter their shared connections. He had a job to do and could afford no distractions. And without his work for the Home Office, how could he possibly honor the men he had served with and who had died in his place?

Yet now he'd gone and made Miss Luna his business, and the frustrating thing was, Sirius hadn't even done it consciously. He'd been chatting with several ladies on the opposite side of the ballroom when he'd glimpsed her dark head disappear down a corridor. Sirius excused himself and immediately followed her, stationing himself nearby to keep watch. When several men had made an attempt to visit the retiring room, he had redirected them elsewhere so Miss Luna's search of Lord Meadows's study was not interrupted. Because of course Sirius knew what she was about, he just didn't know why. Despite having told himself it was none of his business more times than he could count, he was decidedly uncomfortable at the thought of her actions bringing her harm.

But she was in his arms now, and he was determined to get answers.

"Are you finally going to tell me what you're looking for, Miss Luna?"

"I was looking for a good book to read." She huffed a breath. "I'd rather not be here, but as Lady Yardley has insisted upon my attendance, I figured I could read to pass the time."

"Perhaps the viscountess hopes you will find a husband, much as your older sister did."

Miss Luna's chuckle was a dry, husky sound. "Ana María and Gideon's connection is not one that is likely to be replicated. And anyway, I rather doubt I'm the sort to inspire men to marriage."

"And why not?" Sirius's voice was sharper than he intended, but did she not think herself worthy of being courted? Even if gentlemen were not charmed by her obvious wit and curious mind, her fortune alone would be enticement enough.

"I fear I'm not particularly friendly. Haven't you noticed?"

Sirius snorted. "You? Unfriendly? Surely you jest."

Large dark eyes flashed up to meet his, amusement apparent in their depths, though not on her face. "I wish I were. But there are even some fools who seem to think my sister Gabriela is more amiable than I am."

"I pity them." Sirius faked a shudder, although there was some truth to it. The youngest Miss Luna was a fearsome creature.

"You have no interest in joining Gabby's court?" Miss Luna tilted her head. "She's quite popular, you know."

Frowning, Sirius said, "Of course not. Your sister is beautiful, but I know better than to associate with unmarried misses."

"Oh, of course." She rolled her eyes. "Only merry widows and bored ladies for you."

Sirius huffed a chuckle. "Much less troublesome."

"I doubt that," she said, a smirk settling on her lips.

He had no reply, for she was right.

2

It was becoming harder and harder to write these letters.

Isabel stared at the blank sheet of parchment, tapping the end of her pen on the desktop, wishing she were doing anything but detailing her failures for Padre Ignacio once again. She'd even consent to dance with Captain Dawson if it meant saving herself the embarrassment of admitting another defeat.

Actually, no. That wasn't true. Surely nothing could be worse than spending several long minutes in Captain Dawson's arms—

She jabbed at the parchment with the sharp end of her pen, puncturing a hole in the thin paper. The captain had occupied enough of her thoughts the night prior, and Isabel could not allow him to run rampant within them yet again. Despite how her ribs abruptly felt too tight for her lungs when he'd admitted his concern for her safety, Isabel knew she could not let Captain Dawson interfere with her work. To allow him to dominate her thoughts and distract her was not to be borne.

Releasing a long exhale, Isabel shook out her hands and selected a fresh sheet of parchment. Grasping her pen once more, she licked her lips and wrote:

Estimado Padre Ignacio,

*The Meadows ball was uneventful. I did my best to
partake in all aspects of the festivities, and sought out
entertainment where it could be found, but it was not as
fruitful as I hoped it would be.*

Isabel had learned to keep her letters short, the contents
seemingly mundane, her words not hinting at any deeper
meanings. Padre Ignacio knew the purpose of her communi-
cations, so she felt no need to elaborate on the measures she
took to hunt out information. The concise summaries prevented Isabel from giving in to her need to make excuses for
her shortcomings. She'd learned at her father's knee that excuses oftentimes made failure worse.

Unable to resist, she added a line about finally reading *The
Mill on the Floss*, a novel the priest had encouraged her to read
for years. After assuring him she would write about her feelings regarding it in a future letter, Isabel signed her name at
the bottom of the sheet. Folding and sealing it, she tucked it
into her shirtwaist to have it franked later in the day.

Pushing her chair back, Isabel dropped her head and covered her face with her hands. This was the thirty-second such
letter she'd penned over the last two years, and they never became easier to write. In how many different ways, with various
arrangements of words, could Isabel express that she had yet
to discover information that would aid her beloved Mexico in
its fight against the French? She longed for such a boon, a fact
she knew Padre Ignacio was aware of. He knew her better
than almost anyone—although her time in London had allowed Isabel to grow close to her sisters, a development she
was thankful for. But it was the old priest who knew how

desperately she wanted to be of use; to step out from the long shadows of her sisters; to finally see a spark of pride in her father's eyes when he'd only ever looked at her with disappointment. It was why Padre Ignacio had recommended her to Señor Fernando Ramírez for just such a task.

It was the evening before they fled Mexico City when he had found her in the library at the Luna family villa, trying to decide which books she would take on the voyage. The idea she would have to choose between them had gutted her, for her collection of books had been her friend for longer than she could remember. Oftentimes the written word had been her only friend.

"Señorita Isabel," Señor Ramírez had called, coming around the shelf where she was crouched among stacks of poetry, fiction, and history. "Padre Ignacio said I would find you here."

"As if I would be anywhere else." She stroked her hand over the cover of *The Lusiads*. "This room has been more my home than anywhere else in the villa."

Señor Ramírez propped his shoulder against the shelf as he looked down at her. "How will you decide which ones to take?"

Isabel shrugged, although she could not stop her hands from shaking. "How do you decide which child is your favorite?"

He didn't laugh at her comment. Didn't try to placate her or comfort her. Señor Ramírez had simply nodded, as if he understood.

Releasing a shuddering breath, Isabel had taken a moment to appraise her older sister's fiancé. Señor Ramírez was handsome and knew it, his laughs and smiles his social currency. Isabel had noted that the man used his natural charm and winning smiles as a mask to disguise his sharp, cunning mind. She had thought the young politician would make an ideal husband for Ana María, his charisma a match for her sister's golden perfection. But then Isabel hadn't known Ana María as well as she thought she did, for Señor Ramírez was not the only person wearing a mask.

But he had never sought her out before, and cautious curiosity had flared within her.

"Tell me, Señorita Isabel," he'd said, his dark eyes keen on her face, "does Señor Luna know you slip out of every gathering he hosts?"

She dropped her gaze as she lifted a shoulder. "If he knows, he certainly doesn't care."

Isabel had long thought of herself as her father's throwaway daughter, for he had never seemed to find use for or value in her.

"Well, you've certainly taken advantage of his disinterest, and have developed a talent for blending in. Becoming a part of your surroundings."

"I have?" Isabel wasn't sure if he was insulting her or merely stating the truth.

The man crossed his arms over his chest. "Have you thought of how you could use your skill of disappearing in plain sight to help Mexico?"

Isabel's brow furrowed even as she leaned eagerly toward him. "I don't understand."

Fernando crouched down until his gaze was level with hers, his forearms perched on his knees. "You will be in London, but that doesn't mean you cannot serve Presidente Juárez while you're there."

Anticipation tingled along her spine, and Isabel carefully

set down the book in her hand. "Of course I want to help. If I can."

"Padre Ignacio said you would. Because you're a Luna, and your loyalty to Mexico runs in your blood," he murmured, nodding his head approvingly.

"I am," she'd answered, earnest and determined. "What would I need to do?"

Señor Ramírez had *seen* her. Had seen what she was capable of. Had entrusted her with a great responsibility when others struggled to even recognize her existence.

But perhaps everyone had been right not to notice her, for Isabel had been unable to provide anything of use to the Juárez government. Almost two years on English shores and she'd yet to send back any useful information. Oh, she sent along gossip she'd overheard at social events, and speculation about secret scandals, but Isabel possessed no proof of them. She knew that rumors and snippets from tête-à-têtes would not truly aid her countrymen, but then Fernando had not had time to share what specific information she should gather. So Isabel had studied *Debrett's* so she could learn who was who in British society, devoured the morning papers for all manner of news, eavesdropped on the servants' gossip, and listened to chatter at the various social events she attended with her sisters. She recorded names, dates, and titles in a secret journal, and tried daily to piece together her findings, with no success.

Ana María had found love with her new husband and Gabriela charmed the ton, while Isabel had purposely cultivated her quiet, bookish persona, all the better to remain unassuming. Unsuspecting. But it felt like it had all been for naught. One failure after another had withered her confidence to dust. Isabel clenched her eyes shut to hold back the tears. Tears would do nothing to solve—

"I knew I would find you awake," a voice proclaimed into the silence of her chamber.

Spinning about on her seat, Isabel scowled at her younger sister. "Will you ever knock?"

"Buenos días to you, as well, hermana." Gabby plopped on the bed, relaxing back onto her arms. "What are you writing?"

Isabel flicked a hand, hoping she appeared unconcerned. "Nothing of consequence."

"I thought perhaps you were writing out your disgust at having to dance with Captain Dawson at the ball last night."

Gabby's tone was a tad too light. Too innocent. Nothing Gabby did was ever light or innocent.

"I'm surprised you noticed, considering every time I looked your way, you were surrounded by a crowd of admirers," Isabel shot back.

Her sister's expression clouded. "It's quite tedious, really. But then Tío Arturo can't say I'm not doing my part to bolster Mexico's image among the ton."

When they had arrived in Mexico two years prior, their tío Arturo had tasked them with improving the profile of their countrymen, hoping such a thing would aid him in his lobbying effort to win the support of the British government against the French. It was only weeks later they learned how many of those in power despised Presidente Juárez and his Zapotec antecedents.

"I wouldn't dream of wasting ink and parchment on the likes of such a rogue."

Isabel was proud of how nonchalant she sounded.

"He is a rogue, isn't he?" At Isabel's answering snort, Gabby chuckled. "The talk I've heard about the captain would shock you."

"I assure you it wouldn't," she grumbled under her breath.

"So if you're not fond of Captain Dawson, why did you dance with him last night?" Gabby cocked her head to the side. "I know dancing is not your favorite activity."

"I didn't have much choice." Isabel plucked at the sash around her waist. "One minute I was returning to the ballroom after a visit to the retiring room, and the next I was being twirled about the floor."

"Quite rude of him not to ask before he claimed your dance." Gabby's brows rose to her hairline. "Although I suppose some would say it's a bit romantic. Captain Dawson cuts quite a swath."

Rolling her eyes, Isabel bit back the bitter words that perched on the tip of her tongue. "It's only because he's handsome. If he were not so attractive, the ladies of the ton would not look twice at him."

"Perhaps not." Gabby snorted. "But thankfully for the captain, his golden hair and sapphire eyes easily snare hearts." Her sister was deceptively quiet for a moment. "Do you think him handsome, Isa?"

Isabel wished the earth would crack open and swallow her whole. Gabby had always been observant . . . her sister had just never used those skills on her. Now, in an unfortunate turn of events, Gabby seemed to have sensed that something lurked under the cutting animosity between her and Captain Dawson.

Clearing her throat, Isabel infused as much apathy into her voice as she could when she said, "Whether I think Captain Dawson is handsome matters not. What matters is his character, and his is quite deficient."

"He *is* a rake with a capital *R*. But you know what they say about rakes . . ." Gabby raised a palm. "They make the best husbands."

"*Reformed* rakes do." Isabel curled her lip. "And nothing about Captain Dawson's conduct hints that he's been re-formed."

"Goodness, Isa, you truly do not like the man." Gabby held up both hands in surrender. "I don't know what Captain Dawson has done to earn your ire, but I pity him. You are a jaguar when you're threatened."

"Do you think so?" Isabel's chest swelled at the compari-son, for she would never have thought to compare herself to the fierce jaguar.

Gabby nodded, a fond look softening her expression. "One day I hope you learn to see yourself the way I see you."

Before Isabel could press and ask what she meant, Gabby jumped from the bed and walked to the door. "¡Vamos! Let's eat breakfast and learn what her ladyship has planned for us today."

Isabel remained seated for a long moment after her sister departed, contemplating her sister's comment. Gabby wished Isabel could see herself the way she did. Years prior she would have assumed her younger sister thought her dull, but hadn't Gabby just compared her to a jaguar? Her sister did not offer empty compliments.

Although it had crushed her at the time, Isabel was almost happy their autocratic father had sent them away from Mexico City as the French forces approached. The long ocean voyage, and the many long months since then, had allowed Isabel not only to get to know her sisters better, but to actually like them.

Rising to her feet, Isabel smoothed her hand over her shirt-waist, ensuring her letter to Padre Ignacio was still safely tucked inside. With a small smile, she followed Gabby, her mood vastly improved.

. . .

He hated his weekly trips to the Home Office.

His boots clicked on the cobblestone street as Sirius dodged riders, wagons ladened with crates, and swiftly darting street urchins running errands for merchants. Despite Sirius's repeated offers to meet at his gentlemen's club in lieu of a formal meeting at headquarters, his superior had always refused. So despite his distaste for the stuffy, cramped interior of the Home Office with its legion of self-important employees, Sirius squared his shoulders and set off for the building on King Charles Street in Whitehall every Friday, rain or shine.

Holding the door open for a clerk balancing a stack of papers in his hand, Sirius removed his hat as he stepped into the dim interior. His blinking eyes were barely adjusting to the light when a hand clamped down on his shoulder.

"Dawson, let's get this over with, shall we?"

With a crisp nod, Sirius followed the severely dressed man down a crowded corridor until they came to a door at the end of the hall. Throwing it open without ceremony, the older man slid onto a chair tucked under a narrow table. Sirius took the chair on the opposite side without a word.

"What did you learn at the Meadows ball?"

Lieutenant Colonel Walter Green was not one for small talk. He wanted Sirius's report, and preferred it in as few words as possible. It was a quality Sirius always admired about the man. The son of a decorated Waterloo hero, Green had served in the Crimea before an unfortunate injury had him sent from the front lines back to England. But not one to slip into an easy retirement, Green had turned his attention from serving the Crown on the battlefield to serving it through covert assignments within Britain's borders.

When Sirius had returned from the peninsula himself,

physically hale but mentally and emotionally broken, Green visited him. Sirius had been touched that the taciturn former officer had gone out of his way to inquire after him, and when Green offered him a position at the Home Office, he'd accepted. Perhaps the lieutenant colonel knew Sirius would benefit from staying busy. Perhaps he sensed Sirius ached for some way to actually earn the honors that had been heaped upon him. Whatever the case, his work for the Home Office had saved his life in many ways.

"Not much. It was a bore"—Sirius studied the trim on his hat—"but well attended."

Lieutenant Colonel Green's expression remained as neutral as ever. "Was Westhope in attendance?"

Viscount Westhope was Sirius's most recent mark. The young lord had a positive reputation about town for being witty and amiable . . . but whispers of his French familial connections had drawn suspicion among Home Office officials.

Sirius nodded. "I said hello. Exchanged some small talk about the pair of high-steppers he recently acquired."

The other man continued to hold his silence, his expression giving away nothing of his thoughts. Stifling a sigh, Sirius continued.

"And that was it. He had secured dances from several young ladies, and no other opportunity to speak with him presented itself."

If he had not been so distracted by Miss Luna and her continued subterfuge, he might have found another opportunity to engage with the viscount, who seemed a friendly enough fellow.

A slight pucker appeared in the center of the lieutenant colonel's forehead. "That is unfortunate."

Sirius managed to contain his wince. The show of disappointment from the normally unflappable Green cut Sirius to the quick. Licking his lips, he plowed on, words tumbling from his mouth with no forethought.

"But I planned on cornering the viscount at the club. I learned he visits in the early afternoon for billiards and drinks. I figured I could continue our association over a few games."

"Very well," Green murmured, and Sirius released a breath. "It's imperative we learn what the viscount knows. It may be nothing, but it could be everything."

Moving forward to perch on the edge of his chair, Sirius tentatively asked, "Is there a specific reason we should be suspicious of the French *now*? And why would we assume Westhope's cousin would tell him anything?"

"There's always reason to be suspicious of the French." Green scowled before quickly easing his expression back into placidity. "Britain will always keep close watch on any ruler named Napoleon, and for good reason. With much of the world's attention fixed on the States, the French are pushing their advantage wherever they can. Now it's Mexico, but who is to say they'll stop there? It behooves us to be vigilant, and if that means we surveil our own, so be it."

Sirius straightened his spine, allowing a bit of the man's resolve to soak into his own blood.

Green pushed back his chair and rose to his feet. He met Sirius's gaze with his own. "Our fallen brothers deserve for us to expend every ounce of our energy to ensure we protect Queen and country."

"Of course they do, sir," Sirius said, raising his chin.

The older man's parting words played in Sirius's mind as he made the short trek from Whitehall to St. James's Street. He tried to save the memories of his men—his *comrades*—for when he was alone, in his study, with a glass of brandy in hand.

Yet soon Sirius found himself at a table in the corner of the dining room at his club, an empty tumbler in front of him. He thought he'd only had one glass, but he couldn't be sure. His gaze swept over the other members seated at tables nearby, their loud laughter crashing through his skull like the peals of a church bell. Several men had stopped at his table to say hello, and while Sirius had been polite, he had not been particularly welcoming, and his acquaintances eventually left him at peace.

But he wasn't at peace. His mind was roaring with an influx of memories he did not want to entertain but was helpless to fight. Guilt had brought him here, when he should have brought it home to indulge.

"You're not usually here at this time."

Glancing up, Sirius met the cool blue eyes of his oldest friend, Sebastian, the Duke of Whitfield. Without waiting for Sirius to respond, the duke pulled out the chair on the other side of the table and took a seat, ordering a glass of whisky from the footman who appeared promptly at his side.

"How kind of you to join me," Sirius said tartly.

"It is." Whitfield reclined back in his chair and crossed one leg over the other, the perfect picture of a haughty duke. "I don't even know why I'm here now. Only the obnoxious second sons and doddering elders are here at this ungodly time."

"I'm a second son, as you well know," Sirius pointed out.

"Thank you for proving my point." The duke inclined his head. "How is Harcourt anyway? Busy filling his nursery?"

"Last I heard, a spare had joined the heir." Sirius shrugged. "I'm sure Samuel is delighted."

Whitfield narrowed his eyes. "Have you seen him since your return to London?"

Sirius scoffed. "After his initial visit to me in the hospital? No. According to his letters, it's either the business of the earldom, or his pregnant countess, or some other plethora of excuses that have kept him away."

"Of course. Being the head of an old, storied earldom comes with many responsibilities." The duke cocked his head. "Have you been invited to Harcourt Estate?" He snorted a laugh when Sirius raised a brow. "A silly question."

Dropping his gaze to the glass in his hand, Sirius pondered his long friendship with the Duke of Whitfield. For all that Whitfield could be acerbic, sardonic, and biting, he was loyal as the day was long. When Sirius had returned from the Continent a broken shell of the man he'd once been, the duke had never shamed him. He had never asked about his time at war, and yet Sirius knew his friend would listen if he ever wanted to talk about the whole terrible business. Once, when Sirius had been unable to get out of bed for a fortnight, Whitfield had forced himself past his butler and valet, marched into his chamber, and yanked open the drapes, revealing his emaciated form to the blinding sunlight. After dragging him out of bed and into a bathtub, the duke had sat by his side as Sirius ate a small meal. Afterward, Whitfield had escorted him to his study, and sat silently next to him for hours, quietly reading a book. Sirius wasn't sure why the duke had stayed, but he suspected that Whitfield simply wanted him to know he wasn't alone.

"So if you're not usually here at this time, why are you here now?" Sirius asked.

"I had a meeting with my solicitor. The man claimed he could only meet in the early afternoon instead of a more appropriate time after four o'clock." Whitfield's expression was all that was disgruntled. "And since I was awake and out, it seemed a waste to return to Whitfield Place and let my thoughts entertain me."

"An abhorrent idea."

"Indeed." Whitfield sighed, all feigned resignation. "So here I sit with the elders, fortune hunters, and you."

"You've fallen so low," Sirius drawled.

"But at least I've fallen with you." Whitfield raised his glass in a toast.

At just that moment, a group of men walked into the dining room, their voices carrying to their far corner. Sirius glanced over, his gaze landing on Viscount Westhope as he picked up a pool cue, a smile on his face as he spoke with a footman. When he clapped the man on the shoulder, Sirius found he was not surprised by the gesture.

Rising to his feet, Sirius tossed his napkin down on the table. "Fox and I are meeting for lunch tomorrow. Join us?"

The duke pulled his chin back. "Of course. But where are you going?"

"I'm off to play billiards."

"You are?" Whitfield frowned. "I never knew you to like billiards."

"I like all manner of things and don't always feel the need to discuss them with you." Sirius jerked his thumb over his shoulder in the direction of where Westhope was racking balls on a plush red table. "Will you join me?"

"Do I have to?"

Sirius sighed. "Do you object to billiards or Westhope?"

The duke pondered this for a second. "The viscount."

"Truly?" At Whitfield's decisive nod, Sirius snorted. "He seems swell. His reputation for being a genuine fellow appears accurate enough."

"And that's precisely why I don't like him. You can't trust a fellow that nice."

"We're friends and I'm a nice fellow," Sirius pointed out.

"Yes, you are." Whitfield flourished a palm. "But then you also lead a double life, so . . ."

Sirius cut the duke a look. He wasn't sure that Whitfield knew of his work with the Home Office, and he knew better than to ask.

"And what of Fox?" Sirius asked, easing the conversation back on track. "He's one of the most honorable men I know."

"Oh, he is. A paragon of virtue." The duke lifted his glass to the lamp. "But he also tells me to my face when I'm being an arse, so you know he has a bit of the devil in him."

"Or a bit of backbone."

"My father always considered both to be synonymous," Whitfield drawled.

Sirius knew better than to ask any questions about the late duke, so he instead took one last swig from his glass and then tugged on his waistcoat. "In that case, I bid you good day."

"Goodbye, Dawson." Whitfield tilted his head in the direction of the billiards table. "And mind your bets. Westhope is known to be quite the player . . . for all that he's a *swell fellow*."

"I appreciate the warning," Sirius said, a tad more warmly than the duke truly deserved.

But then old, loyal friends were always deserving of a bit more regard.

3

Sirius had not thought aeronautical balloons particularly interesting until he saw Isabel Luna staring up at a rainbow-patterned envelope with her mouth ajar.

The June sun beat down on the crowd gathered in Hyde Park to watch the ascent of three colorful hydrogen balloons owned by French brothers who traveled throughout Europe showcasing their engineering marvels. It was also the reason why Lieutenant Colonel Green deemed it necessary for Sirius to attend for the demonstration. And even without those express orders, Viscount Westhope had asked Sirius if he planned to attend the exhibit during their billiards game the day prior. Not one to let an opportunity slip by him, Sirius had nodded in the affirmative.

Encountering Miss Luna in attendance should not have been a surprise, considering her inquisitive nature. His lips curled up as he took in her curious expression, but Sirius did not approach her. He was here on business and had no time to exchange antagonistic volleys with her.

Linking his hands behind his back, Sirius wandered through the crowd, greeting friends and acquaintances taking in the colorful sights. Many expressed surprise to see him at such an event, and Sirius worked not to bristle. His carefree facade was of his own making and served an important purpose, but it was becoming harder not to resent his own reputation.

Sirius skirted around the perimeter of the gathering, his eyes darting about for a glimpse of Viscount Westhope. His search was halted, though, when a feminine hand grasped his arm. Even through his coat, Sirius felt nails sink into his bicep.

"Captain Dawson, what a delight it is to see you here today."

A flirtatious smile had settled on his lips before he even pivoted about. "Lady Needham, I assure you it's me who's delighted to encounter you here. I had no notion you had an interest in aeronautical balloons."

The pretty blonde dipped her head, the flowers on her fashionable hat complementing the color of her cheeks. The widowed baroness was adept at playing shy and bashful, though Sirius knew her to be anything but.

"Surely you remember how much I enjoy trying new things," she said, her voice a breathy whisper.

Christ, that husky tone used to have a direct line to his cock. Emily, Lady Needham, knew that, if the taunting smirk on her full pink lips was any indication. But now, Sirius felt more annoyance than arousal.

Gritting his teeth, Sirius gestured to the balloon that sat in the grass several yards away. "Are you enjoying the exhibit?"

"I am now," the baroness crooned, pressing her curvy, perfumed body into his side.

"Goodness, your ladyship, you're much more friendly today than you were the other night at the Meadows ball." Sirius patted her hand. "I seem to recall you being quite peeved with me."

"Well, of course I was upset with you. You abandoned me when we were supposed to share a waltz." She pouted, her lips twisting into a perfect moue. "You know how I hate being teased."

Sirius scoffed, his roguish facade slipping for a moment. "You only hate teasing when it's not you who's doing the teasing."

Lady Needham narrowed her eyes. "You've never spoken to me that way before."

"I suppose I haven't." He leaned down to murmur in her ear, "But then you know you deserve it."

Her grip on his arm tightened as she purred, "And what are you going to do to punish me?"

Despite opening his mouth to respond, the words died on his tongue, for at that moment his eyes snagged on the unlikely sight of Isabel Luna tossing her head back in laughter. A frown overtook his face, and Sirius blinked several times, uncertain if what he was seeing was real.

Had he ever seen her laugh? Surely with her sisters, at some point or another. Certainly not with him. He frowned as his mind raced through his memories of the time she spent at Dancourt Abbey. Isabel had appeared to go out of her way to avoid him, but there were occasions in which they had encountered each other in his library, and discussed the books they were reading. She had also recommended several possible additions to his collection, and he had recommended some of his own to her. But try as he might, Sirius could not remember making her laugh. Or smile. And now, as he noted the raspy quality of Isabel's laughter, why did that seem like a great loss?

Isabel appeared to be in deep conversation with a gentleman in an ornate suit, a fancy beaver hat perched on his head. The man was standing next to one of the balloon baskets, and he used his gold-lion-topped cane to point up at the balloon canopy, Isabel enthusiastically nodding her dark head at his words. While Sirius watched, the man opened the basket door and invited Isabel aboard, where he continued to point out various components of the hydrogen release valve.

"Will you come by this evening? I should be free after eleven o'clock."

Sirius glanced at Lady Needham with his brows raised. "I beg your pardon."

The baroness smacked his arm with her reticule. "Sirius, darling, whatever has you so distracted?"

"The balloons." He gestured to the various exhibits surrounding them. Sirius allowed his gaze to touch on Isabel for a passing moment. *Is she going up for a ride? Surely that is unsafe.*

"I would think talk of spending the evening together would be more interesting to you."

Sirius locked his teeth to contain a sigh. At a point in the past, Lady Needham had been his mark, as her late husband had been suspected of smuggling various goods to and from his estate in Cornwall. After the baron's death, Sirius continued to meet with Lady Needham from time to time, for her demands of him were simple and enjoyable.

But his interest *and* patience for her had waned.

Taking a moment to clear his throat, Sirius affixed an easy smile to his lips. "Unfortunately I have plans this evening."

Huffing, Lady Needham asked, "What could you possibly be doing that will be more enjoyable than spending the night with me?"

Sirius intended to spend the evening reviewing the ledgers from Dancourt Abbey and sending letters to his steward and some of the men who now made the abbey their home. He'd also managed to secure the translated version of Dostoevsky's latest novel, something Sirius had been patiently waiting on because his Russian was atrocious. Nothing sounded better than relaxing in his study with a dram and a good book.

But Sirius had no intention of sharing this with Lady Needham.

Instead, he shrugged, smothering a snort when he noticed how the baroness's eyes danced along the breadth of his shoulders. "I will be enjoying dinner with friends."

A familiar face appeared in the crowd, and Sirius snapped to attention. There was Westhope, exactly the man he had hoped to see.

Inclining his head, he flashed Lady Needham a bright smile. "If you will excuse me, my lady, I see a friend I'd like to greet."

The baroness glanced in the direction he had been looking, her hand coming up to shield her eyes from the sun. "Do you mean Lord Westhope? I'll greet him with you."

Irritation flashed hot in his veins, and Sirius nodded tightly. Extending his hand for Lady Needham to precede him, Sirius fell into step behind her, doing his best not to scowl.

That was until he heard a muted shriek. Sirius had no notion how he even heard it above the din, but he turned his head in time to see that the swell of the crowd had inadvertently jostled loose the tethers that secured one of the balloons. Now the basket rocked to and fro, the dark-haired young woman inside it grasping the wicker lip like a lifeline. In the pause of one heartbeat, her terror-filled eyes met his, and Sirius's heart spasmed when he realized it was Isabel.

Without a moment's hesitation, Sirius sprinted to her, his gaze not releasing its hold on hers. The basket now floated several feet above the ground, and Isabel's normally tawny complexion was pale.

"Miss Luna," Sirius called as he pushed and shoved his way through the crush surrounding the basket. When his hands curled around the basket lip, he hoisted himself inside, immediately reaching to grab Isabel's arm. "Allow me to help you out."

Isabel's small gasp met his ears. "I think it may be too late."

Pulling his gaze from her face, Sirius looked around and noticed that the balloon was now almost ten feet above the ground, the collective gazes of the crowd staring up at him as he stared down at them. He noted the gentleman Isabel had been speaking with earlier, no doubt the balloon engineer, was frantically trying to restake the tethers holding the balloon to the ground, several men rushing to assist him. Sirius's stomach gave an uncomfortable swoop as the basket rose several more feet before it jerked to a stop, the ropes groaning with the tension. Peering down again, he spied the engineer waving his hat, before cupping a hand around his mouth.

"Hang tight. We'll have you down in a few minutes," he called.

Sirius lifted his arm in acknowledgment and slowly pivoted to face Isabel.

Her eyes were clenched closed. Her hands were curled about a canopy rope, and if she were not wearing gloves, Sirius was certain her knuckles would be white. The only time he had ever seen Isabel this terrified was when her sister, Ana María, had been abducted. His heart lurched out of rhythm at the sight.

"I can't say I'm surprised you would jump at the chance to soar in a balloon above London," he said, the tension in his chest easing when Isabel's lips twitched around a smile.

"I assure you that a flight above the city was not my intention." Her throat worked on a swallow. "I-I'm actually afraid of heights."

"Are you truly?" At her nod, Sirius took a small step toward her. "I find that quite surprising. You don't strike me as a woman who's afraid of anything."

Her soulful dark eyes blinked open then, and in their depths he glimpsed a perplexing bit of vulnerability. That couldn't be right, and Sirius lifted his hand to reach for her, to reassure her . . . until he remembered himself. His arm dropped to his side with a thud.

"That may be the most flattering compliment I have ever received." Isabel stared at him for a long moment and then her gaze slid away. "Sadly, I find myself afraid of all sorts of things."

Sirius worked his jaw on a pause, unsure of what to say but mindful that his response could either ensure their quarrelsome interactions continued, or perhaps forge a new path toward friendship. And with their connections, friendship seemed an appealing alternative.

Resting his hand near hers on the basket, Sirius maneuvered his body until he prevented Isabel from glancing down to see the crowd below. Being this close to her, he caught a faint whiff of vanilla. Her soap or lotion, perhaps. It suited her.

Isabel looked up at him then, a pucker forming between her brows. Was she wondering why he stood so near to her? Before she questioned his motives, Sirius spoke, still unsure of exactly what he was going to say.

"There's nothing wrong with being frightened of things. The world is a frightening place." Sirius snagged her gaze. "It's what we do with that fear that matters. Do we let it control us? Or do we acknowledge it and move forward anyway?"

The corner of her pink lips quirked. "Is this what you told your men on the battlefield?"

Sirius chuckled, mortified to feel heat spread across his face. "I wish I had been wise enough to think of it then, but alas, such insight was lost to me."

Isabel ducked her head, but not before he spied a flashing glimpse of a smile.

"I read an entertaining little book about aeronautical balloons called *The Balloon Travels of Robert Merry*, and it reignited my curiosity. There was an exhibit in Mexico City several years ago that I had been excited to attend." Isabel shrugged, but the movement was anything but blithe. "However, my father forbade me to go."

"Forbade you?" He blinked. "But why?"

Her shoulders lifted once again, the action stiff and almost defensive. "Because he wouldn't be attending. He only ever allowed us to attend events if being seen benefited him."

Fox had mentioned that Mr. Luna, Isabel's father, had been a demanding and difficult parent. Sirius had not really considered what that meant until this moment, but the dejected wilt to Isabel's frame set his teeth on edge. He had not had much of a relationship with his own father, the late earl never finding interest in his spare. His apathy had stung, but now Sirius wondered if apathy was the better alternative to the casual cruelness Isabel suffered.

Clearing his throat, he waved his hand at the landscape below, mindful not to shift his weight. "Well, it is a good thing he's not here now, or else you would not have been able to go on this adventure."

"Adventure?" Isabel slowly raised her head and gingerly looked at the scenery beyond the basket. Sirius estimated they were about twenty-five to thirty feet above the ground, a considerable height, and yet he was thankful they had not risen further. "I will endeavor to look at this as an adventure and not a terror-inducing disaster."

A grin overtook his face, and a smidge of triumph settled in his chest when Isabel's irises widened. "There's that indomitable spirit I've come to know you for. I knew it wouldn't stay away for long."

"Indomitable? It's a word I've heard used to describe my father." Pink swept across her cheeks. "But . . . I quite like that you used it to describe me. I would never have dreamed there was an association."

"Well, then it's a good thing I am here to inform you." Sirius tilted his head as he stared down at her. "Are you feeling better?"

Isabel nodded, her gaze darting to the ground below for only a second. "It helps that we haven't risen higher. And Mr. Thompson said they purposely didn't bring enough hydrogen for manned flights, so even if the tethers did not hold, we wouldn't soar for long."

"Mr. Thompson is the balloon engineer?" At her nod, Sirius looked over the side of the basket. "It appears he has all the tethers secured, so I imagine he and his men will be hauling us down soon enough."

Sirius turned back to her, curious to find Isabel considering him with her lip tucked between her teeth. He raised his brow in question, and she quickly looked away.

"I find myself surprised that you're here. A balloon exhibition doesn't seem like the sort of entertainment you'd favor."

"I confess that I've never given much thought to aeronautical balloons, but now that I have a front-row view of the contraption"—Sirius tipped his head back to stare at the underbelly of the envelope—"I can see why you find them so interesting."

A shy smile flitted over her face.

"I was invited by a friend to attend. And since it was sunny and the air crisp, it seemed an ideal outing for a spring morning." He jerked his thumb over his shoulder. "And now look at me. High above the ground with a view of London most people will never see."

Isabel shifted her gaze from his to scan the horizon. "I suppose you're right. This vantage point is ideal. Rather breathtaking, really."

Sirius didn't know what changed. But in that instant, being this close to her, with the breeze sending strands of black hair against her cheeks and her vanilla scent to his nose, her expression relaxed and open in ways she had never been with him, Isabel Luna was stunningly beautiful. And damn if that didn't set him back on his heels.

"Breathtaking, indeed."

While her flight above London was over within twenty minutes, Isabel still felt as if the world had tilted.

And it was all thanks to Captain Dawson.

Isabel had been looking forward to the exhibition for weeks. Ever since her father had denied her the opportunity to attend a similar event all those years before, she had been fascinated by the machines, with their colorful envelopes. Mr. Thompson had immediately noticed her interest in the burner, and had been more than happy to discuss the mechanics of it. In fact, he had entertained all of Isabel's questions, his demeanor friendly and open, with none of the impatience she usually encountered when she showcased her curiosity in something. Isabel was grateful.

After a time, though, he had been called away, and Isabel was left to admire the balloon and reflect upon the things she'd learned about its construction. That was until the crowd swelled around her, and she had been forced to seek refuge in the basket to escape being crushed. Or so she thought—until the binds anchoring the basket to the ground were pulled free in the rush of bodies.

Suddenly the only sound Isabel heard was the pounding of her own heart. It roared in her ears as the basket pitched back and forth; the creak of the ropes as they strained against the push of the crowd was like cracks of thunder, and Isabel's lungs refused to draw in breath. Her knees threatened to buckle, and she clutched the basket, unsure of what to do when she had seen Captain Dawson's head above the crowd. Before she had time to blink, he was in the basket with her as it lurched and jerked into the air.

It had been terrifying . . . and yet Isabel knew Captain Dawson would keep her safe because he'd done so before when she'd been a guest at Dancourt Abbey.

And he had again. Contrary to their usual barbed animosity, the captain had been gentle with her. He didn't tease her for her fear of heights or scold her for finding herself in such a predicament. He had called her indomitable, and despite the harrowing situation, he had made her feel as such.

Now as she stood next to him, staring blindly at the rainbow-colored canopy above them, Isabel pondered what to say. A thank-you seemed so inadequate, and yet how else could she express her gratitude? How Isabel wished she weren't so awkward.

Straightening her spine, Isabel turned on her heel to face him, waiting a heartbeat for him to meet her gaze.

"Thank you," she murmured, her throat dry. "I'm grateful to you for—"

"There you are, Dawson. Whatever happened to you?"

Isabel flinched, jerking her head to the side to spy Baroness Needham walking toward them, her green eyes bouncing between her and Dawson. It took every bit of pride not to slink away. Lady Needham had a reputation for being cutting and catty. It would be one thing to endure the older woman's slights when in Gabby's company, for her younger sister's sharp tongue had no match, but to weather the insults alone or, worse, in Dawson's presence . . .

Apprehension unfurled in her chest as Isabel realized how much she relied upon her sisters, especially Gabby, to shield her from uncomfortable social encounters. However, if she were to return to Mexico as she desired, how was she to find her place among the elevated circles her parents occupied if she could not maneuver around cutting remarks and innuendos? She couldn't cling to Gabby's skirts indefinitely.

"I apologize for leaving you so suddenly, but Miss Luna here was in need of assistance." Captain Dawson flashed a smile at her, but it appeared almost manufactured. Certainly not of the sunny variety he had shared with her in the balloon basket. "We ended up taking an unexpected trip above London."

Lady Needham gasped. "Was that you in the balloon I saw slip from its tethers?"

"It was, indeed."

The baroness clasped his arm, pressing her body close to his side. Isabel ground her molars together. "Good gracious, are you all right? Were you injured?"

"I appreciate your concern, my lady, but I am fine." Captain Dawson's indigo eyes swept to her. "As is Miss Luna, thankfully."

For the first time, Lady Needham turned her gaze on Isabel. Isabel had met the baroness once or twice since she had arrived in England, but the older woman had never paid her much attention, and why would she? Lady Needham was a renowned beauty, with gold hair, a porcelain complexion, and pretty, pouty lips. Gabby had once remarked that she looked like a doll, with the empty head to match. Isabel had thought her sister hyperbolic, for the blatant inspection the woman gave her now was quite calculating. Still, she raised her chin. Just a tad.

"Well, you've caught me by surprise." The baroness waved her fan lazily in front of her face as she stared at Isabel. "I had no notion you were a philanthropist, Dawson."

Although his expression remained impassive, a muscle twitched in his jaw. "I'm afraid I don't know what you mean, my lady."

Lady Needham's brows disappeared into her hairline as her gaze darted between him and Isabel. "Come now, of course you do. Why else would you come to the rescue of such a little sparrow?"

A sparrow? Flames of mortification burned across Isabel's skin.

Risking a quick glance at the captain, she found him staring at Lady Needham with a pucker between his brows. "Is that supposed to be an insult? I've always thought sparrows were plucky and clever, and Miss Luna is both those things."

He thought her clever?

"Perhaps," the baroness replied, drawing out the word, "but then they aren't terribly pretty, are they?"

"I've always thought beauty was subjective, my lady." Sirius lifted a shoulder. "Something can be beautiful because it's clever and plucky."

"If you say so."

Isabel didn't have a chance to ponder Captain Dawson's

answer before Lady Needham pivoted on her heel to face her again. Isabel endeavored not to curl her shoulders in.

"Are you here by yourself, Miss Luna?"

"I'm not. Viscountess Yardley and my sister were visiting with friends near the lawn when I walked over here for a closer look at the balloons." Isabel aimed for a smile, but suspected it was more of a grimace. "Neither was as interested in their mechanics as I was."

"Well, of course you were interested." The baroness flicked her fingers in the direction of the balloons. "No doubt you've never seen anything so grand and advanced."

Isabel rocked back on her heels. "I fancy I've seen many amazing sights, both here in England and in Mexico."

Captain Dawson clutched a hand to his chest in faux surprise. "So are you saying England and Europe do not have a monopoly on technological innovations?"

"Indeed not." Isabel pressed her lips together to keep from laughing. "Despite what some people may believe, Mexico City is quite cosmopolitan. It's often called the Paris of Latin America." She tapped her chin with her forefinger, playing coy. "Or perhaps Paris is the Mexico City of Europe."

Isabel experienced a moment of pleasure when the baroness's mien darkened. But her response was nothing compared to that of Captain Dawson, who chuckled out loud, his eyes glinting in a way she didn't think she'd ever seen outside of Dancourt Abbey. "I suppose it's natural for people to believe their home is the center of the world because it is the center of *their* world. I find it refreshing to be reminded that the world is much vaster than my experience on any given day."

Ducking her head, Isabel hoped to hide how his words made her cheeks warm. That Captain Dawson understood her, supported her claim, boosted her confidence more than she was certain it warranted. Nevertheless, his approval made it easier for Isabel to stand a little taller.

"Yes, well, I've never been interested in traveling. Why would I travel when London offers everything a sophisticated woman could ever want?"

Lady Needham adjusted the fit of her fine leather gloves, her head tilted just so to allow the sunlight to glint off the colorful blossoms adorning her bonnet. The baroness was exquisite . . . and it was obvious she wanted Captain Dawson. Isabel could never compete with such a woman. And why would she want to? The captain was a scoundrel of the highest order.

Yet, the baroness's words smarted, and while it wasn't like her to argue a point, Isabel heard herself say, "Not everyone travels for enjoyment, though."

"What do you mean?" Lady Needham asked, lips pursed.

Inhaling quickly, Isabel said, "Some are forced to travel, and they take their culture, their history with them."

"As you have, Miss Luna," the captain said, his tone sober. Looking at the baroness, he tilted his head. "And your point seems rather shortsighted, my lady."

Isabel blinked at Captain Dawson's words. Apparently, she was not the only one surprised, for the baroness frowned outright.

"Whatever do you mean?"

Captain Dawson widened his stance. "What I mean, your ladyship, is that if Britain is providing you with everything you want and need, it's because it was taken from somewhere else."

Lady Needham's brows dipped low. "I don't understand."

"The lace on your bodice, my lady."

Isabel only realized she had spoken aloud when the captain and baroness turned to her in unison.

The set of Lady Needham's jaw was sharp enough to cut stone. "What about it, Miss Luna?"

Darting her gaze to Captain Dawson, Isabel found him staring at her with his brows raised. He was as surprised by her interjection as she was.

Pressing her lips together for a second, Isabel finally said, "Your bodice is trimmed with Spanish lace, ma'am."

"And?" the baroness demanded.

"And, my dear lady, that means it was made in Spain," the captain said with a teasing grin.

Lady Needham brought a hand up to her bodice, her gloved fingers fidgeting with the lace border.

"Do you like pineapples?" Isabel asked.

"They're divine, are they not?" The baroness sniffed, directing her attention to Dawson. "My grandmother told me her parents rented a pineapple for a grand ball they hosted when her older brother announced his engagement. Can you imagine?"

Yes, Isabel could. Meeting Captain Dawson's exasperated gaze, she realized he could as well.

"Well, pineapples were imported to England. As were"— Isabel tapped her fingers as she listed—"sugar, tea, potatoes, silk, cotton, tobacco, and many, many more items."

"What an interesting little lesson." Lady Needham flashed her a terrible look. "Interesting and pointless."

"Not pointless at all, your ladyship." Captain Dawson pulled his timepiece from his pocket and considered it for a second, his mien bored, before he snapped it closed again. "You claimed there was no point in traveling when London is the center of the world, so Miss Luna shared all the ways the world has made life in London better."

"Yes, because the British know how to trade." The baroness twirled her parasol. "Even barbarians know how to trade."

Isabel would have ignored the remark had Lady Needham not slid a glance to her as she said it. Stomping down the anger that threatened to cloud her vision, Isabel forced herself to ponder what Gabby would do if she had been dealt such a slight. No doubt her younger sister would have immediately responded with a sharp retort that would have the baroness scarlet with embarrassment.

But Isabel did not possess Gabby's quick mind, so instead she calmed her temper and ventured, "Trade is always a good thing, but only when it's conducted for the benefit of both parties. It seems to me that the British Empire is not so much engaged in trade as they are in exploitation. They use their might to take what they want by force, often at the detriment of those they have stolen from."

The baroness spread her palms. "Perhaps some people do not understand the resources they possess and require a strong hand to guide them."

A strong hand to guide them? Isabel clenched her teeth so tightly her jaw throbbed. Thankfully Lady Needham appeared not to have noticed how her words affected her, for the baroness's attention was fixed on Captain Dawson . . . whose piercing gaze ensnared Isabel's. For a passing moment it seemed as if he shared her frustration, and Isabel sucked in a breath at the sharp pinch under her ribs.

"Have a care. You wander down dangerous paths." Captain Dawson's tone was light, but his gaze was hard as he stared at Lady Needham. After a tense pause, he changed the subject. "Now if you ever were to travel, my lady, I believe you would enjoy visiting India. An enchanting country with rich, delicious foods, lush textiles and spices, and a fascinating history."

"It's quite hot in India, I've heard." The baroness shuddered. "I'm certain I would not like that."

"It can be quite humid, especially during the summer months." The captain looked to Isabel then. "Mexico enjoys warmer temperatures, too, does it not? It must have been quite an adjustment when you arrived in London—"

"Yes, but I imagine Miss Luna is better built for the heat," Lady Needham interrupted with a dismissive wave of her hand.

Isabel went still. *Built for the heat?* Whatever did that mean? She opened her mouth to ask the baroness, certain the answer would not be at all friendly, when the captain interjected.

"Considering Miss Luna has spent the majority of her life in more temperate weather, she is probably used to the heat a bit more than a pampered English baroness." When Lady Needham smacked his shoulder with her fan, he chuckled. "What offends you, my lady? That I called you pampered? Well, are you not?"

"I've been cared for." The baroness twirled a blond curl around her gloved finger. "As a titled lady, it's only appropriate that I should be protected and pampered."

"And your late husband ensured you were both," Captain Dawson said, patting her arm.

"You've done a wonderful job of caring for me, as well." Lady Needham stared up at him, her eyes wide. "Although you've been neglecting me as of late."

Isabel shifted her gaze away from the fawning expression on Lady Needham's face. Isabel had heard the rumors that the baroness and Captain Dawson were engaged in an affair, but seeing the woman gaze up at him like a subject in a Hayez painting made her almost wish she were back up in the balloon.

As if sensing her discomfort, Captain Dawson took a step back from the baroness. "I've been busy, my lady. Now if you ladies will excuse me, I came here today to visit with a friend, and I should finally see to that task."

"I believe the viscount's left, Dawson," Lady Needham said, pointing her fan at him.

His face fell. "That's unfortunate."

"But now you're free to be a dear and escort me to my carriage." The baroness wrapped her arm around his, flashing a triumphant smile at Isabel. "We never did finish our conversation."

If Isabel weren't watching him so closely, she would have missed the way his chest expanded and then deflated with a sigh.

"Very well, my lady, let's get you out of the sun." A hint of a smile curved his lips as Dawson tipped his hat to Isabel. "Good day, Miss Luna."

With an ache in her throat, Isabel watched the couple amble away. Why she should feel sadness and a sense of loss to see the captain depart, she didn't know. Nor did she like it.

Pushing her melancholy aside, Isabel turned and fixed her eyes on the balloon envelope overhead, willing herself to feel the same excitement she had before her impromptu balloon ride with Captain Dawson. Before he had smiled and laughed with her, and wiped her mind clear of thoughts.

"I know Captain Dawson is a rogue, but I thought he at least had some taste." Gabby came to a stop beside her, curling her lips as she looked at a point over Isabel's shoulder. "Lady Needham? He must be addled in the brain to associate with her."

"She's quite pretty, don't you think?" Isabel said, biting her cheek.

"I don't think anything of the sort." Her younger sister snorted. "Lady Needham is unremarkable. Vapid. Mean-spirited. Enamored with her own consequence."

Isabel looked at her sister from the corner of her eye. "Am I to assume you're not fond of the baroness?"

"Come now, Isa, you know I'm fond of very few people. You. Ana. Gideon. Mother. Sometimes Lady Yardley." Gabby paused, staring into the middle distance. "Perhaps Dove, but only because she's an adorable, empty-headed little beast."

"Five people and a dog?" Isabel chuckled. "I'm surprised, even for you."

"No, you're not. You know I hold little affection or patience for most people I meet, especially when they're idiots." Gabby sighed. "I'm disappointed to see that Captain Dawson may well be an idiot, too."

"I tried to warn you."

"I suppose you did." Gabby leaned into her side. "One day I'll learn to listen to my older sister."

"But today is not that day," Isabel said.

Gabby clicked her tongue. "Indeed, it is not."

And perhaps one day, Isabel would learn not to indulge her romantic notions at the expense of her good sense.

4

As Sirius wandered the hallowed halls of Westminster, he cursed the fact that he even had to be there in the first place.

But despite his best efforts, he'd been unable to pin down Viscount Westhope, and Sirius was annoyed. After missing him at the balloon festival, Sirius had met him again to play billiards at their club, but the gregarious viscount had been surrounded by friends, which made engaging in a deep conversation all but impossible. Sirius tried, though, and Lord Westhope reciprocated his attempts at conversation in that easy manner some men have when they are confident in who they are and their place in the world. Sirius had worked hard to create a similar image for himself, and few people seemed aware that he walked around every day wearing a mask. Whitfield, of course, but then only because the duke was his closest friend, and Gideon Fox, because the man was shrewd and insightful. But seeing as the man wore a mask himself, Fox had never judged him, and Sirius was grateful.

There was now a new person to add to the list: Isabel Luna. She had seemed to look beneath his veneer during their conversations at the festival, and he found it uncomfortable to be the subject of her keen stare . . . especially when he knew it was usually sparked by his roguish actions.

But truly, what choice did he have? Sirius had a job to do, and playing the role of an incorrigible rogue was part of it. He had no business befriending unmarried ladies, no matter how awkwardly charming they were.

Coming to a stop in the middle of the hall, Sirius pressed his fingers to his temples. Now was most certainly not the time to allow his thoughts to wander to the riddle that was Isabel Luna.

After casually inquiring about the location of the viscount's office, Sirius mentally recited the story he had fabricated as an excuse to pay the man a visit. But when he arrived at Westhope's office, the viscount was not in sight. Biting back a slew of curses, Sirius pivoted, staring down one end of the hall and then the other. He tapped his hat against his palm as he contemplated what to do. Would the viscount be at the club? It was still a bit early, but it was possible. Or perhaps Sirius could track him down to—

"I'm surprised to find you here, Dawson."

Jerking his head about, Sirius smiled when his gaze collided with Gideon Fox's.

"I'm not a complete stranger to these halls, you know," he said after regathering himself, holding out his hand in greeting.

Fox shook it, a warm smile in his eyes if not on his lips. His friend possessed a reserved nature, and was a man who kept his emotions locked tight. Sirius thought Fox would have made an excellent officer, leading soldiers with his firm and steadfast example. But Fox had shunned the military in favor of politics. He had made a name for himself in Commons as a firebrand, a reputation he imagined would be bolstered by his marriage to the politically savvy Ana María Luna. Although the pair had caused quite the scandal when they first returned to London after their marriage, they were quickly winning over critics and foes alike.

Truly, Sirius should have assumed Fox would be at Westminster, for if he was not with his lovely wife, he was stalking the halls of Parliament, garnering support for his many proposals, and lending his voice and his vote to all manner of causes.

And it occurred to Sirius that if anyone knew about Westhope, it would probably be Fox.

"Would you like to come back to my office while I finish up a letter, and then we can get a drink?" Fox jerked his thumb at the open doorway behind him. "I don't know about you, but I could use a stiff one."

Sirius nodded and silently followed his friend back to his office. He whistled when he stepped across the threshold and looked around.

"Faith, this space is much different than the one you had when I first met you."

And it was. At least three times the size of the narrow office Fox had been given when he'd first won his borough seat. Now, his friend's large oak desk sat before a set of beveled windows, painting his desktop in sunlight. A bookshelf lined an entire wall, with a plush velvet settee tucked into the corner. It was a space designed to make an impression, and pride for his friend swelled Sirius's chest. Fox had waged numerous battles to find success within Parliament, and Sirius was happy he was receiving the recognition and respect he deserved.

Sliding into one of the armchairs angled before Fox's desk, Sirius gestured to the bookshelf with his head. "If you would like some suggestions for books to fill your shelves, let me know. It appears your collection is off to a stellar start."

From where he sat, Sirius spied a nice selection of both fiction and nonfiction books; poetry collections and philosophy tomes; and history volumes, in what appeared to be both English and Spanish. The sight brought a smile to his face.

"Isabel has been assisting me with building up my library. I had wanted to keep all my books at home, but she insisted that I need a collection here as well. She claimed it solidified the perception of me being a learned gentleman." Fox smoothed his hands down his lapels. "Ana agreed, so who am I to say no?"

Seeing his stoic, proper friend so happy with his wife and marriage had jealousy sinking its claws into his throat. Sirius was of an age where most of his old schoolmates were married and filling their nurseries, and yet he was still perfecting the life of a wealthy bachelor about town, tumbling into beds with various ladies and courtesans, and coloring the gossip pages with his conquests. It was all a facade, of course, meant to hide the true seriousness of his endeavors, and those same endeavors made settling down impossible. And lonely.

But even if he could steal a piece of domestic felicity, Sirius knew he didn't deserve it. Why should he get to marry and have a family, live a full life, when so many of his men—men infinitely better than him—did not have the opportunity?

So instead, Sirius pushed down all those feelings of what could have been, and focused on what was.

"If Miss Luna is assisting you with your book selection, I will graciously surrender the floor, for she has excellent taste," he said.

Fox tilted his head to the side. "I wasn't aware you and Isabel had spoken of books."

"While you and your lady wife were celebrating your vows

at Dancourt Abbey," Sirius began, noting with a twinge of amusement when Fox severed eye contact to dutifully study his desktop, "Miss Luna and I had several conversations about the state of my library and what books I could acquire to elevate it."

"Yes, well"—Fox coughed into his fist—"I am still indebted to you for everything you did to ensure Ana and I could marry, and marry in such fine fashion."

Fox had offered to marry Ana María to protect her and her sisters, and Sirius had hosted them at Dancourt Abbey for their wedding and the first few weeks of their marriage. He'd had an up-close view of his friend's marriage of convenience as it morphed into one of love, and the happy memories of such an event imbued the old abbey with a bright, cheerful light. His staff still spoke fondly of the "pretty Mexican sisters" who had spent the summer with them.

And now Sirius wished he had taken time to actually converse with Isabel beyond a few exchanges, whether about books or her fascination with balloons or her fear of heights, instead of avoiding her. Sirius couldn't help but feel as if he had squandered an opportunity.

"You owe me nothing, my friend." Sirius shook his head . . . to dismiss Fox's suggestion and to clear his thoughts of the younger Miss Luna. "I know if I were ever in need, you would assist me just as readily."

"Of course I would." Fox propped his elbows on the desktop and set his chin in his folded hands. "Now tell me why you're here at Westminster."

His knack for getting right to the point was a reason Sirius liked Fox. "What do you know of Viscount Westhope?" he asked, keeping his voice as deceptively innocent as he could.

But Fox was not fooled, for his gaze narrowed minutely. Still, his friend was discreet, and did not give voice to any of the questions flashing in his dark eyes.

Fox leaned back in his chair, tipping his head toward the coffered ceiling. "Westhope is a nice fellow. Friendly, gracious, easy to converse with. If I find myself at a meeting with him, I try to take a seat at his side, for he will not drone on and on in my ear when I'm intent on following the conversation."

Friendly, gracious, and easy to converse with was Sirius's impression of the man, as well. But such an impression provided no hint of the man's sympathies toward the French, and as long as they remained unknown, Lieutenant Colonel Green would continue to scrutinize him.

"So you would say he's serious about voting his seat?"

"Westhope's participation is not limited to his vote." Fox drummed his fingers on the wooden desktop. "He sits on committees, he works to gather cosigners and supporters for his bills, and he debates policy admirably."

"He sounds like quite the politician," Sirius drawled.

"Honestly, he is. I like him." Fox snorted. "And you know I don't like most of the men who walk these halls."

"Indeed I do." Sirius dropped his gaze to his lap, mentally debating what to ask next. Before he could speak, Fox did.

"Is there a particular reason you are inquiring after the viscount?"

Sirius was shaking his head before his friend finished speaking. "No particular reason."

Fox pressed his lips together, disbelief flashing across his face. But the man was too well bred to push Sirius on this obvious lie, so he nodded. "Since you're here, allow me to extend an invitation for you to join Ana and me for dinner tonight. If you don't have other plans, that is."

"I do not. And I would be very happy to dine with you and Mrs. Fox." Sirius frowned. "Will it just be the three of us?"

"No. Isabel and Gabby will join us, along with Señor Valdés and Lady Yardley." Fox chuckled. "Gabby made me promise not to invite Whitfield, so please do not mention it to him."

It was Sirius's turn to be amused. "She really does not like him, does she?"

His friend shook his head. "I'm not entirely sure why, either. They're so very similar in temperament, I thought surely they would get along."

"Perhaps that's why, though." Sirius rose to his feet, a parting smile on his face. "Neither is quite used to thinking highly of others, so they confuse their emotions with distaste."

"Oh, please share this theory with Gabby tonight." Tipping his head back, Fox let out a bark of laughter. "I do so anticipate her reaction."

"Until tonight, then." Sirius offered a wave as he stepped out the door. "*I'm* anticipating the entire evening."

"Ana, that dress looks divine on you."

Isabel's older sister twirled about, the full skirts of her emerald-green evening gown glinting in the glow of the gaslights. "Gracias. I adore the color and Gideon is quite fond of it on me."

"Gideon is fond of whatever you wear, whether a dazzling gown or a coarse potato sack." A dimple appeared in Gabby's cheek as she smirked. "Although I'm certain he's fonder of when you wear nothing at all."

Ana María pressed her hands to her cheeks as she laughed, while Isabel simply rolled her eyes. Gabby enjoyed shocking people and had been doing it her whole life to earn attention from others. As the youngest Luna sister whom their father had long hoped would be his much-desired son, Gabby had often been pushed to the side and ignored. Isabel was ashamed to think of all the ways she had done the same, confusing her sister's antics as proof of her being spoiled, instead of the frustrated actions of a child who simply wanted to be seen.

This realization allowed Isabel to maintain her patience with Gabby, even when her exuberance became a bit trying.

"You're lucky Lady Yardley is not present. She would be appalled by your innuendo." Any scold contained in Ana's words was softened by the smile in her voice.

"Yes, well, her ladyship enjoys finding fault with me, so I might as well make it easy for her," Gabby grumbled, sliding into an armchair and crossing her arms across her chest.

"Do you need a bit of a respite from the viscountess?" Ana María accepted a pair of earrings from her maid, Consuelo, before she cocked her head at Gabby. "If so, you know you're welcome to stay with Gideon and me for a spell."

"And leave behind Isa?" Gabby scowled. "Never."

Isabel made a noise in the back of her throat. "Lady Yardley's townhome is hardly far. It will not hurt my feelings if you want to spend some time with Ana." She fidgeted with the fit of her gloves. "Although I will miss you both."

"Isa," her older sister crooned, wrapping an arm around her shoulders, "you are more than welcome to come stay, as well."

"Yo lo sé," Isabel murmured. "But it will be good for Gabby to have a break from me and the viscountess." In truth, she might be able to accomplish more without worrying about her altogether too observant younger sister becoming suspicious. "Perhaps I can visit next, though?"

"Definitely." Ana María swayed back and forth with her. "I've longed for our chats. Just the three of us gossiping, in Spanish."

"I miss hearing Spanish all around me." Isabel exhaled loudly. "I become homesick when I think about it."

"Me, too, actually." Gabby's expression turned wistful. "I also crave the warm weather, the delicious food—are the British afraid of seasoning? Everything they cook is so bland."

Isabel met Ana María's eyes, and the pair laughed. Gabby shook her head while she watched them, her own mouth quirking in amusement.

"Laugh all you want, but you know I'm right," she declared.

"It's hard to argue your point," Isabel said, pressing a hand to her chest, "when I reach for the saltcellar before I even take a bite of my meal."

Ana María took a seat next to Gabby, dabbing at her eyes. "You know how I've been searching for a new cook after Mrs. Wheaton left to live with her daughter in Yorkshire?" When her sisters nodded, she continued. "Well, I've found a candidate. And the best part is she's Mexicana."

"What?" Isabel exclaimed. "How is that possible?"

"Many Mexican families have emigrated over the last few years, whether to escape the conflict with the French or the civil war before that. Tío Arturo has kept abreast of their numbers, and frequently meets with many of them to help them get settled." Ana María smiled. "He recommended Señora Gomez to me, and she will start tomorrow."

"And just in time for my visit." Gabby clapped her hands together gleefully. "I cannot wait to taste enchiladas again."

"Let's hope Señora Gomez is able to find the ingredients needed to make them," Ana María pointed out.

A knock on the door interrupted their conversation. At Ana María's call, Consuelo entered again with a letter in her hand.

"Señora, esto es para ustedes. Señor Valdés just arrived, and he wanted you to have it inmediatamente."

Isabel's mouth went dry, and she struggled to swallow as Ana María quickly unfolded the letter and scanned the contents.

"It's from Mother," she said breathlessly. "They've received word that the French may be marching toward their location." Ignoring Gabby's sharp gasp, Ana María kept reading. "They're moving, and she's not sure when she'll be able to write again."

Swaying on her feet, Isabel knotted her hands in her skirts as emotion after emotion crashed over her in unrelenting waves. If the French discovered where her parents—where *Presidente Juárez*—were hiding, all would be lost. The war would be over. Any chance of regaining independence from the French would be almost impossible if the president and his cabinet were captured. Despite her very complicated feelings about her father, Isabel would never want him to fall into French hands.

Nor her mother. *¡Ay Dios!*

"Ana, what can we do?" Gabby jumped to her feet, stalking back and forth as she wrung her hands. "I know we're here and they're there, but surely with Tío Arturo's help, we can do something."

"Maybe Gideon or the duke can help us secure a ship to meet them along the coast and deliver them to safety." Isabel chewed the inside of her cheek. "There are no more blockades to avoid—"

"I don't think that will work, querida." Ana María bit her lip as she crinkled the letter in her hand. "Mother wrote this letter two weeks ago. Possibly three. They've long since moved on to their new hiding spot."

"Or they've been captured," Gabby said, her voice small and broken. It was so unlike her fiery sister that it served as a dose of cold water over Isabel's head.

"No. No, I refuse to believe that. If anyone from the administration had been captured, we would have heard. It would have been blasted all over the papers," Isabel declared, clenching her hands into fists, hoping with every fiber of her being that she was right.

"But the papers have already shown they have no real interest in reporting on the war in Mexico," Gabby sneered, though fear glinted in her hazel eyes. "Many in society approve of Napoleon's actions!"

Isabel spun away to face the window. She could not bear to meet her sister's gaze, for she was right. With the affairs of the empire and the political strife in the States, the British public's attention was divided across many issues. There was little concern for the unlawful French occupation of Mexico, which was why her sisters had been working so hard to make a name for themselves about town to put a human face on the conflict. They had succeeded in so many ways, and Ana María's marriage to Gideon, an emerging powerhouse in Parliament, had been a feather in their cap. Yet they needed to do more to win the public's—the *government's*—support.

Isabel needed to do more. Resolve sparked hot in her gut, and doused with a healthy dose of desperation and fear for her parents, it threatened to turn into an inferno.

"Let's speak with Gideon and Tío Arturo, and devise a plan," Ana María said, her voice hitched. Still, she nodded decisively, and Isabel was thankful for her sister's calm assurance.

"Very clever of you, darling," Gideon said as he paused in the doorframe, his dark gaze sweeping across the room before it settled on his wife. "Señor Valdés just shared the news with us downstairs."

He crossed immediately to Ana María and was followed into the room by Tío Arturo and, surprisingly, Captain Dawson.

The men wore grave expressions, but Isabel's spirits inexplicably lifted when the captain met her eyes.

She sank onto the settee as her uncle immediately launched into a recitation of everything he had learned about the administration's movements since receiving the dispatch, and assured his nieces that their parents were safe. Gideon joined the conversation next, explaining his ideas for how to draw Parliament's attention to the conflict, Ana María and Gabby pelting him with suggestions and concerns.

Isabel tried to follow the conversation, but a headache was building behind her eyes, the steady drum of pain an echo of a single word: *failure.* She was a failure. If she had been successful in finding information to aid the rebel government, her parents wouldn't now be in danger. Why could she not do anything right? Even during her abduction, Ana María had managed to secure information that later helped the Juárez government capture a sizable weapons cache. Her sister had been in a terrifying situation and still had the presence of mind to look for documentation to help their countrymen.

Well, no more. As the heels of her hands pressed into her eyes, Isabel focused her thoughts. Her search tactics thus far had not produced results, so she would study them to determine what she could do differently, because she refused to feel this sting of helplessness again.

She was ripped from her thoughts by a deep dulcet voice.

"Miss Luna"—Captain Dawson kneeled down before her, his blue, blue eyes darting over her face—"I'm so sorry you find yourself in this situation. I presume it leaves you feeling a bit helpless."

A breath caught in her throat, and it took her a moment to say, "It does. And I despise feeling this way. Not knowing if they're in danger or not, and not being able to do anything about it."

Her words were nothing more than a hoarse whisper, and any other time Isabel would have been appalled to showcase such emotions to Captain Dawson. But something in his eyes—a gentleness she'd never noticed before—convinced her that he would treat her vulnerability with care.

The captain nodded. "And with the time and distance between here and there, knowing their current status is doubly difficult."

"Until they contact us directly, I suppose we won't know anything for certain." Isabel sighed, dropping her gaze to her lap. "As you know, I'm no stranger to war, but it's impossible to get used to its realities."

Isabel sensed rather than saw him cock his head to the side. "What do you mean you're *no stranger to war*? Why would three gently bred young ladies like you and your sisters be exposed to war more than once?"

"Because we're Mexican, Capitán." She snorted indelicately. "Someone has always desired to rule Mexico, whether it was the warring peoples of the peninsula or the Spanish or the French. The Mexican people are forever told who they will be, mostly by others but sometimes by their own."

"Aah." Captain Dawson rocked back on his heels, a frown twisting his mouth. "How very frustrating."

"It is." She nibbled her lip as she considered him. It was not lost on her that the captain had approached to offer *her* words of comfort before he had spoken with anyone else. Isabel knew better than to allow herself to think too deeply upon the significance of his actions, especially considering their history with each other. But after Captain Dawson had been kind to her at the balloon festival, and now listening sympathetically as she shared her fears, Isabel couldn't help the pang in her chest.

Lifting her chin, she grasped for composure. "I'm confident that with my uncle's help, Gideon will be able to muster the aid we need to have any chance of evicting Napoleon and his puppet emperor."

When Captain Dawson rose to his feet, Isabel expected him to mumble a word of parting and move away, but he sat beside her. He kept a respectable amount of distance between them, but his tantalizing cedarwood and citrus scent hung in the air, and Isabel still felt the heat radiating from him. Her instincts encouraged her to lean into his side, but instead she knotted her hands together in her lap.

"I have some connections at the Home Office." Captain Dawson crossed his ankles, his foot bobbing to and fro. "Old friends from when I was an officer. I told Fox I would speak with them to gauge how closely they're following the conflict, and what would need to happen to precipitate an intervention."

Her limbs felt frozen in place for a stark second . . . before the sweet heat of relief coursed up her spine. "Is that possible? Would England consider entering the war?"

Captain Dawson raised a staying hand. "It's highly unlikely. From my experience, the military only likes to get involved when British interests are directly at stake. And they're stretched thin with the conflict in New Zealand and Bhutan, as well as the political atmosphere in America."

"I would think that the rebirth of the French empire would be a direct threat to British interests," Isabel pointed out, arching a brow.

A bright smile spread across his lips and promptly took Isabel's breath away. "Another reminder of your cleverness."

To her horror, Isabel felt heat sweep across her chest, neck, and cheeks, and she ducked her head to hide her embarrassment. And delight.

"But I will utilize just that talking point when I speak with my friends." His expression turned calculating. "I have little doubt the Home Office is keeping a watchful eye on Napoleon and the actions of the imperial government in Mexico. I do not think the French expected the Liberal forces to cause them as much trouble as they have."

"They have underestimated our pride." Isabel shifted until she faced him fully, and dropped her voice. "In fact, I would not be at all surprised if the rebel effort has inadvertently aided the Union in their victory against the Confederacy."

The captain's eyebrows shot up, and he leaned closer. "What do you mean?"

After quickly darting her gaze around the room to ensure no one else was listening, Isabel murmured, "This is just conjecture . . ." She licked her lips. "But it occurred to me that the French and the Confederacy could have benefited from an alliance with each other. The French were eager for Southern cotton, and the Confederacy needed French weapons. Weapons the French may have been inclined to offer the Confederate states had they not needed them to fight the Liberal forces."

"Christ," Captain Dawson bit out under his breath, his eyes wide. "If the French had interceded in the war in the States, that would have been disastrous. Not just for the future of that country, but for geopolitical relations across the Atlantic. For free men and women all over the world."

Isabel nodded even as she tried to swallow around the knot in her throat. Late at night, she had contemplated the different scenarios, mindful that while the world often felt enormous, it was small in so many critically intertwined ways.

What happened in Mexico affected their powerful neighbor to the north, which then rippled to Europe and beyond. She was gratified that the captain immediately recognized the gravity of such a circumstance. And if he did, there was hope his countrymen would, too.

She considered the man before her. If Captain Dawson had connections at the Home Office, was it possible he could help her? While it was true he had been kind and attentive to her as of late, it did not mean the captain would be willing to assist her.

And could Isabel stand to be in his presence for so long without her sensibilities falling prey to his charms? Uncertainty, and a healthy dose of caution, had her steeling her spine. Perhaps Captain Dawson wasn't as glib as she had long thought, but that certainly did not mean he wasn't dangerous.

5

The day was unseasonably warm, and for at least the tenth time since she stepped from the house, Isabel cursed the fact that she was required to wear so many layers of clothing. Sweat beaded on her brow and she fanned her face faster, as if the thick, balmy air would somehow cool her.

She had wandered away from the spectator box where Lady Yardley chatted with Tío Arturo and several members of the ton. Isabel couldn't quite remember who had invited them, but after drinking three glasses of ice-cold lemonade, she decided she needed a break from the noise and crowds.

Escape was much harder to find than Isabel had expected. Epsom Downs was a veritable party, with rows of stands selling kites, a rainbow assortment of treats including fluffy marshmallows, various comfits, bonbons, pear drops, and peppermints. There were even milliner stalls with fine bonnets and hats, cobblers showcasing the newest footwear trends from Paris, and flower merchants selling bright blooms of every colorful shade. Isabel had spied more than one woman with a fresh rose in her bonnet or a young man with a daisy pinned to his lapel. In addition to the peddlers and merchants, there were clowns doing silly magic tricks for children, jugglers awing the crowd with their acts, and even a makeshift museum of oddities collected from all over the world. Gabby had squealed with delight over the various entertainments, but Isabel had not known where to look. Her gaze jumped from one sight to the next, the cacophony of voices a slowly building buzz until she was forced to press her palms to her ears to muffle the sound.

Without taking leave of Gabby, Lady Yardley, or her uncle, Isabel weaved and darted her way across the lawn toward the shaded canopy of a large oak tree near the edge of the paddocks. As she stepped under its boughs, Isabel ripped the bonnet from her head and swiped the back of her hand across her forehead.

"Are you all right?" Gabby asked, panting slightly as she came to a stop by her side. "Feeling a bit overwhelmed?"

Isabel nodded. She should have known her sister would ascertain what was wrong. Running away from social gatherings was something Isabel excelled at.

"Well, you look as miserable as I feel," Gabby said.

"I thought you were enjoying the sights," Isabel said, stripping her gloves from her hands to wipe her palms down her skirts.

Her sister sighed as she looked out across the crowd. "Oh, if I were free to wander about and enjoy the festivities without worrying about who may see me and the inferences they may make about my interests or behavior, I'm certain I'd be having a grand time."

A swell of affection surged in Isabel's chest. "I'm sorry that everything you do must be a performance."

Reaching into her reticule, Gabby extracted a white handkerchief embroidered with ivy and patted her face and the hollow of her neck. "Yes, well, at least we have this short reprieve."

With a long exhale, Isabel set her hat back on her head and worked to re-create the bow her maid had tied earlier that day. "Do I really look miserable?"

"No. You look perfectly lovely." Gabby batted her hands away and set about tying the bow under her sister's chin. "But I know you, so I know you're out of sorts. I doubt anyone else can tell."

"That's because no one pays any attention to my presence," Isabel said without thought. She bit down on her tongue when she noticed her sister frown.

"Is that what you believe? That you're invisible?" Gabby questioned, her brows pulled low.

"Does it matter?" she grumbled, looking away.

"I think it matters to you."

Isabel narrowed her eyes at her sister. "Why would you think that? Why should I care about the opinions of people who think I'm beneath them because my skin is darker than theirs? People who think our country deserves to be invaded for no other reason than we're different from them?"

Gabby didn't speak, although her hazel eyes were glassy as they stared back at her.

Smacking her gloves against her thigh, Isabel stepped back and spun about in a circle. "This is not my home and these are not my people. I could not care less if they bestow their fickle attentions on me."

A weight pressed down on her shoulders then, and it felt as if she were being watched. Darting her gaze about, she swallowed a gasp when it collided with Captain Dawson's. He stood in the company of finely dressed people in a private box lining the center of the track, far above the rabble that crowded the inner field. Much like the box she and Gabby had fled. How had he spied her among the throngs of people? And if his pursed lips were any indication, he had witnessed her pique of temper. Knowing he had been watching while she vented her frustrations made Isabel even more frustrated. Why could she not escape the man?

But do you really want to? After their last conversation, Isabel found it difficult to drum up the animosity she usually felt when she thought of the captain.

"It is a good thing we're speaking Spanish, or else everyone in earshot would know of your fiery temper," Gabby said quietly, a hint of laughter in her voice.

Pointedly turning away from Captain Dawson, Isabel tucked an errant lock of hair back into her coiffure before sliding her hands down her skirts again. "I would be not at all surprised if the gossip rags recruited Spanish speakers to follow us around and report on our private conversations. Mark my words, it will eventually come to that."

Gabby groaned. "You're probably right. The papers here are positively ruthless."

"You're being too generous."

"A lowering thought." Her sister approached until she was close enough to whisper in Isabel's ear. "There's nothing wrong with caring about the opinions of others, especially if they're people who care about you."

Isabel met Gabby's eyes and swallowed. "That would make for a very small number of people."

"Could that group possibly contain five people and a dog?" At Isabel's smothered laugh, Gabby pressed a quick kiss to her cheek. "I think your group has more members than that."

Isabel scowled. "Why would you think that?"

Gabby lifted a shoulder. "Just a feeling I have."

"A feeling, huh?" Isabel shook her head. "Well, whatever prompted that feeling, I suspect it's wrong."

"Always so pessimistic."

"Ouch." Isabel pulled back to spear her sister with a look. "And coming from one of the most critical people I know."

"I assure you, Isa dear," Gabby said, patting her hand, "that however critical you may think I am of others, I am doubly critical of myself."

Looping her arm around Gabby's shoulders, Isabel pulled her close to her side. "That's merely because you have high standards, for yourself and others."

"That is a gracious way of considering it, querida." Her sister's shoulders sank with her sigh. "Do you suppose Lady Yardley and Tío Arturo will allow us to hide here in the shade for the rest of the race?"

"I doubt it. Tío mentioned several important members of Parliament would be in attendance today, and he wanted us to greet them with, as he said, our *most charming* smiles." Isabel grunted. "As if there's anything charming about me. I think he may have confused me with Ana, who possesses more charisma in her little finger than I do in my whole body."

"Stop it, Isa."

Isabel jerked her head back. "¿Perdóname?"

"I hate when you do that. Talk bad about yourself as if you aren't intelligent and interesting. As if you don't casually toss out in conversation the most obscure and fascinating bits of information," Gabby said with a sweep of her hand.

"But surely you see how I put people to sleep when they converse with me?" Isabel scoffed. "I never know what to say or how to act when I am with them, and it always feels as if they're staring at me like I'm some exhibit in the British Museum because my nerves make me ramble. It's so disconcerting."

"That's because the ton is full of half-wits." Gabby grasped her arm and shook it. "Their idea of interesting is someone choosing to wear an ascot instead of a cravat. They care for nothing that doesn't affect their carefully cultivated and manicured social circle."

Isabel didn't know what to say, because her sister was right.

"I thought you didn't care about their opinions." Gabby winged up a brow. "They're not *our people*, I seem to recall you saying."

A sound resembling a groan—or maybe even a growl—left Isabel's lips, and she covered her face with her hands. "I don't make any sense. Even to myself. *Especially* to myself."

"Isa," Gabby sighed, her muffled steps on the grass making it clear she was moving closer, "you make sense to me. I know that while you might not want the good opinions of those people, we can't escape the truth that their opinion can be a benefit. Or a curse. Especially now that the precarious situation at home feels so much more real."

That was it exactly. Knowing that their parents' safety, the very future of Mexico's independence, was on the line made Isabel doubly aware of her shortcomings. Not only had she failed to supply any information to Fernando, but she'd also fallen short of winning the approval of the very people who could aid her countrymen. Disgust with herself festered in her gut.

And that disgust made her defensive.

"How much easier would life here be if I were like you, as a darling of the ton?" Isabel slashed her hand through the air. "Your admirers overfill the drawing room during visiting hours, and your dance card is always full. Their favor is readily given to you."

Gabby shook her head as she glanced down at her feet. "And yet I don't want their attentions. I wouldn't be courting their good opinions now if I didn't feel I had to. The only person whose approval I have ever tried to win ignored me as if I were no better than a piece of furniture or a painting on the wall."

Flinching, Isabel exhaled forcibly. "Aren't we an unfortunate pair? Desiring Father's approval as if he could ever be bothered to bestow it."

"Not unfortunate. Perhaps misguided." The light in Gabby's eyes dimmed as she looked at her. "Whatever the truth is, please know that I admire you, Isa, and it breaks my heart that you think so cheaply of yourself."

Swallowing proved impossible around the knot in her throat. Instead, Isabel bit her lip and closed her eyes, completely overwhelmed by Gabby's confession.

"How clever you were, ladies, to locate this gloriously shaded patch of heaven."

The Duke of Whitfield stood several paces away, leaning leisurely on his cane. Always an imposing figure, he was no exception today under the sun's bright beams. A navy-blue, double-breasted frock coat stretched across his broad shoulders, an exact match to the fine blue vest that highlighted the breadth of his chest. It would be easy to believe Whitfield a dandy for all that he cut a stylish figure, but Isabel suspected his right hook was as powerful as his cutting wit.

It took Isabel a moment to notice the duke was darting his gaze between her and Gabby with his brows arched high, and she realized belatedly he was waiting for a response. Thankfully her sister saved her from her inadvertent rudeness.

"Your Grace." Although polite on the surface, Gabby managed to infuse the honorific with disdain. "It is Isabel who spied this little spot of heaven. She's always so clever and observant."

Isabel would pinch Gabby now if she could, but the duke had returned the weight of his attention to her, so she tried to smile instead. Although Whitfield had always been gracious and polite to her, she could admit, if only to herself, that she found him intimidating.

It bolstered her confidence to know Gabby certainly did not.

"Of course I'm not surprised," he intoned, offering her a crisp bow. "It's long been my opinion that Miss Isabel is the intelligent Luna sister."

Ignoring the heat that crept along her cheeks, Isabel asked, "And what of Ana María?"

Whitfield spread his black-glove-covered hands. "Mrs. Fox is the charismatic and diplomatic sister."

She chuckled, for that described her older sister to the letter. Ana María was perfectly fit for her role as the wife of an ambitious member of Parliament.

"And me, Your Grace?" Gabby said, tilting her head in a coquettish fashion. She appeared to all the world as a young lady whose curiosity had been piqued, but Isabel knew better.

So, too, did the duke, for he arched a severe brow. "You are your sisters' defender, Miss Gabriela. Truly, I suspect you belong to the mythical Gorgons, and men cross you at their own peril."

Isabel sucked in a breath, darting her gaze to Gabby to take in her reaction. Her sister could be offended or pleased, and seeing as how Whitfield and Gabby had been at each other's throats since they'd first met, Isabel could envision either being true.

Perhaps it was that long acquaintance that buffered the duke's words now, for Gabby grinned, her hazel eyes sparking with glee. "My, Whitfield, I'm touched by the comparison. Can you imagine how incredible it would be to have the power to turn men into stone?"

Whitfield smirked. "I suspect half the ton would be statues by now."

Gabby flicked her fingers. "Oh, more than a half. And you, Your Grace, would have been my first victim."

Isabel knotted her hands together as she watched Gabby and the duke stare at each other, their bodies canting in such a way that it was almost possible to believe they were on a dueling field. Isabel decided to end this stalemate.

Stepping forward, Isabel placed a hand on Gabby's arm. "I'm forced to agree with His Grace's assessment. You've defended me more than once, querida."

"Para siempre y por siempre. The duke has summed me up perfectly." Gabby turned to bat her long lashes at Whitfield. "A Gorgon? Only to those deserving of such treatment."

Instead of sneering at Gabby or continuing the trade of barbs, Whitfield chuckled. "I'm grateful I can count on you to keep my ducal ego in check."

"Someone needs to," she grumbled, brushing a sable lock from her cheek and looking away.

Whitfield stepped toward Gabby, a taunting grin spreading across his mouth, and Isabel knew she needed to interrupt.

"Who have you come to cheer for at the races today, Your Grace?"

Swiveling his head to her, Whitfield halted, his expression sliding into his usual indifference.

"Dawson asked me to accompany him. He was invited by Viscount Westhope to sit in his box." Whitfield gestured behind him with his head. "The viscount has a colt racing in the derby."

"I haven't had the pleasure of meeting the viscount," Isabel said, darting her gaze to Gabby, who twirled her parasol in apparent boredom. But Isabel knew her sister was following the conversation.

"He's . . . a . . ." The duke paused, tapping his cane on the lush lawn. "Amiable."

"Amiable?" Isabel repeated.

Whitfield nodded. "Friendly. Very . . . loquacious."

Isabel wasn't sure if the duke was complimenting Lord Westhope or not. One never could tell with His Grace.

"Westhope is nice enough, but he smiles too much," Whitfield elaborated.

Now Isabel frowned. "And that's . . . a bad thing?"

Gabby wrinkled her nose. "You can't trust someone who smiles too much."

"Precisely," the duke echoed. He nodded his head in approval at Gabby, who lifted her chin and turned away in response.

While Isabel wasn't sure she understood the issue, it was obvious that Gabby and Whitfield did, and she had no interest in disrupting their newfound accord.

"Regardless of how I feel about Westhope, Dawson has struck up a friendship with the man." The duke leaned on his cane and shook his head. "They're over there now talking about his colt and Westhope's childhood in France."

Her muscles seized as they always did when someone made reference to France.

"Why would they be talking about his childhood in France?" Gabby asked.

Whitfield shrugged. "The late viscountess, his mother, was

French, and Westhope maintains a close relationship with her family. Dawson seemed to find the topic interesting."

"That's nice," Isabel managed, her heart pounding in her ears.

"I suppose." Whitfield glanced back to the box, a disgruntled look on his face. "Apparently his colt—I believe the beast is named Delano—was purchased from a breeder in Normandy."

"Delano?" Gabby snorted. "It's a fine name, but surely they could have come up with something more fanciful."

"I suppose that to French ears, Delano is fanciful," Whitfield drawled.

A diverted smile lit Gabby's face for the shortest of moments before she angled about, her bonnet hiding her expression.

Isabel chanced a glance at the duke, who was staring intently at Gabby, a deep V cut into the groove between his brows.

Licking her lips, Isabel considered this new information. She knew very little of the viscount but seemed to recall that he was active in Parliament. Perhaps Gideon had mentioned him. Whatever the case, with Westhope's close ties to France and the government, it wouldn't hurt for Isabel to learn more about the man. She felt as if she were running out of options, and she was determined to investigate any possible lead, no matter how scarce the suspicions.

Simply put, she needed to meet Viscount Westhope. And while the duke had not offered to introduce them, Isabel was not above manipulating him to do so.

"I would love to learn more about Delano. I haven't selected a horse for the race yet," she said, choosing her words with care to not arouse his suspicion.

It was not the duke who appeared interested in her words, but rather Gabby, who looked over her shoulder at Isabel with narrowed eyes.

"Indeed, Your Grace. Would you be so kind as to introduce us?" Gabby asked sweetly.

Whitfield's shoulders sank, and after a short hesitation, he extended an arm in the direction of the race box. "Of course. Let us hope, ladies, that the footmen are serving lunch, for I fear I will require sustenance to survive the rest of this event."

"Would you care for another dram of whisky? I'm certainly going to have one."

Sirius chuckled, but nodded readily. "With the heat and the noise and the crowds, I would be very thankful to partake of your excellent selection again."

With a slight jerk of his head, Viscount Westhope gestured to a footman, and the man approached instantly, extracting a small decanter from behind his back. As Sirius watched the amber liquid splash in his tumbler, his mouth watered.

Raising his full glass in salute to his host, he said, "To victory on the racetrack."

"And not succumbing to sunstroke," the viscount added with a jaunty laugh.

The liquor hit the back of his throat like a sharp jab, and Sirius ran his tongue over his lips to not let any drop go to waste.

"As fond as I am of my horseflesh, and Delano in particular, I despise race-day festivities." Lord Westhope studied the liquid in his glass before turning his gaze to survey their surroundings. "I often feel as if I'm at a carnival instead of one of the premier races in England."

"Are you telling me you have no interest in watching the

clowns perform or the strongmen wrestle?" Sirius asked, flourishing a hand.

"None at all." The viscount feigned a shudder. "If I could sit quietly off to the side in the shade with a glass of cold lemonade, no one aware of my presence, I would be content."

A frown twisted Sirius's mouth. "Then why invite a whole box full of guests to watch Delano race? It seems as if you could have spared yourself this . . . torture."

"Torture indeed." Westhope sipped his whisky, wincing slightly at the bite. "But I invite guests"—he waved at the expensively dressed people laughing, chatting, and eating behind them—"because a working horse farm needs investors. And if I want investors to go into business with me, I not only need a winning horse, which Delano is, but I need to treat them well."

"Thus this circus show."

"Precisely." The viscount raised his glass to him.

Sirius leaned forward in his chair. "Does this mean you're hoping I will invest in Delano?"

"Actually, no. Although I certainly would not turn you away if you're interested." Westhope barked a laugh. "You just seemed like a fellow who wouldn't try my nerves or patience if we spent an afternoon together."

Sirius chuckled in return. He may have been tasked with befriending Viscount Westhope, but it was not hard to like the man. Truthfully, Sirius felt a bit guilty that he hadn't known how genuinely agreeable Westhope was until now. Until he had been compelled to socialize with him to determine what exactly his French connections were and whether they would be a problem. Britain certainly could not afford to have another traitorous peer working with the French.

Although to compare Westhope with Lord Tyrell, the earl

who had abducted Ana María Fox with the intention of turning her over to his French coconspirators, was laughable. But Sirius knew better than to take people at face value. Hadn't he learned that recently when his annoyance and mistrust of Isabel Luna had changed to admiration? The reserved Luna sister had turned out to be much more than the shy and irascible young woman he thought her to be.

Relishing his next sip of whisky, Sirius propped his elbow on the armrest. "I confess that this most excellent libation is one of the only things helping me to remain pleasant right now."

"No clowns or puppet shows or trapeze performance for you, either?" Westhope cocked his head.

"Lord no." Sirius frowned. "I would much rather be in my library, reading a good book." He raised his glass to study it. "Preferably with a draft of this quality."

"That sounds like a superior way to spend the day." The viscount crossed one leg over the other as if settling in. "What book are you reading right now?"

For the next fifteen or so minutes, the men discussed the books they had read recently, before moving on to politics and the political upheaval in the United States following President Lincoln's assassination. Sirius was not surprised that Westhope was well read and well informed, speaking knowledgeably about various topics, but the viscount also had no qualms about admitting when he did not know something. More than once Sirius cursed in his mind to find Westhope had given him yet another reason to like him.

But with a skill he'd honed over years of covert work, Sirius managed to direct the conversation to France.

"My mother always spoke fondly of the library at her parents' estate in Lorraine. My great-grandfather had the presence of mind to hide the family's extensive library collection before the Revolution, and all those books are enjoyed by my cousins even now," Westhope shared, absentmindedly looking out over the crowd.

Sirius went as still as a fox at its first scent of a hare. This was just the sort of opening he had been hoping for.

He swirled the last remnants of his whisky around his glass. "Do you keep in touch with your family in France?"

"I do. I spent many summers there, running across the hills with my cousins." Westhope slid his gaze to him. "And what of you? Are you close with your family?"

"No." Taking in the viscount's surprised look, Sirius smiled. "My apologies. I've just never been particularly close with anyone in my family. My mother died when I was quite young, and my father was more interested in playing the part of the sympathetic widower, winning the hearts of ladies and tarts alike, than spending time with his spare."

"Ah yes, Harcourt is your brother." Westhope took a handkerchief from his pocket and patted his chin and brow. "I'm terrible at remembering the familial connections within the ton."

"Yes, the Earl of Harcourt is my older brother, although our relationship is more so that of distant relatives than siblings."

"Families are an interesting bunch, are they not?" The viscount exhaled. "For instance, I exchange frequent letters with my cousin Jean-Charles even though he lives in the West Indies, and yet I haven't spoken with my older sister Melody in nigh on two years."

"I'm sorry to hear that," Sirius murmured, and waited a beat before he said, "although I think it's swell that you have a relationship with your cousin."

"Yes, Jean-Charles and I have been quite close the majority of our lives, despite him growing up in France and me in England. But now, he tells me about—"

"I return to your gracious patronage, Westhope, along with two new guests."

Sirius fought back the urge to shove Whitfield out of the box and into the dirt. He had *finally* embarked upon the line of conversation he'd been slowly, methodically leading the viscount toward, and his ass of a friend returned to the box at the most inopportune moment.

Rising to his feet, Sirius managed to relax his scowl into a mundane expression before he pivoted to his friend . . . only to come up short. Isabel Luna and her sister stood on either side of the duke, wearing matching looks of amiability. She met his eyes for a moment, and some of his ire seeped from his muscles. Sirius had glimpsed her earlier in the afternoon, but before he could greet Isabel and Gabriela, Lord Westhope had invited him to have a dram together.

In truth, Sirius had felt terrible when he'd penned a note to Fox to pass along the news that he'd yet to learn anything of note about the conflict in Mexico. His inquiries with several contacts had been unsuccessful, and when he'd called upon Lieutenant Colonel Green at the Home Office, the older man had been unable to meet with him. Numerous times, Sirius had replayed the memory of the frightened, lost look on Isabel's face when she'd learned of her parents' circumstances, and he hated how powerless he was to help.

But seeing her now was like drawing in a lungful of fresh, crisp air, and Sirius wondered at how quickly he was able to regain his composure.

"Your Grace, how clever of you to return with two lovely

ladies," Westhope said, raising his brows as if waiting for an introduction.

A hint of annoyance passed over the duke's face so quickly, Sirius wasn't sure if he'd truly seen it. "Lord Westhope, allow me to introduce to you Miss Isabel Luna and Miss Gabriela Luna. Ladies, this is Viscount Westhope," Whitfield said, immediately gesturing with his chin to a footman for a drink.

The sisters sank into graceful curtsies, and after greeting Sirius in a friendly manner, their attention returned to the viscount. While Isabel smiled benignly but politely, Gabriela fluttered her lashes and said, "You'd do well to know, Lord Westhope, that I made a wager on your beautiful colt before I even knew he was yours."

"Is that so?" A grin brightened the viscount's face. "Well, I hope he runs a race worthy of your confidence, Miss Gabriela."

"Am I to understand that he was bred and originally trained in France?" Isabel's silvery voice was inquisitive, but her onyx eyes were intense. "I confess that I'm not much of a horsewoman, but I didn't know the French were of horse racing acclaim."

Westhope took a step toward her, his mien lighting with curiosity. "And I would not fault you for not knowing, Miss Luna. The French do many things very well. They make exquisite cheese, wine, and pastries, but you are correct that they have experienced little success on the racetrack. However"—he leaned forward, his hand cupped to his mouth as if he were about to impart a great secret—"I believe that will change with Delano."

Isabel winged up a brow. "I admire your confidence, my lord. Tell me, what is it about Delano that has you convinced he's the colt to change France's track record?"

Sirius watched with his teeth clenched as Isabel and the viscount launched into a lengthy discussion of Delano's many qualities, and how they boded well for his success. Eventually, Gabriela and Whitfield wandered away to eat and converse with others, but Sirius could not bring himself to leave with them. Instead, he stood like a silent sentry as Isabel and Westhope bantered, oblivious to his presence. When her pretty red lips stretched around a dazzling smile, Sirius barely managed to bite back a growl.

Pretty lips? Whatever was the matter with him? While Sirius may have just come to recognize Isabel's striking and unconventional beauty, he had no reason to explain the spots that danced in his vision watching how Westhope leaned toward her. And why was it that this reserved wallflower seemed not at all awkward or uncertain of herself with the viscount as she had with any other man Sirius had watched her interact with?

Another truth waylaid Sirius in that moment: Isabel had not glanced in his direction once since their initial greeting. She'd given the viscount the entirety of her attention, and unease crawled under his skin. Was their tentative accord at an end? Was Lord Westhope deserving of all her interest?

Why did Sirius care? Surely he should be more concerned with the fact that his own discussion with Westhope had been interrupted, rather than the uncomfortable realization that Isabel and Westhope's conversation bordered on flirtation. Surely the fact that the viscount showed an interest in her should be no concern of his.

Right?

"I've never seen quite that look on your face before."

Jerking to awareness, his gaze collided with that of Whitfield, who now stood at his side. "I don't know what you mean."

The duke stared at him as he pushed his spectacles up his nose. "You look like you want to punch something."

"Well, this whole event is quite trying." Sirius tugged his hat further down upon his head, shielding his eyes from his altogether-too-insightful friend.

"Yes, I'm sure that's it."

Sirius chanced a look at the duke, who had turned to observe Isabel and Westhope in conversation. When the viscount cupped her on the elbow to escort her toward two chairs situated nearby, Sirius curled his hands into fists.

"Oh yes," Whitfield said again, glancing at Sirius, a single dark brow arched, "quite trying, indeed."

6

It had been a lazy afternoon at home, and Isabel was curled up on her favorite armchair in Lady Yardley's drawing room, a poetry book she'd taken from the library at Dancourt Abbey in hand. She had not meant to leave the abbey with the book and, without success, had been looking for an opportunity to return it to Captain Dawson without alerting him to the fact that she had taken it in the first place. But after seeing him at the derby two days prior and pondering over his uncharacteristic moodiness at the event, Isabel found herself flipping through the pages again, committing the poems to memory. One day she hoped she could think of them without also thinking of the captain—

A knock sounded on the drawing room door, and Isabel glanced up at the same time Gabriela did. They exchanged a quick look, and Isabel glimpsed the same anxiety that pounded through her blood in her sister's eyes. When would a simple knock on the door not send them into a panic that word had finally come from their parents?

"Come in," Lady Yardley called, her gaze glued to the door.

Even Dove, who had been curled in her lap, stood, her little ears perked.

"Your ladyship, Viscount Westhope has come to call," Evans said, stepping aside to allow the gentleman to fill the threshold.

Isabel's shoulders slumped even as a fluttering began in her chest when Lord Westhope paused just inside the doorway. His green gaze touched on Lady Yardley and Gabby, before coming to rest on her. A smile stretched his lips, and Isabel shifted in her chair. Had a man ever looked at her with such anticipation?

She had enjoyed speaking with the viscount about his horse racing enterprise, but had not learned much of his French familial connections. Still, Lord Westhope was smart and interesting, and with his dark blond hair and striking green eyes, Isabel thought him quite handsome. If his appearance now was any indication, the viscount seemed keen on extending their acquaintance. But in truth, the only excitement she felt about his visit was that it afforded her the opportunity to discuss his family ties.

"My lord, how nice of you to call upon us," Lady Yardley said, gesturing with her arm for him to take the armchair near Isabel. "The ladies mentioned they met you at the derby and that they enjoyed watching your Delano claim victory."

Westhope swept his coattails back before he sat, his cheeks coloring. "It was a most excellent day, and I'm very happy the Luna misses were able to celebrate Delano's victory with me."

"You were a superb host, my lord," Gabby said, "and I know I, and most definitely Isa, appreciate the time you took to explain how your yearlings are trained and prepared for the races."

"Yes," Isabel echoed, angling toward the viscount. Now was not the time to revert to her customary shyness. "I was especially intrigued by the science behind selecting specific bloodlines to mix with the hopes of producing just the right set of characteristics to achieve victory on the racetrack."

"Isn't it fascinating?" The viscount turned about in his seat until he faced Isabel fully. "I admit that when I was growing up, I didn't understand why my mother and father reviewed the Jockey Club records so closely, much like other people read the newspaper over their morning tea. It wasn't until I was older that my mother explained what they were studying when they read through the reports. It opened my eyes to a different side of the sport. Breeding and animal husbandry have become deep interests of mine."

"Perhaps we should not be speaking about such delicate topics," Lady Yardley interjected nervously.

Gabby rolled her eyes. "Yes, we don't wish to offend our maidenly sensibilities by speaking about horses."

The viscountess responded in a censorious tone, but Isabel did not hear it. Instead, she cocked her head and asked, "Your mother was a part of the operations at the Westhope stables?"

"She was the heart and soul of it." A fond look settled on Lord Westhope's face. "The horse farm has always been a part of the viscountcy, but my mother is responsible for making it into a racing powerhouse. Her youth in France was spent in the stables, as her father was a breeder who specialized in Arabian horses. She took the knowledge she learned at his knee into her marriage with my father, and thankfully he was smart enough to listen to her recommendations."

"A man—a viscount—who listens to a woman about a topic he already knows a thing or two about is almost unheard of," Isabel said, not bothering to hide the surprise in her voice.

"Indeed. But then it served him and the Westhope stables well." Lord Westhope met her eyes, a curious glint shining in them. "I like to think I have inherited a bit of his modesty."

"As well as your mother's ingenuity and grit," Isabel added.

"Indeed. She was a singular woman, and I think because of her example, I've always admired and respected women who are just a bit . . . different. Who look at the world around them and ask questions." He dropped Isabel's gaze to glance at Lady Yardley and Gabby. "And now I'm being romantic and nonsensical."

"Not at all, my lord," the viscountess declared, fluttering her handkerchief in the air. "The ton has enough rogues and rakes. It's a relief to know there are true gentlemen among the crowd."

"I find it refreshing that you're of a romantic bent, Lord Westhope," Gabby said, sliding her hazel eyes to Isabel. "Don't you agree, Isa?"

"Of course," she murmured, her cheeks turning hot.

Conversation paused for a moment, and Isabel shot her gaze about, unsure whether she should fill the lull, and if so, with what? She did not like being put on the spot, and if she was, Isabel usually made an inane observation that confused others. And with Viscount Westhope staring at her so intently, her palms began to sweat and her mouth went dry.

Thankfully, Viscount Westhope spoke before Isabel descended into a full-blown panic attack.

"I actually came here today with the express purpose of asking Miss Luna if she would like to accompany me on a drive about Rotten Row?"

Isabel pulled her chin back. "Do you mean Gab—"

"Of course Isa would be very happy to take a drive with you," Gabby interrupted, clasping her hands together in front of her chest. "Then you both can continue your conversation about horse racing. And breeding." She smirked as she cut a glance at Lady Yardley. "And all those other topics you both seem to find interesting."

Westhope nodded, his eyes bright. "I can't think of a more enjoyable way to spend the afternoon." He looked to her then. "Do you agree?"

Swallowing was difficult with her parched throat, but Isabel managed a nod.

"Excellent. Perhaps Miss Gabriela can accompany us, for propriety's sake." The viscount turned to look at her sister.

Gabby pursed her lips for a moment, and in that one expression, Isabel read all of her sister's thoughts: that she had no desire to take a turn about the park at the fashionable hour, that she'd rather stick a hatpin in her eye than listen to Isabel and the viscount discuss his horse stables, that she already had plans. Yet despite all that, Gabby eventually nodded . . . albeit very slowly.

"Perfect." Lord Westhope clapped his hands on his thighs and then rose to his feet. "I will meet you ladies at my conveyance outside while you grab your bonnets and parasols."

After he departed, both Lady Yardley and Gabby turned to look at her in unison.

"My goodness, Isabel, a viscount?" Lady Yardley shimmied her shoulders, jostling little Dove in her lap. "And a handsome one at that."

Isabel ducked her head, a stinging heat streaking up her back and across her chest. Reaching into her pocket, she plucked out her handkerchief to discreetly pat at her brow and the hollow of her throat.

"Which is the only reason why I agreed to accompany them," Gabby said with a sniff. "Lord Westhope seems like a nice gentleman, and he obviously has exquisite taste if he fancies Isa."

"I wouldn't say he fancies me." Isabel wrung her handkerchief between her hands. "I suspect Lord Westhope simply enjoys having a willing listener. I'm sure there are few young ladies who enjoy discussions about the inner workings of a horse farm."

"That you know of." Gabby arched a brow.

"Touché." She released her handkerchief to smooth her damp palms on her skirts. "Be that as it may, let's not assume Viscount Westhope has anything more than friendly regard for me."

Gabby and Lady Yardley exchanged a glance, and Isabel's hand itched to reach across the space to pinch her sister over the incredulous cast of her face.

"Whatever you say, Isa. We'll assume whatever we wish . . . we just won't tell you about it."

Sirius never rode this late in the afternoon, preferring to hack out when the rest of the ton was still asleep in their beds. But seeing as how he'd been out later than normal, cavorting with various acquaintances at several gaming hells, Sirius had found it difficult to open his eyes before noon.

Which was why he now found himself attempting to steer his mount through the carriages and phaetons of every member of polite society. It was not an easy task, as riders and drivers alike stopped in the middle of the lane to exchange pleasantries with friends and neighbors, without a care for the queue that built up behind them.

Sucking a bracing breath into his lungs, Sirius turned his mount down a random path, issuing a noisy exhale when he found it blessedly empty. Dropping his head over the horse's neck and loosening the reins, Sirius gave his mount its lead, relishing the warm breeze that whipped by him as his horse thundered over the dirt trail. After thirty minutes stuck on the crowded park lane, he laughed at the space and freedom he'd found, the sound carried away as he raced along.

Sirius was thankful that the pounding in his head was now a thing of the past, for its absence allowed him to focus on recent events. After Isabel Luna had arrived and diverted all of Lord Westhope's attention, the opportunity to speak further with the viscount had been lost in the anticipation of the race, and later in the celebration of Delano's victory. Upon leaving the racing grounds, Sirius had accompanied several gentlemen to a nearby pub, but only because the viscount had indicated he wished to continue celebrating there. Yet the man had stayed for only an hour, an hour in which every patron seemed intent on congratulating Westhope directly, shaking his hand, and wanting to hear the tale of Delano's victory from his mouth. Sirius had watched in mounting frustration as any attempt to continue his earlier discussion with the viscount evaporated. When Westhope had eventually said goodbye and departed, Sirius had immediately ordered a bottle of brandy and proceeded to get smashingly drunk.

He had been so close to finally getting Westhope to discuss his family in France, the connections he had to the Napoleon government, however unknowingly . . . and that had all been derailed, first by Whitfield and then by Isabel. Sirius expected such inconvenient interruptions from the duke, but he had not anticipated how Isabel, with her dark, earnest eyes, thoughtful questions, and deep, husky laugh would snare the viscount's attention. After trying and failing to join their conversation, Sirius had watched them converse for a spell, amazed by how animated Isabel was. It became uncomfortably apparent that Isabel Luna possessed a quick wit, and Lord Westhope had been enchanted by her.

His horse tossed his head back in agitation, and only then did Sirius realize how tightly he was holding the reins.

As he focused on relaxing, Sirius spied a curricle heading in his direction as he rounded a corner. Making a noise in the back of his throat, Sirius brought his horse up and pulled his spine straight, adjusting his hat before reworking the fit of his gloves. He squinted as the conveyance rumbled toward him, and Sirius thought he could make out three heads . . . and when their identities became apparent, he spit out a curse under his breath.

"Dawson, what a capital surprise," Westhope cried as they drew closer. "Miss Luna was just telling us of a book you recommended."

Sirius's gaze swiveled to her like the magnet of a compass, not surprised to find Isabel staring back at him with a challenging look in her umber-colored eyes. She wore a pink striped dress that set off the bronze tone to her skin. With her dark-as-pitch curls bursting from beneath a sleek straw bonnet, and her red lips turned up in that barely there smile she always wore when she saw him—as if he hadn't quite earned a full smile—she looked lovely. Beautiful even. How had Sirius never noticed?

Lord Westhope had noticed, though. He sat close to Isabel's side, the admiration clear on his face as he looked at her. Sirius could respect a man who was honest and open about his feelings.

But he still wanted to punch the viscount in the jaw.

Remembering his good manners, Sirius waited for Westhope's

curricle to pull abreast of him. Tipping his hat in greeting and trading brief pleasantries, Sirius allowed himself to turn his attention to Isabel.

"What book did you mention?" he asked.

"*The Woman in White*," she said, lifting a brow as if to indicate he should have remembered.

And he did. While they had exchanged brief thoughts in passing on any number of books the summer she and her sisters stayed at Dancourt Abbey, it was *The Woman in White* that had sparked an extended conversation between them. When he'd spied Isabel slipping the book back onto his shelf, Sirius asked what she thought of the story, and to his surprise, she seemed eager to discuss it. They proceeded to engage in a full discourse over the intense, frightening feel of the book, including the larger social commentary on women, especially married women in society. They also touched on the changing points of view, and how the various voices made the reader feel off-kilter. Isabel had remarked that the narrative felt almost like an inquest, as if each narrator were a witness being interviewed about what they knew of the crime. Sirius had thought it an insightful observation, and he still did, often remembering that afternoon discussion with fondness.

"Ah." He nodded, releasing Isabel's gaze to turn to the viscount. "It was a compelling book, and if you decide to read it, Miss Luna has perceptive thoughts about it. I appreciated the story and the storytelling more after discussing it with her."

Isabel dropped her chin, but not before Sirius spied the scarlet that swept across her cheeks.

"Well, now I'm determined to read it," Westhope declared, slapping his glove on his thigh. "I find I'm not at all surprised Miss Luna has clever opinions about the book. She is a fount of knowledge and interesting ideas."

Doing his best to ignore how Gabby smirked openly at him, Sirius couldn't stop himself from considering Isabel. Her expression was neutral, but she seemed to sit a bit straighter.

"It would do you well, Westhope, not to take any of the Luna ladies for granted." Warmth bloomed in his chest when Isabel met his gaze. "For just when you think you have them figured out, they surprise you."

Gabby's answering laugh was just this side of wicked. "Captain Dawson, you're spoiling the game. Don't you know that Isa and I covet that look of surprise that crosses men's faces when they learn how foolish they've been to underestimate us?"

"I've spoiled nothing," Sirius retorted, propping his elbow on the saddle pommel and leaning toward her with a grin. "Westhope is trustworthy, and will not disclose your secrets."

"I appreciate your faith in me, Dawson," the viscount said, nodding magnanimously. The effect was ruined, though, when he barked a laugh. "Rest assured, Miss Gabriela, that I wouldn't dream of ruining your fun, especially because I, too, believe I would enjoy seeing the face of any man who underestimated you and your sister."

Lord Westhope and Gabriela continued to trade quips, and while Sirius would normally have joined the banter, it did not hold his attention. Instead, he watched Isabel surreptitiously from the corner of his eye as her head swiveled back and forth between her sister and the viscount, an exasperated indentation between her brows.

Why were she and Gabby alone with Lord Westhope anyway, and on a lesser traversed park path? If Sirius didn't know the man to be honorable, he would be concerned to find the two young women alone in his company. In truth, he was concerned. Sirius had noticed that Isabel appeared uncomfortable in crowds, and the park at this time was a crush. So why would she consent to ride out with Westhope at this time of day? Had she not had a choice? Perhaps Lady Yardley insisted she go, for Westhope was an eligible, titled bachelor. He would need to ask Fox what he knew of the ladies' relationship with the viscountess, because Sirius would hate himself if—

"I beg your pardon, Captain Dawson, but did you hear me?"

Jerking his head back, Sirius blinked as his gaze settled on Westhope, who was staring at him with a frown.

"Please excuse me." He yanked on his lapels. "You caught me woolgathering."

"I wonder what about," Gabby said, a knowing lilt to her tone.

Isabel narrowed her eyes. "Gabby, really. Some of us find our thoughts captured by all sorts of things."

"Is that right?" Lord Westhope turned to face her, that damn smile overtaking his face. "What sort of things ensnare your attention, Miss Luna?"

Before Isabel could respond, Sirius cleared his throat. Loudly. "What was it you were saying, my lord?"

"Oh yes. Right." Squaring his shoulders, Westhope swept his gaze over the three of them. "Invitations have not gone out yet, but I wanted you to be the first to know that I've decided to open Westhope House for a ball the week after next, and I would be quite happy if you all were my guests."

His muscles locked at the viscount's words. Not because he was surprised or even exasperated by the idea of attending yet another ball, but rather because Isabel had proven herself to be a snoop at such events. Would she take this as her opportunity to search the viscount's home? Would such activities even be possible with Lord Westhope paying her such special attentions?

His gaze immediately collided with Isabel's. Defiance lurked in her bottomless eyes, as if she knew the train of his thoughts, and suspicion set Sirius's teeth on edge.

"We would be honored to attend, Lord Westhope." The corner of her mouth tipped up. "Nothing would make me happier."

Sirius bit back a growl.

7

After canceling his evening plans, and in no mood to don his jovial mask when he was feeling anything but, Sirius paced about his library for most of the evening. His mind replayed his conversation with Lord Westhope earlier that afternoon, and what Isabel's taunting expression could mean. Christ, that woman seemed hell-bent on finding trouble, and he really should just let her have at it.

Thankfully, Sirius eventually found a book to hold his attention. With a boot propped on his desk, a glass of brandy dangling from his fingers, and his thoughts now occupied with the tale of a silly Frenchwoman squandering her life by always wanting more, Sirius did not note the knock on the study door for several moments.

Swallowing a sigh, he slid his finger in between the pages to mark his place. "Yes," he called.

The door opened to reveal Stanley, his butler. "There's a man at the back door."

Closing the book with a thud, Sirius set it aside and rose to his feet. "Did you tell him he's welcome to visit at the front door?"

"I did, sir." Although Stanley's expression and tone changed not one whit, he somehow managed to infuse his words with censure. "But the fellow insisted on meeting you in the back garden."

Sometimes pride was all some men had. Sirius repeated this mantra as he made his way through the darkened halls and down the servants' stairs to the kitchens. Cook had already stirred the fire in the stove and put a kettle on the grate, and he flashed her a smile of thanks as he passed. As Sirius stepped through the back door, his eyes took a moment to adjust to the scant lighting in the garden before he spied a tall figure near the gate. He made his way in that direction without a word, gravel crunching under his boots. Coming to a stop several paces away, Sirius planted his feet as he linked his arms behind his waist. He wanted to appear approachable and friendly, but nighttime visits also warranted discretion.

"I'm Captain Sirius Dawson. I was told you asked to speak with me."

The man snatched the hat from his head and pressed it to his chest, swaying back and forth on his feet. "Wilson mentioned you help former soldiers. That true?"

Swallowing, Sirius nodded. "I try." Whether it was helping veterans from the Crimea, or any of the other conflicts the military had participated in, he did his best to help the men find employment or lodgings or even access to medical care. A steady stream of former soldiers found their way to him, referred by other men he'd helped. It wasn't something he advertised, but nor would Sirius turn away a man who needed assistance. Almost every person he employed at Dancourt Abbey was a former soldier or the family member of a former soldier, the old nunnery providing the idyllic place to recover and thrive. The Crown did so little to help those who had protected it, whether on English shores or abroad, and Sirius considered his efforts one small way to atone for having returned when so many others did not.

"Me name's Jack. Jack O'Brien. Rifleman, Fifty-Sixth Regiment."

Sirius bit back a whistle. The Fifty-Sixth's most notable action was in the siege of Sevastopol, where they earned great honors. That a soldier of the Fifty-Sixth needed his help was a travesty because the allied forces should have rewarded him as a hero.

"It's nice to meet you, Mr. O'Brien." Sirius looked over his shoulder to spy Stanley lingering on the back steps. Cook must have refreshments prepared. "Would you like to come inside for a cup of tea? We can speak further in some comfort."

The Irishman shuffled on his feet for a moment, glancing down before he finally nodded. "I'd be obliged."

With a nod, Sirius led the way back up the walk, his mind now absorbed with how he could assist O'Brien. He was thankful for the distraction.

Isabel kicked off her slippers and fell face-first onto her bed, a multitude of emotions churning through her blood.

After almost two weeks of receiving no word from her parents, the sisters had been summoned to have breakfast with Tío Arturo, who had news from Mexico, at his residence on Halkin Street in Belgravia. Over a meal of fried huevos, frijoles, bacon, sausage, and fruit, her uncle read aloud the letter he had received from their mother. Isabel had linked hands with Gabby and Ana María as her mother's missive explained that Presidente Juárez and his officials had found refuge in northern Mexico, but she did not specify where. Thankfully, they were safe if a bit exhausted. Gabby had promptly burst into tears at the news, and Isabel envied her ability to openly express her feelings. Ana María had wrapped Gabby in an embrace . . . and Isabel had longed to join them. She had ached to be held by the two people in the world who understood the terror they had experienced as they waited for word of their parents' safety. To give comfort and receive it in return.

But Isabel did not ask, and although Gabby had clung to her hand as if it were a lifeline, neither she nor Ana María had made any attempts to embrace her. Her rational mind told her this was because they did not wish to make her uncomfortable. Isabel appreciated their regard . . . but if she had ever longed for an embrace, it was in that moment.

Their mother's letter ended with her customary prayers for her daughters, and Isabel could almost hear her voice as Tío Arturo read the words. There was no inscription from their father. Not that Isabel had expected one. The only time Elías Luna deigned to write his daughters was when he had reprimands to impart or instructions to give. Isabel counted herself lucky that he seemed to forget about them the rest of the time.

They left their uncle's house in lighter spirits than when they had arrived. After saying goodbye to Ana María and Gideon, Isabel and Gabby returned to Yardley House, where they were granted a short respite before they departed yet again for a picnic. Lady Vale was known to be a consummate gardener— although Lady Yardley confessed on the carriage ride to Vale House that the countess did not actually garden herself but hired others to do it for her. "As if Eleanor would ever pull a weed or touch a ladybird willingly," Lady Yardley had scoffed, much to Gabby's delight.

But even the viscountess and Gabby could admit that the

gardens at Vale House were impressive. Terraced flower beds overflowing with blooms of every shape, size, and color snagged the eye wherever one looked, and the air buzzed with the sound of bees and the chirp of birds that flitted here and there, snatching insect morsels where they could. Isabel quickly learned to be careful when she sniffed a blossom, as an older gentleman was stung on the nose by one such startled bee.

The terraced steps eventually gave way to cobblestone pathways that led through a small grove of oak trees to a grass clearing on the river Thames. Strands of creeping thyme and the occasional wildflower sprouted in between the stones, while others were hugged close by springy moss, giving the pathway an otherworldly feel.

Isabel had lingered at the back of the group as they meandered down the trail, determined not to be rushed as she filled her senses with the beautiful environment. At one point on the walk, Isabel had lingered in a patch of sunlight stealing through the heavy boughs above, her face turned toward the heavens and her eyes closed. So much about her life in London overwhelmed her. Whether it was the busy social schedule, the feeling of constantly being under a microscope, or the always present pressure to find something—*anything*—to help Mexico end this cursed occupation. Her stress had only been magnified in the time since they learned of their parents' dangerous flight, and Isabel had not been able to regain her footing.

Yet in that moment, with her face bathed in sunlight, Isabel had been at peace.

That peace did not last long, for lunch proved to be a noisy affair. Thick cotton blankets were spread out over the lawn, and footmen served mini ham sandwiches, cold egg salad, roasted chicken, and an assortment of root vegetables. Isabel choked down her meal as fast as was polite so that she might wander through the oak grove by herself again. Much to her frustration, though, she had been roped into a conversation with Lady Vale. The countess had heard talk that Viscount Westhope was paying her court, and the older woman had plied Isabel with questions that left her prickly with embarrassment. Isabel had done her best to deflect, stating that she and Lord Westhope were merely friends.

"I heard he's come to call several times." The Countess of Vale had looked at Lady Yardley with a twinkle in her eye. "Have you ever heard of a man calling so frequently on a young woman he considered a friend?"

Isabel had sent the viscountess a dirty look when she stated she had not. And Gabby proved no help, for she regaled the elderly countess with stories of Lord Westhope's attentions toward Isabel, and her head had been filled with daydreams about pushing Gabby into the Thames.

Thus, the conversation about Lord Westhope and the time they had spent together over the last fortnight was on Isabel's mind as she weaved her way through the oak grove at Vale House, and later as she dressed for the Westhope ball. She had never had a man pay her any particular regard. With a charming older sister and a vivacious younger sister, Isabel was used to being overlooked.

As she considered her reflection in her dressing table mirror now, Isabel thought of her abuela Sesasi. Isabel's earliest memory was of her. She couldn't be certain of the setting, for in her memories it was an obscure, colorless space. But she would have recognized her abuelita anywhere. Perhaps because Isabel saw so much of her whenever she looked in the mirror.

Rarely had Isabel and her sisters visited Abuela Sesasi at her home in that small mountain village in Michoacán, for their father was loath to be away from the capital city. Yet some of her happiest memories had been in her abuela's casita nestled in the terraced steppes her tíos farmed. In the mornings, Isabel would awaken to the scent of flor de mayo in the thick, moist air, and she knew it would be a good day. Abuelita Sesasi had taught her how to prepare tortilla dough and the delicious champurrado that she always craved, as well as how to mix the dyes for the rugs she weaved expertly on her handloom. And every night before bed, she would brush out Isabel's hair. She could close her eyes and still hear her abuela whisper to her in Purépecha, "You have my hair, mi hijita, but it's so much more beautiful on you."

The words, uttered with so much affection and love, came back to Isabel now as she stared into the mirror as her maid, Lupe, arranged her hair. And it wasn't just Abuelita's hair that Isabel inherited from her, she noted. It was her warm olive-toned skin. Her broad nose. Her high cheekbones. Her deep, dark eyes. Isabel knew she'd inherited her bow-shaped lips, as well as her height, from her mother, for Abuelita had been a tiny thing, but it was readily apparent to anyone who looked which side of the family Isabel favored.

Considering the long glances she received when she entered a room, and the arched brows and pinched lips that followed, it was easy to see how some people found fault with her features.

After Lupe had quit the room, Isabel studied her reflection in the mirror again. Gabby had suggested she wear her new gold ball gown, explaining that it flattered her dark skin. Isabel had not thought much of her comment . . . until she considered herself in the gown now. The dress sat off the shoulders, highlighting the sweep of her collarbone and making the line of her neck seem delicate. The bodice narrowed to a belted waist, a detail she adored. The skirt's tulle overlay was stitched with gold ivy that crawled up and down the material and almost appeared to stretch and grow as she twirled about. With her pinned updo displaying her array of corkscrew curls, adorned with a single white feather, even Isabel could admit she appeared graceful. Perhaps even pretty. Tilting her head to the side, she admired the small gold hoops Lupe had fastened in her ears, the understated elegance exactly to her taste.

For the first time in her life, Isabel fancied she looked like a woman who could hold the attention of a viscount. A woman who deserved compliments and praise for her beauty. Oh, Isabel knew her looks could never be compared to those of Gabby, who turned heads with her rich mahogany tresses and large hazel eyes that were framed by thick, inky lashes. But in this gold gown, Isabel felt bewitching and mysterious, like Xaratanga, the Purépecha goddess of the moon. Isabel knew she was being a bit dramatic, but for once she didn't care.

An errant thought brought her up short: What would Captain Dawson think of her in this gown? Would he ask to dance with her again? Would he agree that the gold color seemed to illuminate her skin?

Sucking in a breath, Isabel slashed her hand through the air. Why was she concerned about Dawson when Lord Westhope had already made his interest clear? The viscount was a man of discernible tastes; he was well read and intelligent, and most importantly, Lord Westhope made her feel intelligent and interesting. Plus, he was handsome . . . even if his gilded looks could not compare with Captain Dawson's fiery beauty. But why then did her heart not race like a runaway carriage when she saw the viscount? Why did the mere thought of Captain Dawson seeing her in this gown make her skin tingly and hot?

Turning from the mirror in a swish of gold skirts, Isabel reached for her reticule and ivory gloves, determined to put all thoughts of handsome men from her mind. Tonight would be a key opportunity for her, for she would be granted access to Lord Westhope's home. To the rooms in which he kept his correspondence. His records. His deepest secrets. While the viscount had been forthcoming about his French relatives, there was a possibility one of them had passed along information to him, no matter how innocent. And if they had, Isabel was determined to find it.

Thirty minutes later, Isabel worried the inside of her cheek as she waited with Lady Yardley and Gabby in the receiving line to meet their host. Westhope House was teeming with guests, the din of their chatter paired with the music emanating from the ballroom making her tense and a tad off-balance. Still, Isabel tried to push aside her discomfort and focus on Lord Westhope instead. The viscount had no female relative to serve as hostess for him, so he stood at the end of the queue by himself and Isabel studied him, her heart heavy that he would be alone. For much of her childhood she had felt alone. The odd duck sister struggling to be seen between two lovely swans. But now, her sisters owned her heart, and there was nothing she wouldn't do to ensure their happiness. Their safety. Even if it meant sneaking in and out of strangers' personal spaces.

And if she were to find incriminating information in Lord Westhope's belongings, was she brave enough to use it? Isabel liked to think she would be, but she truly admired the viscount. He had been nothing but generous to her, and his attentions had boosted her confidence. If he were to ask to court her in earnest, would she consent? She fidgeted with her reticule as she scrutinized him. Lord Westhope's comely face was brightened by a smile as he greeted an elderly couple, and it reminded her that while the viscount was handsome, wealthy, and titled, he was also kind. Isabel had been judged by her own looks her entire life, and she would never dream of doing the same to someone else.

And yet despite all the positive things stacked in Lord Westhope's favor, Isabel could not ignore the lack of excitement she felt when she was with him. She enjoyed his company and counted herself lucky to have won his regard and respect. But could she love him? Would she be as keen to spend time with him if he didn't have information she wanted? Isabel frowned as she wondered if her concerns even mattered when her heart urged her to return to Mexico.

Before Isabel had much time to ponder that question, they reached the front of the queue. The viscount greeted Lady Yardley warmly, complimenting her on her beauty and inquiring after Dove. It was the perfect question to ask the older woman because the viscountess did so love to talk about her little dog. Next he greeted Gabby, and exchanged some light-hearted banter with her.

Isabel forced herself not to bite her lip when it was her turn to greet him, but he made it difficult. His green-eyed gaze fixed on her as a large grin spread over his face. Was he truly so delighted to see her?

"Miss Luna, you are a vision," he declared, his eyes bright. "You look like an angel in that gown."

Unable to help herself, Isabel grasped the folds of her skirts and showcased the lace carefully stitched to the hem of her gown. "Thank you, my lord."

Lord Westhope continued to stare at her, until a throat

discreetly cleared nearby. The viscount jolted a bit, and hastily reached out to grab Isabel's hand. "Has your supper waltz been claimed yet?"

She almost laughed aloud. No one had ever secured her supper waltz. Instead, Isabel shook her head.

"Will you save it for me?" the viscount asked.

Isabel nodded again.

"Excellent," he exclaimed. Raising her hand, he kissed the air over her knuckles. "I look forward to it, Miss Luna."

In a bit of a daze, Isabel walked away to rejoin her sister and Lady Yardley.

"I swear, that man's whole face lights up when he sees you," the viscountess said as she led them toward the ballroom.

"If you marry Lord Westhope, Isa, you'll be a viscountess just like her ladyship." Gabby smirked as Lady Yardley looked back at her. "If both of you were in attendance at a dinner, who would enter first? Please say it would be Isa."

"Gabby, stop antagonizing her ladyship," Isabel murmured as they stepped into the ballroom. Her shoulders stiffened for a heartbeat, but she willfully turned her gaze about the space, identifying all the exits of the room. She would investigate where each corridor led soon.

Lady Yardley was greeted almost immediately by a group of matrons, and she walked away with them, chattering happily. Gabby wrapped her arm around Isabel's and led her around the edge of the ballroom, smiling benignly at the people who called out greetings to her.

"Goodness, I hope he doesn't ask for a dance," Gabby murmured into her ear about the Marquess of Clare as he passed. "I'm convinced that man doesn't know what tooth powder is."

"A waltz is a long time to spend with a foul-smelling man breathing down on you."

"Indeed." Gabby shifted her hazel eyes to the other side of the room. "Do you know if Ana and Gideon will be here tonight?"

"They won't be." Isabel dipped her head at an elderly countess as they passed. "They're dining with Lord and Lady Montrose."

"Oh, that's right. Something to do with Gideon's work, yes?"

Isabel snorted. "Have you forgotten that Gideon and Montrose continue their work to sniff out all remnants of the slave trade?"

"Give me some credit, Isa." Gabby bumped her shoulder into hers. "I remembered, but Gideon's abolitionist work is not his only work. He champions a variety of causes. It's something I've always admired about him."

"Me, too," Isabel echoed. She was immensely fond of her brother by marriage, not just because he always treated her with respect, but because he practically worshipped the ground Ana María walked on.

"Do you suppose if we're to stay in England for several more years that you would be open to marrying an Englishman?"

Isabel frowned down at her sister. "Honestly, I never thought I would marry."

"Why not?" Gabby asked with a matching frown.

She nibbled the inside of her cheek, suddenly feeling uncomfortable. "I suppose I've never had romantic notions. Father certainly made it clear he didn't intend to dangle me as bait to his political friends, and when did we have an opportunity to meet gentlemen outside of the events he allowed us to attend?"

"We didn't. We weren't allowed to go anywhere unless he deemed it so." Gabby exhaled noisily through her nose. "And once again I'm jealous of you. Father most definitely had a gentleman in mind for my husband. Probably a viejito with more white hairs than not."

Isabel didn't dare argue that assertion. Their father had made it abundantly clear that he possessed little care for his youngest daughter. While Elías Luna complained about Isabel's behavior on occasion but mostly left her to her own devices, he outright ignored Gabby.

Isabel pulled Gabby to face her. "Mi amor, you know you're worth far more than he ever gave you credit for."

A flush of pink spread across the crest of her cheeks, but rather than dropping her gaze, Gabby laughed. "I know. I've always known. Which is why it always made me so angry when—"

"Good evening, ladies."

Grimacing for a moment, Gabby eventually spun around in a cloud of silk. "Lord Belfry, how do you do?"

"Much better now that you've arrived." Sliding his gaze to Isabel, the teasing smile melted from the baron's face. "Miss Luna."

Isabel barely managed not to roll her eyes.

As if she were simply a part of the wallpaper, Baron Belfry conversed and flirted with Gabby for several long minutes. While her sister repeatedly tried to include Isabel in the conversation, the baron was soon joined by a trio of gentlemen friends, and Isabel was all but pushed aside as the men flanked Gabby in a semicircle. The casual disregard would have stung if she didn't see the outrage coloring every line of her sister's face.

Still, Isabel chose to recognize it as the opportunity it was, for she certainly had no desire to participate in Baron Belfry's inane conversation. As it was, Gabby appeared bored to tears. Thankful for the reprieve, Isabel waved a hand at her sister and melted into the crowd.

Isabel made her way to the refreshment table, where she poured herself a glass of lemonade. Pivoting about, she pretended to drink while she studied the room. Several grand archways ran the length of the space, serving as a barrier between the dance floor and the sitting area, where groups sat at tables chattering and eating a grand assortment of food laid out and meticulously maintained by the Westhope staff. A trio of double doors opened to a large veranda, and Isabel spied several couples in conversation in the cool early summer air.

Turning, Isabel pondered her next moves. The ballroom was designed in an oblong shape, and she noted four different corridors leading from the ballroom, including the foyer guests had taken to enter the room. Isabel nibbled her lip as she decided where to start first. Considering Westhope actively voted his seat in Lords and served on various committees, she imagined that the viscount's study would probably be located near the front of the house. Much easier to welcome guests, she thought. Taking a sip of lemonade, Isabel studied the first corridor, making note of who came and went from it. It appeared to be less used by guests than the two exits located at the other end of the ballroom. Surely that meant those led to the retiring rooms, so Isabel would start her search with the first corridor.

Finishing her drink, Isabel set her glass aside and dabbed her mouth with a napkin. Abruptly, the hairs on the back of her neck rose. Was she being watched? Isabel sucked in a breath as she casually swept her gaze over the guests. No one appeared to be paying her any attention, and Isabel exhaled her agitation. She was always nervous before she embarked on a "scouting mission," a term Fernando used in his letters, and she was doubly so on this night because she would be searching the personal belongings of a man she considered her friend.

And yet, it must be done. Squaring her shoulders, Isabel walked toward the first corridor, a barely there smile on her lips. She returned the greetings of several people she passed, but successfully reached the darkened hall without attracting undue notice. Glancing over her shoulder to ensure no one was watching, Isabel stepped into the darkness, allowing her eyes a moment to adjust to the dim lighting. As the path ahead came into focus, Isabel knew she had chosen correctly. Surely if this corridor was meant for guests, the viscount would have provided adequate lighting to brighten their way.

Grasping her skirts, Isabel moved swiftly down the hall, peeking into the various rooms as she passed them. When she pushed open the last door on the right, her gaze landed on a broad mahogany desk, and a smile crossed her face.

Stealing into the room, Isabel shut the door as quietly as possible, locked it, and leaned back against the wood. A single lamp burned on a side table in the corner, providing enough illumination for Isabel to take in the space. Bookshelves lined every wall, from the marble-tiled floor to the paneled ceiling. There were even bookshelves underneath the two beveled windows that looked down on the street below. Isabel's hands twitched to investigate Lord Westhope's collection. Although he had claimed to have spent a good deal of time and money building up his library, Isabel had not appreciated the endeavor until looking at it now. She'd like nothing more than to peruse the shelves, find a book to her liking, and curl up in one of the armchairs situated near the fireplace. But she did not have time for personal pursuits, for there was no guarantee that Lord Westhope would not come looking for her. Isabel figured she had about twenty minutes to search before her absence would be noted, and she refused to waste any more time.

With a silent exhale, she made her way to the desk. It was a cheerful space, with framed photographs, playful knickknacks, and a stack of books that included a folio of Shakespeare's sonnets. A quick glance at the stack confirmed the rest were all rather bland books about architecture or art history, genres Lord Westhope had indicated a taste for.

Inconveniently, Isabel thought of Captain Dawson. Of the night he found her in his study at Dancourt Abbey and sent her back to bed with *East Lynne*. He had said it was scandalous, and it proved to be just that.

But she couldn't think of the captain now. Definitely not now.

Crouching, Isabel made quick work of the lock on the center drawer, and slid it open with curious eyes. At first glance, nothing stood out as noteworthy, and Isabel pushed aside a quill and pen, a stack of blank letterhead with the Westhope crest displayed prominently at the top, as well as a letter opener with the crest imprinted into the brass. Isabel couldn't help but roll her eyes at such a thing. It was definitely something her father would do with the Luna family seal.

Angling her head to peer in the back of the drawer, her breath stuttered when she spied a stack of letters neatly tucked into the corner. Ignoring how her hands shook, Isabel grasped them and pulled them out. The return address was in Martinique, and the seal on the back indicated it was from the governor's office. Was this correspondence from the cousin Westhope had mentioned in passing? Isabel's heart threatened to lurch from her chest.

With trembling fingers, she unfolded one sheet of parchment and quickly read its contents. It was an innocuous piece of correspondence that communicated everyday events and observations. Isabel refolded it and grasped another letter, her eyes quickly scanning the contents. Soon she had read through the entire stack, learning nothing of importance, but her confidence was bolstered. Lord Westhope and Jean-Charles, his cousin, communicated frequently, so surely Jean-Charles was bound to share tidbits about French movements in the region. Right?

Battling conflicting emotions, Isabel carefully returned the letters to their spot in the corner of the drawer . . . but before she could slide it closed again, the door to the study opened in a whoosh, revealing Captain Dawson standing in the entry.

Isabel jumped back, colliding with the desk chair and almost tumbling to the floor. At the last moment, her hand caught the corner of the desk and she was able to right herself. With panic swelling in her throat, she watched as the captain quietly closed the door behind him, turning the latch. The sound of the tumbler locking into place seemed to echo through her chest.

Captain Dawson advanced several lazy steps toward where she trembled behind Lord Westhope's desk, his face devoid of expression. However, as he came closer, Isabel realized that anger flashed like blue fire in his eyes.

"Miss Luna, this is your one chance to tell me what you're doing in here, or so help me, I will tell Westhope where I found you."

8

Sirius saw her as soon as she entered the ballroom. Her gold gown was bold and vibrant, and paired with her dark skin, Isabel sparkled under the gaslights. From his place with Whitfield and several acquaintances in the corner of the ballroom, Sirius had watched her over his glass as she navigated through the crowd with Gabriela by her side, growing more and more confused that her presence had not drawn more notice. While young men fawned over her sister, Isabel had stood quietly by even as all the light in the room seemed drawn to her. Were people blind? How had they not noticed how arresting she was? Sirius could not keep the scowl from his face.

Which deepened when he noticed Isabel slip from the ballroom into a dark hall. Throwing back the rest of his brandy, Sirius had repressed a sigh. Apparently, he would need to save her from herself once again.

Finding her in Westhope's study had not been hard, although it had taken him a frustrating moment or two to pick the lock. But the time Sirius spent seeing to such an annoying task had been worth it to surprise her as he did. Looking at

Isabel now, her face pale and her dark eyes saucers, filled him with an intense amount of satisfaction.

"Well," Sirius said, advancing another step closer to her, "what is it? Why are you here, lurking in the shadows, and not in the ballroom with the rest of the viscount's guests?"

"I'm not lurking," she hissed, color returning to her complexion.

"Perhaps not . . . but you've not answered my question," Sirius said, slowly arching a brow.

Isabel dropped her gaze immediately. When his eyes landed on her hands, which she was wringing together, she abruptly ceased the motion and dropped them to hang by her sides. "I got lost."

"No, you didn't," he replied, crossing his arms over his chest. "You had to have known the retiring rooms were on the other end of the ballroom, because that is where the crowds congregated."

"Oh, I hadn't noticed," she said, lifting a shoulder.

If she was aiming to be convincing, her performance left much to be desired.

"That's a lie, Isabel. You strike me as a very observant person."

As Sirius had expected, his accusation angered her. Her eyes narrowed into slits, and Isabel prowled around the desk and stopped in front of him, jabbing her finger into his chest. "How dare you."

"How dare I what?" He smirked. "How dare I call you a liar, or how dare I call you one of the most observant people I know?"

Isabel growled in the back of her throat and poked him again. "You know what I mean."

With a quick flash of movement, Sirius grabbed her hand and pulled her closer, until her chest was practically flush with his own. "Tread carefully, Isabel."

"I didn't give you leave to address me by my first name," she said, glaring into his eyes.

Sirius bent down until his face hovered before her own. "I will call you by your Christian name as long as you act like a spoiled child, *Isabel*."

Her mouth flattened. "Spoiled child? You're not my father, Captain Dawson, and you have no authority over me."

"You're right. I don't." His grip on her tightened. "But I have no qualms about telling Fox of your intrusive searches."

Rather than relenting, she grew angrier. Her jaw was granite. "Gideon is not my father, either. Ana María may have to answer to him, but I do not."

"And what of your uncle? I'm certain Mr. Valdés would be appalled if he knew you were sneaking about the private studies of members of the peerage."

Her lips parted as alarm flared in her eyes. In an instant, it was gone, replaced by bright flames of fury. "Why can't you mind your own business?"

"You *are* my business," he snarled down at her.

"Why would I possibly be your business?" Isabel snapped.

Sirius licked his lips to deliver an angry retort . . . but the words died on his tongue when he noticed that her gaze had dropped to his mouth. Desire licked up his spine, and Sirius curled his arm around her back, his fingers pressing into the flesh of her waist. His head swam . . . until she wrenched her surprised gaze up to meet his.

Clarity slammed into him like a locomotive. Sirius stumbled backward, dropping his arms as if she had burned him. This was Isabel Luna, not some willing widow meeting him in a dark library for an assignation. She deserved more care, more consideration, than what his body ached to give her.

"I'm sorry," Sirius mumbled, smoothing his palms down his

lapels and steadfastly avoiding her gaze. "I should not have taken such liberties with you."

Isabel did not answer immediately, but he could hear her throat work on a swallow. "I don't understand why you're here. Why do you care what I do?"

Sirius shook his head, unsure of how to respond because even he didn't understand his need to protect her, as much from herself as from others.

"You are constantly surrounded by a crowd, Captain. Your *exploits*"—she emphasized the word as if it were a slur—"are splashed in the gossip pages. You make friends and command attention wherever you go. Why concern yourself with someone like me?"

"Someone like you?" Sirius advanced a step toward her. "Who do you consider yourself to be?"

Her dark eyes stared up at him, the air between them thick and taut. Sirius knew how others viewed Isabel, but he also knew how wrong they were. So how did she view herself? Did she know she was bright and perceptive, and delivered stinging retorts that replayed in his mind for days afterward? That her barely there smile absolutely beguiled him, for it hinted at all the emotions she kept so tightly contained? Did she know that her sinfully full mouth was made for kisses? Sirius curled his hands into fists at the idea he could show her.

A breath shuddered past her lips. "I'm nobody. Just a Mexican woman trying to be the best sister and niece I can be."

His ribs seized around his heart, and Sirius reached out a hand to her—

A noise in the corridor made them freeze in place. If they were found, alone in a dark room, Sirius was not certain they could survive the scandal. Turning to Isabel, he found her staring at the closed door with panic-stricken eyes.

Taking her hand, Sirius dragged her to the corner of the room and tucked her within the dark drapes, hidden from view by one of the tall bookcases. Sirius swiftly walked back to the armchairs, adjusting his tie and his cufflinks, hoping he appeared relaxed and unruffled, and not like a man waging a war with his emotions. Grabbing a book from a side table, Sirius had just sat when the tumbler clicked and the door swung open.

"Ho, Dawson, what are you doing here in the dark?" Westhope exclaimed, another gentleman standing behind him in the doorway.

Sirius closed the book with a snap and rose to his feet. "Honestly, I was trying to dodge Lady Needham's attentions. She's become quite . . ." He paused, crooking his mouth. "Demanding."

The viscount chuckled, stepping into the room and turning to light another lamp. "Yes, it appears the baroness is determined to make a conquest of you. Pity that her campaign has you hiding in the library when you should be dancing with pretty ladies."

"Indeed. Yet I haven't rushed back to the ballroom, because you have an impressive library, Westhope." Sirius made a show of pulling out his pocket watch. "It would seem that the supper waltz approaches. Should we find our partners?"

"Oh yes, I don't want to leave Miss Luna waiting," Westhope said, hurrying to his desk and unlocking the center drawer. "Let me just grab that printer's card for Andrews."

Sirius nodded in greeting at the other man, and then turned back to the viscount, his teeth abruptly on edge. He cleared his throat. "Have you secured Miss Gabriela Luna's hand for the supper waltz?"

"Miss Gabriela is lovely, but"—the viscount clicked his

tongue—"it's Miss Isabel Luna's quiet, clever demeanor that I'm drawn to."

"I see," he murmured, his pulse thundering in his ears. "She is a singular young woman."

Westhope looked up, a thoughtful expression on his face. "She's incomparable. I have enjoyed spending time with her. Ha, here it is," he finished, brandishing a card in the air.

Straightening his cravat, Westhope nodded. "Here you go, Andrews. Now let's find our dance partners."

With a quick glance to the back of the room, Sirius smiled. "Yes, let's not keep them waiting."

And with that, he followed the viscount and his friend, so many things left unsaid in the air behind him.

Expelling a breath that Isabel had held for entirely too long, she dropped her head back against the wall as the door closed. That had been too close for comfort. If Lord Westhope had walked any farther into the room, surely he would have seen her gold skirts among the dark fabric of the window drapes. She wasn't exactly camouflaged.

But Captain Dawson—Sirius—had delivered the perfect distraction . . . and not just for the viscount.

Inhaling so deeply her lungs felt full to bursting, Isabel ran trembling hands along her brow, carefully tucking loose hairs behind her ears. Once she had adjusted the fit of her bodice, Isabel pushed the drapes aside and stepped into the room. Her pulse was still fluttering, but Isabel knew she could not dawdle, for Lord Westhope would be looking to claim her hand for their waltz, and she absolutely could not be found in this room.

Isabel closed her eyes and squared her shoulders as she counted to ten, before she quietly opened the door and entered the empty corridor. Keeping to the shadows, she reached the ballroom in seconds, but hesitated on the threshold, eyes darting about the space.

She spotted Gabby chatting with several young women on the other side of the dance floor, flashing a bland smile at a gentleman who stopped to greet her, before pointedly turning back to her friends. To the right of her, Isabel found Lady Yardley perched with several matrons watching the dancers performing a reel. Fighting the urge to worry her lip, Isabel took several steps into the room. Suddenly a pair of sapphire eyes snared hers, and her heart kicked into a sprint. Sirius was standing across the room surrounded by a group of people, but his gaze was fixed on her. Isabel couldn't identify what was in the bottomless ocean depths of his gaze—wariness, curiosity, a hunger that made her mouth run dry. No man had ever looked at her that way, and Isabel was helpless to look away from him.

That was until a figure blocked her line of sight.

"There you are, Miss Luna," Lord Westhope said, a friendly smile on his lips and a spark of relief in his eyes. "I had almost feared I wouldn't find you before our set."

"I'm sorry to have worried you," Isabel said, executing a curtsy. "I was merely wandering the room, greeting acquaintances and watching the dances."

The music changed then, and a rush of couples brushed past them to take a position on the dance floor. The viscount held out a hand to her.

"Are you ready?"

Isabel smiled . . . or sincerely attempted to. "I am."

As Lord Westhope led her onto the floor, he placed his hand on her waist and looked down at her. "I've been looking forward to this dance all week."

Unsure of what to say, she dipped her head and allowed the viscount to spin her to the melody.

But not before Isabel felt Sirius's intense gaze drift along her skin, and glancing over Lord Westhope's shoulder, she was not at all surprised to find him staring at her. ¡Por Dios! Something had changed in the viscount's library, but Isabel wasn't sure what. All she knew was that the captain had held her closely against his chest, his fingers pressing into her flesh and his gaze smoldering pools of blue fire. Isabel had been certain he was going to kiss her, but surely she'd been mistaken. Right?

It took two turns around the dance floor before Isabel could attend to the viscount's conversation. Bits of his words floated through her whirling thoughts; something about a book he'd long searched for—a first edition of *Don Quixote*, maybe. Isabel nodded along, hoping she expressed her interest in believable ways. But truly, Isabel found it a herculean task to focus on anything other than the brooding blond man who watched her from across the crowd.

Risking a quick glance in his direction, Isabel found him still standing among a mix of gentlemen and women, the crowd laughing and talking around him. But Sirius's gaze remained fixed on her, and Isabel bit her lip to be the source of such potent consideration. Was he replaying their conversation in the library? Was he contemplating their almost kiss? Or perhaps he hadn't meant to kiss her at all, because why would he want to kiss her when he could have any of the beautiful ladies in the room? And yet . . . the feverish light in his eyes, the one she glimpsed across the room even now, told Isabel that Captain Sirius Dawson possibly had personal reasons for wanting to stop her covert searches.

Suddenly, Isabel wanted nothing more than to return to that dim library and finish their conversation. Had they not heard Lord Westhope in the hall, would Sirius have kissed her? Unlike Ana María, who had confessed to her and Gabby several months into her marriage that she had not known what to expect of her wedding night, Isabel had read enough to know what occurred between a man and a woman behind closed doors. Her books had supplied her with the mechanics, and sometimes the flowery wonders, of the act.

And while Isabel had never thought a great love affair or marriage was in her future, she had absolutely no issue exploring the carnal side of such unions. She knew Padre Ignacio would be aghast at this revelation, but Isabel did not care. A body was just a body, and her spirit was her spirit; she could nurture one while indulging the other.

"Miss Luna, did you hear what I said?"

Isabel wrested her gaze away from Sirius, and blinked up at the viscount. "I do beg your pardon, my lord. I got a bit lost in the music."

Lord Westhope chuckled, squeezing her hand. "I can understand that. This piece by Strauss is one of my favorites. Are you a great fan of music?"

She pressed her lips together for a moment. "I enjoy music as much as the next person. I do miss the gentle melodies my tía Susana used to play on her guitarra on rainy mornings."

"The guitar is not a popular instrument among ladies here in England, and I wonder why that is." The viscount's brow crinkled. "I've heard it played, and it produces a beautiful sound."

"It's probably because it's a Spanish instrument," Isabel tossed out with a shrug.

Lord Westhope frowned. "What do you mean?"

"Come now, Lord Westhope," she said, offering a wry smile, "surely you know that the British don't seem to value much about Spanish culture."

To his credit, the viscount appeared to consider this claim carefully. Instead of responding with an immediate rejection of her statement or even offering an excuse, Lord Westhope screwed his mouth up and stared down at her with a pucker between his brows. Isabel respected his tendency to ponder his response before he said it. And, not for the first time did she wonder why she couldn't feel something, *anything*, for the viscount aside from warm friendliness. For if Isabel were looking for a British husband, Viscount Westhope would be more than ideal.

But as long as she had a choice, her future lay in Mexico.

"I suspect," he began, a teasing smirk playing with the corners of his mouth, "that the British have turned their noses up at the Spanish ever since Sir Walter Raleigh defeated the famed Spanish Armada."

A bubble of laughter burst from her throat. "Ay sí, surely that's it. And I'm certain the Spanish have held a nearly three-hundred-year-old grudge ever since."

"Oh, indeed. National pride is exploited at every chance." Lord Westhope smiled down at her. "And the British have turned their noses up at the Spanish, even if it deprives us of truly excellent music."

Isabel chuckled again . . . but the sound tapered off when she spied Sirius staring at her with a dark glower. Was he upset with her? Because she was enjoying her waltz with the viscount? Isabel had watched him seduce any number of ladies, each time an assault on the armor she wrapped tightly about her. And he was upset now that a handsome man had made her laugh?

Arching a brow in return, Isabel turned away from him and forced herself to focus all of her attention on Lord Westhope.

Their waltz ended some minutes later, and Isabel was

almost sorry for it. When the viscount escorted her into the dining room, a bevy of guests followed them. To her relief, Lord Westhope selected a small table near the front of the room that was large enough for only one other couple to join them, and thankfully that couple was Gabby and her dance partner, a young lord whose name Isabel promptly forgot.

Dinner passed in a pleasant manner, Lord Westhope regaling them with stories of hunting rare books all over Europe, and Gabby's lordling chimed in with funny witticisms that hinted at the charming rake he would one day be. Throughout the time they spent dining, Isabel made a conscious effort not to look for Sirius. The captain had no right to scold her the way he did—and he certainly had no right to cause heat to simmer low in her core. And just because most men had ignored her since she arrived in London, the captain included, did not mean that she was not deserving of Lord Westhope's attentions.

But after Isabel had wished good night to the viscount and prepared to return to Yardley House, Sirius stepped into her path.

Isabel held up a staying hand when Gabby looked back at her in question from the carriage. She reached for her composure as she followed Sirius to the side of the foyer. But just being in his vicinity, inhaling his crisp cedarwood and orange scent that had quickly become familiar to her, threatened all her firm admonitions. Isabel curled her hands into fists, her fingernails cutting into her palms and grounding her in reality.

"Will you hack out with me tomorrow morning?" he asked quietly, his deep blue eyes intent on her face.

"I'm not the best rider—"

"That doesn't matter," Sirius said, his tone curt. "I just want privacy for the discussion we need to have."

She shook her head. "But you know I'll have to bring a groom, so I won't truly be alone."

The corner of his mouth ticked up. "A bit of privacy can be bought."

Isabel rolled her eyes. "Very well. I will be ready by seven in the morning."

"Six thirty," he countered, his brow arching. "I will be at Yardley House not a minute later."

"I'll be ready," she whispered.

Sirius grabbed her hand then, raising it to his lips while holding her eyes. "I look forward to it," he said, the soft pressure of his lips raising gooseflesh across her skin.

Isabel's hand tingled the entire way to Yardley House.

Once she was ensconced in her chamber, successful in evading Gabby's and Lady Yardley's many questions about her evening, Isabel sank onto the chair before her escritoire. Extracting a fresh sheet of parchment from a stack in the top drawer, Isabel paused, nibbling her lip as her mind scripted out various openings before she settled on one. Straightening her spine, Isabel dipped a quill into the ink and carefully wrote out her customary greeting to Padre Ignacio. When she was done, she reread her words, hope swelling in her chest.

Folding the letter, she set it aside to be franked the next day. Then, selecting a book from the stack next to her bed, she climbed under the blankets and propped her back against the pillows. Isabel studied the book she'd grabbed, her selection made unconsciously. It was the folio of poems she had swiped from Captain Dawson's library at Dancourt Abbey.

9

Isabel felt as if she had barely closed her eyes when the drapes were ripped open, assaulting the backs of her eyelids with the harsh light of day.

"Buenos días, señorita," the maid, Lupe, said as she bustled into Isabel's connecting dressing room. "Her ladyship said you were going to be riding out this morning, so I thought the azul habit would be a good choice. What do you think, señorita?"

Isabel grabbed a pillow and threw it over her face, groaning softly. "I don't know why I agreed to such an early time."

"I know why." Lupe poked her head into the room, a large smile on her round face. "Porque el capitán es muy guapo."

Ay, was he ever. He was also observant. Intuitive. Despite his scolds and overbearing actions, Sirius had a way of looking at her as if he really saw her—not the shy, awkward Isabel the ton knew her as, but as the Isabel her sisters knew. The Isabel she was just coming to accept. She supposed the only way she'd know for sure was to dress in the azul habit Lupe had chosen and meet Sirius for their scheduled morning ride.

Thirty minutes later, Isabel paced in front of the windows

overlooking the front walk. What if Sirius didn't come? He said he would, but after several hours of reprieve, he may have changed his mind.

A distant "Good morning, sir" met her ears.

Isabel turned to the window and brushed the drapes aside, her pulse roaring in her ears. Sirius sat astride a large bay colt, dressed in a riding coat a deep shade of blue that Isabel was certain would turn his eyes to the dreamy color of midnight. With buff-colored trousers, crisp and polished riding boots, and his gold locks glinting from under his hat in the early morning sunlight, Sirius looked almost princely. As if he were riding out to rescue a princess from the tallest tower.

Instead, he would find himself saddled with the wallflower Luna sister he felt obliged to protect in some sort of misplaced honor.

Sirius looked up then to the window she stood before, his gaze seeming to find hers. His expression didn't change, but the weight of his stare felt heady.

Without thought, Isabel turned and grasped her crop, before looping the train of her habit over her arm and racing down the stairs. As she neared the last few steps, she slowed, and raised her chin, hoping to appear stately instead of giddy with excitement.

Evans was just opening the front door to Sirius when she stepped into the foyer, and his eyes immediately pinned her in place. Isabel flushed from the tips of her toes to the crown of her head. She hoped he didn't notice.

"Good morning." She cringed at the low-pitched tone of her voice. "Are we ready?"

"Good morning, Miss Luna. You look well," Sirius drawled, his manner perfectly polite, but his blue gaze twinkled in that teasing manner that used to annoy her.

Now that twinkle made her shiver.

Struggling to regain her poise, Isabel dipped her head and severed their eye contact. "Thank you, Captain Dawson. I've been looking forward to our ride."

"Have you?" Sirius's lips tipped up.

Refusing to allow him to assault her aplomb any further, Isabel tapped her crop on her thigh and advanced toward the door. "Shall we be on our way?"

Sirius extended a hand to her as she stepped over the threshold. "Yes, let's. For I, too, have been looking forward to it."

"No doubt so you can scold me, yet again," Isabel grumbled as she walked by his side down the front stairs.

"Not quite," Sirius murmured. "Although you would be deserving of it."

After assisting her to mount her mare, Sirius led her down the street in the direction of Hyde Park. A footman played groom on a gelding twenty or so paces behind them. There was little to no traffic on the street at such an early hour, and the soft click of their horses' hooves mingled with the rumble of supply wagons and the chatter of birds seeing to their business. Isabel was happy for the silence. It gave her an opportunity to settle her nerves. Being in Sirius's presence had always left her a bit defensive; first because he antagonized her, then because he stimulated her, and now . . . well, now because he did both simultaneously.

"How are you feeling this morning?"

His voice was mild, almost polite, but Isabel sensed there was more to his question.

She cleared her throat. "I am well. I had an enjoyable evening at the ball last night."

"It appeared so. You certainly smiled more than I've ever seen."

"I had no notion you kept track of my smiles," she shot back, glancing at him askance.

From the corner of her eye she saw the captain lift a shoulder. "They're such rare events . . . and they change your face so completely, it's hard not to pay attention."

Isabel jerked her head about to look at him. "What do you mean?"

"I mean what I said." The captain fixed his gaze on a point in the distance. "Your whole face comes alive when you smile."

"Oh," she replied dumbly, her thoughts in a whirl. No one had made such an observation about her before, and she was unsure how she felt about it.

"Yes, well, Lord Westhope is a friendly fellow, so I can understand why you would enjoy his company."

"Indeed." Noting that the path ahead was unhindered, Isabel allowed herself a moment to study the reins in her hands. Gathering her courage, she blurted, "You did not seem particularly happy that I was enjoying his company last night."

"I didn't?"

His tone was a shade mocking, which set her teeth on edge. "You glared at me every time I met your gaze after our encounter in the library."

"I wasn't glaring at you," Captain Dawson snorted.

"Come now, I know what I saw," Isabel said with a scoff.

"Apparently you don't," he said, his blue eyes sliding to meet hers, "or else you would know I was glaring at *him*."

Oh. Isabel dropped her gaze, uncomfortably aware of the flush that streaked up her neck and over her cheeks. And yet his words angered her, for why should he care if an eligible, attractive man took notice of her?

"You have no reason to be antagonistic toward Lord Westhope. The man doesn't possess a mean bone in his body."

Isabel tilted her chin as she narrowed her eyes at him. "And why should his kind attentions to me be deserving of your disdain? You've only ever shown indifference to me."

He grunted even as he pulled back on his horse's reins. The beast nickered in agitation as it came to a stop. "Indifference, you say?"

Isabel frowned. How else could the captain describe how he'd treated her for the last two years? She supposed it was true that he had been unerringly gracious when she and her sisters had found themselves unexpected guests at Dancourt Abbey . . . and he'd been especially kind when Ana María was abducted . . . and again when her parents were in danger . . .

With an uncomfortable pain in her side, Isabel realized that Captain Sirius Dawson had been kind and gracious to her more times than she had ever given him credit for. Every time she had spoken to him with sarcasm and barely concealed contempt, he had responded with polite teasing. Captain Dawson had never ridiculed her or mocked her, even when she had done the same to him. Shame nauseated her.

Uncertain of what to say in the wake of such a revelation, Isabel strung random words together that she hoped made sense. "You seemed to avoid me at every turn—"

"Isabel."

She startled, her gaze flying to his.

"If I avoided you, it's because you made it abundantly clear that you were disgusted by me. I'm a gentleman, and have no interest in forcing my company on someone who does not desire it." The captain directed his mount a step closer to hers. "Regardless, I can't help but be concerned for your welfare."

Opening her mouth but discovering she had nothing to say, Isabel closed it with a snap.

"But why?" she finally managed on a whisper.

Captain Dawson cursed under his breath, before he grabbed her reins and led her mount to the side of the riding trail. It took Isabel a moment to realize they were now in the park—she didn't even remember arriving. Apparently she had been so distracted by her tumultuous thoughts, she had not been paying attention to the landscape around her. Gracias a Dios that her mare was content to follow alongside the captain's horse.

Moving his head to and fro, Captain Dawson surveyed their surroundings, no doubt seeing who was close by. Aside from the groom, who respectfully lingered under a tree some distance away, they were quite alone. Isabel wasn't sure what to think about that fact, especially when he moved his horse directly beside hers. Captain Dawson stared at her quietly for several tense heartbeats, his chest visibly rising and falling on a breath.

"Why did I find you in Westhope's study last night?"

Isabel had expected the question, but not the gentle manner in which he asked it. Not the patient way in which he looked at her now. And hadn't she just had an epiphany about Captain Dawson's behavior toward her? He might be a rogue, but he had never disrespected her.

"I'm sure you are aware that my sisters and I were not happy to have been sent away from Mexico, and we've been determined to aid the resistance in the limited ways we can." Licking her dry lips, Isabel continued. "Well, before we left Mexico City, I received a visit from a political ally of my father's. Fernando Ramírcz. You may know that name because he used to be engaged to Ana María."

Captain Dawson's expression clouded. "I knew your sister had been engaged previously, but I didn't know the man's name."

"Well, Señor Ramírez had always been kind to me," Isabel continued, doing her best not to fidget with the reins, "so I was curious when he sought me out before we departed. Padre Ignacio had told him where to find me."

"Padre Ignacio?" he asked, his brows rising.

"Padre Ignacio oversaw my first Holy Communion, and later my confirmation." Her memories turned wistful. "He knew how strict my father was, and through his shrewd persuasion, I was gradually allowed to spend more time at my studies, which he helped oversee. Soon, I was in the library at the rectory more than anywhere else, aside from my own bed. Padre Ignacio possessed books from all over the globe, and loved to talk about them and the new ideas they proposed. He showed me that the world was larger and more diverse than what I knew it to be in my little corner of Mexico City."

"It sounds as if he was a bit of a father figure to you," Captain Dawson murmured.

Isabel swallowed. "He was. He is. I still exchange letters with him regularly."

"Lud," the captain exclaimed, clutching at his chest, "should I assume then that your Father Ignacio knows all about the circumstances of our first meeting?"

A chuckle burst free from her mouth. "He does indeed."

Captain Dawson hung his head in mock shame . . . although based on the look of chagrin on his face, perhaps there was some earnestness there, too.

She grew serious, though, fixing her gaze on the grass below. "It was Padre Ignacio who recommended me to Señor Ramírez."

"Recommended you?" The captain frowned. "Recommended you for what?"

"To . . ." Isabel dragged her eyes to meet his. "Find something."

He leaned forward in his saddle. "What?"

Pursing her lips, Isabel studied him for a long moment, weighing her options. "Señor Ramírez wanted me to locate anything that could be used to convince British noblemen to aid Mexico's fight against the French."

Captain Dawson's brow crinkled and he tugged on his earlobe. "To blackmail them?"

Isabel raised a defiant shoulder. "If need be, yes."

It suddenly felt important to plant his feet on solid ground, so Sirius swung down from his saddle. Leading his mount to a nearby tree, he looped the reins over a low branch, and spun about to face Isabel.

"Let me make sure I'm understanding what you're saying correctly." Sirius rubbed his temple. "This Mr. Ramírez—who may well have been your brother by marriage if your sister had not met Fox—wants you to steal about in the private spaces of peers of the realm to discover incriminating evidence that can be used to blackmail them. Did I get that right?"

This had to be a joke. A great lark of hers. Surely such a dangerous and important task would not have been entrusted into the hands of a young woman with no experience at subterfuge. Surely the people who set her to such a task cared about her safety and would not want her to be harmed. But why, then, would they make her so vulnerable?

Sirius wanted to put his fist through something.

"Sí, that sounds right," she said with a prim nod of her head.

"Isabel," he growled, stalking to where she still sat atop her mare. "What are you thinking? You have no experience conducting such surveillance or successfully navigating such delicate situations. You could be hurt."

"As you can see, I'm perfectly hale," she replied, patting the hand he had placed on her skirts. Sirius blinked, for he hadn't even known he'd done that.

He willed himself to move away, but instead his fingers tightened. "Is that what happened at Tyrell Manor? Why the earl caught you in his study?"

Her eyes shuttered, and Isabel looked away. "It doesn't matter what happened. The only thing that matters is that Ana María and Gideon found their way to each other, just as it was meant to be."

Sirius clenched his jaw. "You have to stop this."

"I don't have to do any such thing." Her expression turned mulish. "Señor Ramírez, Padre Ignacio, and many others are depending upon me to use my access to the most powerful men in England to aid Mexico. And that's what I'm going to do."

A sudden thought occurred to him and he shook her skirts until she met his gaze. "And Westhope? Is that why you're entertaining his court?"

With a growl, Isabel handed him her reins. "Will you please assist me down?"

Sirius obliged her request, ignoring the feel of her waist beneath his palms.

Once her two feet were secure beneath her and she'd shaken out the skirts of her habit, Isabel considered him archly . . . although her cheeks were a dark rose. "If you must know, Lord Westhope's cousin is the secretary to the governor of Martinique. Martinique houses a French garrison, which will sail for Veracruz if called by Maximilian. I would be a fool *not* to exploit my friendship with the viscount to find out what his cousin shares. And I am not a fool."

"And yet you're acting foolish," Sirius shot back, disdain dripping from every word.

Isabel spun away from him and walked under the canopy of a willow tree. She braced her hand on the trunk for a long moment, and Sirius could see how her shoulders shook. No doubt in fury. "Is it foolish to want to help my countrymen? Is it foolish to take advantage of my situation and capitalize on it?"

"It is if it will put you in danger, Isabel." Sirius threw his arms wide. "Isn't it enough that Lord Tyrell caught you in the act?" His jaw twitched. "Isn't it enough that you came across me that night we met, when I was with—"

"I know bloody well who you were with." Her lip curled as she looked at him over her shoulder.

Despite the anger—the fear—blazing like a wildfire through his veins, Sirius felt a pinch right over his heart seeing Isabel so discomfited by the mention of their first meeting. Was there a chance they could have become friends if their first introduction hadn't been so scandalous?

His throat bobbed as he forced down a swallow. "I'm sorry that you met me under such circumstances. It's little wonder you have such a poor opinion of me."

Isabel pivoted to face him, her lip caught between her teeth. "That doesn't matter now. What matters is you are not in a position to stop my search."

Sirius stepped toward her, opening his mouth to deliver a rebuttal, when she held up her hand to stop him.

"No," she cried, stomping her foot. "Don't you see? For the first time in my life, I've been tasked with something important. Isabel Luna, the boring, bookish sister. Not the politically savvy Ana María or the charismatic Gabriela. *Me.* Only I can sneak in and out of the personal chambers of important men to find their secrets. Because no one pays any attention to me. No one seeks my hand for dances, no one engages me in conversation, no one asks to pair with me at the card table. I am a specter, so why shouldn't I exploit that fact to help Mexico?"

"But you're not a specter." Sirius stepped in front of her and grasped her shoulders. "You're dazzling. Your sisters shine . . . but Isabel, you're the entire night sky."

He had no idea where the words had come from. Sirius stared down into Isabel's stunned gaze, certain the same surprise he saw in hers was mirrored in his. And yet the words did not taste like a lie . . .

"Lord Westhope is paying his attentions to you now." He cursed how the light in Isabel's velvet eyes went out when he mentioned the viscount, but it needed to be said. "The scrutiny upon you will be harder to avoid."

Isabel lifted her chin. "I've managed it thus far."

"I don't think you understand the danger you put yourself in when you sneak about these grand houses," Sirius bit out.

She glared up at him. "I assure you, Captain, that my safety is of the utmost concern for me. I would like to return to Mexico one day, preferably hale and unharmed."

"Isabel." He uttered her name with all the frustration he felt. "Surely there are better ways to go about accomplishing your task."

Her mouth flattened in displeasure.

Perhaps it would be best if he tried a different tactic. "I want to help."

"If you want to help, you could start by trusting me," she volleyed.

"Obviously." Sirius dipped his head, before the corner of his lips tilted up. "But . . . I can alert you if someone approaches. Be a distraction if one is needed. And most importantly, I can tell you what I know of these men. I possess a wealth of knowledge about the members of the ton, and with my insight, you won't put yourself in an adverse situation for no reason."

Sirius hadn't exactly realized what he was offering until Isabel's mouth gaped. Christ, why would he volunteer to work with her on this foolhardy mission when he should be putting a stop to it? What was it about this stubborn wallflower that had him rushing to make her happy?

"You would help me?" Isabel whispered, her forehead furrowed.

This was his chance to explain away his offer. To put a stop to any involvement of his.

Instead, Sirius licked his lips and said, "As long as you heed my warnings, with no arguments and no complaints, yes."

Damn it.

Isabel took a step toward him, her hands clenched in her skirts. She practically vibrated like a tuning fork. "But why would you offer your help?"

"Because someone needs to keep you safe," Sirius said, inclining his head, "from yourself as much as from others."

"It's been almost two years since I began my search, and I have been perfectly fine." Her lips twisted in a wry sort of half smile. "Well, aside from the unfortunate incident with Lord Tyrell."

"A very unfortunate incident, indeed." Sirius looked down at his booted feet. "It could have been disastrous, and I don't want you to be in that situation again. You can only claim you're lost so many times before word begins to circulate."

Isabel was silent, and eventually Sirius glanced up to find her staring off through the trees. "I understand I'm taking risks. I've considered all the ways I could be ruined or maimed more times than I can count. This is not something I take lightly, Captain. This is not a grand lark I'm engaging in because I'm bored or looking for entertainment."

Sirius believed her. Of course he did. Everything he knew about Isabel Luna told him that she was passionate about everything in her life: her books, her relationships with her sisters, her fierce pride in her homeland.

What would it be like to have that passion turned toward h—

"I know you're not," he responded, more gruffly than he had intended. But Isabel did not flinch; rather, she arched a black brow with all the censure of a queen.

"But an endeavor such as this requires skill at subterfuge. Espionage." Sirius prowled a few steps away, frustration making his hands curl. "This task you've been given could have serious consequences, and yet you were provided with no training. All the books in the world could not prepare you for this."

This Mr. Ramírez and Father Ignacio took one look at Isabel, with her eager dark eyes, and knew she would do anything to be of use. Anything to help Mexico. Anything to be seen. And they could have gotten her killed for it. Rage locked his jaw.

Firm pressure squeezed around his arm, and Sirius jolted, dropping his gaze to where Isabel's hand held him.

"Nothing and no one has hurt me yet, Captain." Her inky lashes fluttered as she glanced between his face and where her hand held him tight. She did not let him go. "And with your help, I'm certain no one will."

Damn right. Sirius didn't utter the words, but an amused

look touched her face, and he suspected Isabel heard the thought.

Shoving aside his misgivings, Sirius stepped back, silently mourning the loss of her touch. Coughing into a closed fist, he glanced down the riding path. "Tell me, what have you learned about Lord Westhope?"

Sirius heard the gravel crunch as he imagined she swayed back and forth.

"As I've said, my greatest interest in him derives from the fact that his cousin works for the governor of Martinique."

Sirius nodded. "They are inordinately close, from my understanding, and exchange correspondence frequently."

"How do you know that?" Isabel asked, a frown pulling on her lips.

Christ. What did he want to tell her? What was he *allowed* to tell her? Sirius needed to tread carefully until he could speak with Lieutenant Colonel Green. "I believe Westhope has mentioned it a time or two." He added a shrug for good measure.

A loose curl brushed against her cheek as she tilted her head. "And have your contacts told you anything?"

"Contacts?" Sirius said questioningly.

"At the Home Office. After we learned my parents might be captured by the French, you mentioned your contacts there." Isabel's gaze shifted just slightly to the side. "You sent that note, through Gideon, that you had not learned anything alarming from Mexico, so that boded well for their safety."

It was Sirius's turn to look away. Although he had been unable to talk with Green about the situation, Sirius had other friends with the Home Office who had been able to assuage his fears for Mr. and Mrs. Luna. It had brought him a measure of relief to share such news with Fox, for he knew his friend would tell Isabel.

That she remembered his connection to the Home Office impressed him . . . and also made him uncomfortable. Which would not do.

That realization was like a hook pulling his spine straight. "My connections have also told me that it doesn't appear as if Westhope is planning anything nefarious with his cousin."

"Has the Home Office"—Isabel frowned—"been watching him?"

Sirius clicked his tongue as he scrambled to think of a response. "They will always keep tabs on anyone with a French connection . . . especially when France is busying itself with occupying sovereign countries."

"Oh," she cried, her eyes wide, "so the British government has noticed that France has occupied Mexico illegally."

"Of course they have—"

"So they don't care, then," Isabel said, that damn half smile on her lips.

Dipping his head, Sirius chuckled. "As I've said, it's not about caring so much as prioritizing interests."

A bit of her heart glinted in her expression. "So the odds the British will intervene in the French conflict in Mexico remain at zero?"

Rocking back, Sirius shook his head. "The odds are never zero. But again, the British government won't intervene unless British interests are at stake."

"But they are at stake," Isabel cried, throwing her arms wide. "Why can't they see that France won't stop at Mexico? They will bleed my country dry of her resources and wealth and people, and then use those ill-gotten gains to fund their conquests of other countries. And Britain will be on that list. How could they not be? It's only a matter of time."

"I know." Sirius slid his gaze to the groom waiting down the path, desperate to look at anything other than the helplessness in her eyes. "And I suspect those in power know this as well."

He could hear her throat work on a swallow.

"So what is there to do? Is there anything *to* do? Will they only be convinced once French forces arrive on the shores of Kent?"

"I don't know." He canted closer to her, his arms shaking with his desire to reach out and comfort her. "But let's focus on what we do know and what we can control."

"Of course," she whispered, pressing her hands to her cheeks.

"What are your plans for this evening?" he asked, abruptly changing the subject.

Isabel's eyes widened before they glazed over in confusion. "Oh. Um . . . I'm not—"

"Do you know if you received an invitation to the Fairchild dinner party?"

"I'm not sure. Should we have?" she said, frowning.

"I'm certain you have," Sirius said, tapping his crop against his thigh, "because Mrs. Fairchild is on friendly terms with Lady Yardley."

"Right," she said simply, her brows stitched together. "The viscountess has many friends, and I often struggle to keep track of them."

"Understandable. But then it would behoove you to know," Sirius said, dropping his voice as he took a small step closer to her, "that Mr. Fairchild owns various silk production mills in Lyon."

It took a second for Isabel to understand the import of his words, but he chuckled when she gasped sharply. "He does? Surely then that means he has contracts with the French government for silk. Right?"

"His company does." Sirius nodded. "From my understanding, he has several different contracts with the Napoleonic government, not only for silk, but for wool and carpet, too."

Sirius knew this because a fellow Home Office agent was monitoring Fairchild's activities.

"Goodness," Isabel whispered, her eyebrows high on her head as she gazed unseeing at a point over his shoulder. "But if he has so many lucrative connections with the French government, why does he live here in London?"

"He has homes in many places. Here, obviously, but also Paris, Lyon, and an estate in Essex." Sirius shrugged. "Fairchild just so happens to be here in London now. I wager it's because of the wool contract he has with the British military."

Isabel dragged her gaze up to his. "Thank you for telling me. I had no idea Mr. Fairchild was so connected."

Sirius bowed his head. "I told you I would help."

"Indeed you did." Isabel looked back in the direction of where her groom waited. "Captain, if your friends at the Home Office were to learn you were helping me pass secrets to my compatriots, would there be trouble for you?"

No, because Sirius wouldn't be helping her pass along secrets to Mexico. Not really. An idea was formulating in his mind, and he needed to speak with Lieutenant Colonel Green about how he could accomplish his directive while also keeping Isabel out of trouble. Surely between him and the older man, they could determine what information could be shared to aid President Juárez? For while Napoleon was not necessarily Britain's enemy, they were certainly not friends.

Of more concern to Sirius at the moment was how quickly he had agreed to help Isabel. How his gut had clenched and his groin had hardened when she looked up at him with those piercing midnight eyes of hers. How the vanilla scent of her, the way she tucked her teeth into her lips in that endearingly demure manner of hers, masked layer upon layer of fire and grit and determination.

He was attracted to her . . . and that was the real risk he took by helping her. It had made him soft, in ways he had never been with any other woman. Where he'd been able to engage in casual affairs with his past paramours, Isabel deserved so much better than casual.

"We're both taking risks, Miss Luna. With our eyes wide open."

10

Sirius was convinced the only reason he was extended an invitation to the Fairchild dinner party was that Mrs. Fairchild hoped he would be charmed by her daughter, Annabelle.

He considered this idea now as he sat beside the young lady at the Fairchilds' dining table, listening with what he hoped was a patient mien as his hostess regaled him with tales of her daughter's proficiency on the violin. Sirius was quite fond of the instrument . . . or as fond as he could be with only the most basic knowledge of violins, aside from the lovely music they produced when coaxed by a deft hand. According to her proud mother, Miss Annabelle Fairchild was one such musician.

"When dinner is over and the men enjoy their after-dinner drinks, Annabelle will have to play for you, Captain Dawson." Mrs. Fairchild gazed at her daughter, wide eyes filled with hope. "Once you've heard her exquisite skill, I'm sure you will agree with my assessment that there is no more beautiful sound."

"I have no doubt that you're right, ma'am," he said with ready agreement. Turning his head, he found Miss Fairchild with an all-suffering expression, and Sirius suspected she was long used to her mother's machinations.

Sirius patted his mouth with his napkin and angled his chair toward her to ask, "Do you enjoy playing in public?"

Miss Fairchild snorted softly. "Do you want my honest answer, Captain Dawson, or my polite one?"

"I'm flattered you feel comfortable enough to ask." He flashed what he knew to be his most winning smile. "And I will always fall on the side of honesty over politeness. Surely you've noticed that politeness can mask all manner of uncomfortable truths under its veneer of good manners."

"Oh yes. This is my third season out, you see, and in that time I've noticed the need to maintain an air of gentility is more important than actually rectifying errors." The corner of her lips curved. "And as you've noticed the same, allow me to state that I despise playing for a crowd."

Sirius blinked. "Despise? That's a strong word, Miss Fairchild."

"It is. But then it's easy to sour on something that you're forced to do rather than what you want to do."

That was certainly true. And abruptly Sirius was reminded of Isabel. Of how fiercely determined she was to move forward with her assignment, not because she was ordered to see to the task, but because she wanted to. When was the last time he had sought to do something simply because he wanted to and not because he felt compelled, by guilt and shame, to?

He coughed into his napkin and collected his thoughts as he arranged it again in his lap. "Tell me, Miss Fairchild, are you acquainted with Miss Isabel Luna?"

The young woman quirked her head at the change of subject, but her gaze slid to where Isabel sat on the opposite end of the table. She had been situated across from her sister, between Lady Yardley and an elderly baron, and Sirius had watched her throughout the evening, noting that while she smiled and nodded politely as Lord Palmer rambled on at her, Isabel rarely spoke herself. He'd been aware of her shyness in public before, but had not thought deeply about it. But now Sirius couldn't help but recognize how unsettled she was in social situations. He knew Isabel could be charming when she chose to be, for he'd certainly seen the effects of her charisma on Lord Westhope. Yet more often than not, it appeared Isabel was simply uncomfortable in crowds.

He itched to scoop her up and take her away from this infernal gathering. An altogether uncomfortable and foreign urge he'd never experienced before.

"I have not yet had the pleasure, Captain, but had hoped to do so after dinner," Miss Fairchild said, drawing his attention back to her.

Sirius took a sip of wine to wet his lips. "The reason I ask is because I think you and Miss Luna would get along well together. Her sensibilities seem a good match for your own."

And they did. Sirius suspected Isabel would enjoy Miss Fairchild's calm, matter-of-fact demeanor. Selfishly, Sirius also hoped that by having a friend she could converse with during such social engagements, Isabel would feel more comfortable in them.

"Is she forced to perform as well, Captain Dawson?" Miss Fairchild asked with an arch of her brow.

"Aren't all young ladies expected to perform while in company?" he volleyed back.

Her chuckle was light and melodic, and Sirius offered her a genuine smile. Yes, perhaps she and Isabel would make good friends.

Sirius slid his eyes to where Isabel sat down the table,

stifling his surprise when her gaze collided with his own. She didn't smile; merely stared back at him with an emotionless expression. He had thought that after their discussion in the park, Isabel might put aside her animosity and be more genial with him. They were working together, after all. But Isabel stared back at him as if he were just a man she passed on the street. Whatever was that about?

The main course was served then, and Sirius was not permitted further opportunity to ponder it. Mrs. Fairchild, and to a lesser extent Annabelle, monopolized his conversation for the rest of the dinner. The older woman was loquacious but gracious, if a bit direct about her desire to see Sirius court her daughter, but then he was experienced in deflecting the attentions of marriage-minded mamas. He was polite in his replies but noncommittal, and managed to contain his amusement anytime Annabelle rolled her eyes or mumbled tart replies to her mother's words. Sirius had never made a hobby out of conversing with unmarried young ladies more than what was required by etiquette—Isabel being the only young woman he'd truly desired to befriend—but he found he genuinely liked Annabelle Fairchild, and hoped she and Isabel were able to form a friendship.

After dinner, the men retired to Fairchild's study, where they were plied with the finest cigars from his humidor and offered tumblers of his best brandy and whisky. Sirius didn't recall much of the conversation, his eyes too busy mapping out the room and its contents. When he finally met with Isabel later in the night, he wanted to be able to tell her how the room was situated so her search would not be wasted fumbling about unnecessarily.

Plus, earlier that day, Lieutenant Colonel Green had asked that Sirius include a layout of the room when he delivered his next report, stating that it would be useful should they want to search Fairchild's London townhome in the future. This request was made *after* Sirius had taken the better part of their hour-long meeting to persuade Green to put aside his anger over Sirius's offer to assist Isabel's quest. The lieutenant colonel had eventually calmed when Sirius had explained how it could assist his own assignment with Westhope . . . *and* Sirius had consented to the older man's list of safeguards meant to protect not only Isabel, but British intelligence, as well.

Thus, Sirius's interest perked when he observed Fairchild extract a key from an urn filled with an assortment of lilies on a pedestal table behind his desk. When the man glanced about to see whether anyone had noted his movements, Sirius carefully averted his gaze to the glass in his hand, studying it as if the amber liquid contained the answers to his many unasked questions. Once the man was assured no one was paying attention to him, Fairchild used the key to open a small safe just visible under his desk. Sirius could not make out what its contents were, but after locking the safe again, the older man passed around a small silver case containing a brown powder. Sirius endeavored to keep his expression impassive, although the idea of sampling snuff made his stomach turn. The substance reminded him of his time spent near Varna, sitting around a fire with his men, jesting and laughing about the most inane topics. But inanity . . . along with liquor and snuff, helped dull the memories from playing across their eyelids every night.

When the snuffbox made its way to him, Sirius shook his head and held up his glass. One such vice was enough.

Eventually, Fairchild returned the snuffbox to his safe, and Sirius pondered briefly why the man kept the item there. Was the silver container a family heirloom? A sentimental gift?

Whatever the reason didn't matter, for what really mattered was discovering what else was hidden in the compartment along with the silver box. A smile threatened to spread over his lips as he considered how delighted Isabel would be when she learned about the hiding spot later in the evening.

Eventually the men rose to their feet and joined the company of the women in the drawing room. Sirius was one of the last to enter, finding the women engaged in small groups throughout the room. His gaze searched out Isabel, finding her tucked onto a narrow settee with Miss Fairchild, the two women's heads turned toward each other, apparently in deep conversation. As if she sensed his regard, Isabel glanced up and met his eyes. Her expression remained calm, but her gaze narrowed on him. She had seemed almost ambivalent about him during dinner, but now Isabel was glancing back at him warily. Had he done something to upset her?

Whatever the case, Sirius did not approach her immediately. He wanted to. Was almost eager to speak with her. About the safe in Fairchild's study, of course. As inconspicuously as he could, Sirius pulled on his cravat tie. Why did it feel so tight?

Weaving slowly through the guests, Sirius stopped to exchange words with a group of older women and patiently allowed them to introduce their young charges. Sirius fixed a smile on his face as the young women spoke of their time in London and the sights and sounds they'd enjoyed so far. Fairchild's brother-in-law even roped him into a conversation about the conflict in Bhutan, and Sirius contributed comments on occasion, projecting an air of interest he hoped appeared sincere. He stifled a laugh when Gabriela Luna flashed him a jaunty smile. Yet the true object of his attention was a point—a person—on the other side of the room, who continued to sit quietly with Miss Fairchild. By the time Sirius had made his way to them, a half hour had passed by. A long, dull thirty minutes.

"Miss Luna, Miss Fairchild," he murmured, offering them a crisp bow, "you had the right of it by tucking yourselves away here in the back of the room."

"I know better than to place myself in my mother's line of sight." Miss Fairchild employed a mock shudder. "It's a sure-fire way to guarantee I'll be demonstrating my music skills like a pet monkey in a show."

Sirius chuckled, noting that while Isabel did not join him, a genuine smile lit her face.

"While I'm sure I would be gratified to hear your skill on the violin firsthand, I certainly don't wish to see you perform if you yourself do not desire to." Sirius linked his hands together behind his back, well aware the motion drew attention to his shoulders and arms. Shoulders and arms he exercised regularly with fencing and tennis. When he noticed both young women scan their gazes over his form, Sirius bit back a chuckle. While he was not interested in Miss Fairchild's admiration, a flame sparked in the bottom of his stomach to see Isabel's lashes drop low over her eyes. "I've never really given much thought to the pressure we put on young women to perform for audiences under the guise of showcasing their talents. If one wishes to perform, that is one thing, but one should not be compelled to do so by others."

"I quite agree, Captain Dawson, but then sadly no one has ever asked for my opinion." Miss Fairchild nodded her head before turning to look at Isabel. "Are you proficient on an instrument, Miss Luna? Are you, too, expected to entertain on demand?"

Isabel ducked her head. "Unfortunately . . . or perhaps fortunately, I have never shown much musical talent. I've always had a knack for remembering odd details, though. Dates. People's names. The lines to obscure poems or long passages of text." She licked her lip, darting her gaze to his for a moment and then plowing on. "My father thought it would be amusing if I recited several bits of information about each guest at a dinner party he and my mother hosted. I was so nervous to stand in front of the room and speak, I got sick all over my shoes."

"Oh no," Miss Fairchild cried, grasping Isabel's hand tight. "That must have been dreadful."

Dreadful appeared to be an understatement if Isabel's appearance was any indication. Her normally warm complexion had turned pale, and her eyes darted about without landing on one point, as if she were afraid to look at either him or Miss Fairchild. Her confession had no doubt brought up the fear and humiliation she must have felt in that moment so long ago, and Sirius's arms twitched to pull her close. To whisper how cruel that request was.

Instead, Sirius watched her, silently willing her to meet his gaze. But Isabel kept it steadfastly away, and an uncomfortable knot lodged in his throat.

Although her shoulders curled in, Isabel flashed a small, shy smile at Miss Fairchild. "I know that's not the sort of conversation one should engage in, and I apologize. But when you mentioned having to perform, whether you want to or not, that scene burst from my memory like a cannon blast."

"No apologies necessary. I'm terribly sorry that happened to you." Miss Fairchild sighed, her gaze fixing on a spot on the other side of the room. "I know I shouldn't complain. My mother means well. She wants to see me happy and settled. It can be a bit much at times, though. Like tonight during dinner."

"What happened during dinner?" Isabel asked with a cock of her head.

An abashed look settled on Miss Fairchild's face as she glanced up at him. "Poor Captain Dawson was subjected to her matchmaking ploys."

Sirius waved a dismissive hand. "As you said, she wants to see you settled."

"I suppose I should be thankful for her meddling this time, for I'm grateful you suggested I seek out Miss Luna here." Miss Fairchild beamed at Isabel. "I fear I would have missed out on our engaging conversation if I had not listened."

A becoming blush swept across Isabel's cheeks, and her eyes flashed to his for a fleeting second. "The captain thought you should speak with me?"

"He did. He thought our personalities might suit each other." Miss Fairchild bumped her shoulder into Isabel's. "And I think he's right."

Isabel arched a brow. "Even though I spoke of an indelicate topic?"

"*Because* you spoke of an indelicate topic." Miss Fairchild gestured to the guests mingling about. "I've quickly learned that so much about polite society is artifice. I find it quite refreshing whenever the veneer slips and a bit of authenticity is revealed."

"So do I," Isabel said, her onyx eyes sparkling.

Sirius did not tarry much longer with Isabel and Miss Fairchild, mindful that tongues would wag if he spent any more than a polite amount of time with the young women. But before he stepped away, he managed to catch Isabel's eyes. When he did, Sirius looked pointedly at the corridor that led to Fairchild's study, and then back at her. Isabel inclined her head slightly, before returning her attention to her companion.

Sirius took his leave, certain Isabel understood his unspoken message.

A quarter of an hour later, while in the middle of a conversation about overarm bowling in cricket with two gentlemen whose names he could not recall, Sirius spied Isabel slip from the room out of the corner of his eye. He continued to sip idly from his tumbler for another ten or so minutes, and then excused himself with a silent nod. Sirius sidestepped various guests as he made his way toward the opposite end of the room, determined not to let Isabel wait any longer than necessary. When he finally disappeared down the dark corridor, he released a sigh of relief to have finally extricated himself from the crowd.

Walking several paces down the hall, Sirius glanced about, gaze trained on every alcove and open door for a glimpse of Isabel. Where was she? Surely she had not been discovered, for he would have heard the commotion . . . right?

After turning a corner toward Fairchild's study, his steps halted. She was lurking in the shadows before the study door, only a hint of her golden-brown silk gown peeking into view. As he moved closer, her face came into focus . . . and a breath caught in his throat, for Isabel's deep, dark eyes stared at him, and Sirius knew in an instant that he was in trouble.

Without a word, Isabel pressed on the handle and entered the room. Squaring his shoulders, Sirius followed close behind.

Only a single lamp burned on a side table, its glow illuminating a small patch in the corner of the room. Isabel stood in it now, the light glinting on the amber notes in her hair. Her back was to him, her head tilted up at the imposing gilt-framed portrait of some long-deceased Fairchild ancestor. Watching her, Sirius quietly closed the door behind him and rested his back against the wood.

The room was eerily silent, the low hum of voices from the activities on the other side of the house the only sound. Sirius wasn't sure if he should say something or allow her to decide how she wanted to proceed. Despite his frustration on the subject, this was not Isabel's first covert search.

Isabel pivoted then, half of her face burnished by the lamplight, and the other half melding into the surrounding shadows. Sirius rocked back on his heels. What was it about this moment that rendered her so beautiful? Her glinting eyes? The slight pout to her lips? His musings were interrupted when she advanced toward him, not stopping until she stood before him, looking up at him with large eyes.

His brow furrowed as he pondered what to say . . . and then she poked her finger into his chest.

"You didn't have to do that."

"Do what?" Sirius demanded, snatching her hand and holding it against his sternum.

Isabel shook her head, her eyes glued to where he held her. "Convince Miss Fairchild to speak with me."

"I didn't convince her of anything." He waited for her to meet his gaze. "I simply told her you might get along well. I'm happy to have been proven right."

"I'm sure you are." Her gaze fell to his tie. "She's splendid, and I think . . . perhaps if I don't reveal more disastrous personal details . . . that we may become friends."

And that was important to her. For the reserved Isabel, finding friends and making connections was not easy. Sirius could tell by the color that rose in her cheeks, and he was happy to have been the cause of it.

That damnable half smile crossed her lips in the blink of an eye, sparking Sirius to ask, "Why the smile?"

Isabel's mouth flattened into a mulish line. "I didn't smile."

Sirius squeezed her hand. "Yes, you did. You so rarely share your smiles with me, so I pay attention when you do."

Her obsidian eyes blinked up at him before she shuffled about on her feet. "It's just . . . when I—when I saw the two of you laughing during dinner, I was a bit miffed."

Sirius cocked his head. "Miffed? But why?"

Her fingers fiddled with the buttons on his glove, and Sirius realized they still held each other's hands. "Because it appeared you were having more fun than I was with the guests seated near me. And also—"

Isabel snapped her mouth closed, and his curiosity flared to life.

"And what?" Sirius took a step closer. "Tell me."

"I misspoke," she snapped.

"I don't think you did, though." Sirius stroked his thumb over her knuckles. "Were you jealous, Isabel? Was that it?"

Refusing to answer, Isabel tried to pull away, but Sirius held fast.

"I was laughing with Miss Fairchild because she made witty comments about her mother's overbearing tendencies, and not for any other reason."

"She's quite pretty, though." Her voice was so low, Sirius had to strain to hear. But he didn't have to strain to understand the unspoken meaning of her words.

"I suppose she is." He raised a shoulder. "But then beauty is subjective."

"So I've heard."

There was a wealth of disdain in those three words, and Sirius abruptly felt himself to be on unstable ground. Isabel would not take kindly to flowery platitudes, and he would be placating her if he offered them. Instead, he opted for honesty.

"Why would you ever want to settle for pretty? Pretty is

tiresome. It's boring. And you're not boring, Isabel. You're bright and sharp and . . ." He coughed into his fist, his tie abruptly tight. "Memorable."

Her lips parted. "Memorable?"

Sirius nodded, reluctantly releasing her hand. "I certainly haven't been able to forget you."

Somehow Isabel knew Captain Sirius Dawson had never called another woman memorable before.

She didn't have a chance to consider this, for Sirius stepped back, his expression shuttering. "Let's get on with it, because we don't have long."

With a deep exhale, Isabel nodded. She needed to focus. Sirius was right. At any moment, someone might step into the room and find them together. Not only would there be a scandal, but Isabel would have failed to follow through on her real reason for being in Mr. Fairchild's study in the first place. Smoothing her hands along the silk at her waist, Isabel glanced about the room.

"Where do you think we should start?"

Advancing to a table tucked behind the desk on the far side of the room, Sirius stuck his hand inside an urn filled with flowers. His expression turned triumphant as he held up a long key. "Here."

Isabel rushed over as he dropped into a crouch behind Fairchild's desk, maneuvering the key inside the lock of the small safe. She held her breath as he swung the door open.

"Is there anything of note?" Isabel asked.

"This," Sirius said, holding out a silver case.

"Do you use snuff?" she asked, her nose crinkled.

"I used enough of it while in the Crimea. I haven't been able to stomach it since."

She tucked that knowledge away for later. Isabel tried to crouch down to get a better look of what was inside the safe, but her skirts refused to condense enough to allow her to fit, and she huffed in annoyance.

"Don't worry, I'll let you know if there's anything of note inside," he said, flashing her a quick smile.

"I hate these stupid skirts." Isabel batted at the fall of her gown, a snarl curling her lips. "I swear they're designed to keep women under control. They're cumbersome and heavy, and it's impossible to do things when you have to heft around such weight."

His brow puckered. "I have never thought of it that way, but it makes sense."

"Society just loves to dictate how a woman is to live her life." Isabel lifted her chin. "Did you know that some members of the ton thought poorly of Ana María because she smiled too much?"

Sirius chuckled as he peered inside a satchel he'd pulled from the safe. Isabel tried to look over his shoulder, but the dim lighting hid the contents. "I can't say I'm surprised. You and your sisters were at a deficit when you arrived. While you are wealthy and beautiful, you're also foreign. Criticizing such innocuous behavior is another way to maintain the social hierarchy."

"How depressing." Isabel sighed, crossing her arms over her chest. "Find anything interesting?"

"It appears to be deeds and mortgage drafts for Fairchild's estate and his many, many mills." Sirius looked up and met her gaze. "I'm sorry."

"This keeps happening to me." Isabel covered her face with her hands. "No matter where I search or how promising the lead is, I haven't been able to find anything to help my family. I've been hoping Westhope's cousin will pass along information, but so far he hasn't and now my parents are in more danger. I would hate myself if something happened to them while I'm wasting time here in London."

"Nothing is going to happen to them," Sirius said quietly, wrapping his hand around her ankle and stroking his thumb along the bone. The gesture was so scandalous—a man with his hand under her skirts—and yet his touch was comforting. "Despite the French occupation, there are many who are still loyal to Benito Juárez and democracy. They're going to do everything they can to protect him, and the men and women who work for him."

Isabel blinked down at him. "How do you know that about Presidente Juárez?"

The corner of his mouth kicked up. "I have contacts, re-member?"

"Of course." Isabel shook her head. "You certainly didn't learn that from the papers here in London. My sisters and I are always complaining about how rarely the British press writes about the occupation."

Sirius opened his mouth . . . when a noise sounded from the corridor. It was the soft murmur of voices and the steady beat of footfalls on the tile. Isabel went stone-still, her eyes darting about the room for a place to hide. Sirius had managed to hide her in the drapes at Westhope's house, but the only reason she hadn't been discovered was that he served as a distraction. He couldn't do that tonight for he was not supposed to be in this room, either.

"Come here," Sirius hissed, grasping her hand and pulling her toward the desk.

"What?" Isabel scowled at him. "There's no way my skirts will fit under there."

Sirius's expression turned fierce. "We'll make them fit."

Isabel had no chance to protest, for Sirius yanked her down, quickly wrapping an arm about her waist and pulling her flush with his chest. With quick backward movements, he managed to tuck them both under the desk. Before Isabel could point out how her gown billowed from their hiding place, Sirius swept the bulk of it in his arms when he arranged her neatly in his lap. Her shoulder was pressed into his chest, his chin resting against her cheek, every one of his exhales drifting along her temple. Isabel clamped her eyes closed, allowing herself a short private moment to simply enjoy the feel of Sirius Dawson all around her.

"You have a regrettable knack for hiding under desks, Isabel," he whispered on a dry chuckle.

Before she could respond, the study door swung open.

"I told Edward he was a fool to go in with that lot, and now we both know I was right," a masculine voice said, the smug satisfaction in his inflection easy to note. "If he had listened to me, he wouldn't be out at the elbows."

"Some people have to make their own mistakes," another voice said, moving across the room from where they were hidden. The sound of bottles clinking together met her ears. "Edward is one such person."

"Pity that."

What was the true pity was that the men didn't seem inclined to make their stop in Fairchild's study a quick one. Isabel tried to ignore the feel of Sirius's firm thighs under her bottom, or how his crisp scent wove about her. His arm around her waist was firm and soothing, but soon he began to stroke the backs of his hands along her sides, and Isabel shuddered before she could contain it. She had always been sensitive there, and she glanced up in time to see the way Sirius's mouth quirked up when he came to this realization. Meeting her eyes, he danced his fingertips up her sides again, before he firmly dragged them back down.

Isabel bit her lip to keep her gasp trapped in her throat. No one had touched her so intimately, and she wasn't sure if she wanted him to stop or continue.

The men continued to prattle on, sampling Mr. Fairchild's liquor selection, while Sirius waged a silent war with her sensibilities. A war she was losing, because soon Isabel was squirming in his lap, her skin on fire. Her movements halted, however, when her bottom rubbed against something long and hard nestled in his lap. Her eyes flew wide. Isabel darted her gaze to his, her tongue sticking to the roof of her mouth to find him heavy lidded.

"Have a care, darling," he whispered, "I'm only a man."

And he inhaled deeply from the spot behind her ear, sending her eyes rolling to the back of her head.

The chatter of the men not a handful of yards from them continued, but Isabel could only focus on the man before her. The man beneath her. The man who suddenly dominated all of her senses and left her aflame.

Yet Isabel was determined to not burn alone. Curling her lip, she met his gaze as she slowly swiveled her hips, acting on instinct alone.

Sirius released a heavy breath as he tipped his head back to rest on the desk.

A thrill of delight—power—shot through Isabel, and she moved again, with more force, committed to eliciting a response from him.

Goodness, but she had no notion such activities could be so exciting. Isabel wished she had the room and privacy to remove her voluminous skirts and explore the sensations building within her core, her curiosity . . . her desire, overriding her timidity. Sinking her nails into Sirius's thighs, Isabel moved with abandon, her body undulating over his, chasing some unknown destination that seemed just out of reach.

Sirius grasped her hips then, slowing her frantic movements, even as he leaned forward to rasp, "Let me help you."

His large hands flexed, coaxing her to move again, and Isabel readily complied. Held enthralled by his sapphire eyes, Isabel surrendered to his ministrations, allowing him to maneuver her body over his.

Nothing else existed beside his blue-fire gaze. Nothing else mattered but the feverish awe on his face as he stared at her moving over him. And suddenly Isabel was beset by the need to touch him. To convey how much she was feeling and how desperately she hoped he felt the same. Planting her hand on his shoulder, Isabel surged up to snare his lips with her own. She had no idea what she was doing, and had desire not muddled her mind, she would have been mortified by her actions. But Sirius took her face between his hands, tilted her chin, and brought his mouth down over hers.

He tasted like every decadent, heady thing she'd ever craved. Ever denied herself. Sirius kissed her like he'd been starved to kiss her. His hand slid along her jaw to grip the back of her neck and hold her close. And Isabel went boneless under his touch, Sirius's lips moving over hers in an elegant mimicry of her movements in his lap.

A great peak loomed before Isabel could catch her breath, and she arched her back as her pelvis moved frantically, intent upon finding some sort of relief. Sirius leaned forward and trailed his lips down the long line of her neck before he stopped at the base of her throat, licking her pulse point with one broad stroke of his tongue.

"Come for me," he grated softly.

And every muscle in Isabel's body seized, her eyes screwing shut as towering waves of pleasure crashed over her, rippling through her body as she writhed over him. Isabel's lips fell open at some point, a moan of ecstasy poised on her tongue when Sirius slammed his mouth over hers, stifling the sound with his kiss. His taste seemed to radiate through her body, colliding with her rippling pleasure until Isabel wondered if she were capable of enduring such bliss. Collapsing forward, she sagged against his chest, all but purring when Sirius stroked a large hand over her shoulder and down to her waist.

Tension she wasn't aware she carried seeped from Isabel's bones, and she snuggled further into his chest, a cloud of sunset silk nestled like a cocoon around them. No one had ever made her feel this special, this cherished, and that it was the rakish Captain Dawson to do so caused unease to wrap tightly about her chest. Isabel wanted to trust him, but she also knew his reputation, which was not so easy to overlook.

Still, he was here with her now, hidden away, rather uncomfortably really, under a desk in a gentleman's study. He allowed her to kiss him, and kissed her gently in return, helping her find pleasure when he had taken none for himself. He could have easily wiped his hands of her and her silly antics a long time ago. Instead, he had tried to help her . . . so shouldn't she be grateful?

Pulling back, Isabel met his eyes, intent on saying something—anything—of her thoughts, when the voices of the gentlemen in the room snared her attention.

"Dawson was supposed to be Armstrong's partner in the card game, but apparently the man couldn't find him. Armstrong was chafed when I stepped away to join you here."

Isabel smiled at the look of chagrin that settled on Sirius's face.

"I'm surprised Dawson's even here tonight. This isn't usually his crowd."

"That's true." The other man paused, and Isabel imagined he was taking a sip from his glass. "I so rarely see him outside gaming hells."

"And if you do see him at a ball or some other such nonsense, he has this widow or that widow hanging from his arm."

The other man snorted. "The good Lord has his favorites, it seems."

The blood in her veins turned to ice, and Isabel froze, careful not to meet Sirius's gaze. His grip around her grew tighter, and even when he gently shook her, Isabel stubbornly kept her eyes trained on the back side of the desk they were crammed under.

Nevertheless, Sirius leaned forward and ran his nose along her cheek. "What's wrong?"

Isabel shook her head. How could she possibly tell him how the reminder of his rakish pursuits was a bucket of cold water over her head?

Her throat worked on a swallow, and unshed tears scorched the backs of her eyes.

"I wonder if he attended tonight because Lady Needham was supposed to attend," one of the men said. "Rumor is that she's been angling to get him back in her bed. Perhaps he's finally ready to do so."

Now it was Sirius who stiffened under her, and Isabel curled her hands into tight fists to resist the urge to look at him. Isabel knew it would break her if she saw guilt on his face.

The conversation turned to other topics, but Isabel could not keep up. Was that truly why Sirius was in attendance? Because Lady Needham was supposed to be here as well? Isabel thought his presence at the dinner party was to help her with her search, but had he told her that, or had she assumed it? The possibility that she had misread his intentions stung in the worst way, and Isabel was suddenly desperate to escape. Desperate to be as far away from Sirius Dawson as she could be.

How was it possible for a man who took her body to such great heights to reduce her heart to such depressing lows?

To his credit, Sirius did not attempt to speak again. He simply held her, his arms tight around her.

When the study door finally closed behind the men's retreating backs, Isabel stumbled from their confined hiding space, her chest heaving as she greedily sucked in air. She needed to expunge his scent from her lungs and exorcise the feel of him from her mind.

And yet Isabel knew it was a pointless task. Sirius Dawson had imprinted himself on her, and while he might view her as a silly girl he helped find pleasure, Isabel knew she would never be the same.

She was adjusting the fall of her skirts, fastidiously ignoring her damp drawers, when Sirius spoke into the silence.

"Isabel, I hope those men didn't offend you."

"Of course not." She waved a hand.

"Because what they said was untrue."

Pivoting, Isabel finally met his gaze. "What part was untrue, exactly? That you only attended tonight's event because you agreed to help me, or because you expected Lady Needham to be here?"

A muscle flexed in his jaw. "I attended because of you, Isabel. Lady Needham has never mattered, and will never matter."

She loved how he said her name. The back of her throat ached at that familiarity, and yet her heart refused to soften.

"I think that's the point, though, isn't it? Your romantic

entanglements don't matter to you. They're casual affairs. Just as this"—Isabel moved a hand back and forth in the space between them—"was casual."

A cloud passed over his visage. "And has *this* been casual for you?"

Of course not. Isabel bit her tongue until the urge to say the words passed. "It has to be."

His shoulders dropped a tad. "I know. I agreed to do this, to help, not just so you could aid your countrymen, but so that you'll remain safe."

Isabel crinkled her brow suddenly. "And what do you get out of it? Why help me?"

Sirius pressed his lips together for a long moment, his blue eyes sweeping over her face. When he finally spoke, his voice was sad. "Because I can, Isabel. Because I can."

11

He hadn't seen Isabel in a week.

Was he avoiding her, or was she avoiding him? Sirius wasn't sure he knew.

When she did not attend the Venetian breakfast hosted by Countess Abernathy, Sirius had been a tad relieved. He certainly hadn't recovered from their encounter in Fairchild's study—he was haunted by Isabel's vanilla scent, the phantom pressure of her grip on his thighs. Her sister Gabriela had mentioned in passing that Isabel had been nursing a headache for most of the day, and Sirius had spent the rest of the evening trying to figure out whether he should send her a posy of willow bark to alleviate the pain. The following day, his relief turned to disappointment when he learned she had stayed in rather than accompany Lady Yardley to the musicale the older woman had specifically mentioned they would be attending. Sirius had managed to secure an invitation.

Isabel was the reason he was now sitting at a narrow table next to Lord Westhope, within a private room at the British Museum. The viscount had reserved the space so his guests could admire the newest Maqdala acquisitions from Ethiopia on display before hosting a dinner party, and Sirius had immediately accepted the invitation. While it was true Sirius had already visited the museum to admire the collection, he could hardly send his regrets when Westhope indicated the Misses Luna would be in attendance. After a week of not seeing her exquisitely expressive face, Sirius was determined to corner Isabel and find out why she had been avoiding him.

He stared into his glass of brandy now, the amber liquid a backdrop for the memories playing out in his mind. Memories of Isabel sinking her teeth into her plump bottom lip as she moved on top of him, using his body to find her pleasure. The way she shivered when he'd nibbled on her earlobe. How her expression morphed from satisfaction to despondence when those two jackasses had mentioned Lady Needham. As if Sirius had thought of the baroness since that day in the park when he had taken his impromptu balloon ride with Isabel.

Now there was only her, and her foolhardy mission . . . with only her quiet charisma and gentle beauty to hold his attention.

But Sirius had not had a chance to explain these things to her. After they had extricated themselves from under Fairchild's desk, Isabel had promptly slipped from the room, rejoining the festivities as if she had never left. No one remarked upon her absence, but much was made of his return when he finally ventured back to the Fairchild drawing room. Sirius had lied about taking a turn about the gardens to smoke a cheroot, silently praying that no one noticed that his person was devoid of smoke. He'd tried to catch Isabel's eye after he had appeased his inquisitors, but she had immersed herself in a conversation with her sister and Miss Fairchild.

Never had Sirius ever worried about the women he had taken to bed, outside of ensuring their pleasure. They both understood the nature of their association, and knew better than to involve inconvenient emotions in their bed sport. And yet here was Sirius now, fretting and stressing over Isabel Luna, whom he had shared *one* passionate—albeit mind-numbing—encounter with. He hardly knew himself.

"I'm glad you agreed to come tonight," Westhope said, sliding onto the chair next to him. The viscount raised his glass at a passing couple before he swung his gaze to Sirius. "I had hoped you might find the cultural treasures from Africa as interesting as I do."

"And I do." Sirius gestured with the glass in his hand toward the exhibition beyond the reception doors. "I was here on opening day for a tour of the collection. The items are quite remarkable."

"Indeed they are." Westhope leaned back in his chair and speared a glass of wine between his fingers. "I hope the rest of my guests find them remarkable as well."

Sirius shrugged. "Some will. But most are here to partake of your excellent company."

"No doubt you're right," the viscount said, taking a sip of his wine. "If only the ton knew how wrong your reputation was."

The change in topic caused Sirius's thoughts to stumble, but he quickly recovered. "Oh, but it's not wrong. The ton may not know of my intellectual pursuits, but I am still a rake and knave." Sirius tossed back his brandy in one stinging gulp. "And will be for the foreseeable future."

Sirius fought the urge to fidget with his cuff links, certain his action would not go unnoticed by the viscount, who had proven himself to be quite perceptive.

Westhope scoffed even as a smile crossed his face. "Still,

I've learned over the weeks of our acquaintance that there's much more to you than you reveal. It's almost as if you use your roguish reputation to keep others at bay."

Perceptive indeed. Sirius pressed his lips together to keep from smiling. "People see what they want to see and believe what they want to believe. They think me a merry rake, and I'm content to allow them to think as much. Therefore the only actions they choose to note are those that support their assertions of me."

"Like your interest in North African cultural objects."

Sirius grinned. "Precisely."

"Well. I'm glad to know that bit of information about you. It makes you more real," Westhope said with an answering smile.

"More real?"

"Come now, Dawson." Westhope slapped him on the back. "You're an earl's son, a famed hero from the Crimean War. Plus, your gold curls and blue eyes have snared the admiration of one half the population of the ton. That could be a bit intimidating for us simple folks."

Sirius looked at the viscount askance. "Westhope, you're a bloody viscount. Even if you were missing all your teeth and were as old as Methuselah, women would be intent on earning your notice and winning your hand."

"Oh, no doubt." Westhope tossed back the remainder of his drink. Patting his mouth with a napkin, he set his empty glass on the table. "And I've never been particularly interested in marrying, especially because I knew the chances were high that any bride I chose would be just as interested, if not more so, in being my viscountess as she was being my wife."

"There's a difference," Sirius agreed.

"I'm glad you understand that. And truly, I can't blame a

woman for thinking of such things when their choice of a husband determines whether their future will be one of comfort
or not." Westhope turned his gaze to the other side of the
room, the corners of his green eyes crinkling. "But I'm beginning to think that perhaps I have found someone who is more
interested in me as a person than my title, and I am quite
pleased about it. If you'll excuse me."

Sirius watched as the viscount walked away to greet new
guests who had just entered the room. The man seemed quite
serious in his admiration for Isabel, and how could Sirius
blame him? But what would Westhope think if he knew Sirius
had kissed senseless the woman he sought to make his viscountess? His imaginations were petty, but Sirius could not
stop the satisfaction that coursed through his blood at the
thought.

Yet the prospect of watching Westhope court Isabel turned
his stomach.

There was a break in the crowd by the door at just that moment, and Sirius's breath stuck in his throat when his eyes met
a pair of familiar dark brown ones. Isabel stared back at him
for the length of two heartbeats before she blinked and looked
away. She turned to greet a couple who had come up to welcome them, before she smiled up at Lord Westhope, who was
grasping her gloved hand. Sirius hated that Westhope was
touching her, greeting her with smiles and warmth as if all of
Isabel's smiles and warmth should be reserved for him and
him alone.

Sirius's blood pounded in his ears throughout dinner.

Dinner and drinks were a lively affair, and much laughter
and interesting discussions were had. It appeared Westhope
had tailored his guest list to friends and members of society
who would most appreciate the private viewings of the Maqdala

treasures, for much of the talk during the meal revolved around the objects and how the museum was able to bring them into the country.

"I do wonder how the British Museum had the authority to acquire historical artifacts from other countries." Gabriela Luna ran a finger around her glass. "I'm curious, hypothetically of course, of a situation in which a member of the Austrian Empire was to acquire a prized painting from the Elizabethan period. Do you believe England would allow such a seizure to occur so easily?"

"Definitely not," an older gentleman said, his voice harsh. Sirius narrowed his eyes as he tried to remember the man's name. Pfeiffer? Pearson? A professor at Oxford, he believed. "The British government has done much to protect British antiquities and keep them safe within British hands."

Gabriela nodded, her pretty face contemplative. His grip on his utensils tightened because Sirius knew better than to underestimate the youngest Luna sister. "That is good for the British, I would say, but unfortunate for other countries who are in the midst of war or colonization and who cannot protect their own histories from those who would exploit their vulnerability."

"Vulnerability?" Professor Pfeiffer wrinkled his brow. "Surely you are not claiming the museum took advantage of Maqdala's political turmoil to acquire these objects."

"That's exactly what I'm saying, sir." She chuckled and waved her hand, as if Professor Pfeiffer had told a joke. "It is a move that comes from the colonizer's script, I'm sure. Identify a region in flux and sweep in to either grasp power, destabilize the current government"—Gabriela ticked these items off on her fingers—"or loot what resources or treasures can be found while the local people are unable to protect it. I'd wager that is exactly how *this* museum came to possess the objects in this collection, and possibly a good deal of other items on display."

The older gentleman opened and closed his mouth for a moment, before he grasped his glass of wine and took a drink. "Artifacts need to be protected, and if a mother country cannot do it, it is the responsibility of others to step in to do so."

"Responsibility?" Isabel interjected. "Why is it that there is a responsibility to *things* and not to people?"

Sirius's heart stuttered a beat at Isabel's question. It was not like her to enter a conversation in an argumentative way, and he almost smiled as he took in the proud tilt of her chin and the flashing light in her eyes.

"I don't understand what you mean, Miss Luna," Professor Pfeiffer murmured with a frown.

"You spoke of responsibility. Of how artifacts and historical items should be protected, and I am asking why such *things* warrant more protection than the people who made them." Isabel winged up a brow. "I'd wager that whoever swept into Africa to save these cultural objects we have been admiring this evening did not even think of how they could assist the Ethiopian people, whether by offering them food or shelter or aid."

The older man laughed, and several other gentlemen at the table snorted. Sirius ground his teeth together.

"It's not the museum or the British government's responsibility to aid the people—"

"Just to *protect* their riches," Isabel interjected.

Professor Pfeiffer scowled, jerking on his tie. "I'm sure this is a difficult thing for a young woman like you to grasp, but the workings of government have priorities—"

"Christ, Professor, if you are attempting to excuse the museum's culpability in this, you are doing a poor job of it," Sirius called, fixing a lazy smile on his face. "Just be honest. It's easier and certainly more profitable to focus on looting the historical treasures of warring countries than it is to provide humanitarian aid."

"I will say no such thing," Professor Pfeiffer growled, "and I think it grossly unfair to place this sort of responsibility on the museum or even the British government."

"You keep speaking of responsibility, Professor, and yet you seem quite adept at assigning responsibility only when it serves your needs." Isabel smiled, the gesture not meeting her eyes. "A bit disingenuous, don't you think?"

The older man gaped and stuttered, and Sirius simply took a sip of his glass and enjoyed the show. With a twitch in his lip, he noted the look of pride Gabriela flashed her older sister, and Sirius was certain his own expression mirrored hers. So often Isabel was overshadowed by her fiery younger sister, but she was fierce and strong in her own right. His Isabel was not to be overlooked.

His Isabel? Sirius took a mouthful of wine and welcomed the burn as it singed down his throat. He had no right—no interest, really—in claiming anyone, least of all someone as singular as Isabel Luna.

Her gaze met his then before it quickly flitted away. In the next moment, Westhope patted Isabel's hand on the table next to him and leaned close to whisper in her ear. Red flashed before Sirius's eyes. Gripping his glass with stiff fingers, Sirius willed himself to remain calm even while he battled the urge to throw the viscount across the room. Whatever was wrong with him?

"I've known Professor Pfeiffer for a good long while, and I can speak confidently that his intent is not to be disingenuous," Westhope proclaimed to his guests. Yet when Isabel arched a brow, the viscount cocked his head at the older man. "Still, the Misses Luna bring up excellent points about how our society values tangible goods—property—while turning a blind eye to humanitarian issues."

"I suspect the Misses Luna are more aware of this issue considering what is happening in their country," Sirius said, pleased he managed to unlock his teeth. "Seeing how Mexico is now occupied by French forces and an Austrian grand duke is now their supposed emperor, I think their concern and frustration is more than warranted."

Isabel met his eyes, the corners of her lips tilting ever so slightly up.

"I'm glad you think so, Captain Dawson." Gabriela folded her hands demurely on the table in front of her, but her chin was lifted proudly. "When one is forced to flee their homeland in the middle of the night to escape an advancing army, sadly one's thoughts are not of protecting hundred-year-old artifacts from the Mexica empire."

"There is no excuse for fortune hunters and foreign dealers to prey upon such dire circumstances," Isabel said with a firm note.

"I quite agree, Miss Luna," Viscount Westhope interjected, flashing a look to the gathered guests that made it clear the topic would not be argued further. "Speaking of Mexico, what news is there of the war with France? Since we've become acquainted, I've tried to pay attention to any reports of it in the papers, but coverage has been lacking."

"It has indeed," Gabriela said tartly, "but Señor Valdés has managed to keep us abreast of the developments at home."

Sirius listened with half an ear while Gabriela relayed what they knew about the moves Emperor Maximilian had taken to solidify his power within Mexico. He had made a number of liberal decisions that had surprised the monarchists who had aided the French, and Isabel chimed in to emphasize how the emperor's decisions could undermine his support among his advocates. And now that the American Civil War had ended, the United States government was sending aid to Juárez supporters, and there was reason to be optimistic that the tide was turning. Several of the guests asked questions about the Mexican people's attitudes toward the French and how political turmoil over the preceding years had paved the way for such an occupation.

It was obvious that the sisters were well informed about the topic, and although Gabriela did most of the talking, Isabel interjected on occasion with her own passionate words. Sirius knew he needed to be circumspect, especially at such an intimate gathering, and yet he found it difficult to look away from her. Everything about Isabel suddenly captivated him, from her quiet beauty to her unflappable composure. When Westhope inadvertently snagged his attention, the viscount's brow crinkled in unspoken question, and Sirius hastily looked away.

He stayed at the table long after the other guests had embarked on a private tour of the Maqdala collection, nursing his wine and silently waging a battle with his riotous emotions. Westhope asked if he intended to join the group, and Sirius nodded, stating he would follow as soon as he was done with his drink. But he was in no rush. Truthfully, watching Westhope plant a hand on the small of Isabel's back as he ushered her forward left Sirius seeing red.

He needed to do *something*. Something to finally discover what, if anything, Westhope knew about the French and their intentions. Because if his uncharacteristic agitation tonight was any indication, Sirius could not stand idly by and watch the viscount court Isabel. Two things were bound to happen if

Westhope touched her again: the viscount would come to harm, and thus Sirius's career with the Home Office would be at an end. Sirius had never considered himself a masochist, and he certainly was not going to become one now.

As he grappled with his turbulent thoughts, Sirius spied Isabel step away from Westhope and disappear down a side antechamber while he was in conversation with his other guests. Sirius knew the ladies' room was on the other side of the building, so where was Isabel headed? Throwing back the rest of his wine with one acerbic gulp, Sirius rose to his feet and followed her . . . a smile pulling his mouth taut.

He did not search for long, finding Isabel standing in front of a large gold and silver processional cross, her mouth ever so slightly ajar as she looked up at it. It was an impressive sight, and Sirius couldn't fault her for wanting to steal some time to study it alone.

And yet because they were alone, Sirius intended to take full advantage.

A door marked with a sign that read MUSEUM STAFF ONLY was situated not far from where Isabel stood, and without a second thought, Sirius approached her and grasped her arm.

"Come with me," he whispered in her ear as he pulled her along after him.

Isabel scowled, but did not fight him. "What do you want, Captain Dawson?"

"Don't play coy with me, Isabel Luna." A sigh of relief slipped past his lips when he found the door unlocked. The room was empty, so Sirius ushered her inside, locking the door behind them. Turning to look at her, he narrowed his eyes. "Now, whatever is wrong?"

She planted her hands on her hips. "The only thing wrong is you stealing me away and locking me in this room."

"You stole away on your own." He spread his palms. "I simply took advantage of the moment to speak with you privately."

Curling her lip, Isabel spun about and walked to the opposite end of the room. It appeared to be the office of a museum administrator or manager, and he watched as Isabel fidgeted with the pens and trinkets that lined the narrow desk. A small, high window offered a view of the darkening sky outside, emitting faint rays of light to illuminate Isabel's raven hair as she paced around the desk. She was once again refusing to meet his eyes, and Sirius clamped his jaw in frustration.

"Isabel, have you been avoiding me this week?"

He hadn't meant to ask the question so baldly, but Sirius could admit he wasn't in full grasp of his faculties.

"I don't know what you're talking about," she replied, still not looking at him.

"You most certainly do." Sirius took a step toward her, even as he linked his hands behind his back. "You're too smart for me to believe you."

"Only because you cavort with simpletons," she snapped over her shoulder.

Well, she had him there.

"Do you think *I'm* a simpleton?" His voice was a growl, his patience beginning to slip. "You expect me to believe you suddenly canceled all of your engagements—even though your sister and Lady Yardley attended—because you weren't avoiding me?"

Isabel shook her head, her lips a firm line.

Sirius advanced a step toward her, clearing his throat. "Was it because of what happened in Fairchild's study?"

"Of course not," she exclaimed, throwing her arms up.

But she still avoided his gaze, and Sirius's shoulders sank.

"Isabel," he whispered, flexing his fingers instead of reaching out for her, "what happened between us is nothing to be embarrassed about. You know that, right?"

She nodded, her stare fixed on the desktop.

"I quite enjoyed it, if you must know," he murmured, dipping his head in an attempt to snare her gaze.

Isabel looked up, her eyes wide. "You did?"

Sirius took a step closer. "Of course I did. You were beautiful."

"You know many beautiful women." She scoffed. "Isn't that what those men said in the study? That you always have an attractive woman seeking your attention?"

"I suppose to others it would appear that way." Sirius took another step until he was close enough to sweep a loose curl off Isabel's cheek with his fingertips. "But then those women weren't particularly memorable."

"They weren't?"

Sirius tracked how her throat worked on a swallow. Christ, he knew what her skin tasted like there. Had taken himself in hand all week to the memory. "No, Isabel. I don't daydream about them in my lap, making little sounds of pleasure."

Her long lashes swept down to cover her gaze, before she peered up at him through them. Sirius doubted she knew how alluring she was at that moment. "Who do—"

Sirius cut her words off with his lips.

He couldn't possibly . . .

And like dandelion fluff, Isabel's thoughts scattered to the four winds as she melted under Sirius's touch. All she knew was him. His mouth on hers. His arms enfolding her against his firm chest. His scent invading her senses and leaving her pliant in his hands.

"Watching Westhope touch you, whisper in your ear was

driving me mad," he rasped against her mouth, only to press searing kisses down the column of her throat. "Do you want him to touch you, sunshine? Do you hope he will?"

Isabel shook her head, aghast he would ask her such a thing. "Never."

Sirius nipped at her earlobe and Isabel shivered. "And yet you keep welcoming his attentions, darling."

"Because I need to know," she tried not to pant, but he made it so hard when he nibbled along her jaw, "I need to know if information is passed to him, however innocently."

His chuckle was like a caress down her spine. "Ah, so you're doing it for country?"

Isabel gasped as he licked at the pulse point at the base of her neck.

"And now?" Sirius dipped his fingertips beneath the bodice of her gown, just lightly grazing over one pebbled nipple. "Are you allowing me to touch you for Mexico?"

"No." The word started as a whisper but ended as a moan as two fingers enclosed her nipple and pinched it tight.

Sirius pulled back, and Isabel blinked open her eyes to look at him. In the light filtering through the one small window in the room, she took in his wide pupils and mussed hair. In all the months Isabel had known him, she'd never seen Sirius anything less than urbane and sophisticated. But she had left him undone.

Her. Isabel Luna was capable of bringing Captain Sirius Dawson to his knees.

And to his knees he suddenly dropped. Grasping her hips, he ushered her backward until the back of her legs hit the office chair. Isabel sat with a huff, her skirts rising about her in a cloud. She tucked her lip between her teeth when Sirius looked up at her, a devilish light in his blue eyes.

"Can you be quiet, darling?"

Isabel quirked a brow. "Why?"

"Always so inquisitive." His hands moved over the tops of her feet before encircling her ankles. "Because I would like to give you something."

"What do you want to give me?"

"Pleasure," he purred, dragging his hands up her legs to caress the insides of her knees. Isabel swallowed a gasp at the delicious sensation. "Will you allow me to touch you?"

Sirius was the *only* man whose touch she desired. Isabel nodded.

His mouth curled into a smirk. "If you can hold your silence, I'll make you feel so good."

"What do you intend to do?" she asked, in a breathless voice she didn't recognize. Already the thought of Sirius touching her . . . intimately . . . made her squirm in her chair in anticipation.

Sirius's eyes were midnight pools. "I intend to taste you. To kiss and lick every part of you I can reach, until you are begging to come on my tongue."

Isabel whimpered in the back of her throat, her hands curling around the armrests. ¡Híjole! No one had ever spoken such crude words to her, and while she knew she should be scandalized, instead Isabel was eager. Daring. Desperate in a way that made her feel as if she'd vibrate out of her skin.

"But I can only do this if you're quiet." Sirius's thumbs traced patterns on her thighs. "Can you be quiet for me?"

"Yes," she breathed, without hesitation. Isabel would be so good for him.

"Good girl," he said, his voice like smooth black coffee. Taking hold of her hem, Sirius lifted the bulk of her skirts until Isabel felt the cool air on her bare legs. Tucking the taffeta around her waist, he met her gaze. "And good girls get rewarded."

The heavy weight of her skirts made it impossible to see anything but the top of his blond head, but Isabel certainly felt the smooth glide of his palms down the insides of her thighs, and the shift of her drawers when he hooked a finger inside the hem to pull them aside. When his warm breath coasted along her wet cleft, Isabel bit down on her fist to contain the moan that bubbled up from the depths of her core.

"This is the prettiest cunny I've ever seen." The back of what she thought might be his knuckle brushed across the sensitive nub at the top of her sex, and a tremor shook her frame. "And I have no doubt it will be the best I've ever tasted."

Before Isabel could even think of a coherent response, Sirius licked her from the bottom of her sex to the top, where his tongue flicked her nub. Her back arched, and only the sharp bite of her teeth in the back of her hand kept her grounded.

"I'm so proud of you, darling," Sirius crooned, catching her eye as his tongue swiped along his lips. "And I was right. You're delicious."

Isabel dropped her arm over her face as a shiver shook her frame.

When Sirius began his ministrations again, his strokes were firmer, the attentions he laved on her nub wet and messy and so intense Isabel's eyes rolled into the back of her head. Sirius pulled back after a moment, and craned his head to meet her gaze.

"Do you know what this is called here?" he asked, rubbing the pad of his thumb over her nub and causing her to tilt her hips into his touch. Somehow she managed to nod. "It's called the clitoris. It's said to be the center of a woman's pleasure. Do you feel pleasure when I do this, darling?"

Isabel opened her mouth to respond, but Sirius leaned forward to suck the little pearl into his mouth, and she twined her fingers in his hair as she bit back a wail. Her pelvis swiveled against his tongue, his chin, desperate for more. Desperate for relief from the rising inferno boiling inside her.

Sirius paused again, and Isabel whined in frustration. "I know, sweetheart. Let me help you." She watched as he held up two fingers and popped them in his mouth, holding her gaze as he ran his wicked tongue over them. When they glistened, Sirius flashed a triumphant grin. "Remember, you said you could be quiet."

He traced those two fingers up and down her cleft, and Isabel's breath hitched in her throat when Sirius hooked them in her opening, pressing them firmly but gently inside. Isabel shifted her hips to adjust to the sense of fullness, but abruptly he twisted his fingers about and pressed them to the front wall of her sex at the exact moment his tongue lapped at her nub and Isabel's body clenched. Every muscle, every cell, every inch of her tensed . . . and then exploded in an eruption of light and sound. Her body trembled with the force of her release, and the only reason Isabel knew she had not made a sound was the tinge of iron that filled her mouth from having bit her tongue so forcefully.

Isabel was unsure of how long she lay there panting, her mind scrambled and her limbs loose. Was copulation always this earth-shattering? This overwhelming? This—she ran a hand along her temple, pushing back sweaty strands—messy? Chest heaving, Isabel glanced down at Sirius.

With his cheek resting against her thigh and his blond hair askew, he looked exhausted. Isabel reached down to brush errant locks back into place. Her hands lingered near his neck long after she had put him to rights. Sucking in a breath,

Isabel looked for his eyes. They were shuttered, and with a clarity born of his ministrations, Isabel knew he was conflicted. Perhaps he felt a bit vulnerable. Lord knew she did, especially because she was still bare to his gaze.

Probing her thoughts for something she could say to put him at ease, Isabel blurted out, "Why do you call me sunshine?"

Sirius lifted his head and sat back on his haunches, a small frown on his lips. "Because everything seems brighter when you're there."

"Oh," Isabel said dumbly, her mouth trembling. He'd uttered the words so simply, as if the reasons were clear. And yet he'd knocked her completely off her axis.

If she was going to survive this affair—for that's what it had become—with her dignity intact, she needed to set some boundaries.

Straightening her spine, Isabel said, "We should return. Our absence will be noted."

Sirius dragged his hand through his hair. "Yes. Of course. Although I'm loath to converse and laugh with Westhope and his guests as if the time we spent in this room didn't occur."

So was she. Still, Isabel pushed her skirts down and stood, her legs shaky. "I admire Lord Westhope a great deal, but you know the true reason I'm encouraging his attentions."

"He is quite taken with you," Sirius murmured, his blue, blue eyes intense on her face. "And I don't blame him."

Although her throat was tight, Isabel forced herself to say, "And if my future was in England, he would make a fine husband."

Sirius's mouth compressed into a thin line, but he said nothing. No comment about how he would make her a better husband. About how he understood her better than Westhope ever could. How he, Sirius Dawson, had seen her and given her a chance to prove herself in ways so many others had not. Not a single word on how he would love her and endeavor to make her happy as she longed to make him happy.

Her heart fractured, the jagged pieces an outline of his dear face.

"But"—Isabel worked on a swallow, tears like glass scouring her throat—"I don't fit in here. Ana, and even Gabby, have made friends and connections, and I still feel so out of place."

"But what of Miss Fairchild?" Sirius shook his head. "What of . . ."

He snapped his mouth shut and closed his eyes. What had he meant to say? Isabel's heart lurched with hope in her chest, but her mind screamed at her not to be foolish. Sirius had taught her about passion. Offered her assistance when she needed it the most. But that wasn't enough.

Isabel twined her hand in her skirts. "England has no future for me."

"And what do you want for your future?" Sirius asked, his expression guarded.

"I'd always hoped our time in England would be short." Isabel shrugged, the movement meant to be carefree, though it felt anything but. "And yet the weeks have turned to months and now years, and I'm no closer to returning to Mexico than I was when we first left Veracruz."

"So you want to return, but what then?"

What then, indeed. Isabel hadn't allowed herself to think past her mission of aiding the Juárez government's fight. If she proved herself, what did she want?

Isabel nibbled on the inside of her cheek. "Ideally, I would like to work for Presidente Juárez. I could translate documents, perhaps. Write correspondence."

184 · Liana De la Rosa

His brows drew together. "You'd want to be a clerk?"

"Maybe."

"But, won't your parents object?" Sirius shook his head. "I don't see how they would allow you to work a menial job or any job, for that matter."

An exhausted sigh slipped past her lips. "They would not be pleased by the prospect. Young Mexican women of my station are raised to run a household, but in an ideal world, I would be able to make decisions for myself and my future. And I want to do something worthwhile. I want to be someone other than Elías Luna's middle daughter. I don't want to be the wallflower Luna sister anymore. I want to be something *more*."

The muscle twitching in his jaw was the only indication Sirius was moved by her words. "And if you find a way to help the Juárez government, you'll be able to be someone different?"

She nodded, his form obscured by the tears that filled her eyes. "At least I'll have done something. Helped in some way. I've spent my whole life in the shadows. In the pages of books, dreaming of exciting adventures and daring acts. And here I am now, with the chance to do something tangible to help my people, and I would never forgive myself if I didn't try."

Spinning away from him, Isabel wrapped her arms about her waist. "I just want to make my father proud. I want to *earn* the right to return. My sisters and I weren't given an option when we were sent here, and I don't want to feel that powerless again. I refuse to."

"Sunshine," Sirius whispered, the word ragged. He reached for her and placed a hand on her arm, patiently waiting until she turned to look up at him. "I don't understand how anyone could not be proud of you."

Isabel dropped her eyes to his chest, her emotions threatening to overthrow her tenuous hold on them. She wasn't certain anyone had ever looked at her that way. But it didn't matter. Sirius's life was here, where he was a beloved member of society, and hers was in Mexico . . . as soon as she was able to make a place for herself.

Daring to smooth her hand down his lapel, Isabel shook her head. "I just have to find something, *anything*, to send home."

Sirius leaned down and bussed her temple, remaining there for a heartbeat. "I promised I would help you, and I intend to."

12

Isabel was leaving.

Even a day later, Sirius had still not recovered from that damning revelation. He'd been winded from his ministrations, his cock aching and begging for release, when Isabel had declared her wish to return to Mexico.

Sirius stared down into his coffee cup unseeing. Why did everything about his life feel off-kilter? He didn't recognize himself anymore.

She was returning to Mexico. Of course she was. Mexico was still her home, the place she was courting danger to protect. But until Isabel said the words, Sirius hadn't fully understood what that meant. No longer would he sigh in frustration when he saw her disappear down a dark corridor. No longer would her brows snap together and her ebony eyes burn with devil fire when they saw him. And shouldn't that make him happy? Sirius had enough responsibilities to concern himself with.

So why then had he been daydreaming about bundling Isabel up in cotton and absconding with her to Devonshire?

Damn it, what was wrong with him?

Scrubbing a hand down his face, Sirius pushed all thoughts of Isabel into the ether.

Lieutenant Colonel Green was due to arrive for their weekly meeting at any moment, and he needed his wits about him. Taking a sip of coffee, Sirius held the bitter liquid on his tongue for a long moment and willed it to ground him. He'd never had trouble focusing on the task at hand, a skill that had helped him in battle.

When Green finally arrived at the coffee shop and took the seat across from him, Sirius was vaguely confident he appeared as unfazed as he hoped himself to be.

"Is it any wonder why I prefer to meet at my office at King Charles Street? It's too damn busy here. And noisy," Green grumbled as he glared disdainfully around the coffee shop.

Sirius signaled a server with a flash of his hand, and soon a steaming mug of coffee sat on the table in front of the lieutenant colonel.

"So why the change of venue?" the older man asked, stirring several sugar cubes into his cup. He took a sip, his face contorting at the taste.

Sirius made a show of swirling the coffee in his cup around the rim. "Sometimes a change of scenery is good for the mind. I know you dislike leaving the comforts of your office, so it was very good of you to venture out and meet me here today. Thank you, sir."

The older man's eyes became slits of displeasure. "Do not think to placate me with your ill-placed flattery, Dawson."

"Come now, sir," Sirius said with a snort, "when have you ever seen me deploy flattering as a weapon." When Green's gaze turned menacing, Sirius chuckled. "All right, fair enough. But when has it not been productive?"

The lieutenant colonel waved his hand in dismissal. "So tell me how things have gone"—his gaze darted to the tables around them, before he dropped his voice—"with the Mexican chit you were so eager to help."

Sirius managed to contain an internal cringe. Instead, he folded his hands together over his waist and glanced up at the ceiling. "As I had hoped, keeping an eye on Miss Luna has not only allowed me to keep her from trouble, but also permitted me to spend more time with the viscount."

"Yes, the papers have mentioned he seems quite smitten with her." Green drummed his fingers on the tabletop. "And what of Westhope?"

"We have become steady acquaintances over the last few weeks"—Sirius raised a shoulder—"and I attended his private showing of the Maqdala collection at the British Museum last night."

Green lifted a brow. "And have you learned anything new or pertinent?"

Oh, he definitely learned something pertinent, but he knew Green would not care about that.

Sirius cleared his throat. "Unfortunately, nothing of importance yet. However, this was all about earning Westhope's loyalty. How am I to expect him to tell me anything if he doesn't count me as a friend?" Sirius tilted his head. "Surely you can't fault me for wanting to build a trusting rapport with the man."

"I can find fault with all manner of things about you, but I am willing to see how this situation plays out." Green took a drink from his cup, wincing again at the bitter taste. "When do you plan to take advantage of his attachment to the Luna girl?"

"Soon. He already hangs on her every word," Sirius murmured, shifting in his seat.

"Good. After that whole ghastly business with Earl Tyrell, I refuse to be caught unawares again." The lieutenant colonel propped his elbow on the table and rubbed his brow. "I don't know how the man thought he could just abduct the wife of an MP, and from your home, of all places."

Sirius didn't, either. "Hubris was Tyrell's fatal flaw."

"Indeed." The older man cocked his head. "Now back to Miss Luna. What do you know of her?"

That she was brilliant. Clever and passionate. That Sirius hadn't noticed how beautiful she was right away because he'd been so preoccupied with his own tasks, his own pursuits, until Isabel had quite literally snagged his heart in her small hand and squeezed it tight.

But of course, Sirius made no such confession.

"Isabel Luna is reserved. A bit shy, even a little awkward in a crowd. But she's incredibly intelligent. When she's comfortable with you, she shares her wit and charm." Sirius lifted a shoulder in what he hoped was an airy fashion. "It's easy to see why Westhope is so enchanted by her."

Green's gaze narrowed slightly, before he turned to study his coffee cup. "Enchantment is something you can work with. Coach her on what line of conversation to begin with him to determine what he knows. Encourage an attachment, which I doubt will be hard to do. Westhope is a bloody viscount, after all."

A detail Sirius had not been able to ignore. It would be quite the feat if Isabel were to secure the hand of a peer.

". . . and with the dispatches we've received from contacts in Mexico, you can tell Miss Luna—"

Sirius blinked, his spine straightening as his attention focused on the lieutenant colonel. "I beg your pardon?"

The older man arched a displeased brow. "We've received some reports of activity in Mexico. You can use it as enticement for Miss Luna's cooperation."

Sirius slid to the edge of his chair, the hair on his arms standing at attention. "What sort of activity?"

Green stared at him impassively for a moment, and Sirius hoped he didn't appear as anxious as he felt. Finally, the older man leaned back in his chair, crossing his arms over his barrel chest. "There have been increased campaigns to the north. The monarchists have taken Coahuila and are reported to be making campaigns into other northern Mexican states."

That was probably why Isabel's parents had been forced to flee their last location. "What do you know of their movements? That would be excellent information to pass along to Miss Luna."

After spending several minutes discussing the monarchists' movements in northern Mexico, Sirius licked his lips. "And what of Maximilian? At dinner last night, the Luna misses mentioned that he's championed several reforms that have angered some of his supporters."

Sirius had found the discussion fascinating. He had tried to learn what he could about the French occupation of Mexico after he hosted Isabel and her sisters at Dancourt Abbey two summers prior, but he wouldn't dare say he understood the complexities of the situation. Isabel and Gabriela were a fount of knowledge regarding their homeland, but Green had access to updated information that they did not.

"Yes, well"—Green tapped his finger against his coffee mug—"it would seem the monarchists should have known better than to get into bed with a Napoleon, especially now that the Americans are free to lend their support to Juárez."

An idea suddenly occurred to Sirius, and he pressed his

tongue to the top of his mouth as he wrestled with the right words to express it.

"You look as if you drank sour milk, Dawson. What's wrong?"

Goddamn Green and his perceptiveness. Releasing a silent sigh, Sirius said, "If you were to learn . . . of possible threats to members of the deposed Juárez government, would you tell me?"

A fraught silence stretched between them. Green stared at him intently, and Sirius knew what he was thinking. They had agreed to share information with Isabel, but what that information would be was decided solely by the lieutenant colonel. Yet both men knew this topic was different because Green was aware that Isabel's father was an adviser to the Mexican president. If the Home Office had intelligence that her father and President Juárez were in danger, how could Sirius not tell her? It was unthinkable.

Green rose to his feet, tossing several coins on the table. Snaring Sirius's gaze, he nodded. "If I learn anything, I will let you know."

Pressing his lips together, Sirius inclined his head.

"Now it's your turn," the lieutenant colonel growled softly. "Find out what you can from the viscount. Encourage Miss Luna to take advantage of Westhope's infatuation. There's a suspicion I can't shake that he knows more than he understands, even if inadvertently."

Sirius nodded.

Green clapped a hand on Sirius's shoulder. "I know I don't have to remind you, but I'm going to anyway. Have a care, Dawson. Westhope is a respected peer with connections, and if he is keen on making this Miss Luna his bride, it would be for the best to maintain some distance from her."

"But of course—" he began, but the lieutenant colonel squeezed his shoulder, cutting Sirius short.

"Explanations are not necessary." Green shook his head. "Just don't throw your career away so easily. Your men would not want that for you."

Sirius tried to contain his wince, but he was certain it showed on his face. For Green to make such a statement, to bring up his men in such a way, was a blow he had not seen coming, and his head swam with the implications.

Green placed his hat on his head and moved toward the coffee shop door. "Until next time, Dawson."

Sirius sat unmoving for several long minutes after the lieutenant colonel departed. Why had the older man brought up his men? Had he not worked hard to provide for them—to atone—since he'd returned to England? He employed one of his former lancers as a valet, and the gamekeeper and manager at Dancourt Abbey were former troopers of his regiment. He sent yearly stipends to both Taylor's and Robinson's families, for they had had the unfortunate luck of dying on the battlefield when Sirius, the lucky bastard, had somehow survived. He had thrown himself into his work for Green and the Home Office for the last eight years, maneuvering, outwitting, and seducing whomever was necessary to discover the information he needed so that his wretched life had a reason for being spared. For a higher purpose.

And when he had finally indulged his emotions with a respectable and altogether alluring young woman, suddenly he was letting his men down?

A sudden loud sound jerked his attention back to the moment, and Sirius stared down at his coffee mug, which now lay in cracked pieces on the tabletop.

Pressing his fingertips to the center of his brow, Sirius

inhaled deeply, counted to five, and released the breath in a loud whoosh. Now was not the time to become frustrated or angry with Green. He knew the lieutenant colonel was only doing what he felt was best, because he was aware of how much Sirius struggled when he first returned to London. How he still struggled, although the nightmares were fewer and farther between.

Sirius pushed back his chair and rose to his feet. He tossed a few coins on the tabletop, jerked on his tie, and placed his hat on his head. Stamping his cane on the floor, he contemplated what to do next. Hunt out Westhope at the club? Return to his home and toss back an entire bottle of brandy while he cursed his errant emotions? Sirius instead stepped out into the midafternoon sunshine and directed his steps toward the club. He had a job to do.

"Ay, Isa, you haven't turned a page in at least ten minutes."

Isabel jerked her head around and met Gabby's amused gaze. Glancing quickly down at the book in her hand, she noted her sister was right. She'd been on page fifty-five for far longer than the story warranted.

"I—I." She stopped to clear her throat, quickly flipping the page to fifty-six. "I've had to reread it several times."

"Is that so?" Her sister arched a black brow. "So what's it about, then?"

"Um . . ." She pressed her lips together, frantically skimming the page for any notion of what was occurring in the story. "It's about—about, uh . . ."

"Right." Gabby clicked her tongue. "So what were you really thinking about?"

"Nada," Isabel answered, a tad too quickly.

With slow movements, Gabby folded the newspaper she

had been reading and set it down on the table next to her. Planting her hands on her knees, she leaned toward Isabel, her gaze intense. "You've been distracted all day. I assumed you were concerned about Mother and Father, as we've yet to hear from them again, but you were distracted last night, too."

"I am worried for them"—Isabel toyed with the corner of the page—"so I don't know what you mean."

"You disappeared for quite some time at the museum," Gabby continued as if Isabel had not spoken. Her hazel eyes were far away. "I thought you were wandering the galleries, intent on viewing the exhibits without Lord Westhope hovering at your elbow."

Her lips twitched. "He's very attentive."

"Por supuesto," Gabby said with a roll of her eyes. "Please don't misunderstand. I like Lord Westhope. Very much. He's kind and handsome and intelligent, for he fancies you. But you don't feel the same way about him, do you, Isa?"

A great sigh sank Isabel's shoulders. "No, I don't. I like him, too, but my feelings do not go any deeper than that."

Gabby nodded but continued to study her sister's face. "I realized today, as I watched you stare at that page, that Captain Dawson disappeared last night at the same time you did."

The blood in Isabel's veins turned to ice. "Did he?" She smothered a cringe over how high-pitched her voice sounded.

"He did. And when he returned later, I noticed his face was flushed," Gabby said, continuing to stare intently at her. "Captain Dawson is one of the most composed, disciplined men I've met."

Isabel shrugged. "Yes, well, I'm sure he flushes easily considering how fair he is."

"That's true . . . but then I noticed the same of you." A

teasing smile settled on Gabby's mouth. "Your face was flushed and your eyes sparkled."

Dropping her sister's gaze, Isabel glanced down at the book in her hands. Why must Gabby turn her critical eye upon her *now*?

"That's because I was finally able to see the Maqdala exhibit without having to squeeze through the crush that's usually packed around it," she said, pleased with her flippant tone. Reaching for the teapot on the tray situated nearby, Isabel poured herself a cup. Studiously ignoring her sister, and any dubious look on her face, Isabel took a sip.

"Is that why your skirts were all wrinkled, too?"

The tea shot from her mouth on a gasp, and Isabel immediately pressed her napkin to her lips as she choked out coughs. Even through her blurry eyes, she noted Gabby's pleased expression.

Once Isabel's hacking coughs had subsided, Gabby clapped her hands together and pressed them to her chest. "I didn't think you had it in you, Isa."

"I don't know what you're talking about. I didn't have anything in me," she bit out, determined to concede nothing.

"I bet you did last night, though," Gabby drawled, waggling her brows.

"Gabriela Luna," Isabel gasped, truly scandalized.

Her sister rolled her eyes. "Act as offended as you'd like, but that doesn't negate the fact that you are having an affair with Captain Dawson."

"We're not having an affair," she grumbled, her tongue heavy with the lie. "We're just friends."

"Friends who kiss and leave love marks on each other's skin, it seems." Gabby gestured at her with her chin.

Isabel clapped a hand to her neck, panic crawling up her throat. She thought she had hid the mark Sirius had sucked into her skin with the cut of her gown, but apparently not. And if Gabby had noticed the mark, had Lupe as well? Or Lady Yardley? Her stomach abruptly turned at the thought of the older woman discovering the liberties she had granted Sirius.

But why should she be ashamed of her actions with Sirius? True, she had been raised within the church, had been taught to be pure and godly, and that she must be untouched and virginal for her future husband. But not once had Isabel regretted what she shared with Sirius.

Of course, a lack of shame did not mean she wanted to discuss the particulars with her sister.

So, mustering as much pride as she could, Isabel dropped her hand and picked up the book again, turning back to page fifty-five to begin again.

"When did it start?"

Isabel shook her head but did not answer.

"Was it here in London or at Dancourt Abbey?" Gabby pushed.

Isabel turned a page.

"Isabel, will you look at me?"

Shaking her head again, Isabel refused to glance away from the book.

"Isa, at least tell me he's been respectful." Gabby was worrying her lip when Isabel turned to her. "Captain Dawson has always struck me as a courteous man, but then the image a man presents to the world is often very different from the reality behind closed doors."

Exhaling a deep sigh, Isabel crossed to her sister and took

her hand. "Sirius—Captain Dawson has been nothing but kind to me. Gentle and attentive. He respects me, querida."

Gabby pressed her lips together for several heartbeats, simply staring at their knotted hands. "I'm happy to hear it. I've always liked Captain Dawson. Ever since he welcomed us to Dancourt Abbey on such short notice, and gave Ana and Gideon their beautiful wedding, and then helped Gideon recover her after that pendejo tried to steal her away. And I know that you two have not always gotten along . . ." Gabby glanced up at her then, a light shining in her hazel eyes. "But perhaps that was all foreplay."

Isabel bit back a laugh. "How do you know what foreplay is?"

Her sister waved a hand. "I know all sorts of things, many of which I learned from reading your books."

She had no reply to this, so Isabel merely shook her head.

"Does he intend to marry you, Isa?" Gabby asked, her expression abruptly serious again.

Dropping her gaze, Isabel frowned. "Of course he doesn't want to marry me."

The thought that Captain Sirius Dawson would want to marry her was laughable . . . and yet only unshed tears filled her throat.

"But why not? If he is capable of . . ." Gabby raised her brows meaningfully. "Surely he is capable and willing to marry you."

Opening and closing her mouth, Isabel grappled with what to say. She'd known that getting involved physically with Sirius would be a gamble, for there was no agreement between them. He had not promised to marry her and made no such offer after they had become intimate. Even with Lord Westhope paying her court, Sirius had still not offered her more. It stung, but at least she knew where he stood. He was willing to help her with her search, and pleasure her until she was boneless, but there would be no emotions involved.

"I was aware of Captain Dawson's reputation well before *this*." Isabel cleared her throat. "I don't have any illusions now."

"Well, I think that's nonsense."

"Why do you say that?" Isabel asked, pulling back to glare at Gabby.

Her sister narrowed her eyes in turn. "Because how could Captain Dawson not ask you for more? You deserve more. You deserve *everything*, and that man should be tripping over himself to give it to you."

Isabel looked away.

"Isa, do you still not know what you're worth? Do you still settle for scraps and fleeting bits of affection because that is all you think you deserve?" Gabby's palms pressed to her cheeks, and Isabel was forced to meet her sister's blazing eyes. "Father gave you—gave us—only the smallest hints of affection, and then only to keep us in line. But that doesn't mean that's how it should be. That doesn't mean you can't want more."

Any words Isabel wished to say were trapped by the lump of tears burning in her throat. Pressing her hand to her lips, she shook her head, willing her emotional dam to hold.

But Gabby seemed determined for Isabel to confront her emotions, for she gently smoothed back the escaped curls from her face, her gaze intent on Isabel's. "Do you not want to marry Captain Dawson? Are you happy with an affair and nothing more?"

Isabel shook her head. "I—I don't know what I want."

"That's fair. After everything we've been through, it's hard to know much of anything."

"It's just . . ." Isabel hiccuped, and she paused while her throat worked. "I don't want to stay here, Gabby. I want to return to Mexico. We've been gone so long and I still feel like a stranger here."

Gabby's expression softened. "I understand. It's been hard to make f—"

"But you *have* made friends," Isabel interrupted with a scowl. "You have the women's group you attend, and you're invited to parties and events all the time. People want you here. You have a place. Ana has a place. I don't, hermana."

"I assure you that whatever place you think I have here is not permanent." Before Isabel could ask what she meant, Gabby gripped her fingers so tight they hurt. "And anyway, *I* want you here. Ana wants you here. Gideon does, too." She jerked on Isabel's hand until she met her eyes. "And Captain Dawson wants you here. Isn't that enough?"

It should be. Her mind recognized her sister's argument, and Isabel knew, to the depths of her soul, that she was loved and wanted. And yet her heart wanted what it wanted.

"I wish it was, querida. I really do," she whispered, bringing their clasped hands to her face and rubbing Gabby's knuckles along her cheek.

Her sister was silent, her hazel eyes simply watching Isabel as if she were a riddle she was determined to solve. Isabel let her watch, uncertain of what to say or do to make this situation easier for either of them. The thought of leaving her sisters behind felt like a chasm cracking open in her chest and sucking the joy from her world. And yet the thought of staying in England, always feeling like an outsider looking in, was a fate she was resolved to avoid.

"Do you think it's possible, Isa," Gabby began, her words halting and cautious, "that Captain Dawson has not asked for more of you because he knows of your wishes to return to Mexico?"

Isabel swallowed and then shook her head. "I only told him of my wish to return very recently."

Gabby pursed her lips. "I wonder if his hesitancy is on his side. Perhaps there is something in his past that is keeping him from pushing for more."

"Why must there be some great motive for his disinterest?" Isabel's laugh was harsh. "Let's not skirt the truth. He never has. He's a rake. A rogue, and I've never expected him to act differently. As if I could possibly change him."

"Of course you couldn't. A person needs to change himself." A faraway look turned Gabby's eyes glassy. "But I've seen the way he's looked at you, Isa. Once I realized there was something happening between the two of you, I thought back to prior interactions you've had with him, and noticed it. He's different with you. He's more . . . genuine. I don't know how to explain it, I just know it when I see it."

"I suspect you're seeing what you want to see."

"And I suspect you are, too," Gabby retorted, a smug smile playing on her lips.

Isabel gritted her teeth and looked away. After a pause, she plowed forward. "Regardless of what you think you see, Sirius's home is here. He's well liked and well respected, and never wants for company. He would gain nothing from a marriage to me—"

"He'd gain you, Isa." Gabby's expression was implacable. "You are a prize without measure."

Clamping her eyes closed, Isabel released a watery laugh. Before she could respond, a knock sounded on the drawing room door. Smoothing her hands over her cheeks, she tried to calm herself while Gabby called for the butler to enter.

"Lord Westhope is here to see you, Miss Luna," he said from the door. "Should I tell him you're in?"

The sisters exchanged a loaded glance before Isabel nodded. "Please do, Evans. Thank you."

After the door had been closed again, Isabel rose to her feet and crossed to the opposite end of the room to peer at herself in the gilded mirror that hung there. Aside from a faint tinge of red lining her eyes, her appearance looked unfazed by her recent discussion with Gabby, and Isabel released a breath. She was almost glad Lord Westhope had come to call, for she needed the distraction. He was friendly and witty, and she always enjoyed the time she spent with him.

"You know, Isa, that the viscount wishes to make you his bride," Gabby said into the silence.

Isabel did not respond, merely meeting her sister's gaze in the mirror's reflection.

"Have you told him about your desire to return to Mexico?"

"I haven't." Isabel swallowed. "As I have no notion of when I will be returning, it didn't seem appropriate to bring up."

"If that's the case, why, then, are you using it as an excuse to hold Captain Dawson at bay?"

Biting back a curse, Isabel yanked her gaze away.

Isabel had no more time to consider her sister's question, as the door opened and Viscount Westhope appeared on the threshold, a smile brightening his handsome face.

"Miss Luna, Miss Gabriela, how good it does me to see you this day," he exclaimed, stepping into the room. Although his greeting encompassed Gabby, his gaze remained fixed on Isabel.

Sinking into a curtsy, Isabel fashioned a smile on her face. Perhaps it would be a good day to see Lord Westhope as well.

13

"I'm so happy you're both here."

It was obvious Ana María was telling the truth, for her velvet eyes sparkled, a grin brightening her face. It had been more than a week since they had seen one another, her sister and Gideon having been busy with political dinners and such. Isabel and Gabby were aware of their older sister's duties as the wife of an MP, but sometimes they smarted. However, any frustrations they may have felt were extinguished by Ana's excitement for their visit, which was infectious. Gabby grabbed Ana's hand and twirled about, laughing gaily. When they stopped, Isabel smiled as Ana turned to her, grasping both of her hands.

"Querida, I've missed you."

And Isabel had missed her older sister. So much so that she reached out, wrapped her arms about Ana's waist, and tucked her face into her shoulder. Ana María's arms came around her instantly, holding her tightly in a manner Isabel had always desired but never known how to ask for.

"Isa, has something happened?" Ana asked softly, rubbing a soothing hand along her back.

Isabel shook her head but did not lift it from her sister's shoulder.

"I suspect she's feeling a bit . . . emotional right now."

She slid her eyes to Gabby and glared.

Ana María's hold tightened about her shoulders. "Why would you be feeling emotional, Isa?"

Her grip on her sister increased.

"Is it Westhope?" Ana María's voice turned hard. "Has he hurt you?"

¡Ay Dios! How could she have forgotten how protective her older sister was? Sucking in a breath, Isabel pulled back and met Ana's gaze. "He did not."

Gabby snorted. "It's Isa who's breaking hearts. Lord Westhope is enamored with her."

Isabel could not stop the rush of heat that swept up her neck, over her cheeks, and to the roots of her hair. While she knew Gabby was just teasing her, she had not told her younger sister how Westhope had seemed poised to kiss her in the shadows of the terrace at the Harrington ball . . . until Isabel had feigned a cough and scuttled back inside the ballroom. She had felt terrible, a feeling that had not dissipated, but the thought of kissing anyone but S—

"And are you enamored with him?"

Faith, what should she tell Ana María? She certainly couldn't admit that she was encouraging the viscount's affections to learn what he knew about French movements in Mexico, and the special push and pull between her and Sirius seemed too uncertain, too precious, to discuss in her sister's drawing room. Without thinking, she slid her gaze to Gabby, desperate for an idea of how to respond.

"I think," Gabby began, flopping onto a settee in a mass of

crinoline, "that our dear Isabel is fond of the viscount but is hesitant to engage his affections."

"Why?" Ana María slowly sank onto an armchair, her gaze glued to Isabel's face.

Isabel paced around the matching armchair, her hands curling around the seat back. "I don't intend to stay in England."

Understanding swept across her older sister's expression. "Oh. Of course."

And with those three words, uttered with such forlorn sadness, a stone settled in Isabel's gut. She'd always known that when Ana María married Gideon, her sister's home would forevermore be in England. Gabby knew it, and so did Ana María. But they had never discussed what it meant for the three of them, and how one day their futures, their day-to-day lives, would be spent far away from one another. Two and a half years ago, this would not have bothered Isabel, for her sisters had been polite but indifferent strangers. Yet now . . . now that reality was enough to steal her breath away.

A melancholia settled like a cloud over the drawing room. Ana María busied herself with the tea tray, her mien pale as she prepared their cafecito. Gabby stared out the window to the little garden beyond, her hazel eyes clouded over. Exhaling, Isabel settled her gaze on a painting that hung over the unlit fireplace. Gideon had it commissioned from a visiting Mexican artist, and it featured a sweeping view of the Mexico City skyline, with the snowcapped mountains far in the background. And in the center of the foreground was a woman looking out on the view, her black hair tossed about on the breeze. An intense wave of homesickness crashed over Isabel whenever she looked at it, and she suspected it did the same for Ana María. Sliding her gaze to her sister, Isabel found Ana looking at it, as well, her lips pursed and her face in a frown.

Abruptly, Ana María dropped her spoon on the tray with a clatter. "I don't like to think about you two leaving. Just the thought of being left here, alone, makes my heart feel like it might lurch from my chest."

"But, Ana, you're not alone." Isabel leaned toward her. "You have Gideon."

"And think of all the friends you've made, especially at the parish," Gabby added.

After her marriage, Ana María had become involved in the parish church where Gideon had been raised. Isabel enjoyed visiting for Mass, but Ana had taken it upon herself to organize all manner of events for the congregation. Palm Sunday and Easter festivities, a fundraiser for the small parish school affiliated with the church, health clinics for parishioners, and more were overseen by her older sister, and Isabel was in awe of Ana María's leadership abilities. Her sister had bloomed in her marriage to Gideon, and Isabel knew that despite how she ached for Mexico, Ana María would never call it home again.

"I know," Ana mumbled, aggressively stirring cream into her coffee, "and I know Gideon loves me. But you are my *sisters*."

Isabel swallowed down a painful knot of emotions and turned away. The sound of rustling fabric met her ears, and she peered back to see Gabby had taken a seat next to Ana, an arm wrapped around her shoulders.

"Ana, please don't cry. It makes me uncomfortable."

An amused snort slipped out before Isabel could contain it, and both her sisters glanced up at her, Gabby's gaze full of mirth and Ana's tinged with fond exasperation.

"Gracias for reminding me you are not deserving of my tears, pendeja," Ana María grumbled.

"Ana!" Isabel and Gabby exclaimed in unison. When had their older sister said such a foul word?

It was Ana María's turn to laugh, and soon the tense atmosphere was dispelled by the trio's shared laughter. Over cups of coffee, they conversed and shared all manner of chatter about society gossip, the parliamentary bills Ana María was helping Gideon find support for, Gabby's increased participation in her suffrage group, as well as speculation over what was occurring in Mexico.

"Oh, I can't believe I forgot to tell you," Ana María said, jumping to her feet as she dashed to a cherrywood escritoire situated on the other side of the room. "Tío Arturo passed along a letter from Mother and Father. They are safe and well, gracias a Dios."

Cupping a hand to her mouth, Isabel swallowed down tears of relief.

Ana María rejoined them, but held out an envelope to Isabel before she sat. "There was also a letter from Padre Ignacio for you."

Hoping her hand didn't tremble, Isabel reached out and grasped the yellowed, dirt-smudged envelope, her throat thick. Without hesitation, she tucked it into the small reticule at her side.

"Don't you want to read it?" Gabby asked with a shake of her head.

"I'll wait until tonight." Her sister opened her mouth as if to argue, so Isabel turned to Ana María and quickly asked, "Will you read us Mother and Father's letter?"

The deflection worked. Soon the sisters were discussing the news their parents shared, and what it meant that imperial forces were heading north to Guaymas in Sonora. Isabel hid a secret smile, for she had shared that information with Padre Ignacio after learning it from Sirius. But her smugness was short-lived because she knew it wasn't enough. The constant worry for her parents made Isabel keenly aware of the letter in her reticule, and she pondered what words Padre Ignacio had written until her head pounded. She needed fresh air. She needed to read the letter in solitude. Isabel needed to escape.

Rising to her feet, Isabel smiled at her sisters . . . or hoped she did. "I'm going to walk to that little bookstore around the corner."

Her sisters blinked at her, their mouths twisting, twin frowns on their faces. It was Gabby who spoke first, though. "Por supuesto. I figured you would want to visit because we were so close."

Isabel nodded, silently praying for blessings for her ornery sister who always made her feel understood.

"Oh," Ana María murmured, her gaze darting about. "Let me ask Consuelo to accompany you."

"No." Isabel realized she said the word sharper than she intended when her sisters jerked back their chins. Licking her lips, she tried again. "The shop is not far. Surely I can walk there and back without encountering trouble."

"You would think," Gabby murmured, taking a sip of coffee.

Ana María rolled her eyes. "Very well. Enjoy yourself."

On the short walk to the bookshop, Isabel allowed herself a moment to contemplate what it would mean to return to Mexico and leave her sisters behind. Because while neither of them had said it, Isabel knew her younger sister would be in England for longer than she would. Despite her sister's claims to the contrary, Gabby had made friends and established relationships with an ease that made Isabel jealous, and she didn't think her sister would rush to abandon them. She could be wrong, of course, but if Gabby followed her back to Mexico, it would be several years still.

Straightening the hat on her head, Isabel pushed open the door to the bookstore.

"Good afternoon, miss," the proprietor called, a stack of books in his hands. With a quick dip of his head, he disappeared into a back room.

Thankful to have been spared the awkward practice of small talk, Isabel looked around. She had been pleasantly delighted when she discovered this little nook of a store nine or so months ago. It was tucked between a butcher shop and a bakery and had an impressive selection of books, from philosophical tomes to penny dreadfuls. Isabel had also found several Spanish translated works, and had eagerly thanked the shopkeeper for stocking them. Surrounded by rows of books, the air filled with their musty, slightly vanilla scent, Isabel expelled her stresses with a great exhale.

That was until she turned down an aisle and promptly collided with a firm chest. Stumbling backward, she would have fallen except a strong pair of hands gripped her upper arms and stopped her descent. Isabel looked up, her breath catching in her throat.

"Isabel! Are you all right?" Sirius asked, drawing her closer until his chest was almost pressed against hers. His sapphire eyes were large with concern.

After a heartbeat, she nodded. Isabel willed her body to step away from his warmth, but she was suddenly unable to control her limbs. It had been a handful of days since she'd seen him at the museum . . . where he'd brought her to release against his tongue. Heat singed her cheeks as she stared up at him.

"What are you doing here?" she eventually managed.

The corner of his mouth ticked up, his eyes tracing her face.

"I live only two blocks away, by the park." At her questioning look, he added, "The town house with the blue door?"

That sounded vaguely familiar. Isabel dipped her head.

Sirius glanced over her shoulder, and she assumed he was checking to see where the proprietor was. "I was selecting books to send to Dancourt Abbey."

"For your library?" she asked, knowing he took pride in building up his collection.

"No, actually." Sirius dropped his hands and stepped back a half step. "I periodically send books to the families who live there. Any books they don't keep they donate to the local schoolhouse. Sometimes they send requests." He pulled a scrap of parchment from his coat pocket and showed her.

A fluttering feeling began low in her belly, and Isabel clasped her hands together tightly. Sirius sent books to his country estate simply for his employees and their families to enjoy? His thoughtfulness didn't surprise her. Not really. When she thought back to the weeks she spent as a guest at Dancourt Abbey, it had been apparent to Isabel that Sirius was greatly respected and esteemed by his employees. There was always someone, whether a local farmer or man from the mill, who stopped by to chat with him, and it was not uncommon to hear their combined laughter echoing about the halls. Once, Isabel had stepped outside for a walk when she'd encountered Sirius and Whitfield playing cricket on a makeshift pitch with a handful of boys from the village. She'd watched them covertly, not wanting to seem at all interested in their antics, until a bend in the path had obstructed her view. He shared his charm and consideration with everyone.

It was probably why he had agreed to help her in the first place, and nothing more. Anything that occurred between them after that was a matter of opportunity and convenience.

And yet he said you weren't boring . . .

Sirius took a step closer to her, a pucker between his brows. "What's wrong, Isabel?"

She instantly bristled. "Why do you think anything is wrong?"

"I can tell," he said cryptically, his gaze softening.

Isabel didn't know what to think about that, nibbling her cheek as she glanced about. The shop owner was still in the back storage room, and she could hear him rummaging about, leaving her and Sirius alone. Just standing this close to him, his scent in her nose, left her a bit breathless. Isabel risked a glance up at him, finding him considering her patiently.

Something about his calm countenance had her blurt out, "I received a letter."

He nodded. "From whom?"

"Padre Ignacio," she said quickly, as if saying the name might make her voice tremble.

Sirius widened his stance, concern filling his eyes. "Is it news of your parents?"

"No," she blurted out. Catching Sirius's surprised expression, Isabel clarified, "We received a letter directly from my mother stating they were well."

"I'm relieved for you." He raised his hand to her cheek but abruptly paused . . . before letting his arm drop. "So why do you seem so perturbed to hear from him?"

"Because . . . it's just . . ." She mashed her lips together as her gaze darted about, her mind racing to explain all that she was feeling. Glancing back at Sirius, her shoulders sank. "I—I don't have anything new to share with him."

Not wanting him to see the embarrassment on her cheeks, Isabel pivoted to face the nearest bookshelf. Her gaze fell on the cover of *Five Weeks in a Balloon*, by Jules Verne. How

Isabel wished she could ascend in a balloon again, but instead of being tethered to the earth—to her problems—it would carry her away. Far, far away from her sense of failure. From the kind man who sought her company but left her cold. From the man who stood behind her, whom she wanted for herself despite knowing he could never be hers.

"Do you expect Father Ignacio to shame you?"

"No." The answer was immediate. Not once had Padre Ignacio ever shamed her. And yet the idea of failing him made her nauseated. "It's just . . ." Isabel shook her head as she trailed off, dipping her chin so he could not see her expression.

After a tense moment, he exhaled, long and loud. "Have you read it?" When Isabel shook her head again, Sirius's tone turned soft. "Would you like to read it now, while I'm with you? Sometimes it's easier to do difficult things when you have a friend for support."

What a lovely sentiment, and even lovelier that Isabel finally had a friend who might be supportive of her. With a nod, she extracted the letter from her reticule and slowly unfolded it. Her eyes skimmed over the writing and stopped, a frown pulling on her mouth.

"It's not from Padre Ignacio," she whispered.

"Who's it from, then?" Sirius asked.

Isabel looked up at him, panic cinching around her throat. "Fernando Ramírez."

The only thing Sirius knew about this Fernando Ramírez was that he used to be engaged to Ana María Fox, and had tapped Isabel with her irksome task. Yet the dread that contorted Isabel's face at the realization the man had written to her was enough for Sirius to hate him.

Instead, Sirius grasped Isabel gently by the elbow and

ushered her farther down the row, until they came to an armchair tucked into a narrow corner. A ginger cat lay nestled in a
circle on the seat, and though Sirius was loath to chase it away,
he wanted Isabel to be comfortable. So Sirius scooped up the
grumpy feline and set it on its feet, and he rolled his eyes when
it bared its teeth at him before sauntering away. Without waiting for her leave, Sirius sat, Isabel bundled in his arms. Her
skirts made the position a tad uncomfortable, but his need to
hold her overrode any discomfort.

"Sirius, really?" she scolded, her mouth pursed in reproach.
Yet she didn't attempt to escape his grip.

"Mr. Johnson is getting a bite to eat. I told him I would
keep an eye on the shop," Sirius said, squeezing her side, "so
we have all the privacy needed to read that letter."

Isabel rotated her head to look at him. "You truly want me
to read it to you?"

Sirius resented the doubt in her voice, but did not mention
it. Instead, he tucked a silky strand of black hair behind her
ear and nodded. "Go on, then."

With a sigh, Isabel unfolded the letter again, smoothed out
the corners with her fingers. "It may take me a moment to
translate."

"There's no rush," he said, making a show of settling more
comfortably in the chair.

A fleeting, perhaps fond, smile lit her face. Clearing her
throat, she began.

Señorita Luna,

*I hope this letter finds you well. Current circumstances
have made communication a trying affair, so forgive me*

for not being in touch more frequently. However, Padre Ignacio has told me that you have a new suitor.

The word *suitor* made Sirius clamp his teeth together.

I'm sure I don't have to tell you to employ your charms to learn of his connections, but circumstances here are precarious. We must rely upon our friends, and perhaps your new suitor can be of assistance. I know your father would be very proud to know your affiliation with this gentleman has borne fruit.

Isabel's mien paled at the mention of her father, and Sirius dared to hold her a bit tighter. How dare Ramírez use her father to manipulate her. Sirius allowed himself a fleeting moment to daydream about choking this faceless man—

However, if you do not feel comfortable pursuing an attachment or his attention wanes, then maybe your sister, Señorita Gabriela, would meet with more success. Do not hesitate to use any advantage at your disposal.

Sirius snatched the letter from her hand, folded it carefully, and slipped it back inside her reticule. "That's quite enough of that, I think."

He'd expected Isabel to respond with indignation at his high-handed ways, but instead she sank back against his chest and covered her face with her hands. Grappling with what to do or say, Sirius settled on burying his face in the curve of her neck, his arms locked snugly around her.

The sound of Isabel's throat working met his ears, and

while he didn't think she cried, it was obvious her emotions had been rattled. Sirius longed to ask her what she was thinking, but held his tongue. She would tell him when she was ready, if at all. And Sirius would learn to be satisfied with that.

He suspected he'd have to content himself with whatever Isabel was willing to give him.

Isabel tipped her head back to meet his gaze. "I can't imagine why I thought I could do this. Me, timid, awkward Isabel Luna."

"Stop that," Sirius growled, dragging his hand up to cradle her face. "There is nothing about you that is timid or awkward. The Isabel Luna I know is fearsome. Sharp-witted. Quotes *Frankenstein* with clever ease." When Isabel chuckled, he ran his thumb over her smile. "You dazzle me. Please don't allow the words written in that letter to speak louder than the words I'm telling you right now."

Her obsidian eyes glinted with her unshed tears. "You're just saying that because you're kind to everyone. I know, because I've been paying attention."

"Not close enough, it seems." Sirius held her gaze for a long moment before he leaned forward to slowly press his lips to hers. It was a short kiss, and still it rocked him to his core. "Instead of hearing Ramírez's words in your mind tonight as you lie in your bed, hear mine, Isabel. The man who doesn't want anything from you aside from your happiness."

It was a lie. An acrid lie, for Sirius wanted too much. Much more than he could ever venture to deserve.

Determined to chase away his morose thoughts as well as hers, Sirius rose and set Isabel on her feet. "Johnson will return soon, and we certainly don't want him to find us curled up like two rabbits in a burrow."

Isabel shook out her skirts while her gaze never left his face. "Certainly not."

Gripping his lapels . . . while he tried to keep a grip on his self-possession, Sirius gestured to the shelves with a jerk of his head. "Will you help me select some books to send to Dancourt Abbey?"

A sunrise emerged across her expression. "I would love to."

Sirius smiled, thankful to steal a bit more time with her.

14

Isabel had left the bookstore that afternoon with her heart much lighter than it was when she had entered it. Sirius had successfully managed to dampen the stress she felt over Fernando's letter by simply being his charming self. They perused the bookshelves for a long while, exchanging lighthearted banter, and Isabel quizzed him on whom he intended to buy books for. With that knowledge, she made recommendations, a feeling of triumph glowing in her chest whenever Sirius commended her taste. Eventually, Mr. Johnson returned and chimed in on occasion with his own picks, but overall he was content to allow Isabel and Sirius to search about his store and fill the air with their teasing.

When she realized it had grown late, Sirius escorted her back to Ana María and Gideon's home, although it was in the opposite direction of his own, and the satchel on his shoulder contained a large stack of books. Sirius bade her goodbye on the front steps, his gaze moving between hers and her lips, and Isabel almost wished he would kiss her, not caring if her sisters saw. Instead, he lightly squeezed her elbow and departed. Isabel followed his retreating back until he turned the corner and disappeared from view, taking a bit of her happy mood with him.

Once she had rejoined her sisters, Isabel learned that she and Gabby had been invited to stay the night and enjoy a big Mexican breakfast in the morning. While she shared Gabby's excitement for such a treat, Isabel had decided upon other plans as she had watched Sirius walk away. If her sisters were surprised when she politely declined the invitation, they did not show it, and Isabel was grateful.

Now, Isabel waited impatiently in her room at Yardley House for the staff to turn in for the night. It was nearing midnight, and since she and Lady Yardley had stayed in, Isabel was hopeful she would not have to wait much longer. A small pile of books lay scattered across her bed, as she had tried to distract herself among their pages, but her mind would not stop whirling. Since spending the afternoon with Sirius, she had been consumed with turning her carefully considered idea into reality.

The grandfather clock in the foyer announced the midnight hour, and Isabel bit her lip. She'd told herself to linger for a quarter of an hour more, which felt like an excruciating amount of time with her nerves so raw. But Isabel had turned waiting and watching into an art form, so she paced across the floor, quoting lines from "A un samán" by Andrés Bello.

When she was certain the house was still, Isabel wandered to her dressing room, where she donned a dark gown and the same black cloak she wore the night she and her sisters escaped from Mexico City. Pulling her curls into a bun, she slipped a small knife into her pocket. Wandering to the mirror to consider her reflection, Isabel pondered how much her opinion of Sirius had changed in the last couple of months. Oh, he was still the same rogue he'd always been, but now she knew there was much more to him beneath that merry exterior. There existed a man she genuinely liked, whom she enjoyed spending time with, and who seemed to understand her when so often she struggled to understand herself. What surprised her, even now, was that Sirius seemed to like her, too.

Isabel tried to envision what Sirius saw when he looked at her. But all she found was her same old dark eyes, broad nose, and black-as-pitch curls in the mirror. Isabel had always thought her features plain, but perhaps she had been unfair to herself. Hadn't she caught the attention of a viscount? Didn't one of London's most notorious rogues call her remarkable? Isabel certainly didn't want to tie her confidence to a man and his opinion of her, but perhaps the time had come to finally cast aside her insecurities and embrace the Isabel she'd always wanted to be. Fearless. Resilient. Beautiful. And she would do so tonight.

Peeking into the hallway, Isabel released a quiet sigh to find it empty. Slipping out of the town house several minutes later, Isabel clung to the shadows as she made her way through the Mayfair streets. She was thankful that Sirius's home was closer than Ana's and she didn't have to skulk past where her sisters slumbered. Isabel wrapped her newfound bravery tightly about her shoulders and hoped fervently it was not misplaced.

The town house with the blue door was not hard to locate, and Isabel tucked herself behind a copse of trees in the adjacent park to allow herself time to study it. A row of three windows lined the first and second floors, with two narrow dormer windows situated on top. Unlike at Yardley House or even Ana María's home, no flower boxes brightened the windows, the blue door and brass knocker the only adornment. Yet it was elegant and stately.

Of course Sirius lived there.

After studying the house for several minutes, Isabel noticed a lamp burned in the far right window, and if she squinted her eyes, she could make out a figure pacing back and forth behind the drapes. That had to be him . . . right? Her pulse pounded in her head and her palms were clammy, but Isabel did her best to focus on her surroundings. Was there traffic on the road? Was anyone in the windows of the neighboring houses? Confirming her path was clear, Isabel darted across the cobblestone street and tucked herself as best she could in the narrow hedge growing under the window. Ignoring how a branch jabbed her in the back, Isabel curled her fingers over the windowsill and pulled herself up to tug on the window. When it wouldn't budge, Isabel extracted her knife and made quick work of the lock. Pushing loose strands of hair from her face with the back of her arm, Isabel pressed her hands against the windowpanes to slide it open. Grasping the skirts of her gown, she crawled through the dark window as gracefully as possible, a sigh slipping free when her feet hit the floor.

Suddenly, Isabel was wrenched by an iron grip on her arm, a thick bicep encircling her throat and cutting off any scream she would have emitted. Forcing down her panic, she strained her head back to meet Sirius's gaze.

Sirius had just poured another finger of whisky into his glass when a noise outside the window abruptly snagged his attention. Sirius went stone-still, his ears craning to listen for what had disturbed the quiet stillness of the night.

There it was again. A soft rustling of the bushes outside his window. Silently walking to his desk, Sirius extracted a pistol from the top drawer and stealthily made his way to the window, pressing his body flat against the casement. If a robber thought to make a target out of his home, he would not like the reception.

In the dim moonlight creasing through the cracks in the drapes, a shadowy figure appeared from below. Sirius watched with his tongue pressed to the back of his teeth as the person picked the window lock and slid the casement up. Within moments, two feet softly thudded to the floor, and as the figure moved to push the curtain aside, Sirius leapt up and wrapped his arm around their neck.

A string of strangled Spanish words met his ears, and Sirius jerked back in surprise. Hastily depositing his pistol on the desk, he quickly turned to rip the black hood from the figure, stifling a gasp when sable eyes met his.

"Isabel, what in God's name are you doing here?" he demanded, grasping her shoulders and shaking them.

Her face crumpled in derision, and Isabel yanked herself from his grasp, stumbling to the side. "You don't have to be so rough."

"My apologies," he mumbled, running a hand down his face. "Now answer my question."

Isabel's chest rose and fell with her breaths, her eyes darting about but carefully avoiding him. "I—I just—"

Advancing toward her, Sirius crowded her back against the drapes, planting his hands on either side of her head. "*I just* . . . what? You were brave enough to come here, in the middle of the goddamn night, so you should be brave enough to tell me what your intentions are."

Her full lips parted on a sigh . . . before irritation flared in her dark gaze. Planting her hands on his shoulders, Isabel shoved him back.

"First, don't curse at me. Second, you're forgiven for accosting me—"

"You crawled through my window in the dark, and I'm supposed to apologize to you?" Sirius quirked his brow. "You have a lot of nerve."

"Third," Isabel continued, ticking off a finger as if he hadn't spoken, "I needed to speak with you."

Sirius froze, his interest piqued. What could have possibly driven Isabel out in the dark to speak with him? "About what?"

Her hands twisted in her cloak, her teeth nibbling on her bottom lip. "I—I wanted . . ." She swallowed. "I wanted to a-ask if you would show me how to use my feminine . . . *wiles* to learn what Lord Westhope knows of the French?"

A buzzing sound filled Sirius's ears, and his mouth fell open as shock chased away all his thoughts.

Noting his stunned silence, Isabel clenched her eyes closed. "Lo siento. I don't know what I was thinking coming h—"

"You want me to teach you how to seduce Westhope?" Sirius bit out.

Isabel's throat worked on a swallow, but she nodded. "It's the only thing I haven't tried, and time is running out."

This infuriating woman. Sirius dragged a hand through his hair and yanked on it for good measure. The sting helped settle his mounting frustration.

Or so he thought, until he opened his mouth and said, "If you think I'm going to help you seduce another man, you are cracked."

Outrage swept scarlet across her cheeks. "You said you would help me!"

"And I have been. But understand this, Isabel Luna." Sirius

stalked toward her, an unholy roar echoing in his head. "I would break every bone in Westhope's hands if he ever laid a single finger on you."

Isabel gasped, pressing a palm to her mouth. But soon her eyes narrowed and she abruptly pushed past him, stripping her black cloak from her shoulders and draping it over an armchair as she went. Her simple purple day gown should not have looked so tempting on her, but Sirius locked his arms at his sides to keep from reaching for her. Isabel might be standing in his dark library now, but she was a tempting handful he *knew* he should not touch again.

"You know I'm not interested in the viscount romantically," she said, dragging her slender fingers along his book spines.

That motion, done so artlessly, sent heat streaking to his groin. Sirius shifted on his feet to relieve the pressure. "I know you've said that, but your feelings could have changed. Westhope is quite amiable."

Sirius forced himself to say the words, although his body recoiled. He did not want to talk about the viscount, especially not with Isabel before him, surrounded by the books that used to bring him so much joy but now only reminded him of her.

"He is. And handsome, too." Isabel glanced at him over her shoulder, a smirk twisting her lips. "But while you may be capable of trifling with more than one woman at a time—"

"It's not what you think."

Isabel blinked, her mouth slightly ajar. "I don't understand."

"My supposed exploits." Sirius rubbed a hand along the back of his neck. "My rakish reputation. I've cultivated it for a reason."

"What reason would that be?"

The pucker of confusion between her brows urged Sirius to take a step closer to her. This revelation had to be done with care. "You know how Mr. Ramírez wanted you to use your access to members of London society to search for their secrets? Well, I use my status as a war hero"—Sirius spit out the word—"and an earl's son to do the same."

"You do?" Isabel's gaze swept over his face. "D-does that mean you work for—"

"I come by my connections in the Home Office naturally." He smiled. "I started when I returned from the peninsula."

There were days when the war felt like a long-ago memory, and others when the memories were so vivid and wretched they kept him awake at night.

Isabel's eyes darted about with her thoughts, and Sirius could see her putting puzzle pieces together. "So does that mean that all those times I saw you with different women, or heard salacious whispers of your affairs, you were . . . working?"

His shoulders tensed, and then fell on a long exhale. "More times than not."

That barely there smile of hers curved her lips, but her expression darkened. "Is that why you know so much about Westhope? Is he one of your . . ." She frowned. "Targets?"

Sirius hesitated. Lieutenant Colonel Green never told him to withhold such information from Isabel, but admitting to spying on the gregarious viscount seemed akin to kicking a puppy. "Westhope has close ties to the French, and after what happened with your sister and Earl Tyrell, we are remaining vigilant."

Her brief scowl told Sirius she had noted his nonanswer, and he was thankful she didn't push the topic. Instead, she broached an equally unnerving one.

"Am I one of your targets? Is that why you're suddenly showing interest in me?"

Isabel uttered the questions with her shoulders back and

her head high, but her bottom lip trembled. Her large doe eyes stared up at him with defiance . . . but also an endearing amount of anguish. It would not do.

Planting his hands on her shoulders, Sirius gathered her against his chest. "No, sunshine. The curious workings of your mind, your reckless courage, and steadfast loyalty are what snagged my interest."

Silence ebbed between them, and Sirius wondered what she thought of his confession. He imagined Isabel was considering his words and judging his sincerity. It seemed like a very Isabel thing to do. So to save her from overthinking, Sirius pulled her back and waited until she met his gaze.

"I enjoy spending time with you. I look forward to hearing your thoughts on whatever topic captures your fancy. Throughout the day, I ponder ways I can make you laugh." Sirius brushed a curl from her cheek, allowing his fingertips to dance across her skin. "And I anxiously anticipate the next time you'll let me touch you again."

Surprisingly, Isabel's expression was unreadable. Or maybe it was just guarded. Sirius didn't have long to ponder it before Isabel slipped from his grasp and moved away. He let her go, his chest uncomfortably tight. Did she believe him? Sirius had never said such things to another woman before, and he hoped Isabel understood that his candor was in earnest.

Once she was outside his reach, Isabel stared at him and Sirius stared back . . . until one of her slim brows arched sharply. "You know, I don't just let anyone touch me."

A bolt of desire threatened to turn him into a human torch. "You've let me touch you, Isabel. You've let me *taste* you. What, then, does that make me to you?"

Isabel dipped her head but looked up at him through her thick lashes, and Sirius bit back a groan. She thought she needed help learning the art of seduction? Christ, she could have him on his knees with a slight tilt of her head.

Turning back to the bookshelf, Isabel studied his selection until her hand paused over one volume. Sirius smiled when he saw which book had snared her attention. Slipping the book from the shelf, Isabel held it up.

"Why do you have this?"

Sirius leaned his elbow on an adjacent shelf, his gaze glued to her profile. "Because I appreciate her work."

Isabel pivoted about, color high in her cheeks as she clutched the book to her chest. "You have the complete works of Sor Juana Inés de la Cruz? You've never spoken of having an interest in her writings before."

His gaze dropped to the volume she held so tightly, his jaw rolling as he pondered what to say. He could tell her it was a coincidence, that he had found it in passing. And not that he had asked Mr. Johnson to locate a copy for him, and had waited months for the man's search to bear fruit. All because of her.

"You mentioned her that summer. At Dancourt Abbey." Sirius lifted a shoulder. "You spoke of Sor Juana, as you called her, with such respect and admiration, and I suppose I had to know why."

Her dark eyes widened as they held his. "And . . . what do you think?"

Sirius shrugged again. "I think she was quite brilliant. It was easy to see why the men of her time were so threatened by her. She eclipsed them in every way."

Isabel licked her lips as she moved toward him. "Everyone doubted her simply because she was a woman. But she wasn't content to allow others to define her. Sor Juana knew who she was and what she wanted to do, and although society at the time would not allow her to pursue her passions, she managed to create a life for herself that was fulfilling and memorable."

She looked down at the book in her hand. "I confess that Gabby reminds me a bit of her. She's fervent and sharp. She will change the world."

Sirius's fingers itched to brush a curl from her brow. "And I was just going to say that Sor Juana reminded me of you."

"Of me?" Her mouth formed a perfect O.

"Of course. I'm a bit offended that you seem so surprised." Sirius smiled when Isabel chuckled, but he quickly sobered as he debated whether he wished to steer the conversation down a road she had avoided before. "And now you want to direct that passion toward Lord Westhope."

Her teeth sank into her bottom lip. "I don't want to do anything of the sort. Not really. I just don't know what else to do. When Fernando recommended I ask Gabby for help, it was like a punch to the gut. I know I haven't found anything yet, but I'm *trying*. I want to help, and I just know I can do this."

"I know it, too." And Sirius did. Isabel was the most determined, focused woman he had ever met.

"Perhaps I should ask my sister." Isabel huffed a breath. "She's never met a stranger, you know. Even as a child, Gabby gathered admirers wherever she went."

"And what of you?" Sirius asked.

Her snort was indelicate. "I'm a stranger even to myself."

But not to me. The words sat on his tongue, but Sirius didn't dare utter them. He knew they would chase her away, like a timid fawn. Yet he suspected Isabel saw the claim in his eyes, for she stared at him for a long moment, and spun about, Sor Juana's works still clutched in her hand.

"So what do you suggest I do?" she asked, sinking onto the

settee. "I know the viscount is fond of me, but how do I encourage him to be more . . . amorous?"

Fighting back the surge of anger that sparked in his chest, Sirius spread his arms. "Be yourself? Darling, you're desirable all on your own."

A bashful smile curved her lips. "You're just being nice."

"I'm being honest. There's nothing nice about me."

"That's not true." Isabel shook her head, more wiry strands slipping from her bun to brush against her face. "The Captain Dawson I know has turned his estate into a haven for the men he served with, where they can rebuild their lives surrounded by the beauty of the Devonshire countryside. He selects books to send to the families who live there." Rising to her feet, she approached until she could grip the loose hem of his untucked shirt. "He befriends a shy wallflower, whom most people ignore, and listens to her chatter on and on about books and science even when it must be very vexing."

Emotions he refused to identify singed the back of his throat, and Sirius forced them down with a rough swallow. Unable to have her so close without touching her, Sirius dragged his knuckles along her temple. "*Vexing* is not the word I would use to describe it."

"What word would you use, then?" she breathed.

"*Intoxicating. Mesmerizing. Hypnotic.* Are those enough words?" A tear streaked down her cheek, and Sirius brushed it away. Overwhelmed with the urge, the *need* to kiss her, he cradled her face in his hands. The obsidian pools of her eyes blinked up at him, and Sirius would have done anything for her in that moment.

"Only you think those things of me," she whispered.

Sirius swiped his thumb across her bottom lip. "I doubt that, but then most people are fools."

And he leaned down to kiss her.

Their first kisses had been fueled by all the wild emotions combusting between them and the threat—the thrill—of being discovered. But this kiss was different. There was no fear of discovery, no one to find them wrapped up in each other. Here, within the walls of his townhome, Sirius could take his time with her . . . and a woman like Isabel deserved to be worshipped.

Cupping the smooth curve of her cheek, Sirius trailed his other hand down her back until his fingers snagged on the simple eye closures that held her dress together.

"May I?" he murmured in between kisses.

Isabel nodded, her hands curling about his shoulders.

While he trailed kisses along her jaw, down her throat, to the sensitive valley between her neck and shoulders, Sirius plucked free every clasp, biting back moans with each patch of warm skin he felt under his fingertips. Eventually her bodice sagged, and Sirius paused, his lungs laboring with every breath.

"Sunshine, come with me," he said gently, pulling her by the hand toward the settee.

Her red-tinged lips quirked. "I love that you call me sunshine."

"It's the perfect name for you." Sirius encouraged her to straddle his lap, for he knew she would appreciate the level of control the position gave her. If she was uncomfortable, he wanted her to be able to halt their interaction as soon as possible. "You blaze brighter than anything else in my life."

"Ridículo," she whispered, leaning forward to kiss him.

While he allowed Isabel to dictate the kiss, Sirius put his restless hands to work pulling the pins from her hair. When her inky curls tumbled about her shoulders, he leaned back to study her. "Christ, you're stunning."

Isabel surprised him by laughing. "I'm really not . . . but you make me feel beautiful. You're the only person who ever has."

"Darling, that's an unforgivable sin," Sirius hissed between his teeth as his hands hooked around the edge of her bodice and dragged it down her arms, revealing her golden skin to the light. "Look at you. I can't believe you let me touch you."

Sirius jerked his gaze to hers when Isabel gently grabbed his chin. Soft velvet eyes stared back at him. "And I only want *you* to touch me."

Clenching his teeth, Sirius simply held her, his hands firm on her waist and his gaze locked with hers. How had he been so blind? With her black curls falling about her smooth shoulders, Sirius was speechless. How had he not seen all this beauty right in front of him? Once again, shame was his old friend.

He hesitated with the bindings of her corset, although his mouth watered at the thought of seeing the curves her gowns only hinted at. Even now, the swells of her breasts rising above her corset tempted him . . . but he didn't make any moves to unwrap her. Although he ached to taste her and touch her again—to finally fill her—Sirius wrestled his desire into submission, for he knew this was Isabel's first time with a man, and he refused to frighten her. Refused to pressure her or coerce her into an act that could not be undone. If she did allow him to take her to bed, Sirius intended to apply every ounce of experience he had ever gleaned into pleasing Isabel Luna so that this moment, with him, would be forever synonymous with pleasure. She would soon return to Mexico, but tonight Sirius was determined to make sure she never forgot him.

15

Did she really want to do this?

Yes, her mind screamed, which almost made Isabel laugh, because it was usually her mind that approached things logically. But logical thinking told her it didn't make sense to give her virginity to a man who was the rogue of all rogues . . . or who at least pretended to be.

And yet Sirius Dawson sparked a slew of emotions in her chest that she tried so very hard to suppress. From the moment she met his sapphire eyes from under that desk, no other man had commanded her attention. Not even dear Lord Westhope, who treated Isabel like a queen. Still, the viscount did not send flames licking up her spine at his nearness. Didn't make heat coil in that place between her thighs that she hadn't been able to forget since Sirius had caressed it with his tongue.

The only man to make her feel thus was sitting beneath her now, his gaze almost adoring as he stared up at her. When she returned to Mexico, Isabel desperately wanted these memories to cherish. To keep her warm when she was alone, for Isabel knew she would never feel these emotions with anyone else.

Sirius had loosened her bodice and pulled it from her arms but had made no attempt to remove her corset or chemise. He hadn't tried to remove her skirts, which were thankfully lacking the bulk they usually had, since she left her crinoline at home. With his hands on her thighs, he simply looked at her. And suddenly Isabel understood. Sirius was waiting for her to make the first move.

Which was definitely something she could do.

Sinking her teeth into her bottom lip, Isabel curled both ends of the corset knot around her fingers and pulled. Ignoring how his breath hitched and the path his hands took as they traced the muscles of her thighs, Isabel made steady work of the ribbons until finally they were loose enough to pull the corset up and over her head. Her hands trembled with the urge to shield herself, knowing all too well that her white chemise hid little of her figure beneath. Instead, Isabel straightened her spine and met Sirius's gaze head-on, determined for him to look his fill.

"Isabel," he breathed, his pupils blown wide as his gaze drifted over her. The delicate hairs on her skin rose even as heat surged like a torrent through her blood, pumping not just desire to her limbs, but power. Sirius's admiration of her beauty, yes, but also of every one of her awkward and tenacious traits, made her feel powerful. He made her feel deserving of good things . . . and in this moment, Sirius's hungry gaze promised *very* good things.

Her skin abruptly felt too tight, and Isabel shifted in his lap, her hands curling around the hem of his loosened waistcoat. Sirius groaned, his eyelids dropping to half-mast as he stared up at her. "Have a care, darling. We're not hiding under a desk this time, and my desire for you knows no bounds."

Isabel shuddered at the dark note in his voice. Surging

forward, she wrapped her arms around his neck and pressed her lips to his.

Faith, kissing Sirius Dawson sent a bolt of lightning sizzling along her skin. The logical part of her brain noted this as hyperbole even as it quickly melted under the onslaught of his mouth. And when his tongue flicked along her bottom lip and she opened for him, coherent thoughts were incinerated in the rush of sensations. Isabel dragged her fingers along his scalp to run through his glossy hair, moaning into his mouth.

She needed to feel closer to him. She wanted to make him feel as overwhelmed as she felt.

Without lifting her lips from his, Isabel grasped the hem of his shirt and broke away to lift it off his shoulders and over his head.

"Off," she ordered, smiling when he mumbled something about her being bossy.

Any response she would have offered died on her tongue as soon as she took in the broad expanse of his chest. Blond hairs ran over his torso and down his sternum to disappear into the waistband of his trousers. Isabel ran her fingernails through the wisps, chuckling when gooseflesh spread in her wake. A raised scar streaked with shades of mauve and rose ran over several ribs, and she bit her lip to keep from touching it. Instead, she reached for one tan nipple and traced it with her nail, flames flaring in her core when he shivered.

"Shall we see if yours are as sensitive as mine?" Sirius asked in a growl.

Before she had a chance to respond, he grabbed the delicate straps of her chemise and ripped them down her arms, baring her to his hungry gaze. Her nipples immediately pebbled, whether from the coolness of the room or the heat in his eyes, she knew not.

"Darling, I should have known." Sirius stroked his thumb along the underside of her right breast, while he blew his warm breath across the puckered peak. "Of course you would have the most delectable breasts I have ever seen."

"You're such a liar," she said . . . the words turning to a hiss when he flicked a hungry tip with his thumb.

"I would never claim to be a paragon of truth and honesty," he said, cupping her right breast in his hand and kneading it gently. "But I don't tell lies in the bedroom."

"An honorable rogue, are you?" Isabel breathed, arching her back and pushing herself more fully into his hand.

"Only with you, Isabel." Sirius looked up and snared her gaze, his eyes dark and stormy. "Only with you."

And then he drew her nipple into his mouth.

Isabel sank her nails into his thighs as she lost herself in his lovemaking. Sirius kissed and caressed, nibbled and kneaded her flesh until she was crying out inarticulate babbles and grinding her hips in his lap. When he finally released the tip with a loud pop, Isabel felt as if her skin barely contained her and she needed something—*anything*—to appease this sudden desperate need clawing through her.

"Bloody hell, let's get this nonsense off you," he said, tugging on her dress.

Standing on trembling legs, Isabel helped Sirius pull down the bulk of her skirts with impatient hands, kicking the dress aside when it finally pooled at her feet. Sirius paused with a slack jaw to take her in, his scalding blue gaze fixed on the juncture between her legs. Isabel knew she should have been embarrassed to stand in front of a man in such a scandalous state, but her core pulsed with an unfulfilled need she knew, from experience, Sirius could satisfy. He was the *only* one she wanted to satisfy it.

Without a word, Isabel straddled his lap again, tackling the belt and the fall of his trousers. Her fingers were clumsy and awkward, and after she bumbled several attempts, Sirius stopped her movements with his hand.

"Take a deep breath." He brushed his palms along her temple to smooth back her wayward curls. "I'm not going anywhere. I'm here. With you."

Isabel sat back on her haunches, her tongue sticking to the roof of her mouth. "It's just . . ."

"It's just what?" Sirius pecked a kiss to her chin.

Her fingers curled into the firm flesh of his thighs. "It's just . . . I don't want you to change your mind. I don't want you to remember whom you're with and think of all the reasons why this is a bad idea."

Sirius's face crumpled. Twining his hands in her hair, Sirius tugged her head back until the long line of her neck was bared to him. "I know exactly who's in my arms. Whose smooth, fragrant skin is stretched under my lips. Whose perfectly decadent breasts fill my hands." He sucked on her pulse point, causing her toes to curl. "And I know whose cunny I will be filling."

Isabel shivered at the crude promise of his words.

With a groan, Sirius surged up to fuse his lips with hers, wrapping his arms about her and pulling her flush with his chest. The feel of his coarse hair abrading the tender skin of her breasts made her squirm, her pelvis bearing down on the hard ridge of flesh still encased in his trousers.

"Sirius, por favor," she pleaded, clutching his hair and holding his face close to hers.

"Say it again," he gritted as his grip tightened around her.

"Make me feel good." Isabel rolled her hips, moaning at the hard feel of him *there*. "Por favor."

In a whirl of movements, Sirius spun her about until she lay tucked under him, looking up into his boundless indigo eyes.

He said not a word, instead placing a quick kiss to her lips before walking to his desk to extract a small box from a compartment. Undoing the remaining buttons on his placket as he returned, Sirius pushed his trousers and drawers over his narrow hips and knees, kicking them aside when they fell at his feet. Seizing her gaze, he opened the box and pulled out a narrow sheath of some sort. Grabbing his length, which stood hard and pressed against his abdomen, Sirius gave it a firm stroke before he pulled the sheath over himself. Isabel had heard of condoms before, especially after Charles Goodyear had successfully vulcanized the rubber used to create them some years before, but she hadn't dreamed of seeing one herself. A bubble of gratitude lodged in her throat that Sirius had thought to protect her in such a way.

"Is this the first time you've seen a man undressed?" he asked, propping a knee on the settee near her thigh.

Isabel shook her head. "But he wasn't like . . . *this*."

His brow quirked up, and the corner of Sirius's mouth followed suit. "He wasn't erect?"

"No," she whispered.

"Do you know what it means when a man is erect?"

Swallowing, Isabel nodded.

Sirius grasped the inside of her thighs and spread them wide. Wide enough to fit his hips between them. Gripping his thick flesh, he pumped it once, twice, before cocking a brow. "It means the man is aroused. Eager to copulate."

Isabel trembled, her body pulsing at his words.

"It means the man wants to fuck." Leaning down, Sirius kissed her, sucking on her tongue until she whimpered. "May I fuck you, Isabel?"

A sob lodged in her throat, and Isabel could only nod.

"Are you sure?" he panted against her lips. "If we do this, there's no turning back. There's no returning what I'm about to take."

Arching her back to grind against his swollen flesh, Isabel moaned. "There's no taking when it's freely given."

With a stifled groan, Sirius captured her lips with his own.

Even while his mouth played a hypnotic melody over hers, Isabel was still aware enough to know when he ran a thumb along her seam, cutting off her gasp with a kiss. But instead of pulling his hand away in embarrassment or chagrin, Sirius hooked his other hand under her knee and spread her legs wide. Pulling back, he stared down into her eyes as he ran his member up and down her sensitive flesh. Isabel panted, her heart threatening to lurch out of her chest.

Sirius clenched his eyes closed, a harsh sound slipping from his lips. "Christ, I'm not even inside you and you already feel so good."

Isabel grasped the seat back with one hand, the other clutched at his hip, and dug her heels into the cushion underneath her, anything to gain purchase. Anything to moor herself for the onslaught of sensations—*pleasure*—he was subjecting her to.

"Por favor," she begged, tossing her head back as he finally notched his member at her opening.

"Look at me."

Isabel dragged her gaze to meet his. Sirius looked down at her as if she were the sunrise after a long, dark night, and slowly pushed inside her. Gritting her teeth, she willed herself to relax. Not to shy away from the sting, the uncomfortable pressure and stretch she felt as his body made a home within hers. Instead, Isabel kept her gaze connected with his, the glimpses of pleasure in his blue eyes the salve she needed to withstand the discomfort.

When his hips eventually met hers, a breath shuddered from his chest, and Sirius dropped his head forward to press it to hers. "Are you all right?"

She jerked a nod. "Are you?"

Sirius hissed between his teeth as he slowly pulled his hips back, and then thrust them forward again, his gaze avid on her face. "You feel unbelievable." He buried his nose in that hidden spot beneath her ear and inhaled deeply. "You're unbelievable."

Soul-deep bliss licked up her spine, and Isabel tentatively arched her back into his next thrust, sighing in delight. "This feels unbelievably good."

He smiled down into her eyes then, grasping her hips as his next stroke surged deeper. "Oh, sunshine, I'm going to make you feel so good."

And Sirius set out to do just that. Every movement of his powerful body elicited starbursts of euphoria that whited out her sight and stole the breath from her lungs. The only thing that seemed to exist was the ecstasy he coaxed from her with each stroke of his hips, for how could life possibly exist outside this moment? How would she ever be able to go back to being the Isabel of seasons past after she'd been shot into the heavens and given a glimpse of pure, unadulterated pleasure?

Before she knew it, Isabel teetered on the edge of that crevasse again, the one Sirius had taken her to before. Her thighs quivered around his, and sweat trailed between her breasts. Reaching up, Isabel twirled his short blond hair between her fingers and yanked him down to kiss her.

"I'm so close," she whimpered, writhing beneath him. "I feel like I'm about to crawl out of my skin."

Sirius smoothed his palm down the center of her chest, over her abdomen, and to the top of her sex. "We can't let that happen. Let me help you."

And he pressed the pad of his thumb to the nub tucked into the hood of her sex.

It wasn't until moments later that Isabel realized the ringing in her ears was caused by her own shriek. Violent pleasure quaked through her flesh, and Isabel sank her nails into his thighs as she squeezed around him, her body intent on pulling him under just as sure as she had been. She was vaguely aware of Sirius's movements growing erratic, of his grip tightening almost painfully on her hips, before he dropped his head to her chest as his body stuttered.

Isabel panted softly as Sirius climbed from the settee and returned moments later after discarding the sheath. He maneuvered himself onto the narrow settee next to her, his chest pressed to her back. Scooping his shirt from the floor, he draped it over her like a makeshift blanket and then wrapped his arms about her. With his thumb rubbing over her knuckles and the gentle rise and fall of his chest behind her, Isabel's limbs relaxed. Cocooned in his embrace, she felt precious. She felt treasured.

The soft tick of a clock sounded from somewhere in the room, and Isabel allowed its steady rhythm to lull her heartbeat, and soon it was impossible to keep her eyes open.

Suddenly, Sirius's embrace grew tight about her.

"I'm sorry, Isabel," he breathed, burying his face in her hair. "You deserved to have your first time in a bed, surrounded by comfort and luxury. And all I offered you was this uncomfortable settee in my dark library."

Running her nails up his arm, she pressed a finger to his hand. "Sirius, I can't think of a better place for my first sexual experience. I'm surrounded by the things that have brought such solace and joy to my life. I am more comfortable here, with you, in front of all these books than I would have been in the grandest bed."

She craned her head to meet his gaze. "This is poetic, don't you think? Every one of our most contentious encounters occurred within studies and libraries. First at the Meadows ball, then at Dancourt Abbey, and then in Westhope's library." Prickles of guilt spread like ripples down her spine, but Isabel aggressively pushed the sensations away. "And now here, at your home."

His throat worked for a long moment. "I don't quite understand why you would grace me with such an honor. You've seen the worst side of me, over and over again. I've felt your disdain—your disappointment—so often. And though I'm used to disappointing people, it always hurt more acutely knowing it was you whom I had displeased."

Sirius was used to disappointing people? *What does he mean?* He continued before Isabel could voice the question.

"But you're here with me now. Why, Isabel?"

Why indeed? Isabel didn't know how to respond. Should she tell him the truth? The truth that she was in love with him, despite her future in Mexico and his roguish life here in London. And yet Isabel did not know how to tell her heart not to love him.

But knowing better than to admit as much, and already feeling vulnerable in his presence, she twined her fingers with his and squeezed.

"Because I want to be."

16

When had Everhart ever looked so young?

The thought pinged in Sirius's mind as he grasped his old friend under his arms and hauled him to his feet. Without a word, the pair dashed through the underbrush away from the pounding of horse hooves and ring of cannon fire.

"You should have left me, you daft idiot," Everhart panted, limping along beside Sirius. "I can't possibly outrun these Russian bastards with my ankle in this shape."

"Perhaps if you stopped complaining and focused on surviving, you'd have no trouble outrunning danger," Sirius bit back, pressing them to an oak tree and peering around its broad trunk.

They were being pursued, but try as he might to peer through the surrounding murkiness clinging to the forest floor, Sirius could not make out the enemy. Prickles of unease crept like spiders' legs across his neck.

"It's not complaining to speak the truth," Everhart had tossed back on the acrid breeze, his devil-may-care tone unchanged despite the threats lurking like unseen monsters around them. "And even if I can't outrun them, I know you'll be there to protect me."

Suddenly, without warning, the oak tree Sirius had been hid-

den behind shifted under his hands, and he stumbled back and
fell on his arse as the largest serpent he had ever seen uncoiled
from the ground before him. Yellow eyes glared down at him,
and a scream froze in his throat as Sirius scrambled to grab his
friend. But Everhart lay prone and unmoving on the ground, his
complexion waxy and pale. The serpent lunged for him, and Sir-
ius dove to block it, his fear fleeing as bloodlust surged through
his limbs like opium. He wrapped his arms around the beast's
neck and squeezed—

"Wake up, Sirius."

He moaned in the back of his throat, confusion cutting through the vision before him like a hot knife through butter until the serpent dissipated. With frantic jerks of his head, he searched for Everhart, but he was nowhere—

"Sirius, you're dreaming. It's just a dream."

A dream? Sirius attempted to open his eyes, but it was a herculean task, for while his mind screamed at him to awaken, his body refused to do so.

A solid, warm hand pressed to his chest, and heat spread through his blood, yanking him back to reality like a shepherd's hook.

Kisses rained down upon his brow, a familiar vanilla scent descending over him like a springtime shower, washing clean the memories. Blinking his eyes open, Sirius found Isabel staring down at him.

"That's it, cariño. You're here with me, at your library in London. I'm so impressed with your collection."

Sirius moved until he could bury his face in the crook of her neck, his arm going around her waist and pulling her flush with his chest. Wishing dearly that he could soak her into his skin.

"It must have taken you years to build it up," she said, her breath shifting the hairs along his temple.

Licking his dry lips, Sirius tried to attend to her words. He knew why she had mentioned it. Or rather he thought so. If Isabel was attempting to anchor him to the moment, she had succeeded. "Since I was released from the hospital after I returned to England."

Her breath hitched for a moment. "You were in the hospital?"

Sirius nodded.

"What happened?"

Her voice was gentle. Curious. Sirius didn't want to discuss it, not with his dream—his *nightmare*—so vivid in his mind, but it was impossible to deny her.

"I took an artillery shot to the side. The surgeons said it was a miracle that it missed my internal organs." He swallowed, memories of the pain returning to him during inconvenient moments. "I was lucky enough to be carted from the field not long after the injury, and field doctors tended to me immediately. They saved my life."

"And I'm grateful to them." Isabel ran her knuckles across his cheekbone. "You don't appear particularly happy about your good fortune."

Sirius barked a hoarse laugh. "It doesn't feel like good fortune when so many of my fellow soldiers were not as lucky."

Isabel dropped her head to rest over his heart. "Lo siento. I—I can't imagine how devastating that was." She pressed a kiss to his skin. "How devastating it still is."

He'd thought the burden of his grief, of his guilt, would become easier to bear the more time passed, and yet they were his constant companions. Sirius's nightmare had been inconvenient after so many weeks without one, but perhaps Providence sought to remind him that he was undeserving of the small doses of happiness he managed to steal from a life devoted to penance.

"It's why you have so many former soldiers working for you. Why so many of your men make their homes at Dancourt Abbey." Isabel lifted her head, her eyes darting between his. "Why you try so hard to take care of them all."

They weren't questions. Isabel may not have understood the guilt that motivated so many of his actions—and he was not ready to tell her—but she grasped his intentions. That he didn't have to explain it to her was a relief . . . but Sirius still wanted to try.

"This country doesn't do enough to care for the men who serve it. Who fight for it." It abruptly felt like he'd swallowed nails, but he pushed down the sensation. "So many of them return injured and scarred, most with internal wounds that will never heal. And they grapple with slipping back into a mold that no longer fits the jagged edges of the men that war shaped them to be."

Although Sirius did not say it, Isabel's hold on him tightened, and he knew that she understood he was speaking from experience.

"And so you do what the Crown does not." She pressed a kiss to his cheek. "Is that why you also work for the Home Office?"

Closing his eyes, Sirius let his silence answer.

They lay quietly next to each other for a time, the steady rise and fall of his chest almost syncing with hers. Isabel ran her fingers through his hair, her touch soothing his frayed sensibilities. But after a time, she sighed.

"I need to leave. The sun will rise in an hour or two."

Sirius wished she didn't have to go. He longed to spend the day with her, preferably on the expansive bed in his chamber, tangled in the bedsheets. But just like his nightmare, their dreamlike stasis could only hold back reality for so long.

"I'll walk you back," he murmured, kissing her cheek.

Dressing silently, Sirius helped her with the laces of her corset and refastened her dress, and Isabel adjusted his cravat tie until it lay respectably against his white shirt. He watched her fix her hair, tucking the sweet-smelling black curls into a sensible bun, the suffocating feeling of despair, of loss, twisting tight around his chest. Could they possibly go back to their lives as if their night together had never happened? As if she had not just reordered the structure, the composition of his chemistry, with the taste of her lips?

When her person was put to rights, Sirius helped drape her black cloak over her shoulders, before he spun her about and cinched it closed under her chin. Holding her eyes, he pulled the hood up over her head, shrouding her in shadows.

"Are you ready?" she asked, reaching out to grasp his hand.

Was he? Was he ready for matters between them to return to how they'd been before? Was Sirius prepared to watch Viscount Westhope continue his courtship when he now knew the bliss to be found in the tight, wet heat of her body? Could he meet her gaze from across a crowded ballroom and not want to immediately go to her and pull her into his arms? Was it possible to watch her laugh and converse with another man when he knew the narcotic rush of being the sole focus of her attention?

"I am," he said instead, for he didn't deserve the rest.

If Stanley, his butler, was still awake at this obscene hour, he had enough sense and discretion not to alert Sirius to his presence. He was grateful, because the fewer people who saw him smuggle Isabel Luna from his home the better. As much as he wished to keep her reputation intact, Sirius also had a great deal to lose if they were discovered. Surely his work for the Home Office would suffer, and his older brother, Harcourt, would be livid if Sirius were to bring scandal to his doorstep. It was enough that he'd returned to England injured but alive. When Harcourt had visited Sirius as he convalesced, he said it would have been better if Sirius had perished as a hero rather than returning to British shores as a shattered man.

His older brother's callousness, especially when Sirius was already so low, was a blow he doubted he would ever recover from.

Yet Harcourt's condemning voice whispered in his ear the entire walk back to Lady Yardley's townhome. Although pink was beginning to streak through the early morning sky, Sirius kept a wary eye on every shadow they passed. His vigilance reminded him that Isabel had come to him without an escort, and the possibilities of how she could have been maimed turned Sirius's grip on her hand into steel.

Although Isabel held her silence, Sirius sensed her agitation. Her hand on his arm trembled slightly, and her steps on the walk became wooden and awkward. Sirius knew he was the reason for Isabel's uncharacteristic moroseness, and a dozen reasons clanged about in his head. Was she embarrassed by what he revealed of his injury? Did she regret losing her virginity to a man whose polished veneer hid so much brokenness?

Instead of asking, he said nothing at all. Everything seemed to have changed during their hours spent together, and for once, he didn't know how to proceed. His confusion and uneasiness poisoned the air around them, and Sirius could feel Isabel's eyes return to his face again and again as they walked. When they finally reached their destination, Isabel abruptly grabbed him by the bicep and thrust him into the shadows that lurked near the servants' entrance. Sirius frowned down at her, frustrated he could not see her face.

"We can't linger here, but I have to know what's wrong," she whispered.

Sirius was shaking his head before Isabel was done speaking. "Nothing is wrong. I was just focused on the walk."

Her scoff echoed in the small garden. "Querido, your expression was frustrated, not focused. A-are you irritated you had to walk me home?"

"Of course not," he snapped.

"Then what is it?" Isabel demanded.

"I—I . . ." Sirius's brain scrambled to find a viable excuse to cover his tumultuous thoughts. "I was just thinking about when I would be able to see you again."

There. That sounded believable. It was also true.

"Oh." Isabel turned to look up at the house, the sole lantern burning near the back walk illuminating the fall of her nose and plump shape of her lips. "I believe Lady Yardley canceled our engagements for the next day or two because she was feeling unwell."

"That's fortuitous." At Isabel's snort, Sirius hastened to add, "For us, not for her ladyship."

At least he didn't have to worry about Westhope trying to steal a kiss from her.

"Would you be willing to meet me?" A breathless note filled her voice. "To decide what I can do next?"

"Of course," Sirius said promptly. "I'm not terribly certain of where we can meet that will shield us from detection, but I will think of options from now until then. How about I send a carriage to the corner this afternoon, and you can meet me there?"

Isabel nodded. "That will work. Thank you."

Without another word, Sirius pulled her into his arms. Isabel stiffened for a moment, but eventually the starch left her form. Twining her arms about his waist, she tucked her face into his chest.

"Someone may see us," her muffled voice said.

"They might."

"It would almost be worth it, because you smell so good," Isabel hummed.

Sirius buried his face in her hair. "I'm delighted you think so."

They stayed in each other's arms for several more heartbeats before Isabel stepped away. "I'll see you later today."

He nodded, and watched her disappear into the house, his heart pounding in his throat. As he pivoted to depart, Sirius scrubbed his jaw as he allowed all his warring emotions to fall over him. He certainly didn't regret the night he spent with Isabel—Sirius could *never* regret it—but with sinking clarity, he realized how vulnerable she made him. A decidedly frightening development.

Isabel made it to her chamber in time to see Sirius disappear around the corner at the end of the block. Letting the drapes fall back into place, she wandered to the bed and collapsed upon it in a heap.

Sirius had whispered the sweetest sentiments in her ear as he stroked within her body and brought her to heights of pleasure Isabel did not even know were possible. And when he stared into her eyes, she could almost believe he loved her. *No,* she declared to herself. Isabel couldn't allow her thoughts to venture down that path. Covering her face with her hands, she pushed the memories of the night into the corner of her mind, where she could make herself believe they wouldn't haunt her.

Isabel felt as if she'd only just rested her head on the pillow when a hand gripped her shoulder and shook her awake.

Grumbling obscenities, she rolled over and glared at Gabby, who sat perched next to her on the bed.

"I returned from Ana's an hour ago." Her sister's gaze roved over Isabel's face. "You never sleep this late. Are you unwell?"

Smoothing the hair back from her brow, Isabel flung an arm over her eyes. "I'm fine. Just feeling a bit tired."

"Obviously." Gabby paused, and Isabel could practically hear her thoughts whirling about. "What did you do last night that made you so tired today?"

"Nothing of note. Lady Yardley and I had dinner, we sat together for a spell afterward, and she retired early." Isabel snorted. "It's not like I'm the most engaging conversationalist."

"I beg to differ." Gabby paused again, and when the silence stretched a tad too long, Isabel peeked out from behind her arm to look at her. Gabby stared back at her with her brows raised. "Is that it?"

A frown tugged on Isabel's lips. "Well, I read for a while, and then retired myself."

Gabby's eyes narrowed. "I don't know that I believe you."

Isabel pulled herself into a sitting position, tucking the sheet about her, and glared at her sister. "What are you implying?"

"I'm not implying anything. I'm stating"— Gabby enunciated the word with harsh *t*'s—"that I think you were somewhere else last night, and that's why you're so tired today."

"Don't be silly," Isabel shot back, although her voice was high-pitched to her own ears. Of course her sister—her altogether too perceptive baby sister—would notice Isabel's out-of-character behavior. An ache pulsed behind her eyelids. Still, she refused to admit anything, not at all ready to share *whatever* was happening between her and Sirius.

"Do you always sleep in your cloak?"

Isabel jerked her gaze down at the question, a stone settling in her stomach when she realized the sheet was actually her black cloak. *Mierda.*

Panicking, she tried to rally an excuse. "I forgot to take it off when I came in from my walk in the garden."

Her sister just stared at her, her hazel eyes unamused.

"Where would I even go? And with whom?" Isabel threw up her hands. "You and Ana are my only friends."

Gabby scowled. "Well, I know that's not true."

"What does that mean?"

"What that means, Isa," Gabby growled, reaching out to grab her arm, "is that Captain Dawson is your friend, too."

Just hearing Gabby say his name sent flames searing across her cheeks, and Isabel ducked her head. She didn't dare meet her sister's gaze.

Clearing her throat, she eventually answered, "Yes, well, that certainly doesn't mean I was out with him last night."

Lies! Alarms sounded in her head, her mind noting that she had never lied so blatantly to Gabby before. And it was apparent her sister didn't believe her, because she rolled her eyes.

"I don't understand why you won't tell me the truth." Gabby cocked her head, her lips twisting into a smirk. "It's not like I'm asking if he's a good kisser or if he takes his time—"

"Ay, why must you always be so much?" Isabel snapped, even while she fought back an exasperated laugh. "Whatever is happening between Sirius and me will stay between us."

"Que aburrido." Gabby considered her for a moment longer and exhaled loudly. "Very well, then. But please know that you are more than welcome to confess all your sins to me instead of Father Duncan should you feel the need to unburden yourself."

Isabel tutted. "That's sacrilegious, traviesa."

Rising to her feet, Gabby shrugged as she walked to the door. "What are your plans for today?"

Isabel licked her lips. "I don't have any. Lady Yardley canceled our engagements for today because she's under the weather, so I thought I would spend the day reading. Maybe go for a walk."

She was pleased by how normal she sounded . . . although her heart was still lurching in her chest.

"Perhaps I can accompany you on that walk," Gabby said, her tone just a tad too blasé.

"T-that"—Isabel coughed into her fist, unease scratching at her throat—"that would be wonderful."

Gabby inclined her head and then opened the door, stepping into the hall. "See you downstairs."

Isabel stared at the closed door for a long moment and then dropped her head into her hands. How was she ever to meet with Sirius if Gabby insisted on accompanying her?

Dragging herself from bed, wincing at the twinge of discomfort between her thighs, Isabel wandered into her dressing room. As she stared unseeing at her selection of day dresses, Isabel fervently prayed to Saint Jude, the patron saint of lost causes, for a way to keep Gabby from ruining her assignation with Sirius.

Her nerves gradually abated when she joined Gabby and Lady Yardley in the drawing room. Although she felt her sister's gaze on her throughout the afternoon, Isabel did her best to ignore her. Instead, she listened to Lady Yardley's long list of complaints about her health, and feigned interest when she shared the bits of gossip she gleaned from the newspapers. Isabel had never been particularly close with the older woman, whose spirited personality both complemented and clashed with Gabby's, but she genuinely liked and respected the viscountess. Lady Yardley had welcomed her and her sisters as if they were her own family, and provided them with the opportunity to build a new life in England. So if she had to be an audience member to the woman's chatter, Isabel would do so willingly.

Eventually, Lady Yardley was distracted by the post, which Bauer, her lady's maid, brought to her in a basket. While she read aloud the invitations, often with added commentary about the sender, Isabel snuck another look at the clock on the sideboard. Sirius had said the carriage would be waiting for her at three o'clock, which was in an hour. Fighting the urge to nibble on her lip, Isabel slid her gaze to Gabby . . . to find her sister staring at her.

Gesturing with her chin to the clock, she asked, "Should we prepare for our walk?"

Damn it.

"Good idea," Isabel replied, hoping she appeared nonplussed.

Gabby didn't allow her a moment to plan for a diversion, instead following Isabel into her chamber and dismissing Lupe. She proceeded to rifle through Isabel's walking dresses while she clicked her tongue. Selecting a turquoise ensemble and holding it up to Isabel, Gabby hummed.

"I don't care that some people think blue is unsuitable for brunettes," she grumbled, spinning Isabel about to unbutton her day dress. "This color looks stunning against your skin."

Isabel glanced at her sister over her shoulder. "I adore the color, but I haven't worn it because I thought it might make my skin look darker."

"And why is that a bad thing?" Gabby asked.

Without waiting for a reply, she pushed Isabel's day dress over her hips and then promptly dropped the turquoise walking dress over her head. After Isabel had managed to slip her arms through the sleeves, she waited patiently for Gabby to lace up the back. Once that task was complete, her sister grabbed her by the hand and led her to the small dressing table. Encouraging Isabel to sit, Gabby set out tweaking her curls until they cascaded down her back in a style Isabel would never have dreamed of trying but would readily admit looked flattering on her. When the coiffure was to her liking, Gabby produced a decorative hat from her own collection. It was simple by Gabby's own standards, with a modest brim and a black velvet bow whose ribbons would drape over the back of the wearer's head. Isabel had always thought it quite pretty, but when Gabby perched it on her head and pinned it in place, pleasure warmed her chest.

"Do you like it, Isa?" her sister asked.

"I do. Thank you for letting me wear it."

Gabby nodded, but didn't say anything, fussing with the fall of the ribbons instead. Isabel watched her, confusion knotting her tongue. Finally, she asked, "Hermana, we're just going for a walk. Why are you dressing me as if I'm meeting someone special?"

Lifting her head, Gabby met her gaze in the mirror. "Because perhaps you will."

A prickling sensation crept along her scalp, and Isabel dropped her eyes. After a long moment, she finally said, "Would you like me to help you dress?"

"I'll be fine." Gabby clasped her shoulder and squeezed. "I'll be downstairs shortly."

Isabel nodded, watching in the mirror as her sister left the room. Turning back to her reflection, she smiled. The turquoise color did look striking against her dark skin . . . and suddenly Isabel wondered why she had let other people's opinions of her looks become her own opinions. She was striking, she was appealing . . . she was memorable, not despite her Purépecha ancestry, but because of it.

With that revelation in mind, Isabel made her way downstairs. After accepting a shawl from Evans, the butler, Isabel lingered in the lobby, waiting for Gabby to appear.

Instead she was met by Bauer.

"Miss Gabriela asked me to tell you that she has come down with a megrim, and won't be able to walk out with you."

Isabel's mouth gaped. "Gabby's not coming?"

"She's not, miss," Bauer said, bobbing a curtsy before walking away.

Even as she stood on the front step, blinking against the bright sunlight, Isabel tried to make sense of what had just happened. Her sister had picked out her best walking dress, styled her hair, and made her feel beautiful . . . only to leave her to walk on her own? Glancing up at the window to Gabby's chamber, Isabel would swear she could see her sister lurking behind the curtains. Gabby must have guessed that she planned to meet Sirius, and had taken the time to make Isabel feel confident in her appearance before she did.

A powerful wave of love surged through her, and Isabel blew a kiss up at the window, before spinning about and heading down the street.

As she approached the corner, her half boots clicking on the walk, the snouts of first one horse and then the other came into view. Her pulse pounded erratically, eager to see Sirius's handsome face and hear his rich voice. Increasing her pace, Isabel turned the corner, a smile already stretching her lips . . . when she stumbled to a halt. For there stood Sirius, with Lady Needham wrapped around his arm.

17

Watching the smile slip from Isabel's lips was like a punch in the face . . . but knowing he was the reason sucked all the air from his lungs.

Sirius had been on a knife-edge all day since he'd said goodbye to Isabel, anxiously glancing at the clock, waiting until he could see her again. Dressing with care, Sirius had then paced around his study, flipping through first one book and then another, distracting himself by keeping a mental list of the books he wanted to discuss with her. Sirius had wasted so much time since he'd met Isabel, time he could have spent watching her face light up when she was interested in a topic, listening to the quirky workings of her mind, quoting poetry to her while they made love . . .

When the time came to finally ask for the carriage to be brought around, Sirius checked his reflection in the mirror, accepted the cane Stanley held out to him, and walked outside. As the conveyance rumbled over the streets, Sirius daydreamed about pulling Isabel into the carriage cab, kissing her senseless before dragging his kisses lower. And when the tremors had finally left her limbs and her eyes turned dreamy,

Sirius would gather her in his arms and finally discuss her search.

The driver pulled the carriage to a stop, and Sirius hopped out without waiting for a footman to open the door. Tapping his cane on the walk, Sirius peered down the street toward Yardley House. He tried to imagine Isabel getting ready to meet him. Was she as nervous as he was? As eager? Sirius ripped his hat off his head and dragged a hand through his hair. Had he ever been so flustered in his life? Despite his many years of service with the Home Office or in the cavalry, this moment left him feeling completely off-balance. His friends—his men—would laugh if they could see him now.

"Dawson," a feminine voice called, "whatever are you doing here?"

His stomach dropped to his feet. Clamping his teeth together, Sirius spun on his heel, his gaze landing on Emily, Lady Needham.

"Your ladyship, how do you do?" Sirius asked, executing a crisp bow.

Mayhap if he was polite but distant, Lady Needham would lose interest because he was no longer a willing participant in her flirtations.

"I'm doing much better now that I've seen you," she said, her voice saccharine sweet.

Or not. Sirius bit back a sigh.

"Why are you waiting here with your carriage?" The baroness rotated her head to look up and down the street, her green gaze keen. "Are you waiting for someone?"

"Indeed, I am," he replied. Lady Needham raised her brows, as if expecting him to continue, but Sirius held his tongue. He didn't owe the baroness an explanation.

Lady Needham studied his face for a moment, before looking

about them again. She seemed to come to some sort of decision, for her lips tipped up into a hungry smile, and she sidled
closer.

"It's been so long since we've spent time together." She
wrapped her arm around his, pressing into his side. "Why
have you not come to see me?"

Sirius stepped backward, hoping to create some distance
between them, but the baroness clung to him tighter. "I've
been busy, unfortunately. I'm hoping to sojourn to my estate in
Devonshire soon, and have had much to prepare."

It was not a lie. Sirius had been itching for several months
now to return to Dancourt Abbey and the relaxing change of
pace it offered. Plus, he wanted to see how Jack O'Brien and
his family had adjusted to life at the abbey. His steward had
mentioned the Irishman had been praised as a hard worker by
the stable manager, but Sirius wanted to follow up personally.
Plus, the wheat and orchard harvest would happen soon, and
Sirius intended to be present for both.

If not for Isabel, he would have found a way to be there now.

Lady Needham moved closer still, pressing her breasts
against his arm. "You know I would love to visit your estate.
Does your brother, Harcourt, visit frequently?"

Harcourt? His brother had never deigned to call upon him
at Dancourt Abbey, and Sirius doubted he ever would.

Resisting the urge to roll his eyes, Sirius opened his mouth
to respond, when he spied Isabel come around the corner.
Outfitted in a stunning blue-green dress, with a jaunty hat on
her black curls, she was bewitching . . . until her expression
shuttered. And she looked at him now as she had all those
months before when she thought him nothing but a cad.

A knot lodged in Sirius's throat that he doubted he'd ever
be able to swallow.

Despite that strangling thought, Sirius pried himself free from Lady Needham's grip and took a step in Isabel's direction. "Good afternoon, Miss Luna. It's a pleasure to see you."

Isabel's obsidian eyes searched his face before they slid to the baroness, who stood behind him. "Captain Dawson," she said simply, inclining her head.

"Miss Luna," Lady Needham crooned, stepping forward to stand beside Sirius, "where are you about on this sunny afternoon?"

"I—I was just . . ." Isabel stopped, her throat bobbing on a swallow. "I was on my way to visit my sister, Señora Fox."

It was a believable lie, even if Isabel's cheeks turned scarlet.

"Ah, an afternoon visit sounds lovely." The baroness cocked her head as her gaze traveled up and down Isabel. "That color is also lovely on you. It makes your complexion look darker, but that's all right. It's quite fetching nevertheless."

"Thank you, your ladyship," Isabel murmured. Smoothing a glove-covered hand across the waistband, she raised a shoulder. "My sister said it made my skin look luminous, which I admit made me quite pleased."

"As it should," Sirius interjected, moving toward her a half step. "It looks beautiful on you."

Isabel's gaze darted to his, her eyes softening a degree.

"I'd be happy to escort you to your sister's," he blurted out, desperate to escape the baroness and spend time with the woman he had been thinking about all day. "I haven't seen Fox in a week or so, and it would be nice to visit with him for a spell."

"Oh, that's a very kind offer—"

"Dawson, I thought you were waiting to meet someone."

Sirius whipped his head about to the baroness, who was staring back at him with narrowed eyes. Why was this woman determined to be so damn troublesome?

Quirking his mouth, he extracted a timepiece from his pocket and considered it. "I was. But the gentleman I was supposed to meet is now twenty minutes late, so it would seem . . ."

Sirius trailed off when he spotted Daniels, one of his footmen, lingering several paces away, his face blotchy and his chest moving rapidly up and down as if the man had run to meet him. Alarm crept up Sirius's spine.

He flashed a quick smile at Isabel and the baroness and said, "If you ladies would excuse me for a moment, it appears my appointment has arrived."

Before either lady could respond, Sirius stepped away, his gaze fixed on Daniels's. When he came to a stop in front of the man, Daniels shoved a square of parchment into his hands.

"Lieutenant Colonel Green had this delivered. The page indicated it was of great importance, so I came to find you," the man whispered.

"Fuck," Sirius growled, ripping the letter open without delay. It was only two sentences long.

They've found him. Visit if you want more information.

Rocking back on his heels, he reread the words. Did Green mean that the French had discovered President Juárez's hiding spot? Good God, he had to find out what the lieutenant colonel knew, and once he was confident of his intelligence, Sirius would let Isabel know.

"Thank you, Daniels," he said, clapping the man on the back. "I appreciate you bringing this to me as soon as you could."

"Of course, sir," Daniels said, dipping his head before departing.

Setting his shoulders, Sirius turned back to the women, intent on extracting Isabel from the situation as quickly as possible, but halted. Isabel no longer stood with Lady Needham, but instead was sitting in a well-sprung curricle that had parked behind his carriage. At her side, holding the reins, was Lord Westhope.

What the hell?

Surprise stole his words, and before Sirius could even call out to her, the curricle pulled away. Westhope offered him a friendly wave as they passed, but Isabel simply looked at him, her expressionless mask back in place. Sirius watched them drive away until they disappeared into the park, and he cursed under his breath.

"Now that we're alone, say you'll return with me to my house, Sirius," Lady Needham said, tapping him on the arm with her fan. "I've missed you."

Biting back unkind words, Sirius turned to look at her. "Unfortunately, my lady, that will not be possible. But I hope you have a good day."

And with that goodbye, he climbed the steps of his carriage. "Take me to the Home Office," he called to his driver, before stepping into the cab and slamming the door.

Clenching his head in his hands, Sirius groaned. How had the day turned so disastrous?

"How fortuitous it was to see you on the street, Miss Luna, when I was on my way to Yardley House to call upon you," Lord Westhope said, flashing a bright smile at her.

Isabel attempted a smile in return. "A happy accident."

"Indeed." The viscount tipped his hat at a passing carriage. "Lady Needham seemed quite pleased that I had whisked you away when I did. Rumor is that she's been pursuing Dawson for some time, and no doubt she knew your clever wit would showcase what a bore she is."

Turning about in her seat, Isabel stared at him. "You think Lady Needham is a bore?"

Westhope's brow crinkled. "Please forgive me if that sentiment was rude, but while the baroness is perfectly amiable, she is a bit empty-headed, don't you think?"

She opened her mouth, but paused, uncertain of what she was going to say. Lady Needham had not been friendly to her, and her remarks were sometimes barbed. But more often, she simply ignored Isabel, which made her one of many. It certainly wasn't the baroness's fault that she was smitten with Sirius and wanted more from him than he could give her.

It was a feeling Isabel was acquainted with.

Isabel faced forward again. "Not everyone is as quick-witted and intelligent as you, my lord."

Westhope's gaze was heavy on her face; Isabel could feel it even though she steadfastly avoided looking at him. "I'm not sure about that."

They rode in silence for several minutes, and Isabel was content to watch the scenery roll past. Summer had arrived and the landscape eagerly welcomed it, the trees dressing themselves in juniper and sage, flowers in lavender and cerise. Pulling her shawl from her shoulders, Isabel inhaled a fragrant breath of air. This was one thing she would miss when she returned to Mexico, for summer looked different in her homeland.

"Did I tell you the good news? That the manager at Hatchards sent a note to my secretary to let me know that he had finally managed to secure a first edition of the first part of *Don Quixote*?" Westhope asked abruptly, snaring Isabel's attention.

Isabel shook her head. She knew she should be excited he'd finally found the edition he'd long coveted, and yet she struggled to find the necessary enthusiasm. Still, she tried. "What an incredible find."

Lord Westhope laughed. "I can't tell you how thrilled I am at the prospect of finally possessing one. It only took three years, four shopkeepers, and two rare book hunters."

She reached for a smile. "I daresay I would be filled to the brim with excitement to own a first edition of *El ingenioso hidalgo don Quixote de la Mancha*."

"I love the way you say that." Westhope slid his eyes to look at her, the color rising in his cheeks. "The way you shape the words is so enchanting."

"Oh, well, thank you." Isabel ducked her head. She was so rarely complimented on her Spanish that it always caught her unawares. "Gabby and I discussed not long ago how much we miss hearing Spanish. Speaking in Spanish with others. It is a very different experience than speaking English."

"That makes sense. I know speaking French, especially speaking it with a native speaker, uses my brain in ways it doesn't when I converse in English." A wistful look settled on Westhope's face. "It makes me a tad melancholy for my French family."

The hairs on Isabel's arm rose, and she held her breath. It was just the sort of opening Isabel needed, and she released a long exhale as she contemplated how to advance. "You mentioned previously that you are a frequent correspondent with your cousin in the Caribbean, is that right?"

The viscount flashed her a pleased grin. "I'm flattered you remember. Yes, Jean-Charles lives in Martinique, where he works for the governor of the island. We communicate quite regularly. I actually received a letter from him today."

When Westhope extracted a letter from his front pocket to

show her the postage mark, elation surged through Isabel's chest. The letter was new. Did it finally contain information she could use? The possibility left her almost lightheaded, and Isabel knotted her hands together so she was not tempted to pluck the correspondence from his fingers.

"Even reading French is a different experience," the viscount continued, unaware of Isabel's tense silence. "For instance, he was just telling me—"

The conveyance jerked to a halt, and Isabel reached out a hand to brace herself against the front panel. Frowning, she turned to Westhope, who was already leaning over the edge of the curricle to inspect what might have occurred.

"I think one of the horses may have slipped a shoe." He sat up and passed the reins to her hands. "I'm going to give it a look. I shouldn't be more than a few minutes."

"O-of course," she stuttered, watching as he climbed from the curricle and jumped to the ground.

Stifling a sigh, Isabel looked about. The walk wasn't particularly busy, but nor were they alone. If Westhope was in need of assistance, help would arrive in no time, a fact Isabel was grateful for, as holding the reins made her a bit nervous. She was comfortable enough on the back of a horse, but had not had many opportunities to drive a team. The thought that two powerful bays were controlled by the strips of leather in her hands had perspiration beading at her hairline.

Isabel squared her shoulders, holding the reins more firmly. She was in control. The beasts would not be able to move if she—

The letter! Stifling a gasp, she whipped her head about trying to locate it . . . until she spied the parchment near her feet, where it must have fallen. Craning her neck, Isabel spied the viscount kneeling next to one of his bays, the beast's right back hoof nestled in his lap. Isabel knew she had only a few moments before he returned and her opportunity was lost.

Without a second thought, she quietly unfolded the letter and quickly read. It was written in French, and she murmured a prayer of thanks that her father had insisted she and her sisters learn the language as part of their studies.

The letter was not a long one, and was mostly filled with irreverent observations and tidbits of Jean-Charles's day. Isabel gritted her teeth in frustration at its mundane contents . . . that is until she reached the last paragraph, and terror cinched her chest tight.

> *I don't know when my next letter will reach you. We're leaving for Mexico tomorrow because Maximilian has called upon the French garrison stationed here. Word is that the imperial army has discovered the rebel president's hiding place, and the emperor wants to stamp him out and finally put an end to this rebellion.*

She felt as if her entire body had been dunked in ice water, and she stared unseeing at the parchment. The French had finally found Presidente Juárez? And if they had found Presidente Juárez, they had found her parents. Her chest rose and fell as her breaths turned into pants, and Isabel clenched her eyes closed, her mind reeling. She needed to tell Tío Arturo. *Now.* Without delay. Surely her uncle would be able to get the message to the president before the French captured him.

A rattling breath slipped past her lips, and Isabel carefully refolded the letter and placed it back on the squab, where the viscount had left it. Twisting her hands around the reins, Isabel desperately tried to calm her breathing. It would do her no good to arouse Westhope's suspicions. Jean-Charles's lack of circumspection about sending such sensitive information to him made her uneasy; did the viscount know more about the imperial government in Mexico than he let on? Isabel didn't think so, but with her parents' lives and freedom on the line, she could not afford to trust him.

"Well, he'd definitely thrown a shoe, but we should be able to make it back to Yardley House without issue, as long as I don't push the team past a walk," Westhope said as he climbed into the carriage. He paused when he looked at her, his brows knitting together. "What's wrong, Miss Luna?"

¡Ay! "I just . . ." Isabel pressed a hand to her temple, excuses pinging about in her mind. "I wanted to ask if you would be kind enough to bring me to Señor Valdés's home? I was on my way there when I encountered Captain Dawson and Lady Needham."

"The Mexican ambassador?" When she nodded, Westhope blinked but immediately grabbed the reins from her. "Oh, of course. His residence is not far from here, and I would be happy to take you."

"That's very kind," Isabel murmured, daring to pat the back of his hand for a brief moment. "I intend to ask him if he can help me get a letter to my parents in Mexico City. I've been feeling quite homesick lately."

Westhope rotated his hand until their palms met, and he grasped hers tightly. "Well, then I won't be too disappointed that our ride is ending. I will try to get us to Mr. Valdés's as quickly as I can, but unfortunately with my lame horse, our pace may be a tad slower."

"I appreciate it," Isabel said with a nod before lapsing into silence. She hoped Westhope would take her silence as a wistful one filled with memories, and not because dread and fear for her parents had coiled in her gut like a venomous snake.

But the viscount was ever a gentleman, and did not engage her in conversation, instead making general observations about the people or sights they passed.

When they finally arrived at Tío Arturo's stately townhome, Isabel felt ready to jump out of her skin, and wished Lord Westhope a polite but swift goodbye. If he was taken aback by her brusque manner, his expression did not reveal it, and Isabel was thankful. All she cared about right now was alerting her parents to the danger that awaited them and Presidente Juárez, and nothing else.

"I look forward to seeing you again soon, Miss Luna," the viscount called as he took up the reins again and departed.

Offering a hasty wave, Isabel clasped her skirts and sprinted up the front steps. Before she could grasp the knocker, the door opened, revealing Señor Alvarez, the butler. Isabel slipped past him into the foyer, pacing to look down the hall toward Tío Arturo's study.

"¿Está aquí ahora?" she asked, a bit breathless.

Alvarez nodded his graying head, his brows knotted together. "¿Algo está mal, señorita?"

"Sí," Isabel said succinctly, before grasping her skirts and dashing toward the study.

Without waiting, she burst through the door. Her uncle was seated at his desk, reading a letter. At her abrupt entrance, he snatched his spectacles from his face and rose to his feet.

"Sobrina, what's happened?" he asked, coming around the desk to grasp her hands.

Swallowing down the sob that surged up her throat, Isabel managed to say, "The French have found them."

18

Isabel arrived at Yardley House after dark.

Gabby and the viscountess met her in the foyer, demanding to know where she had been. Mentally and emotionally drained, Isabel assured Lady Yardley she was well, but then grabbed her sister's hand and dragged her up the stairs to her room. Thankfully, Gabby held her tongue until Isabel had shut the door, and then whirled on her with large eyes.

"Dios mío, what happened?" she demanded, grasping Isabel's hands.

Somehow Isabel made it through a quick recitation of what had transpired in Lord Westhope's curricle, and then the notes she and Tío Arturo had written to those in Mexico. Her sister bombarded her with questions, and Isabel did her best to answer them, but some required more explanation than she had the energy for.

"Hermanita, I know there is more you want to know, but can your questions wait for the morning?" Isabel rubbed the heels of her hands into her eyes as she yawned. "The stress of the day is catching up with me."

"Bien," Gabby murmured, kissing the top of Isabel's head.

"Get some sleep, because I'm sure Ana will be here early to ask the same questions."

Just the thought exhausted her.

After Gabby left, Isabel allowed Lupe to strip off the turquoise walking dress that made her feel so beautiful, and pluck Gabby's fetching hat from her hair. Slipping a simple cotton nightdress over her head, Isabel shook out her curls and watched as Lupe fixed her hair in a single plait over her shoulder before bidding her good night. Wandering into her room, Isabel paced to her bookshelf and considered her selection. Lady Yardley had given her the six-shelf bookcase for her last birthday, and Isabel had been ecstatic to move her books from the trunk she'd stored them in since they escaped Mexico City. Seeing them on display, her favorite volumes organized by author and title, filled her with joy.

But even her oldest friends could not chase away the dread that sat on her chest.

Her chamber door opened behind her, and assuming it was a maid with a food tray, Isabel gestured to her desk with a hand. "You can put it there. Gracias."

At the sound of the door closing, Isabel pivoted . . . only to jump back, clapping a hand to her mouth.

"I'm sorry for scaring you," Sirius whispered, whipping off his hat and rushing forward to grasp her shoulders.

Isabel slowly dropped her hand and stared up at him with wide eyes. "What are you doing here? How did you get in here?"

"You're not the only one with a talent for slinking about." Sirius curled the tail of her braid around his finger. "And I came because I had to see you. Fate conspired against us this afternoon, but we still need to speak."

Without hesitation, Isabel wrapped her arms around his

waist and buried her face in his chest. "I'm so glad you did, because fate was actually on our side today."

"What do you mean?" Sirius asked, craning back to look into her eyes. "Did something happen?"

"I hope not. Not yet, at least." Isabel pressed her lips together for a long moment. "I pray my letter arrives before something terrible occurs."

Sirius bent down to hold her gaze. "Tell me."

"I finally found something. Some way to help," she whispered. "Westhope received a letter from his cousin, and I read it when he wasn't looking. The French have discovered where Presidente Juárez is hiding. They're preparing to capture him."

Her voice broke off with a hitch.

What if she was too late? What if the French found them before her letter could? What if a storm swept the ship bearing copies of her letter off course, and they never made it to her parents? Isabel had managed to block out all the horror of what could happen, of the precarious position her parents were in, by focusing on the task at hand. Her tío Arturo had hastily written several letters, each bearing the same message, and had them dispatched within minutes of her arrival. He assured her at least one of the letters would arrive before the French did, and Isabel clung to his confidence.

Yet, in the privacy of her room, pressed against Sirius, all the possibilities became too much. Isabel didn't know how she'd survive the guilt if something happened to her parents—to the president—because she had taken too long.

As if sensing how much she needed him, Sirius gathered her in his arms and carried her to the bed, where he cradled her against his chest. Tears streamed down her face as sobs rattled from her throat, and he stroked a hand along her back and brushed her tears away with his knuckles.

"If the warning doesn't reach them, or it gets there too late, I'll never forgive myself," she confessed around her tears.

Sirius pressed his lips to the crown of her head. "It'll get there, sunshine. I know it."

"I wish I had your confidence," she mumbled into the folds of his coat.

"Well," he began, an odd note to his voice, "I'm confident because you're not the only one to have sent notice."

Isabel reared back to meet his gaze. "What do you mean?"

"What I mean is that the Home Office also received intelligence that the French were marching north to capture President Juárez." Sirius smoothed his thumb over the crest of her cheek. "So a message was dispatched to British contacts within Mexico to alert the president. I signed your name to it."

Cotton seemed to fill her ears, and Isabel stammered, "M-my name?"

Sirius nodded. "I indicated that the intelligence had been discovered by a Mexican operative named Isabel Luna."

Isabel's jaw went slack. "But . . . but you didn't know what I had learned before you sent that note."

"I didn't." Sirius lifted a shoulder, his eyes trained on his knuckles as they swept down her cheek. "But I wanted them to believe the veracity of the warning, and I knew they would believe you because you're one of them."

Her eyes stung, and she blinked rapidly as she stared up at his dear face. "I don't know what to say."

"You don't have to say anything. You truly did unearth this information all on your own, and because you are a shrewd, discerning woman"—Sirius bussed her temple—"you immediately knew what to do with it to ensure it was delivered into the right hands. I'm proud of you, Isabel."

Clamping her eyes closed, Isabel let his words sweep over

her like a comforting breeze. The fear that froze her veins just moments ago had been tempered, and she was now infused with the warmth of rekindled hope.

"I'm so glad you're here," she whispered, opening her eyes and smiling.

His blue gaze turned tender. "Are you?"

Isabel nodded, the temperature of her blood quickly spiking. Her fingers plucked at the buttons on his coat before her hand moved up to play with the tie of his dress shirt, her fingertips brushing against the patch of skin hidden there.

"You've been so stressed, darling. Do you need to be soothed?" When she jerked her head in assent, Sirius smirked. "You know I can give you what you need," he whispered against her neck.

Her hand curled around his lapel as she nodded again.

"Because you know I'll keep you safe." Sirius kissed her jaw, his lips lingering against her skin.

Isabel turned to snare his lips, but he moved his face away.

"And you know I'll do anything to make you happy," he purred, his soothing scent filling her lungs.

She pressed closer into his chest, emotions she refused to name pulsating through her. "You're just saying that."

"I'm not." Sirius grasped her chin and brought her head up. "Isabel, I mean it."

"Why, Sirius?" Isabel placed her hand over his, twining their fingers together against her cheek. "Why me?"

"You know, sunshine." His throat bobbed. "You know why."

"Say it," Isabel whispered, her breath coming in pants.

"Because I want you. I want you in ways I've never wanted another woman." Sirius dragged his fingers to cup the base of her neck. "I'll never want anyone else the way I want you."

Her ribs squeezed tight around her lungs, and her heart abruptly thundered in her throat. Could Sirius be in earnest? Dare she trust him? Isabel wanted to, but her insecurities clung to her with eagle talons. "That's what you say now, but—"

"But nothing, darling." Sirius pressed a finger to her lips. "I know nothing I say will ever convince you, so let me show you. Please let me do that."

Faith, she was desperate to believe him. "Very well," she breathed. "Show me."

Sirius didn't need another invitation. Lifting her chin with his hand, he crashed his mouth down upon hers. His scent curled about her, leaving her lightheaded, even as he gripped her tighter, as if impatient to consume her. Isabel was more than willing to surrender.

Without lifting his lips from hers, Sirius ran his hands down her sides to clutch the hem of her nightdress. Isabel raised her arms, and he pulled it up and over her head with an impatient huff. Reaching for him, she scrambled to remove his jacket, uncaring for where it fell.

"Relax, Isabel. There's no rush." He stopped her anxious hands with his own. "I'm not going anywhere."

"You may not be, but we could still be discovered," she said, tension prickling along her scalp. "If Gabby or Lady Yardley were to check on me, they would get a shock."

Squeezing her fingers, Sirius waited until she met his eyes. "This is our first time together in a bed. I've daydreamed of stretching you out and kissing every inch of your body, so let me. Put your worries aside for now. They will still be there when I am done with you."

The backs of her eyes burned, but Isabel remained quiet as Sirius lowered her to the mattress, sighing deeply when he kissed her. Before she could deepen the kiss, however, Sirius moved his mouth to the valley between her neck and shoulder. To her collarbone. To the swell of her breasts.

"You are so beautiful," he whispered, dancing his fingers down her arms to trace along the underside of her breasts. "Your skin is so soft, like the most decadent silk."

Isabel tried to rise up on her elbows to kiss him, but her long braid caught under her arm, yanking her head back. Sirius tsked under his breath, freeing her plait. With a hint of a smile on his lips, he unraveled her braid, sifting through her black curls until they fell loosely about her shoulders and across the sheets.

Wrapping a strand around his finger, Sirius watched as it sprang back when he released it. "I wish you could wear your hair loose for all to see, for it truly is magnificent. And yet . . ." He buried his face in her locks. "I don't want anyone else to glimpse you this way. So free. So uninhibited. So completely enthralling. You would sink ships and start wars, I'm convinced."

"You're ridiculous," Isabel murmured, her voice choked.

"I am." Sirius nodded as he gathered her curls and pushed them back from her face. "You make me ridiculous every time I am with you. And even when you're not, because my every thought has been consumed with you. When you're not with me, I wonder what you're doing. What you're reading. Are you safe? Do you think of me, too?"

Isabel twined her arms around his neck and pulled him down until nothing but a breath separated them. "Always. I think of you always."

And she kissed him.

Yet that one kiss was not enough. Could never be enough. Soon they moved their mouths over each other as if they'd suffocate if they weren't tasting each other's skin and teasing moans from each other's lips. Isabel dragged her hands from Sirius's hair, down his back, and around to the front of his waist.

"Off, por favor," she begged, "I need to feel you."

Sirius pulled himself away long enough to shuck off his trousers and smallclothes and peel his waistcoat and shirt from his torso. In the dim, warm glow of the lamp on her side table, Isabel took in the sight of him towering over her. He was so perfectly formed, from his angelic face to the broad sweep of his shoulders, to the dips and dents of his waist and abdomen. But it was his cock, surrounded by curly, dark blond hair, that held her gaze. A feeling of empowerment surged through her as she watched desire firing bright in his eyes. Isabel crawled to the edge of the bed on her knees, preening when Sirius groaned.

"May I taste you?" she dared to ask, the words nothing but a whisper.

There was no doubt Sirius heard her, however, for he clamped his eyes closed and dropped his head back. "Christ, you're going to be the death of me."

Somehow Isabel managed not to grin. Slowly wrapping her hand around his length, she gave it a tentative squeeze, his answering moan telling her she was on the right path.

"Will you show me what to do?" she asked, peering up at him through her lashes.

"Of course," he said, shaking his head eagerly.

His instructions were helpful, even if she had to coax the words from him because he often communicated only through moans. Sirius instructed her on how firmly to hold him, and how to twist her hand at his tip. When she opened her mouth around the head, he stroked his cock across her tongue, mumbling broken curses. But it was when she swallowed as much of his length as she could and then hollowed her cheeks that Sirius bit down on his fist to keep from cursing.

It was a messy business, and Isabel's jaw ached, but she reveled in having this beautiful man so completely in her thrall. Captain Sirius Dawson, the man half the women of the ton desired for themselves, trembled under *her* touch. And the words he spoke to her while she worked him soon had her squirming and looking for relief.

You're so good, darling.

Fuck, you take me so well.

Do you like the way I taste, sunshine?

Isabel increased her ministrations, enraptured by his response to her, and determined to bring him to release against her tongue. But Sirius had other plans, for he gently pulled free from her lips, his chest laboring. Stroking his hand along his cock, he rolled on a condom, and then pointed at the bed behind her.

"Lie down, Isabel."

Hastening to obey him, Isabel scrambled onto the bed, reclining back on her elbows. She bit back a moan when Sirius roughly pulled her legs apart, his gaze possessing hers as he leaned forward and stroked up her slit with every inch of his tongue.

Isabel tossed her head back as her hands twisted about in the coverlet, seeking purchase.

Sirius ruthlessly teased her until she lay quivering beneath him, hoarse supplications falling from her lips in Spanish and English. Eventually, he crawled over her, pressing his mouth to the flesh over her heart as he settled his hips between her thighs. Isabel tilted her pelvis up, shaking with desire and the need for the release he kept just out of reach, but Sirius made no move to enter her. He simply stared down at her with his midnight eyes, until he opened his mouth and recited slowly, in halted Spanish,

Acá en el alma te vía,
acá en el alma te hablaba.

A tear slid down her cheek as Sirius continued to quote "My Lady," by Sor Juana Inés de la Cruz, his words punctuated by caresses and fevered kisses to her skin. When he finally thrust into her, Isabel gasped against his lips. She clung to him as he undulated his hips and shifted her farther and farther up the bed, completely overcome by his sweet words. By his greedy kisses and possessive hands. And with each poem he breathlessly quoted, whether penned by Donne or Barrett Browning or Byron, Isabel fell a little more apart. For while he didn't say the words, Sirius showed her his love, and she endeavored to show hers in return.

When her release finally crashed down upon her, Isabel could only hold on to Sirius, and hope this moment, filled with all their unsaid love, would be enough to sustain her.

Sirius lay sprawled on top of Isabel, his face tucked into her neck. His heart raced like a runaway Thoroughbred, but the steady drum under his ear told him that Isabel's did, too.

Eventually, he pulled free of her body, causing Isabel to hiss between her teeth at the slow drag. Sirius quickly climbed to his feet and found a wet strip of cloth on a water basin in her dressing room. Returning to the bed, he gently applied the cool cloth to the sensitive valley between her thighs, taking all due care to tend to her, for Sirius knew he had been more rough with her than he had intended.

With his ministrations complete, he climbed into bed next to her, drawing her into the circle of his arms. Isabel fit against him like a missing puzzle piece, her curves and dips nestling perfectly against the long line of his body. Sirius inhaled a great breath, soaking her vanilla scent into his blood, before he released it in a whoosh of air.

"Content, are you?" she drawled lowly by his side.

"How could I not be?" he answered, kissing her head. "That was marvelous."

Isabel nestled her head on his chest with a sigh.

"Did you enjoy it, too?" Sirius couldn't help but ask.

"You quoted Sor Juana Inés de la Cruz's poetry." He could feel her swallow. "It was the most beautiful thing anyone has ever done for me."

"That's a crime," he murmured, warmth pulsing under his ribs. "Or perhaps my deplorable Spanish was."

"Claro que no," Isabel said, running a hand up his chest and resting it right over his heart. "It was perfect."

He snorted. "Now I know you're being untruthful." A smile stole over his mouth when she swatted him. "I am but a servant to your pleasure. I quite like the role."

"That's a good thing, as you are quite apt at it."

They were quiet for a time, a silly, lighthearted bubble surrounding them. Sirius indulged in the moment, deciding that his post-release bliss was more enjoyable when he could spend it with Isabel in his arms.

But all good things eventually had to come to an end, and when Isabel rotated until she could look up at his face, Sirius knew he could no longer put off the inevitable.

"So do you now intend to return to Mexico?"

Sirius had not meant to ask so bluntly. There were a dozen other things he wanted to say to Isabel—questions he wanted to ask—but his mouth shaped the words before his mind had even conjured them.

Isabel went still against him, and dread tumbled about like ore in his gut.

"I hope to. At some point."

It was a direct answer with no embellishments, and Sirius was not surprised by it. It was so like his Isabel to respond in such a way.

"And when do you think that point will come?"

Her hand on his chest curled into a fist. "I don't know. Perhaps when I receive word from my parents that they are well."

"So soon, then." When she opened her mouth to argue, Sirius silenced her with a kiss. "I have every expectation that they will receive the warning in time."

Isabel released a long sigh. "I hope you're right."

"I hope I am, too." He smoothed damp strands of hair back from her face. "So my time with you is coming to an end."

"I suppose it is." She grasped his hand then, bringing it up to press against where her heart pounded in her chest. "I wish it wasn't. I have loved our time together."

"Have you, darling?"

"Of course I have." Isabel smacked him lightly. "How can you ask that?"

Sirius aimed for his next words to be insouciant. Perhaps even playful. But he was certain they came off as petulant instead. "Because you're still leaving."

"I am." Her voice dropped to the lowest of whispers, and Sirius had to lean close to hear her words. "I've never felt like I belonged here."

He ran his nose along her jaw. "I'm sorry you've felt that way. I'm sure there are many in your life who would argue that point."

She snorted. "If you mean my sisters, yes."

He craned back his head to meet her eyes. "Not just your sisters."

Isabel's expression turned pained. "You're being nice again."

"I had no notion you thought me so disingenuous." Sirius could not keep the hurt from his voice.

"Not at all." Isabel pressed her palm to his cheek, forcing him to meet her gaze. "But, mi amor, you have charmed your way into the beds of many women of the ton. You've been a rogue with a silver tongue, with the golden looks of an Adonis. Forgive me for thinking the words you've whispered to me might be a part of your ploy."

"Ploy? I thought you understood the reason for my reputation." It stung to say the words, but not as much as it ached to think she thought so little of him. "*Our* interactions, the connection *we* share, both physical and otherwise, have never been a ploy."

Isabel kissed his chin. "I've never once thought of staying in London for longer than I had to. I've been so uncomfortable here. It's loud and crowded everywhere I turn. And I routinely say the wrong thing at the wrong time to the wrong person. And yet I was tasked with something important, and I failed at every opportunity. I've felt like I've let down everyone, Sirius. Over and over and over again."

She kissed the corner of his mouth. "That was until we became friends, and suddenly there was another person who seemed to understand me. Took the time to know me." Isabel clamped her eyes closed. "That seems unfair to say because Gabby and Ana María have loved me and accepted me unconditionally, but they're my sisters. Their judgment cannot always be trusted."

"And yet everything you've told me of them—that I know of them myself—convinces me their judgment is sound," he grumbled.

"You dear man," she whispered to his lips. After a time, they broke apart, quietly panting for air. "You've always seen me, Sirius, and I will forever love you for that."

He was paralyzed. Every one of his muscles locked. Even his heart stumbled in its beat.

"Yes, I do," she said, a shy smile lighting her face. "Since I first saw you, I think. There I was, hiding under a desk while two people made animalistic noises above me—"

"Christ, how appalling," he groaned, hiding his face against her neck.

"Yes, well, I've pushed that aside in favor of remembering how incredibly piercing your eyes were." Isabel ran her knuckles over his cheek, her gaze far away. "You have the bluest eyes I had ever seen."

"And you had the fiercest scowl."

Her laugh was the sweetest sound. "You deserved my scowl then."

"And now?" Sirius asked, a bit breathless.

"Now you deserve my love."

She was so staunch. So sure. That this stunning woman who battled her own sense of inferiority could be so sure of *his* worth brought Sirius to his knees.

"I'm not deserving of your love, sunshine." His throat bobbed as he swallowed a knot. "My sins are great. In the war, I committed horrible acts in the name of the Crown. I did what I was ordered to do, but that knowledge does not eclipse my shame."

"But are you doing those horrible things now? Still?" Isabel asked.

Abruptly, he thought of his work for the Home Office. The lies he told to friends and foes alike. The ways in which he manipulated his targets, many of them innocent women whose only crime was being associated with men capable of treason or espionage.

But Isabel knew of his work with the Home Office, and why he did it. And not once had she expressed disappointment in him. That disappointment he'd seen his whole life; first from his father, then his older brother, and later from the men he'd been forced to abandon on the battlefield. Isabel had never shunned him for what he felt compelled to do in the name of the Crown. In his quest to assuage his guilt . . . the source of which he thought he might be ready to share.

Because Sirius realized he would walk through the bowels of hell before he'd ever give Isabel Luna cause to be disappointed in him again.

Remembering her question, Sirius exhaled. "No. I don't do those things anymore."

A fierce look settled on her face, and Isabel kissed the skin over his heart.

"We've all done things in the moment that we wish we could take back. That, given the chance again, we would change. Make another choice." Her obsidian gaze was mesmerizing. "But since we can't, we have to learn to let go of the guilt, the shame, so that it doesn't distort and discolor the rest of our lives."

He wanted to believe that so dearly, but his conscience screamed that such a pardon was not something he deserved.

"Do you remember the nightmare I had in the study?"

Isabel nodded, her eyes wide and a tad guarded. Good. She needed to know that although he wanted her, she would be wise to remain wary.

"I've had nightmares since I've returned from the peninsula." Sirius paused, his nerves suddenly on the surface of his skin. "If I'm lucky, I don't remember them when I awake. But more often than not, I do. Every one is reliving the day I was shot."

Isabel wrapped her arms around his waist, cocooning him in her embrace. "What happened?"

Sirius took a moment to form the words. He'd only spoken of the events after he'd awoken in the hospital days after he was shot. His tale had been promptly told to senior officials, and they latched on to it as the perfect propaganda ploy. The young, handsome son of an earl almost lost his life saving his men, when he was really the reason so many lives were lost.

"We'd received intelligence that the enemy would be redirecting their supply wagons to avoid the barricades and checkpoint we had erected across a narrow portion of land we had managed to take from the Russians." His chuckle was humorless. "As you can imagine, we were determined to hold our line and not let the enemy slip past our defenses. Our pride depended upon it."

Sirius covered his face with his hand, unease heavy and thick in his lungs. "Except I learned from my senior officer that the generals were switching tactics, and their priority had become the western line. My company was the only one they were leaving in place to defend the swatch of land we had won."

"They expected your company to hold the line on your own?" she asked, her voice rising an octave.

"They did. The western front was under constant bombardment from enemy forces, so additional support was needed. The tract of land we maintained had remained relatively calm, but only because the military had assigned so many companies to defend it. But they underestimated the people who lived in the region and used this specific area as a trading route. It was a vital thoroughfare for many of the Russians and Tatars, and when we cut off their free access to traverse it, we earned ourselves dangerous enemies. And suddenly we no longer had the troops to withstand an assault."

"Ay no," she breathed. "Did they attack?"

He pressed his lips together for a moment, willing them not to tremble. "They caught us completely unawares."

Her arms around his waist tightened.

"I tried to set up a defensive line on the outer flank, and a runner escaped with a missive asking for help, but I was shot before the real fighting had even started." Sirius closed his eyes, clouded memories of that day flashing behind his eyelids. "I don't remember anything else. I awoke in a field hospital several days later."

Isabel's hand touched the puckered flesh on the right side of his stomach. "I may never have met you."

The thought of never having known Isabel made his whole body tingle with thankfulness, and he kissed her brow.

"I was very lucky, but so many of my men were not." The words were like glass on his tongue, but he forced himself to continue. Isabel deserved to know what happened. She needed to know the awful legacy he carried with him. "All but five of the men in my company were killed, yet they were able to hold the line until reinforcements arrived. They were the true heroes, but it was I who received all the fanfare when I returned to London."

"Sirius, it's not your fault you were shot—" Isabel began.

"But I wasn't there to help—" His voice broke.

"You were the one who was shrewd enough to order the men into that formation. They were trained and prepared to defend the position because of your leadership." Isabel rubbed his chest. "You made sure a runner went for help as soon as possible, and—"

"I could have done more. I *should* have done more. I should have been more assertive with my senior officers." Sirius wrenched a hand through his hair. "I should have demanded reinforcements beforehand. Instead I was used to deflect negative commentary on the war. I was given honors and medals I did not earn. I failed my men."

Once again, everything he touched fell apart. His mother died giving birth to him, and his father blamed him for it. His older brother had wanted no relationship with him, and had rebuffed every attempt Sirius had ever made to forge a connection with him. His work with the Home Office had been perfect for him, for it allowed him to keep every relationship he engaged in superficial. With the exception of his friendships with the Duke of Whitfield and Gideon Fox, every aspect of his life was shallow and empty.

Until Isabel.

Her hand swept over his cheek now, her dark eyes glinting in the dim light. "And yet you employ your men."

He held his silence.

"You allow them to live at Dancourt Abbey."

Sirius nodded.

Isabel seemed to ponder this for a moment, her expression considering. "And I suspect you pay yearly stipends to the families of the men who were killed."

Sirius jerked his head up. "How do you know that?"

"My tío Arturo told us." Her fingertips traced along his cheekbone to his nose, and she dragged her finger down to the tip. "Back when we stayed at Dancourt Abbey. He wrote and assured us you were an honorable man who would do his best to keep us safe."

"And Earl Tyrell was able to abscond with your sister from right under my nose," he replied with an angry growl.

Isabel silenced him with a finger to his mouth. "You helped Gideon rescue her. You organized the entire effort. Gideon said he will forever be grateful to you for taking charge when he was too overcome to do it himself."

Sirius didn't know how she could say that. How she could have so much faith in him when he had so little in himself.

He worked to clear his throat. "Thank you," he said simply.

"I've never felt comfortable opening up to others. Sharing my feelings or thoughts." She squeezed her earlobe between her fingers. "Despite how close we are now, my sisters and I were not friends as children. My father sowed discord between us, so we were more at odds with one another than sisters ought to be."

"He kept you friendless and isolated." Sirius's mouth lifted into a sad smile. "I'd guess it was easier to keep you all obedient that way."

"Indeed. We all strived so hard, in our own ways, to make him proud. And none of us were successful." A sigh made her lips tremble. "I didn't know that, though, until we came here. But that knowledge hasn't made it any easier to be open and honest with Ana and Gabby. In many ways, it's harder because now that I truly know them, I would be crushed if I disappointed them."

"You could never disappoint them, sunshine." His tone was firm, for Sirius needed her to understand. "I see it every time Gabby looks at you. She's so proud of you."

The darkness could not hide the pink that touched her cheeks.

A comfortable stillness enveloped them, and Sirius stroked his hand over her shoulder and down her arm, thankful to have this quiet moment with her. Eventually, Sirius remembered the book he had slipped into his cloak before leaving his house, hoping he would have a chance to share it with her. "I brought a book with me," he said, breaking the silence.

"You did?" There was a smile in her voice. "Will you read to me?"

Contentment surged through his body. "I'd be happy to."

Slipping from her embrace, Sirius padded to his discarded cloak, plucking the book from its pocket.

"What is it?" Isabel asked as he rejoined her on the bed.

"*Don Quixote.*" Sirius handed it to her before turning to switch the gas valve on the bedside lamp. "It's a first edition. I found it when I was in Varna. One of the only good things to come out of my wretched time there."

A bemused look passed over her features. "Westhope was searching for a copy."

Sirius tilted his head. "Was he?"

Isabel nodded, settling into his side. "He had rare book hunters here and in Paris looking for one."

An odd warmth spread to his fingertips as he opened the book. Sirius grinned as he met her gaze. "Well, then, make sure not to mention you've seen one before him."

19

Isabel awoke before Sirius did, certain she had heard someone outside her bedroom door. She had made sure to lock it the night before, but she didn't put it past Gabby to pick the lock. Somehow, Isabel was certain her sister would know such a skill.

Thankfully, the house remained silent and still, and Isabel eventually relaxed into the embrace of the furnace pressed close against her back. Sirius had his arm wrapped around her waist, his nose tucked to the delicate spot in the back of her neck. A smile curved her lips. She could get used to this . . . if only she believed this could be for forever.

Isabel mashed her lips together as she replayed the words Sirius had shared with her just hours before. He'd been an attentive lover, coaxing pleasure from her body until she hadn't known which way was up. But somehow he'd been different. Intensity simmered in his cerulean gaze. It turned his touch electric, his kisses overwhelming. Every move he made hinted at his desperation, but desperation for what? It was almost as if he were afraid she would leave for Mexico directly, and his hold on her had been ironclad. Sirius hadn't returned her love confession, and such an omission would normally have sent her into a downward spiral of screaming insecurities. Yet he had shown her, hadn't he? With every kiss. Every caress. Every strangled moan spoke of his love.

Suddenly, Isabel was at a loss of what to do. She still wanted to return to Mexico—*yearned* to—and hoped that one of her many missives was received in time. Isabel prayed that it was Presidente Juárez himself to invite her to return, because her father would be less likely to object. But if the president did issue an invitation, could she turn it down if Sirius made an offer of his own?

Isabel thought she might be able to. And that would not do.

Carefully twisting about in the circle of his arms, Isabel studied Sirius's slumbering form. His face was soft and peaceful, his unfairly long lashes fanned across the crests of his cheeks. His breath slipped from between his parted lips, and Isabel smiled. Sirius looked so innocent in sleep. So incredibly dear.

And he was dear. Sirius Dawson was the gentlest, kindest, most intelligent man she knew, and it would have been impossible not to fall in love with him. His confession of heroism made her heart ache in her throat. Sirius believed himself unworthy of the accolades he'd received, but Isabel saw them as his due. His role in the battle that returned him to England injured may have been exaggerated, but everything he had done since, from caring for his men and other veterans of the war, to working for the Home Office to uncover enemies of the Crown, and helping young women with more ambition than skill, told Isabel that Sirius was worthy of every good thing.

So how could she possibly ask him to give up the home, the sense of purpose, he had created for himself?

Gently extracting herself from his embrace, Isabel reached for her chemise, slipping it over her head before she pulled on her stockings. She was just sliding her corset around her waist when a pair of masculine hands smacked hers away.

"I wish we didn't have to rise," Sirius said, nibbling along the side of her neck as he pulled the laces taut. "I could stay in bed with you all day."

Isabel arched her head back into his touch. "That sounds wonderful, but I don't wish to court trouble, especially with my sister so close."

Sirius paused in the middle of tying her corset laces. "Ugh, yes, I would prefer to avoid Miss Gabriela as well."

Stifling a laugh, Isabel rested her head on his chest. "Tío Arturo is supposed to arrive later this morning so that we may discuss the cabinet's next moves. I'm sure Ana and Gideon will be here, as well."

Kissing the top of her head, Sirius said, "There is only so much you can do from the other side of an ocean, but with so many clever people in the room, I'm certain you all will think of something."

"You're right. I have to learn to temper my expectations or else I'll go mad." She bit her lip. "I just can't help but think of all these horrible scenarios of what would happen if all of the letters we've sent were lost."

"I'm sure a missive will reach the necessary parties in time." He perched his chin on the top of her head.

Isabel released a long sigh. "It will take time for the garrison at Martinique to reach Sisal or even Veracruz," she said slowly, processing the logistics.

"Exactly." Sirius rubbed her back. "All the more reason to have hope."

He was right, of course, but then Isabel knew that trying to temper her worries was a fruitless exercise. Until she received confirmation that her parents, the president, and the cabinet members had escaped to safety, Isabel was convinced she would not be able to sleep.

Taking a step back, Isabel looked up at Sirius. A tender light burned in his gaze as he stared down at her, and when he carefully brushed her curls back from her face, Isabel suddenly felt as if her lungs were too tight to draw in breath.

Be brave. She recited the mantra several times, painfully aware their affair had to end if she wanted to survive Sirius with her pride intact. Her heart, in comparison, was already in tatters.

"Thank you for coming to me," she managed, moving a step away.

Sirius let his arm fall. "Thank you for letting me stay."

She lifted a shoulder, her palms clammy. "I should freshen up. Lupe will be here soon."

He nodded, his blue eyes narrowing.

"And I'm sure you have plans," Isabel babbled, her hands gesturing nervously. "You've always kept a busy social schedule."

"A bit of a job requirement," he said.

Her chuckle sounded odd to her own ears. "You're probably more than ready to focus on your work again, and not follow me, ensuring I don't find trouble."

Unable to hold his gaze a moment longer, Isabel spun about and fussed with the items on her dressing table. A silent moment passed, and a small piece of Isabel died with every second that ticked away on her bedside clock.

"Isabel," Sirius finally said, a frown in his voice. "Why does it feel like you're saying goodbye?"

Isabel shifted back and forth on her feet, her fingers curling to bite into her palms. "It's not goodbye. It—it just occurred to me that our time together has come to an end. You helped me discover the information I was looking for—"

"You did that yourself, sunshine." Isabel looked over her shoulder to find him with a small half smile on his lips. "Westhope was smitten with you because you are everything that is charming and lovely."

Tearing her gaze from his, Isabel dropped her eyes to the tabletop. She couldn't do this if he continued to be so wonderful. Dread pumped through her veins like acid, coalescing around her heart with a crippling sting.

"Whatever the case may be, you offered to help me and you did." Isabel pivoted, leaning back against the dressing table. She tried to smile and hoped it didn't appear as broken as she felt. "You can get on with your life now. The cosmopolitan, sophisticated life you led before you agreed to help me."

A deep groove appeared between Sirius's brows. "Get on with it?"

"Of course." She gestured at him with a hand. "I'm sure the Home Office has been so thrilled by your *work* with me, and are ready for you to get back to the business of defending England. I don't want to monopolize any more of your time."

Sirius simply looked at her, and a sob threatened to burst free from her throat at the shuttered look in his eyes. "Any more of my time. Right."

The flat tone in which he said the words battered her resolve.

Isabel barreled on, her mind searching for things to say to help him understand why this had to end, when all she truly wanted was to curl up in his arms. But she couldn't trap him. Sirius had too many responsibilities, too many people who depended on him, too many people he loved and supported to abandon them for her. Isabel's pride refused to even broach the subject.

"I can't thank you enough for everything you've done to help me get to this point." Isabel ignored how her voice cracked, determined to set him free before he realized how precariously she held herself together. "I would have searched, in vain, for a very long time."

Sirius took a step closer to her, and Isabel flinched. If he touched her, she would crumble. He jerked to a halt, though, his face turned ashen. "Isabel." He paused, his throat working. "Is this the end?"

Oh God. Isabel clamped her eyes closed and pressed her tongue to the roof of her mouth until she was certain she wouldn't cry. "I know you're busy, Sirius, and I don't want you to have to waste any more of your time on me."

"You could never be a waste of time, Isabel." Sirius grasped her shoulders, shaking her until she met his gaze. "I want—"

Her hand shot out to press against his chest, and Isabel struggled not to curl her fingers into the soft hair that ran down his sternum. "Your home is here, and mine"—she swallowed—"is not. I can't continue to be this close to you knowing that what we share has a time limit."

Sirius shook his head. "But it—"

"Sirius, please," Isabel cried, sidestepping him. Crossing to the door, panic and despair warring in her chest, she held his gaze as she willed herself to say, "I have to fall out of love with you, and I would appreciate it if you gave me the space to do so."

Everything about that moment seemed suspended, the tension

raising the hairs on the back of her neck. If Sirius argued with her—if he confessed his feelings for her—Isabel would not have the fortitude to push him away again. The thought of never seeing him again, of one day learning from Ana and Gideon that he had married, would be a father, threatened to reduce her to ash. Yet he could be happy here . . . and she could not.

So Isabel pushed down her grief, pulled her spine straight, and risked a glance at his face.

His resigned expression sent a tear streaking down her cheek.

Isabel watched as Sirius dressed silently, the only hint of the emotions roiling under his somber facade the muscle flexing in his jaw. When he put his hat on his head, he finally turned to her, his eyes devoid of the light that had long shone in them.

"I wish you the best, Isabel. You are a singular woman capable of great things. Don't let anyone convince you otherwise."

Sirius bowed crisply, avoiding her gaze. Wordlessly, Isabel held open the door for him and watched as he slowly slipped past her. When Sirius melded into the darkness of the hall, she quietly shut her door and threw herself on her bed. The sheets still smelled of him. Gathering them to her chest, she buried her face in them as she wept.

20

Time seemed to stand still, each second, every minute of the clock painful and endless. But it also seemed to rush past with every sunrise and sunset.

Or at least it appeared so to Isabel as she watched the world pass by through her bedroom window.

In the weeks since she had ended her affair with Sirius, Isabel had left the house only a handful of times. She visited Ana María and Gideon, and attended Mass a Sunday or two, but couldn't bring herself to go anywhere else. Isabel made no trips to the lending library or museum. No meandering walks in the park with Gabby. When her sister and Lady Yardley dressed in the evenings to attend one event or another, Isabel declined their increasingly frustrated requests to accompany them. But Isabel was incapable of feigning interest in such things any longer.

When Tío Arturo received the letter that Presidente Juárez and her parents had managed to escape before the French troops surrounded their location, he had delivered the news to Isabel in person. She'd been overwhelmed with relief, thankful the message had reached them before Maximilian's army could, and yet Isabel didn't cry. Couldn't cry. Her chest felt hollow, and she could think of nothing to fill it.

Isabel wanted to go home, but home still seemed so very far away.

A soft knock on her chamber door drew her head around. "Entra," she called.

The door opened, and Gabby stood on the threshold, her brow puckered in concern. She stepped inside, but paused, glancing about her.

"Aren't you tired of this room?" she said, her tone gentler than her words.

"What do you want, Gabby?" Isabel said, turning back to the book in her hand.

"Viscount Westhope is here to see you."

Isabel went still, her gaze flying to meet her sister's. The last person she wanted to speak with was Westhope. He had called two times already, with Gabby or Lady Yardley claiming Isabel was feeling unwell. She knew that excuse would last for only so long. "Did you tell him I was in?"

"I did," Gabby said succinctly.

"I wish you hadn't," Isabel said, groaning.

Gabby flung a hand up. "I thought you liked the viscount."

"I do like him," Isabel said, snapping her book closed. "And that's the problem. I do not wish to hurt his feelings."

"Why would you hurt his feelings?"

Isabel stared at the cover of the book in her hand. It was a collection of poems by John Donne. She did so love to hurt her own feelings. "Because I would have to tell him I'm not interested in being his bride."

"That will be hard." Gabby's voice was sympathetic. "But the viscount deserves to know."

She was right, of course. Westhope deserved her honesty,

especially now that she had used their acquaintance to gain what she wanted. Guilt festered in her gut.

The room went silent . . . but the tension screamed in Isabel's ears. When she glanced up, Gabby was considering her closely. "Lord Westhope is not why you have cloistered yourself away like a medieval nun, right?"

Smothering a chuckle, Isabel nodded. "Correct."

"Then why have you, Isa?" Gabby demanded. "Why do you refuse to leave this room? What happened?"

Rising to her feet, Isabel walked to the window and peered out, desperately wishing she could escape her sister's questions. "It doesn't matter."

"It does matter." Gabby's hand slipped into hers, spinning her about to meet her gaze. "I don't like seeing you like this."

And I don't like being like this. But a malaise had settled over Isabel, and she had no notion of how to free herself from it . . . other than to leave. Without Sirius, London had become unbearable.

"I'm fine." Isabel tried to smile but wasn't sure whether she was successful. "Truly."

"You're a terrible liar, Isa." Gabby spun about in a cloud of skirts. At the door, she glanced at Isabel over her shoulder, her lip curled in irritation. "If you're going to lock yourself away, you may as well move to one of the attic rooms so you can haunt the house like a proper ghost."

Isabel snorted . . . and it quickly turned into a laugh. A full-body laugh that soon had her wheezing. Gabby watched her with an exasperated, if fond, look on her face.

"Go tell Westhope you're not interested in being his bride. He deserves to hear it from your lips." Her sister opened the door and stepped into the hall. "The cowardly thing to do is hide. And you're not a coward, Isa."

Staring at the open doorway, Isabel covered her face with her hands and groaned. Gabby was right; she wasn't a coward.

Setting her book aside, Isabel checked her reflection in the mirror, thankful she didn't look as terrible as she felt. Straightening her spine, she headed down the stairs.

The viscount was chatting with Lady Yardley when Isabel entered the room, and his face lit up when he spotted her. After exchanging greetings, Isabel sat in the armchair next to his, and politely answered his questions about her health and her recent absence from society. But something about her bearing must have alerted Westhope that Isabel had not been entirely truthful, for he turned in his chair to face her directly, a tightness to his expression.

"Has something happened, Miss Luna?" The viscount shook his head. "I get a sense there's something you're not telling me."

Isabel slid her gaze to Lady Yardley, who looked back at her with disgruntlement.

Knotting her hands in her lap, Isabel lifted her chin. "You're right, my lord. I haven't exactly been honest with you."

Westhope moved to the edge of his seat. "What do you mean?"

"What I mean," Isabel began, sinking her nails into her palms, "is that I haven't told you that I plan to return to Mexico."

"Soon?" he asked, rotating his head to look at Lady Yardley.

The viscountess grimaced as Isabel murmured, "No. I do not have immediate plans to return."

Lord Westhope rubbed the back of his neck. "Why did you decide to tell me this now? If you will continue to live in London for the foreseeable future, why are you thinking of returning to Mexico?"

"Because I'm *always* thinking of Mexico. I have never planned to make my stay here permanent." Isabel dropped her gaze. "But the more time I spent with you, the more I came to admire and respect you, and the more it became clear that you wanted more of me than I could give you."

Isabel pressed her tongue to the roof of her mouth, fearful she had said too much. Worried she might have misread the situation and attributed feelings to the viscount that he did not feel for her. Setting her jaw, Isabel prepared for his response.

Thankfully she did not wait long, for the viscount stood and stalked to the fireplace, gripping the mantel with a firm hand. "It seems foolish now to admit it, but since you have been honest with me, Miss Luna, I will be honest with you."

Lord Westhope turned to face her, a pained light in his eyes. "I had hoped to one day make you my bride. You're the first woman I've met whom I find interesting and clever. And your life in Mexico has given you a different perspective on society. On culture and literature! I've enjoyed our conversations, and feel as if I learn something new whenever we speak." He glanced down, the tips of his ears turning red. "And you're quite pretty. Very unique and striking."

It was Isabel's turn to dip her head, overcome by the sentiments the viscount had shared. But the heart wanted what the heart wanted, and Lord Westhope deserved to have a bride who desired his.

"I am more honored than I can say that you hold me in such high esteem," she said.

"But honor does not a happy bride make," he replied with a self-deprecating smile.

"Any woman would be honored to be your viscountess," Lady Yardley interjected with a tsk.

"Perhaps," Lord Westhope said, his eyes wistful as they

landed on Isabel, "but then I only wanted that honor from one woman."

Taking a moment to fight back a blush, Isabel said, "You know, my lord, I have a friend you should meet. She's witty and beautiful, and I believe you would get along splendidly."

The viscount cocked his head in interest.

After he departed, Lady Yardley asked Evans to bring them two glasses of wine, stating they were in great need of it. As they sipped an excellent red vintage Isabel didn't know the name of, the older woman considered Isabel over her glass.

"You could have been a viscountess." Her blue eyes were far away, no doubt imagining the wedding announcement. "What an achievement that would have been."

"I want to achieve more than marriage, my lady." Isabel held up her glass, rotating it, mesmerized by the red liquid that swished about. "There are so many things I'd like to try—"

"Well, you'd have to get your nose out of your books to do so," Lady Yardley said with a dry laugh.

"I know." Isabel smiled at her. "And I will."

The door opened, and Evans walked in, a sealed letter on a tray. But instead of presenting it to the viscountess, he extended it to Isabel.

"Mr. Valdés just sent this by courier. He said you need to read it immediately."

Blinking up at Evans, Isabel nodded, gingerly lifting the letter from the tray. Studying the seal, Isabel's eyes widened. Ripping it open, she gasped, raising a trembling hand to her mouth.

"Who's it from?" Lady Yardley asked.

Lowering her hand, Isabel released a shaky breath. "Presidente Juárez."

. . .

"You look like shit, Dawson."

Sirius glanced over his shoulder to grumble at the intruder, but paused when his gaze landed on the figure in the doorway. Setting down his book, he dropped his feet to the floor and rose, inclining his head respectfully. "Sir."

Lieutenant Colonel Green stepped into the study, his eyes sweeping over the room, before turning to examine Sirius. His inspection felt tangible, and Sirius stood straighter, struggling not to shift on his feet. Yet Sirius had so much to feel ashamed of.

Finally, the older man pulled out a chair on the opposite side of the desk and sat. "You missed our meeting today," he said without preamble.

Sirius gradually sank back onto his own chair. "I apologize."

"You missed last week's as well. And the one before that."

Hunching his shoulders, Sirius nodded. "I've not been feeling"—his throat bobbed—"myself."

"So it would seem." Lieutenant Colonel Green raised his brows. "Although I suspect what's ailing you is not physical."

Sirius fought back a wince . . . as well as a desire to defend himself. But there was no defense, so he pressed his lips together in what he hoped was a friendly smile. "What would you like to discuss today, sir?"

"Your retirement."

"My what?" Sirius cried, slapping his hands on the desk as he leaned forward.

"Your retirement, Dawson." Green slipped a letter from his coat pocket and held it out to Sirius. "You've served the Home Office honorably for the last eight years, and have proven yourself to be an asset to the Crown multiple times."

"And yet you want me to retire?" Sirius growled, taking the letter and brandishing it in the air. "Why?"

The older man leaned back in his chair, folding his hands over his belly. "Because it's obvious you don't enjoy the work anymore."

Sirius scoffed. "It's work. Was I ever supposed to enjoy it?"

"When you had a beautiful woman on your arm, it appeared you did." Green peered at him over his spectacles. "Dawson, we both know you don't have to work. Regardless of your relationship with Harcourt, your parents left you a sizable fortune. You don't have to do this job, so why continue to do so when it's obvious your heart is no longer in it?"

Standing, Sirius crossed to the sideboard and grabbed a glass. Lifting a half-filled decanter of brandy, he poured himself a finger before tossing it back in one burning mouthful. "I do it because I feel that I *have* to."

Good breeding won out over frustration, and he poured Green a glass, depositing it on the desk in front of the man. Too agitated to reclaim his seat, Sirius paced in front of the window.

Green lifted his tumbler and took a sip, whistling as he set it down. "Excellent bite." Sighing, he looked at Sirius. "You did it because of your men. I know. I've always known. The occupation seemed to be good for you, so I didn't say anything."

Sirius glowered. "What could you have said?"

The lieutenant colonel considered the glass in his hand. "That no matter what you do, or how hard you work, you won't be able to bring them back."

Clenching his jaw, Sirius pivoted, his gaze unseeing out the window.

"I know, because I've tried."

Despite how his heart raced, Sirius tried to keep his breath measured. Even. But his emotions were too raw for this discussion. Hadn't losing Isabel because of his own reticence been enough? And now he was being forced to retire when he needed the distraction of his work the most?

The urge to kick something, to crush something within his hands, nearly overwhelmed him.

But Sirius had already destroyed too much.

Swiping a hand down his face, Sirius poured himself another tumbler of alcohol. "What about Westhope and the information I was trying to get from him?"

"We already have someone else on it"—Green shrugged—"although from what you've reported, I don't think the viscount knows much."

Unsure of what to say, Sirius filled his mouth with brandy.

Sirius watched as Green stood and walked to the door. "Go to your abbey in Devonshire. Hack out across the meadow, help with the harvest, and let those early country hours lull you to sleep. With those bags under your eyes, you look as old as me."

"Not quite," Sirius shot back with a hoarse chuckle.

Green smiled. "Get out of this godforsaken city, Dawson, and let old ghosts lie."

Sirius stared at the open doorway for an indeterminate amount of time after Lieutenant Colonel Green departed, and contemplated what his life would be like now that he no longer had to spy for the Crown. Boring, no doubt. Infinitely less stressful. For so many years, his work had given him a sense of direction, a piece of stability, and his pay helped him fund the renovations and expansions he'd made not only at Dancourt Abbey, but the nearby village as well. Now that work was done, and Sirius felt a bit like a fish flopping about on the seashore.

And curse his silly broken heart, but the only person he wanted to talk about this news with was Isabel. She would know exactly what to say to strip away this lump in his throat, and the next phase of his life wouldn't be so uncertain because she would be a part of it. But Isabel would be returning to Mexico. To a life she wanted and deserved. Sirius respected her enough to allow her that happiness.

Dropping his head into his hands, Sirius considered Green's suggestion to retire to Dancourt Abbey. It was true that he felt more himself, more at peace, within its aging walls than he did anywhere else. And what was keeping him in London now? Sirius could cancel the lease on his townhome, and invite Stanley and the other men to accompany him to Devonshire or pension them, if they'd prefer. Glancing at his bookshelves, Sirius could admit that he liked the idea of blending his collections into one large library. Isabel would have loved organizing them together—

Sirius rubbed his chest as if it could ease the razor-sharp pain that festered there. He couldn't wait for the day that Isabel Luna didn't haunt everything he did.

The move to Devonshire proved to be easier than he anticipated, and Sirius settled into the daily routine of a country gentleman. Rising with the sun, he hacked out with Monroe, the gamekeeper, to survey the land. Sirius did so love the early hours when mist still clung to the grass and made the world seem a bit magical. Soon, though, the sun burned away the fog, and Sirius busied himself with visiting the nearby mill before stopping at the various farms located on Dancourt Abbey land. Many of the farmers who worked the land had served in the Crimea, as had a large portion of the mill workers, and the men who tended to the orchards or whom he had hired to restore the old abbey. He had purchased the dilapidated estate after he'd been released from the hospital, and within its quiet walls and sun-dappled meadows, Sirius healed and rebuilt his life. Seeing it provide a place for other men and their families to do the same would always bring a warm glow of satisfaction.

Now Sirius longed to find contentment there again, but it just didn't feel the same without Isabel's quiet, calm presence.

"You've been staring at that colt for so long, I'd almost think you were expecting it to sprout wings."

Blinking back to the moment, Sirius shifted back and forth on his feet. "I got lost in a bit of woolgathering."

O'Brien's mouth quirked. "You've seemed to do that a good deal since you've arrived."

"Have I?" Sirius winced when the other man nodded. "I suppose I have a lot on my mind."

"The abbey is a great place to think through it all"— O'Brien shrugged—"or so I've found since I been here."

It had been many long weeks since Sirius had met the Irishman in the back gardens of his London townhome, and in that time O'Brien had found a place for himself among the stable hands and trainers who cared for the draft and heavy horses. Sirius had taken to stopping by the stables to chat with the man almost daily, finding him sharp-witted and droll. Oftentimes their conversations led to Sirius assisting him with one duty or another, a fact O'Brien was scandalized by.

"The lord of the manor can't be mucking out horseshit," he'd declared the first time Sirius grabbed a shovel to help him.

"I'm not a lord, and I've done every job at this manor at least once." Sirius had chuckled. "I've never been afraid to get my hands dirty."

And Sirius desperately needed anything to keep his mind busy and his hands active.

"I was going to attach Angus and Goliath to the hay wagon, and bring them to the southeast field." O'Brien cocked his head. "Do you want to come?"

Sirius blew out a noisy breath. "I don't have anything better to do."

"Still haven't finished putting all your books away?" At Sirius's curt nod, O'Brien looked at him askance as they walked to the draft horses' stall. "Mrs. Ormsby said your library is your pride and joy, but I always see you here in the stables or out in the fields."

His books, and their memories, were for the night, when sleep fled him and all Sirius had to keep him warm was the written word and his regrets.

"Organizing a library takes careful consideration, and I'm doing just that."

Thankfully, O'Brien did not push the conversation, and soon he couldn't if he wanted to, because the sound of pick-axes striking rock as several field hands worked to extricate debris to prepare for new plantings drowned out every other sound. It was why Sirius did not hear the approaching horse hooves until Monroe had stopped his mount next to the wagon. A flicker of unease sparked in his gut when the man thrust a piece of paper at him.

"Telegram was just delivered. Mrs. Ormsby said it was marked urgent."

Sirius accepted it wordlessly, hastening to open it. The message was short, but it almost knocked Sirius off his feet.

Isabel departs for Mexico. Wednesday, 2 p.m. Fox

21

"So you got your wish. It seems you're leaving."

Isabel looked up from the letter she was writing to Padre Ignacio, her pen hovering over the paper. Sitting back, she lifted a shoulder. "I am. It wasn't much of a struggle to accept."

"Indeed." Gabby wandered into the room, sitting on the edge of Isabel's bed, her mien pale. "When you're thanked personally by the president of Mexico and invited to serve as an assistant to the First Lady, it's hard to say no." Plucking at a loose thread on the counterpane, Gabby considered her. "Is this something you want to do, Isa, or do you feel like you can't say no to it?"

Tossing her pen onto the desk, Isabel rotated in her chair to face her sister. "No, I'm very happy to have been offered this opportunity to work with Señora Maza de Juárez. I'd always hoped I would be able to return to Mexico and help with the war effort, and I've been working to do that this whole time."

Gabby made a face. "What do you mean?"

Isabel bit her lip. Did she want to tell Gabby her secret? Did she trust her sister with such a truth? Looking into her sister's eyes now, she realized how holding herself back from others had only ever hurt her. And hadn't Gabby, and Ana María, earned her loyalty?

Squaring her shoulders, Isabel said, "Have you ever wondered why I always escaped during balls and other events?"

"I assumed you just didn't want to be there." Gabby snorted. "And I've envied you for it. I wish I could run away whenever I wanted."

She was running away, to a small extent, but Isabel didn't think that truth was the pressing issue of the moment. "Yes, well, you're right, but that's not the only reason I would slip away whenever I had a chance."

"Well, this sounds interesting," Gabby murmured, wiggling about.

Her sister's eyes continued to widen and her mouth eventually slipped open as Isabel explained how Padre Ignacio had connected her with Fernando Ramírez, who then gave her the task of uncovering information the rebel government could use against the French.

"So all those times I thought you were reading, hiding away in the libraries and studies of pompous peers, you were searching through their belongings instead?" Gabby clapped her hands together. "Ay, are you serious?"

Isabel chuckled. "I am. I've been searching for anything that could help our people in their fight against the French. Sadly, I've not been very successful . . . until I read that letter in Westhope's carriage."

"¡Vaya! No me esperaba esto." Gabby chuckled. "Here I was annoyed with you for fleeing these tedious events I'm *made* to attend, all to charm these gringos for Mexico, and you've been putting yourself in harm's way in the name of espionage." Her sister looked at her with starry eyes. "You're amazing."

Pressing her lips together, Isabel looked away. "No, I'm not. I'm terrible at this. I hadn't found one useful bit of information during the years we've been here. I have been a horrible failure before now."

"How could you call yourself a failure? You had no instruction, no tutelage, nothing but rushed directions on the eve of our departure." Gabby tossed her hands up. "You had to teach yourself not only who was who, and who might possess useful information, but how to get into and out of rooms without being spotted. I repeat, that is amazing."

Isabel tucked her chin to her chest. "You wouldn't say that if you knew that was how Lord Tyrell found me in his study."

Gabby gasped, her hazel eyes owlish. "That's why you were in his study?"

She nodded, shame sweeping up her face.

Her sister made a rough noise in the back of her throat. "Too bad you didn't find any of his secrets before he discovered you."

Frowning, Isabel shook her head. "Y-you're not upset with me?"

"About the situation with Lord Tyrell?" Gabby scoffed. "No. I don't have to tell you that the incident in the earl's study forced Ana María and Gideon together, and look how happy they are now. I could never be upset with how that turned out."

Isabel's brow crinkled as she considered that. She'd carried an enormous amount of guilt on her shoulders for how her lack of circumspection had brought such danger into their lives and changed the trajectory of Ana María's future. Despite knowing how happy her older sister was, the guilt had always been a nagging ache in the back of her mind.

"Isa, no matter the failures you think you experienced, you ultimately found information that saved Presidente Juárez's life." Gabby's hazel eyes swam with unshed tears. "Your quick thinking very well may have saved democracy in Mexico."

Overcome with emotion, Isabel pressed her lips together and looked away. She certainly didn't think her efforts deserved such praise . . . but it consoled her nevertheless.

Gabby said nothing else for a spell, and Isabel was thankful for a quiet minute to reflect on how much she would miss these moments with her sister once Isabel left for Mexico.

"Is there another reason you were so eager to accept Presidente Juárez's invitation?" Gabby asked into the silence.

She wouldn't miss her sister's uncanny ability to knock her off-balance.

Isabel cleared her throat, feigning nonchalance. "I don't know what you mean."

"Yes, you do, Isa." Gabby slid off the bed and approached Isabel's chair, crouching down to look up at her downturned face, her skirts pooled about her. "I haven't pushed you, but now that you're leaving, I have to ask if you've been nursing a broken heart over Captain Dawson?"

Isabel flinched before she could contain her reaction. "N-no. I told you there was nothing serious between us. This has nothing to do—"

"I heard you two talking. In your room." Gabby placed a hand on her knee. "I saw him leave, Isa."

She thought she had been so careful. Isabel was certain no one had heard them. Had heard the argument between her and Sirius, and later her throat-scouring tears. Neither Gabby nor Lady Yardley had mentioned it. Isabel had allowed herself to mourn the loss of Sirius and what could have been between them in solitude. Yet her sister had known the whole time.

Wrapping her arms about her waist, Isabel choked down the rush of emotions she'd worked so very hard to stifle.

Waiting while her throat worked convulsively, Isabel finally said, "My time with Captain Dawson was a finite thing. It was destined to come to an end."

It was a truth Isabel repeated to herself over the next week as she prepared for her departure. She packed her books with care, setting aside several novels she thought Gabby would like. When she came across the book of poetry she never returned to Sirius, Isabel shed a few tears, thankful no one was about to question why.

Gideon had secured her a first-class ticket to Altamira, and Tío Arturo had coordinated with emissaries for the president to deliver her to the location where the cabinet had moved ahead of the French. Neither Isabel nor her uncle knew exactly where that was, but Tío Arturo speculated it was somewhere in Nuevo León. Isabel had never been to the northern state, but she looked forward to exploring it . . . well, as much as she could with her new responsibilities. She also looked forward to seeing her mother again and being enfolded in her firm embrace.

However, Isabel was apprehensive to be reunited with her father. She may have uncovered information that ultimately saved his life, but that didn't necessarily mean Elías Luna's opinion of her had changed. She knew Padre Ignacio had lobbied hard on her behalf, and the invitation to assist Señora Maza de Juárez was an honor not bestowed lightly. However, her father's approval was a constantly moving target. Such a realization would have gutted her in the not-too-distant past, but now Isabel allowed it to touch her only with a passing sadness.

Isabel pondered that change of perspective as she watched Lady Yardley's footmen unload her trunks from the carriage. Gabby stood on her right and Ana María on her left, their arms looped with her own. Neither of them spoke during the carriage ride from Yardley House to the docks, and Isabel was grateful. She had spent the last week with them, whether they dined together for meals, took walks in the park, or simply laughed over their shared memories. Ana María had even stayed in her old room at Yardley House for several nights, claiming she didn't want to be away from Isabel for a moment. It had been a long goodbye, filled with deep discussions, lighthearted jesting, and heartfelt confessions. Her sisters had become her best—her *only*—friends, and she was leaving them behind. Isabel was just beginning to understand who she was as a person, and now she would have to be that new Isabel without the two most important people in her life. Her grip on her sisters tightened.

Was she making the right decision? Isabel thought she knew the answer, but now that she stood on the windy docks, the expanse of the Atlantic looming before her, she wasn't sure.

"I'm so proud of you, Isa, and all you've accomplished." Ana María leaned into her side. "And working with Señora Maza de Juárez will give you the opportunity to do so much more than you ever could have done here."

Isabel swallowed audibly. "I hope I always make you proud, querida."

"I have no doubt you will," Ana replied, her dark eyes glassy.

"You were too much for London, Isa. Too intelligent, too brave." Gabby's voice broke, and she pressed her cheek to Isabel's shoulder. "And too brilliant for this gray city."

"Gabby," she choked out, all other words strangled by her unshed tears.

"The only consolation I have in your leaving is that you will

finally be able to show your worth for all the world to see."
Her younger sister patted her arm. "No hiding, when you were
meant to shine."

Gabby's words were reminiscent of those someone else had
uttered to her once before, and Isabel gritted her teeth against
the memory.

Instead, she enfolded both her sisters in her arms and cried.

Isabel wasn't sure how long they held on to one another,
their sniffles and shuddered breaths the only sounds they
shared, but eventually Gideon informed them that passengers
were boarding the ship. Isabel clung several more moments to
her sisters before she finally stepped back, patting her cheeks
with a handkerchief.

"This is not goodbye forever, Isa," Ana said, cupping her
face and bussing both of her cheeks. "Once the war is over, we
will visit. Perhaps you will be kind enough to introduce us to
Presidente Juárez."

"I'll think about it," Isabel replied archly and then chuckled at Gideon's expression of mock offense.

After saying goodbye to her brother-in-law, and reminding
him to care for Ana María, she shared her thanks and well-
wishes with Tío Arturo and Lady Yardley. Finally, Isabel
turned to Gabby. Her sister was no longer crying, her expression stoic and resolute. Isabel was not used to seeing her so
somber. Without hesitation, she wrapped her arms around
Gabby's shoulders and buried her face in her neck.

"I don't know what I'm going to do without you there to
defend me. From others, but more so from myself," she sniffed.

"You've never needed a defender, Isa. You've always been
the bravest of us all. But I've always needed a big sister"—
Gabby held her tighter—"and I will miss you more than I
can say."

Soon Isabel stood on the ship's deck, away from the other passengers on the rail, who waved to family and friends on the docks below. From her solitary spot, she considered her sisters, who stood side by side with their arms linked. It felt foreign and disconcerting not to be standing with them, and the realization that she didn't know when she would get to be with them again made Isabel rock on her feet. If she weren't so desperate for a second chance, would she be leaving now?

That dull ache that had taken residence in her soul pinged anew, and Isabel knew her answer. She yearned to pull a full breath into her lungs and not think of *him*. So much of London was now haunted by ghosts of what could have been.

And suddenly her gaze snagged on a figure in black standing on the far end of the dock. Even across the distance that separated them, his eyes were the bluest of blues, and Isabel could not look away. Not as the ship pushed from the docks, or as it eased into the sea-lane. Isabel raised her arm in goodbye to her sisters, blowing kisses on the breeze, but then she turned back to Sirius. She didn't wave or call out a goodbye. Instead, Isabel clutched a hand to her empty chest and hoped that somehow, one day, she'd find a way to fill it again.

It took Sirius a moment to realize the banging he heard was not in his head, but rather a visitor at the door.

Lurching to his feet, he padded to it, grumbling with every step. He'd rented a room at the Grosvenor Hotel, assured it would provide him with the privacy he desired for such a trip to town. And yet somehow there was a visitor, pounding so loudly it would surely wake the dead.

Flipping the lock, Sirius threw open the door. "Who the hell do you—"

"Well, hello to you, too, Dawson."

The Duke of Whitfield looked him up and down over his spectacles, before pushing past him into the room. Sirius watched his old friend prowl about, picking up the empty bottle of gin Sirius had finished after he'd returned from the docks. After he'd missed Isa—

"Gin? Lord help us," Whitfield groused, shaking his head in disgust.

"He's upset you didn't let us know you arrived in town."

Sirius whipped his head about, his gaze landing on Gideon Fox lingering on the threshold. His gaze moved over Sirius's face, but whatever he saw there didn't change his own expression. Fox was adept at keeping his thoughts concealed.

"I left quite abruptly." Sirius stepped to the side to allow Fox to enter, and then shut the door. Leaning against the wood, he shrugged. "My only concern was getting here before she departed, but I couldn't even do that."

The ship had sailed away, taking Isabel with it, and the only thing Sirius could do was watch helplessly from the docks.

"You could have sent a telegram," Whitfield snapped. "Given Fox time to delay matters."

Fox frowned. "I don't know that I would have been able to. Isabel was one of the last passengers to board as it was."

Sirius recoiled hearing her name spoken aloud for the first time.

"How did you know about . . ." He trailed off, unable to say the words. In his current state, filled with cheap gin and bone-crushing despair, Sirius wasn't certain he wouldn't sob.

"Gabby told Ana." Fox shrugged, picking up the copy of Sor Juana's writings that Sirius had brought with him from the abbey. He studied the cover for a moment before glancing up at Sirius, a sympathetic tilt to his mouth. "She thinks you're in love with Isabel."

"I am," he said candidly. Thumping his head back on the door, Sirius contemplated how much he wanted to tell them. "But I couldn't ask her to stay. Not when she was so determined, so eager to leave. Now she's gone, and there's nothing left for me to do."

There. He'd confessed the gist of it, and now perhaps Whitfield and Fox would leave him to nurse his battered heart and fractured pride in peace.

"Nothing left for you to do? Are you mad?"

Heat swept up his neck and cheeks, and Sirius glared at the duke. "What the fuck do you want from me, Sebastian? Isabel wanted a life in Mexico. She longed to prove herself, and I wouldn't dream of stopping her." Sighing in exhausted frustration, Sirius pushed off the door and plopped into a nearby armchair, burying his head in his hands. "I just wish I hadn't taken so long . . . to truly *see* her. I wasted so much time."

The duke scowled. "Did you ask her to stay?"

"Why would she ever want to stay *here*, with me?" Sirius demanded.

"Maybe you should have given her an opportunity to decide for herself." Whitfield threw his arms wide. "You could have confessed your love for her and expressed how you wanted to build a life with her." The duke's eyebrows drew low. "You did tell her you loved her, right?"

Sirius shook his head, not daring to look up. He was more comfortable staring at his bare feet than at his fiery friend. "My love wouldn't have been enough. It never has been."

Not for anyone in his life. All he deserved was the casual—

"Goddamn it, Dawson, stop this self-flagellation once and for all." Whitfield grabbed Sirius by the shoulder and shook him. "That anguish you've carried since you were a boy?

Release it. Harcourt is a selfish fool who's jealous of your good looks and charm. A real idiot, that one."

Fox emitted a low chuckle but quickly covered it with a cough.

Whitfield kept a firm hand on his back. "I can't pretend to understand what you endured on the peninsula and in the dark times after, but I've seen how it's colored everything you do. If you're not working to give something to someone, then you seem incapable of allowing anything for yourself."

Sirius closed his eyes, but he couldn't drown out his friend's voice.

"There's nothing wrong with wanting a bit of happiness. Did Miss Luna make you happy?"

He nodded.

"Then go to Mexico and get her," Whitfield declared. "Christ, you fight for everyone else, and now it's time to fight for yourself."

Could he do it? Travel to Mexico and ask Isabel for a second chance? Would she say yes? He had to try.

A new thought occurred to him, and Sirius deflated. "I can't ask her to give up her home, *again*, to live with me here. It would be selfish to ask."

The duke ran a hand along his jaw as he exhaled.

"So move to Mexico yourself."

Sirius turned with a frown to Fox. "Move to Mexico?"

His friend raised a shoulder. "What responsibilities do you have here in England?"

"The abbey, for one—"

"Your solicitor could set up a trust to oversee it," Whitfield interjected, the shadow of a smile curving his lips. "I'm sure there are dependable men who can tend to the day-to-day operations, right?"

His steward had cared for the abbey during the long months he spent in London, and Monroe was smart and loyal, and probably loved the land more than Sirius. And O'Brien had quickly learned the workings of the home farm, and would probably welcome more responsibilities. Perhaps the suggestion had merit . . .

Yet could he really move across the ocean? To a war zone? Where they spoke a language he didn't know? The uncertainty made his palms wet and throat dry.

Rising to his feet, Sirius took a moment to steady himself, before looking at Fox. "Would your wife and Gabby be upset if I tried to win their sister?"

His friend snorted. "Their main concern will always be Isabel's happiness, and if you can make her happy in Mexico, they will be delighted for both of you."

A sunbeam of hope pierced through his sadness. "And would Mr. Valdés help me organize my trip? I don't know anything about the country."

Fox chuckled. "I believe he can be persuaded."

Sirius looked back and forth between his friends, errant thoughts and possible plans churning about in his mind. He could do this. He needed to do this. For himself and for Isabel, because no one would love her, would understand her, quite like he did.

"So have you decided?" Whitfield asked, his tone all suffering.

The heaviness that had clung to him since that night in Isabel's room lifted a tad, and Sirius nodded. "I believe I'm going to Mexico."

"As much as I'm happy for you, I'm also slightly perturbed that you will see my wife's homeland before me." Fox smiled when Sirius laughed, but his expression turned grim. "One thing I do not envy you for is that you will meet my father-in-law, the infamous Señor Luna."

That detail left Sirius off-kilter. The whole situation left him off-kilter. But he would do it for Isabel. For the chance to bask in her bit of sunshine again.

22

Four hundred and fifty-six steps lay between her front door and the fountain in the center of the town plaza. Isabel knew because she had counted them every day since she arrived in Villa de Santiago.

Walking that well-traveled path now, Isabel no longer looked around in wonder. The lush mountains that flanked the village no longer stole her breath. Neither the colorful stucco homes nor the twin spires of the Parroquia Santiago Apóstol made her pause with a smile. Her excitement to work for the Mexican First Lady had waned, and the feeling of triumph that swelled in her chest when she stepped from the ship in Altamira had dissipated on the long journey to Santiago. For her heart was heavy, and it seemed to grow heavier every day since she departed England, and no amount of praise or recognition could lighten it.

Isabel sat on the fountain's edge and peered down into the blue waters that rippled beneath her. Her reflection stared back at her, unchanged from the last time she had looked. Oh, but her mother remarked upon the changes every day. María Elena lamented the dark circles under Isabel's eyes, the gauntness to her cheeks, the pallor of her skin. While her mother always inquired after her health, and insisted Isabel take her meals with her instead of alone with a book as she would have preferred, María Elena never asked Isabel directly about her time in England. Never asked about the friends she may have left behind. While the Isabel of old would have thought that meant her mother didn't believe her capable of making friends, now she suspected that Ana María or Gabby had informed her of what had transpired before Isabel left. And even if they hadn't, Isabel still didn't possess the words to discuss it, with her mother or anyone.

Reaching into her pocket, Isabel extracted the latest letter she received from Gabby. Receiving mail was difficult, as it had to be redirected several times before it found its way to this small hamlet outside Monterrey, oftentimes arriving soiled and damaged. Miraculously, this particular letter had been delivered unscathed, and Isabel traced her fingers over her sister's swooping handwriting. Gabby had written of her work with her women's group, and described a fundraising event they were planning for John Stuart Mill to stand for Parliament. The man had apparently advocated for a universal education system that included women, among other things.

Isabel closed her eyes for a moment to offer up a prayer for her sister and her safety. She'd certainly read enough news reports to know how suffragists were treated by the authorities, both in England and the United States.

After sharing details of the latest dinner party Ana María and Gideon had thrown to drum up support for a new initiative he was introducing, Gabby mentioned she had met with Lord Westhope while on a walk in the park. He'd been escorting Miss Fairchild, a development that had Isabel smiling ear to ear. The viscount had been kind, inquiring after her health, and specifically asking how Isabel was doing, and not for the first time did Isabel wonder how different her life could have been if she had deeper feelings for Lord Westhope. He was the first man to show an interest in her from first association, and her recollections of the times she spent with him were fond ones. Isabel wished she could write to him, tell him of the books she was reading, her work with Señora Maza de Juárez, and the effort to win back Mexico from the French . . . but then the viscount's loyalties lay elsewhere. She was happy he'd turned his attentions to Miss Fairchild, and thankful to Gabby for passing along his well-wishes. She stored them away with her memories of him.

It was Gabby's parting lines that drew her eyes again, as they had the first time Isabel had read the letter.

I miss you, hermana. Every day. All day. But I am happy you have found contentment in your work for the rightful president, and I pray your chance to find true happiness arrives for you soon.

Arrives soon? What an interesting sentiment, but then Gabby possessed a fanciful flair that used to exasperate Isabel but now charmed her.

True happiness. What did that look like? Isabel pondered the question as she refolded her sister's letter and clutched it in her hand. Not long ago, she thought it meant contributing to the war effort. Being recognized for her intelligence. And Isabel had achieved that. She experienced immense satisfaction helping Señora Maza de Juárez and her daughters raise funds for soldiers and their families, and ensuring hospitals were stocked with the supplies needed to support the Mexican troops. Isabel also regularly sent the First Lady, who was living in exile in the United States and acting as a Mexican diplomat, translated reports to share with allied American officials. In addition, she acted as an intermediary between Señora Maza de Juárez and her husband, and their letters to each other were funneled through Isabel, a responsibility she did not take lightly.

Her father had initially pushed back against the idea of Isabel working, even though it was at the president's request, but Padre Ignacio and Fernando had eventually convinced him that Isabel's talents were best utilized serving the republic. Elías Luna had never thanked her for the intelligence she'd uncovered or congratulated her on the accolades she'd received from Presidente Juárez, yet he was quick to introduce Isabel as his daughter to members of the cabinet. The first time he'd done so had shocked Isabel so completely, she had excused herself after the introduction and rushed outside to compose herself.

Isabel was busy. Her life was interesting and challenging . . . and yet she felt empty. A yawning cavern existed where her heart used to be, and no amount of praise, whether from the president or her own father, could fill it.

Tipping her head back, Isabel let the sun soak into her skin. Let its warmth permeate her bones. She had missed this while in England. For the first month they were in London, Isabel was certain she'd never be warm again. Now she feared that coldness had crept into her chest, where it sank in its claws and created a lair.

"Enjoying the sunshine?"

Every muscle in her body froze as that voice swept over her. Fluttering her eyes open, Isabel gasped when she saw him. Standing not four feet away, in an impeccable suit, was Sirius. His blond hair was a bit longer now, the curls she knew were soft as down brushing against his ears, and his cheeks were tan, as if he'd spent days toiling in the fields at Dancourt Abbey.

Or on the deck of a ship sailing toward Mexico.

Slowly rising to her feet, Isabel gaped at him, certain he was an apparition she had conjured with the yearning ache in her heart. She ripped her gaze from his face to look around, certain she must be dreaming, but the plaza looked as it always did. All was well . . . except for the panicked roaring in her ears.

Licking her lips, Isabel opened her mouth to greet him, to demand to know what he was doing there. Instead, a choked cry rushed up her throat.

"Oh, please don't cry, darling," Sirius murmured, stepping forward with his hand outstretched. He paused before he touched her, a shadow falling over his expression. "I didn't come here to upset you."

"I don't understand," she rasped, moving closer. "Why are you here?"

His Adam's apple bobbed, the pupils of his blue eyes large as they stared back at her. "Because you're here."

Isabel wrapped her arms tight about her waist. "You left England . . . because of me?"

Sirius nodded, taking a step. "There was nothing left for me there after you left."

"B-but what about your work for the Home Office?" Static filled her mind. "What about Dancourt Abbey and the men who live there?"

The corner of Sirius's mouth kicked up. "I was offered retirement from the Home Office. My work no longer brought me purpose, and there were other, younger men to take over my assignments."

"And the abbey?" she whispered, her hands flexing in their urge to reach for him. "What of Dancourt Abbey?"

Sirius shrugged, glancing down at his feet. "The abbey will always be mine, but with the help of my solicitor, I have drawn up guidelines for how the land and the manor will be used in my absence. They've provided a level of control and independence to the men who live there, and my hope is that they will be content to live there for years to come."

"That's wonderful," she murmured, understanding why that was important to him. Sirius had worked so hard to care for the men who had cared for him, and he had readily, unselfishly, offered Dancourt Abbey as a refuge.

And he walked away from it for her?

"So as you can see, darling, I had no reason to stay in England." Sirius reached up to gently brush a curl from her temple. "Especially when my heart lay elsewhere."

Leaning into his touch, Isabel closed her eyes as she dared to ask, "Where?"

"Right here," he answered, dragging his knuckles across her jaw. "It's always been right here, with you."

"Did you know that before or after I left?" she asked archly.

"Before." He pressed his lips together, gaze roving over her face. "And yet I couldn't bring myself to say it."

Isabel could only nod, overcome with a dizzying mix of confusion and hope.

"Is it too late for us?" His other hand grasped hers, his palm warm. "Will you forgive me? For not being honest with you about how I felt? For not *seeing* you sooner?" Sirius hesitated, his eyes darting between hers. "Will you let me care for you, for the rest of my days?"

"You care for me?" she whispered, feeling lightheaded.

"Sunshine," he breathed, bringing both hands up to cup

her face. "To say I care about you is an injustice to the thunderstorm of emotions I feel whenever you're near. Or not near. Whenever I think of your name or imagine your face. I don't just *care* about you, Isabel Luna. I'm in love with you."

Isabel stared up at him, completely dumbfounded. Sirius loved her? "B-but why didn't you tell me? I would have given up the future I envisioned for myself here in Mexico to stay with you. Why didn't you ask?"

His eyes turned glassy, and Sirius tore his gaze from hers to stare at the ground. "How could I ask you to give up everything you worked for? I watched as you struggled to find a place for yourself in London, and I didn't want to tarnish the rewards of your success with my selfishness."

"Selfishness?" Isabel shook her head. "How could confessing your love for me be selfish?"

Sirius released a long exhale and slowly slid his gaze back to lock with hers. "Because you seemed so sure of yourself. So confident of what you wanted and what was best for you, and I couldn't bear to say it. I didn't want to burden you with my love."

A choked sound slipped from her mouth, and Isabel realized belatedly that it was a sob. Throwing her arms around his neck, she buried her face in his shoulder. "Mi amor, if anything has been a burden, it's the ever-present ache of what could have been if I had only been braver."

"The regret I've endured for having let you go has been the greatest burden of my life," he whispered hoarsely, his arms holding her tight. "I'm so sorry, Isabel."

"And I'm sorry, too." Isabel pulled back to meet his gaze. "I would have loved you until my last breath."

Without a moment's hesitation, Sirius leaned down to press his lips to hers. When he broke the kiss several moments later, they were both gasping.

"I don't deserve you," he panted, his eyes reverent as he rubbed his thumb along her bottom lip, "but if you let me, I will spend every day showing you how great and deep and all-encompassing my love for you is."

"Sirius," Isabel said firmly, "you are the most admirable man I know, and deserve to be loved for all that you are and all that you give. Will you let me spend my days showing you how much you deserve to be loved?"

He nodded, the color high in his cheeks. "Only because it's you."

Happiness so potent, so dazzling, shot through her, and Isabel closed her eyes to withstand it. Pressing close to Sirius again, Isabel allowed his familiar, dear scent to fill her lungs and lessen the pain that had settled in her heart. Because he was here, in Mexico, because he loved her.

"I can't believe you came." She brought his hand to her mouth. Kissing his knuckles, she pressed it to her cheek.

"I would have come sooner, but it took me a while to understand that I kept trying to repay a debt that had never existed outside of my own mind and heart."

Ignoring the people in the plaza, many whom she knew would tell her parents about this meeting with Sirius, Isabel pressed a kiss to his cheek. His jaw. The bridge of his nose, which made him chuckle. "Oh, cariño, you didn't owe anyone anything, yet you gave to them so unselfishly. It's one of the things I love about you."

"I should have fought for us," he growled, leaning his cheek against hers. "I should have told you I loved you, instead of letting you chase me away."

Isabel released a shuddering breath. "Neither one of us wanted to hold the other back."

"How very silly of us," Sirius murmured.

"Indeed." Isabel tucked her head in the crook of his neck, the sun suddenly brighter in the sky. "But we're together now." She paused when a new thought occurred to her. "Are you ready to meet my parents?"

"I already have."

Jerking back, Isabel met his amused gaze. "You have?"

Sirius nodded, his arms still firm about her waist. "If I spoke better Spanish or your father spoke better English, I'm certain I would've heard an earful from him by now. But his abundance of *pendejo*s gave me a good idea of his opinion of me."

Isabel mashed her lips together to keep from laughing. "How do you know the word *pendejo*?"

"I paid the scullery boy on the ship a crown every week to give me Spanish lessons."

"Ay, no wonder. I can only guess at the other words he taught you." She hiccuped between laughs.

"Yes, well, I was determined to know some Spanish to help me—" Sirius stopped to press a tender kiss to her lips. "Navigate my new home."

"Are you home, Sirius?" Isabel asked, a bit breathless.

"Now that I'm with you? Yes."

AUTHOR'S NOTE

Writing *Isabel and The Rogue* was an experience I had not expected.

When I first "met" Isabel while plotting *Ana María and The Fox*, I very much viewed her as a Jan Brady character; the middle daughter frustrated at being overlooked and outshined by her sisters. Then I spent time in Isabel's head. First in the scene that appeared in *Ana María and The Fox*, and later when I stepped into her shoes to write her book, and I realized how much I'd misjudged her. But misjudging Isabel is a central part of her story. Her parents were the first offenders, then her sisters, then Fernando Ramírez, and then later Sirius Dawson. But like any good romance hero, Sirius quickly learned the error of his ways.

And so did I. Once I realized how wonderful and special the middle Luna daughter was, I knew her book had to be special. It had to be filled with growth and discovery, of course, but it was incredibly important for me to show Isabel learning to accept herself, not because of Sirius's love for her, but because of her own.

Isabel and The Rogue takes place a couple of years after the first book in the series, and circumstances in Mexico and the United States have shifted. The Civil War ended in April 1865, Reconstruction had begun, and sadly President Lincoln had been assassinated. With the great war over, the US government could finally turn its attention to other matters, one of which was enforcing the Monroe Doctrine, a long-standing tenet of US foreign policy stating that any European intervention in the Americas could be viewed as a hostile act toward the United States. And with the US embroiled in the war between the states, France had invaded Mexico . . . an act the United States fiercely opposed. It's rumored that when Maximilian, the emperor of Mexico under Napoleon III, learned of the Union's victory, he exclaimed, "This is the end of the empire!" In many ways, it was. Now able to offer Mexico assistance, the United States military supplied Benito Juárez supporters with weapons and ammunition, and imposed a naval blockade. The pressure was on Maximilian and the French, and in early 1866, Napoleon III ordered the withdrawal of French forces. It is in this environment that Isabel returns to Mexico. The war is not yet won but the tide is turning, and Juárez and his supporters know it.

An interesting aside of the French occupation in Mexico is the belief that the ongoing conflict with Juárez's supporters kept the French from siding with the Confederacy in the US Civil War. In the book, Isabel serves as the mouthpiece for this theory from historians, outlining how an alliance between the French and the Confederate states could have changed the outcome of the war. There are some who believe that the US government, led by new president Andrew Johnson, was so keen on aiding Mexico after the Civil War as a means to repay it for keeping the French from interceding for the South.

I'd like to take a moment to highlight two real-life Mexican women who appeared in this book: Señora Maza de Juárez and Sor Juana Inés de la Cruz. Both women made their impact upon history and in the story, upon Isabel's life.

Sor Juana, as Isabel referred to her, was a colonial Mexican writer and the first published feminist in the Americas. In one word, she was a badass! Born in 1648 in what was then called New Spain, Sor Juana was a poet, dramatist, scholar, and nun, and during her time at the Convent of Santa Paula, she acquired one of the largest private libraries in the New World. A role model Isabel could aspire to! In a time when most women did not have access to an education, Sor Juana maintained a correspondence with scholars and members of court, and received the patronage of the viceroy and vicereine of New Spain for her scholarly pursuits. Her many writings are studied to this day, almost three hundred and thirty years after her death, because of their range of emotions, themes, and even languages. In one infamous example, her poem "Hombres necios" ("Foolish Men") implicates men of the same nonsensical behavior that they accuse women of. Sor Juana was a brilliant trailblazer . . . which also made her a target, and after immense pressure from members of the Catholic Church, she set aside her literary pursuits and renewed her religious vows. Her expansive library was even sold for alms. Sor Juana Inés de la Cruz died in 1695, and is revered as a national icon of Mexico and Mexican identity.

During the 1860s, upper-class Mexican women, like Isabel and her sisters, led very insular lives. While of course social events and parties were commonplace, a Mexican woman's place was in her home as a wife and a mother. Although wartime saw women stepping into support roles, whether as nurses, cooks, or in some cases, soldiers, for the most part women occupied a very narrow domestic role. But there were exceptions, and one such example was Señora Margarita Maza de Juárez, the first lady of Mexico. Born in Oaxaca a handful of years after Mexico won its independence from Spain, Margarita received a genteel education as a member of a wealthy family. Due to her family's status, several Zapotec people worked in the home as domestic servants . . . including a young Benito Juárez. After Juárez attended university, earned his law degree, and was appointed a judge, he became part of the city of Oaxaca's educated professional class. Finally at a more comparable social class, Juárez and Margarita married in 1843 and went on to have twelve children together. Their marriage shocked some of their contemporaries, as Margarita was a white woman and Juárez an indigenous Mexican. Margarita was by Juárez's side as he climbed through the political ranks, and she experienced persecution, banishment, and prolonged separation from her husband. During the French occupation, Margarita lived in the United States for several years, and acted as a diplomat when she met with politicians and government officials, including President Lincoln. Margarita and her daughters worked to raise funds and support causes that aided families affected by the war . . . a cause Isabel was only too happy to support. Sadly, Margarita passed away at the young age of forty-four, but is fondly remembered for the life she spent in service to Mexico.

One last point I would be remiss not to comment upon surrounds the Maqdala collection. If you are a history buff, I have no doubt that when you reached the British Museum chapter in this book, you may have screeched, "That didn't happen until 1868!" And you would be right. In the early 1860s, Tewodros II, Emperor of Ethiopia, was incensed by the British government's refusal to support his military campaigns, and in response, he took several British missionaries hostage. After failing to negotiate an agreement, the British military sent an expedition to Ethiopia in 1867 and killed hundreds of Tewodros's soldiers. The emperor himself committed suicide to avoid being captured, which immortalized him to many Ethiopians. According to the British Museum, accounts from soldiers report of widespread looting of the Maqdala fortress, where Tewodros had amassed an extensive collection of "ceremonial crosses, chalices, processional umbrella tops, weapons, textiles, jewelry and archaeological material, as well as tabots (altar tablets that consecrate a church building that are highly sacred objects within the Ethiopian Orthodox tradition)." The items were auctioned, as a supposed way to generate prize money for the British troops, and one of the principal buyers was an archaeologist from the British Museum, Richard Rivington Holmes. Holmes returned to England with a majority of the looted objects, which then became the "property" of the British Museum. Representatives from Ethiopia petitioned the museum for years to have the pilfered items returned, but the museum has claimed their hands are tied by laws that prohibit valuable items from being sent out of the country. Another excuse the museum has utilized is that it was better equipped to protect the antiquities and valuables in their possession than the countries they belonged to . . . a claim undermined by the August 2023 discovery that an employee of the museum had stolen approximately two thousand artifacts and sold them on eBay. In 2021, a nonprofit group based in the United Kingdom was able to purchase a significant portion of the Maqdala collection from the British Museum with the aim of restituting it.

The calls for the return of stolen cultural relics are growing louder; as a result of the eBay scandal, China demanded that the British Museum return Chinese antiquities in their possession, and took it a step further to demand the museum return all of the stolen relics they possessed to their home countries . . . a call Isabel and Gabby would fervently support! The museum has a list on their website of the contested items in their collection, which includes the Rosetta Stone (Egypt), the Parthenon Marbles (Greece), the Benin Bronzes (Nigeria), and some six thousand human remains from all over the world. The debate over whether Western museums have a right to the contested items in their collections is part of a greater discussion regarding cultural identity and history, and who gets to own it. It's a discussion Isabel would have been passionate about, considering her life in England was brought about by French colonialism.

This is just some of the history that appeared in *Isabel and The Rogue*. One of my favorite parts of being a historical romance author is immersing myself within the era I'm writing, and deciding which details, historical figures, and events will add to or influence the story I am crafting. My hope is that readers' curiosities will be sparked by Isabel and Sirius's story, and they'll research this moment in history and these various topics for themselves . . . and if you do, please let me know so we can chat about it!

ACKNOWLEDGMENTS

While my name may be on the front cover of *Isabel and The Rogue*, I have the honor of having been surrounded by a talented team of professionals who were just as invested in ensuring Isabel and Sirius had their happily-ever-after as I was.

I owe a wealth of thanks to Sarah Blumenstock, my savvy, ever-patient editor. I submitted a knot of ideas, dialogue, and themes to her, and she pulled at the threads to help me bring Isabel and Sirius's story to life.

To Rebecca Strauss, my superb agent, who has been a steadfast supporter, and who knows exactly how to bolster my confidence and calm my nerves when publishing can be a bit much.

To the entire team at Berkley, including Liz Sellers, Yazmine Hassan, Jessica Plummer, Hilary Tacuri, Katie Anderson, Lila Selle, Kristin del Rosario, Tiffany Estreicher, Jennifer Lynes, and Andrea Hovland. They embraced Isabel and Sirius, and worked hard to launch their book into the world with all the fanfare it deserved.

Special thanks to my friends Elle Pond, Elizabeth Bright, and Lisa Lin, who read very early copies of this book, and provided not just helpful feedback, but enthusiasm and fierce defense of my middle sister.

To my LatinxRom crew, who are a continuous blessing I will forever be grateful for. Adriana Herrera, Natalie Caña, Angelina M. Lopez, Sabrina Sol/Annette Chavez Macias, Diana Muñoz Stewart, Alexis Daria, Priscilla Oliveras, Mia Sosa, Ofelia Martinez, and Zoraida Córdova, I'm so lucky to call you friends!

To the Berkletes—thank you for being a safe space to discuss, and often vent about, publishing, entertainment, and everything in between.

To my wonderfully supportive family, including my own romance hero husband. I'm so thankful for all of you, especially because of your unfailing belief that my books will one day hit the *New York Times* bestseller list, despite all my pragmatic arguments to the contrary.

Last but not least, a huge thank-you to my readers! Thank you for embracing the Luna sisters and sharing your excitement for their stories on social media or in real life with your friends and fellow bookworms. Publishing is a hard business, and readership for historical romance as a genre is down. So to write historical romances with Latina main characters, featuring history from outside the Eurocentric lens most readers are used to, was a gamble, and I'm thrilled readers are invested in the lives and happily-ever-afters of Isabel, Ana María, and Gabby. I hope to tell more stories with smart, savvy, and, of course, proud Latina women living their best lives in history and beyond!

Isabel
and
The Rogue

A LUNA SISTERS NOVEL

Liana De la Rosa

READERS GUIDE

DISCUSSION QUESTIONS

1. As the middle sister, Isabel often feels overshadowed by her sisters and ignored by her parents. When she is approached by Señor Ramírez with a plan to help Mexico, she jumps at the opportunity to be useful. If you were in her shoes, would you have accepted Señor Ramírez's proposal?

2. Sirius is a man who has struggled with guilt, not just for his mother's early death, but for the death of his men in battle. If he hadn't struggled with this guilt and shame, do you think Sirius would have understood Isabel's burning need to prove herself?

3. Isabel and Gabby's dynamic involves Gabby serving as her older sister's defender, while Isabel gives the fiery Gabby a safe space to be herself. Do you have a sister? What part of Isabel and Gabby's relationship is true of your own experience?

4. In many ways, Sirius and Isabel have been shaped by the inattentiveness of their parents. Sirius was the spare who was ignored by his father and despised by his older brother, and

Isabel was continuously overlooked by her father because he didn't find "value" in her. How would their relationship with each other have been different had they not come from similar circumstances?

5. Isabel and Sirius bond over their shared love of literature. Of the various books or authors mentioned within *Isabel and The Rogue*, were there any that you have read? Are there any you plan to read now that you've been introduced to them?

6. An intense discussion transpires at the British Museum regarding the acquisition of the Maqdala collection—a collection the museum still possesses to this day, which would have appalled Isabel and Gabby. Do you feel the British Museum, and other museums around the world, have a responsibility to return the items in their possession that were obtained through colonization or war? Or do you feel museums can operate on a "finders keepers" basis?

7. Within Mexican society, women of Isabel's station were expected to be wives and mothers, and working outside of the home was a very rare occurrence—not unheard of, but rare. Yet Isabel's work as a secretary for the First Lady of Mexico brings her a sense of accomplishment and suits her strengths. If not a secretary, what other job or occupation do you think would suit Isabel?

8. The bond between Sirius, Whitfield, and Fox proves to be incredibly tight, especially when the men help Sirius to see that a future with Isabel is possible. Do you enjoy reading about male friendships? How can the portrayal of male friendships within romance novels challenge how the patriarchal

structures in our society dictate that men should engage with one another?

9. It is not uncommon for a female protagonist to give up parts of her life to live happily ever after with a male protagonist. But in *Isabel and The Rogue*, Sirius gives up his life in England to have a future with Isabel in Mexico. Did this ending feel believable to you? Do you feel Sirius's actions were justified by the story?

Photo courtesy of the author

Liana De la Rosa is a historical romance author who writes diverse characters in the Regency and Victorian periods. Liana has an English degree from the University of Arizona, and in her past life she owned a mystery shopping company and sold pecans for a large farm. When she's not writing, Liana is listening to true crime podcasts and pretending she's a domestic goddess while she wrangles her spirited brood of children with her patient husband in Arizona.

VISIT LIANA DE LA ROSA ONLINE

LianaDelaRosa.com

LianainBloom

LianainBloom

LianainBloom